TABLE OF CONTENTS

KNIGHTS
OF
MALSDON

BOOK ONE

First paperback edition 2024

978-1-80541-655-5 (paperback)
978-1-80541-654-8 (ebook)

KNIGHTS OF MALSDON

N.K. NASH

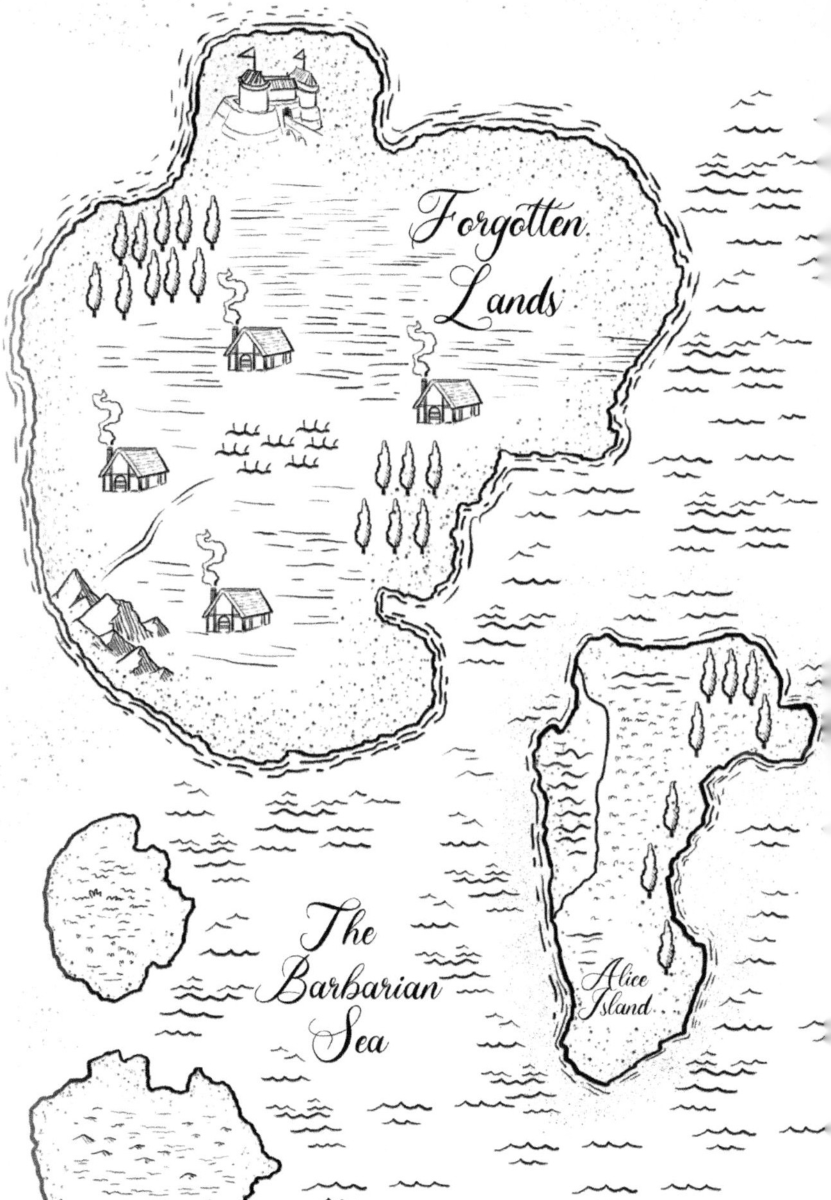
Forgotten
Lands
The
Barbarian
Sea
Alice
Island

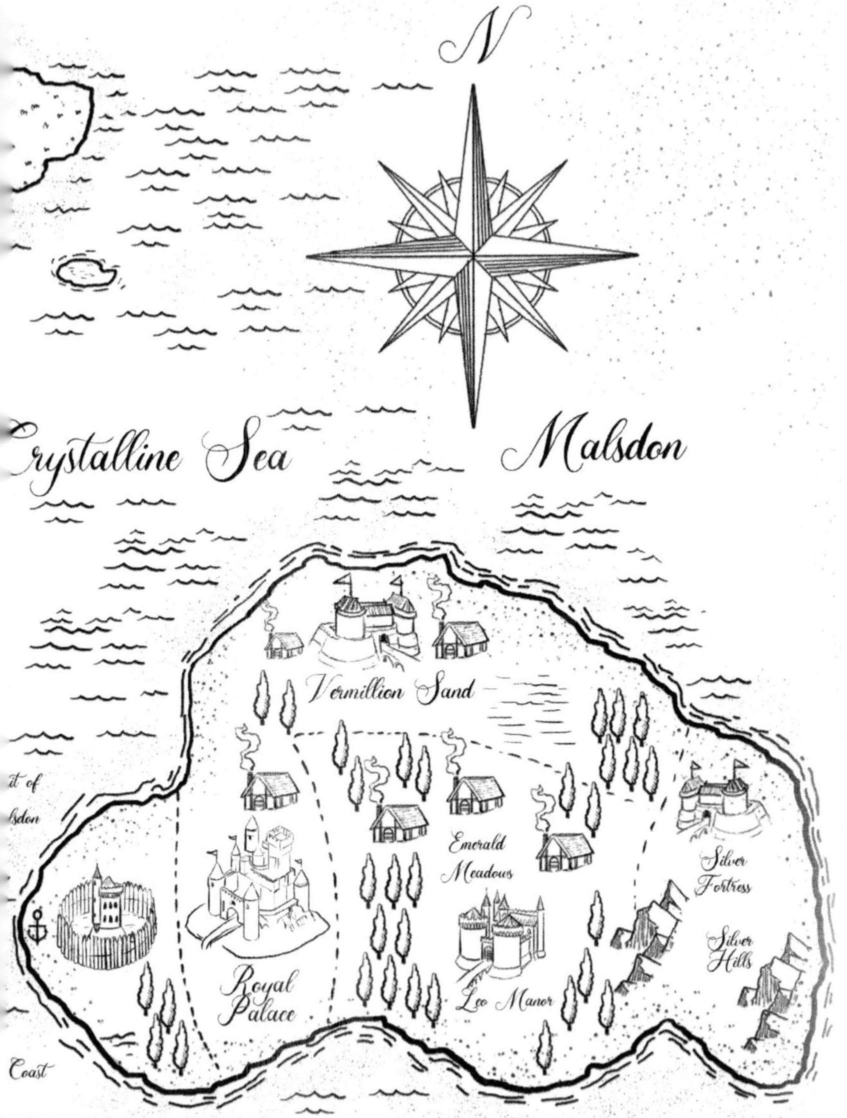
N
Crystalline Sea
Malsdon
Vermillion Sand
Emerald Meadows
Silver Fortress
Silver Hills
Royal Palace
Leo Manor
Coast

MALSDON

The island of Malsdon holds magic at its core, infusing everything that grows and everyone who partakes of its bounty with a unique enchantment. Vast and diverse, the island boasts a multitude of climates.

At the western point of the island lies the Iron Coast, where the air is damp, the skies are often grey, and rainfall is a constant companion, a stark reminder of the scars left by the war against the mages nearly two decades ago. The House of Graw asserts its lordship over these weathered lands.

Set in the north of Malsdon, one encounters the Vermillion Sands, a region where minor houses vie for power amidst slightly arid landscapes that nonetheless support a thriving ecosystem. Exotic plants and animals flourish, and the houses in this area exploit these rare species for economic gain.

In the eastern reaches of Malsdon, the Silver Hills rise in majestic mountains, some composed entirely of pure silver. The House of Silverlight, one of the oldest on Malsdon, holds sway over this mountainous domain.

At the heart of the island, surrounded by lush forests, stands the Royal Palace. From there, the royal family, the House of Lucius, governs all of Malsdon.

To the south, the Emerald Meadows unfold with vast fields of emerald-coloured grass and towering forests that rival mountains in height. This region is home to the House of Leo, who rules over the verdant expanse.

Part One
Shadows Reborn

Chapter One

House of Leo

It was summer on the island of Malsdon, and the Emerald Meadows were in full blossom; the local flora and fauna teemed with life. Around midday, Xavier began to stir from his bed. With a sigh and a lazy yawn, he mumbled to himself, "No more late nights."

Slowly, he climbed out of bed and stumbled towards his bedroom window. "What a view! I love this place," he said as he observed the vast green meadows in the distance, with the wind playing over the hill slopes.

A deep, thunderous roar interrupted his daydream. Xavier shifted his attention to the trail leading to the manor, where he witnessed his father, Lord Darius Leo, riding his gigas lion, storming down the path and into the courtyard of the manor.

"Xavier, why are you not out of bed and ready yet?" Darius asked, looking up at his son.

"Well, Father, I am out of bed, as you can see."

"Don't get cheeky with me, or I'll tell Captain Artemis to give you extra days of training," Darius replied with a playful smile on his face.

"All right, Father, I'll get ready. I'm just tired from last night."

"There's a good lad. But, in all honesty, son, the king is on his way to meet with us, so be quick." Darius jumped off Tiberius and patted him on the head. "Thanks for the help, old timer. You can go and rest in the fields."

Tiberius nodded and walked off.

Xavier finished getting ready and descended the stairs towards the courtyard. He pushed open the large double oak front doors and spotted his father standing there, engrossed in conversation with Captain Artemis.

Captain Artemis turned with a sarcastic look. "Oh, Xavier, I heard you wish to have extra training days with me and the rest of the knights."

"Well, if you're not grumpy and moody, then I might," Xavier teased.

"Are you ever going to stop being cheeky to your elders?" replied the captain.

Before Xavier could reply, the king's horn sounded as they approached the manor. King Theo Lucius, along with four bodyguards and his daughter Princess Isabella, was making his way up the trail.

"We all know why Isabella is here," said Artemis to Xavier, poking him in the side.

"Shut up, old man. She's married now."

"It's never stopped her from taking a few trips here to the Emerald Meadows, if you know what I mean," Artemis replied, winking at Xavier.

"Quiet, the both of you, before I knock both your heads together," Darius said, "Artemis, you should know better, and you say nothing, Xavier."

"Hope I'm not interrupting anything, Darius," laughed the king.

"Nothing important, my lord, just two idiots—my son and the captain of the Knights of Leo—acting like children."

The king dismounted his horse and looked at Darius. "What is this, a handshake?"

"My lord?" Darius replied.

The king sighed, knocking his hand aside, and pulled Darius in for a hug. "The two of us have been through many perils, and

I see you as my brother and equal, so we embrace as brothers," the king said as they hugged. "It's good to see you again as well, Artemis. General Brock sends his regards."

"Thank you, Your Majesty," Artemis replied.

Princess Isabella dismounted her horse and walked towards the group.

"Your Highness," all three greeted her.

"Hello, Lord Darius, Captain Artemis," she replied in a soft tone.

Xavier thought, *Why didn't she greet me? Is she shy or embarrassed?* However, his train of thought was broken by his father's deep voice.

"My king, I will lead you to my war room for us to discuss matters."

"Very good, Darius, lead the way," the king replied. "Oh, young Xavier, could you keep my daughter company?"

"Of course, my king."

The king and his four bodyguards followed Darius and Artemis into the manor towards the war room, leaving Xavier and Isabella outside alone.

"Hello, my Xavier, I haven't forgotten you," she said with innocent eyes but a mischievous smile.

Xavier walked over to her and embraced her with a tight hug. "I've missed you," he whispered.

*

The king, Darius, and Artemis gathered around the large oak table at the centre of the war room. The king's joyful demeanour changed as he reached into his side bag, pulling out an oddly shaped arrowhead and placing it on the table. Darius looked at it in confusion, but Artemis appeared shocked. The king observed both of them.

"Artemis, you look like you've seen a ghost," the king said in a concerned tone.

"I haven't seen this type of arrowhead in decades. Only found on the Forgotten Lands north of the Iron Coast. It belongs to the barbarian tribes," Artemis explained, his shock evident.

"Correct," the king replied.

"How did you come by it?" Darius asked.

"Hera was doing her weekly scout along the coast and over Alice Island. Just before the Forgotten Lands, she returned injured with the arrowhead stuck in her talon," the king explained.

"She was shot over Alice Island? That's too close to the Iron Coast. On the other hand, how could someone shoot a gigas eagle? They fly at great heights," Darius mumbled.

Before Darius could utter another word, Artemis whispered, "Magic."

"Yes," the king replied. "The war with the mages ended with many of their kind dead and buried. However, we never caught Matriarch Delilah, and the Patriarch Dax was injured fleeing Malsdon."

"We have to do something," Artemis urged.

"That is why he is here now, to see us," Darius said to Artemis.

The room fell into silence, and then was broken by the king. "I have asked Sol Silverlight to forge armour and weapons resistant to magic for you, your son, and the Knights of Leo. I must ask you to go to Alice Island and investigate."

"It will be done, my lord," Darius replied.

"What about the Graw family?" Artemis asked, "They control the Iron Coast; they could check the matter quicker than we could."

"I do not trust Ginn Graw. He's only married to my daughter to strengthen our houses' alliances. With his father dead, Ginn and his brother Gavel are wild and reckless. It's too easy to corrupt weak hearts such as theirs with magic," the king explained. "That is why I must ask one more thing from you."

"Anything, my lord," Darius said.

"Xavier has to marry Arabella, to prevent the kingdom from

falling into their hands if anything goes wrong."

Darius nodded in response.

"I know of Isabella and Xavier. She has been told the plan, and if anyone can cure Arabella's cruel heart, it will be Xavier," the king said with a smile.

While the others were inside the war room planning the future, Xavier and Isabella strolled through the vast fields of the Emerald Meadows.

"It's so peaceful here," Isabella said, taking in a deep breath of the fresh air, "I can feel my soul recharging."

"I take it palace life is draining. Maybe you should run away and live here," Xavier replied with a smirk.

Isabella playfully shoved him off the path. "Don't tease like that," she said, with a hint of sorrow in her eyes.

Xavier walked towards her, gently taking hold of her hands and bringing them to his chest. "I'm sorry. Have you been wishing that was so?" he asked softly, looking into her eyes. "I know what will cheer you up."

A small smile appeared across Isabella's face.

Xavier turned away from her, closed his eyes, and called for his two gigas lions. *Saya, Jupiter, come to me.*

The sound of two roars echoed across the fields.

"Here they come," Isabella said with excitement.

The two lions came running towards them, their golden fur glistening in the sun. Xavier hugged both lions before jumping onto Saya's back.

"Come on, Isabella, jump on Jupiter, and we'll go for a ride through the forest," Xavier said, trying to hurry her up.

Isabella climbed onto Jupiter's back, and the two set off.

Xavier and Isabella rode deep into the forest, discovering a serene spot where the forest ceiling opened up, allowing a cascade of sunlight. The two found a comfortable spot on the ground to sit, while Saya and Jupiter wandered off into the forest.

"Isabella, are you okay?" Xavier asked.

"The more we're together, the harder it is for me to accept what is about to take place," Isabella replied.

Xavier could hear heartbreak in her voice. He held her hand as they turned and looked at each other. Her long, dark brown hair covered the sorrow on her face.

"Tell me what is bothering you," Xavier said as he brushed aside her hair.

"Father told me you have to marry Arabella. He has also asked your father to take you and your knights on a dangerous mission, so either way, I'll lose you," Isabella said, tears rolling down her cheek.

Xavier dropped his head, and then embraced her tightly. "I will always love you, and our hearts will be forever joined no matter what happens."

"I love you too," Isabella replied, resting her head on his shoulder.

The two stayed in the forest for a while, lying in silence, savouring each other's company while they listened to the enchanting music of the forest. However, the melody was interrupted by the thumping footsteps of Tiberius.

"Princess, your father is waiting for you. We'll escort you back to the manor now," Darius said.

The sun was setting over the manor, and all were bidding their goodbyes.

"Darius, Sol will meet you here in two days with your new armour and weapons," the king said, "Then, you must make haste to the Iron Coast."

"It will be done, my lord," Darius replied.

The king, Isabella, and his bodyguards mounted their horses and left through the manor gates. Just before they vanished from sight, Isabella turned around and mouthed the words, "Farewell, Xavier. I love you." Then, they faded away from view.

Chapter Two

Gifts

Darius and Xavier sparred with wooden swords in the practice hall, preparing for the task ahead.

"Ah, very good form, my son, but put more power behind those overhead strikes," Darius said as he skilfully blocked Xavier's attacks.

"I know, Father, but it's only practice. I don't need to go full strength," Xavier replied, attempting to find gaps in his father's defence.

Darius stopped and looked directly into Xavier's eyes. "Xavier, experience is a cruel teacher. It gives the exam first and the lesson after. This will be your first taste of real combat, which is rare for someone your age," he told him in a stern but reassuring tone. "I was fifteen when I was thrown into combat, and the person opposite you doesn't care how old you are or how well you practise. They will try to kill you for their cause."

"I know, Father. I'm lucky to reach twenty without having to kill anyone in war, and that's thanks to you and others for winning the war," Xavier said with great humility, glancing at his father's scars that covered his warm honey-toned skin—a reminder of battles past. "This isn't going to be a simple scouting mission, right?"

"I have a feeling it won't be, my son," Darius replied. "Then you'll have to marry Arabella; she might kill you."

Xavier laughed, shaking his head, and the two resumed sparring.

Artemis entered the hall, walking with great haste towards them. "My lords, Lord Silverlight and Master Victor have arrived and are in the courtyard."

"Very good, Artemis. We're coming," Darius replied.

Darius, accompanied by Xavier and Artemis, stepped into the courtyard. Before them were four wagons full of equipment being unloaded by Sol and his men. Sol and Darius exchanged nods of recognition.

"Artemis, get some men and bring the armour and weapons into the barracks. Muster the men; we march at sunset," Darius commanded.

Artemis replied with a nod and got straight to work.

Victor approached Xavier with a gift in hand. Despite being only twelve, Victor was a talented craftsman, a trait synonymous with the Silverlight name.

"Mighty Xavier, I come bearing gifts," Victor said, attempting to deepen his voice.

Xavier chuckled and replied, "Thank you, Master Craftsman," ruffling Victor's hair.

Victor handed over the package, saying, "It's a long coat for you to wear over your armour. It will protect you from all types of weather, and it's very stylish."

Xavier smiled and unwrapped the coat. It was made of black-dyed leather with grey stitching, featuring two lion faces sewn into the lapels and infused with the magical silver found in the Silver Hills' mountains.

"A mighty gift, my young friend," Xavier said.

Victor bowed dramatically and then ran back to the wagons to help unload the rest of the supplies.

Sol dragged two oak chests towards Darius and Xavier. "Still holding onto the salt and pepper look?" Sol teased Darius.

"And your hair is as silver as those mountains of yours," Darius laughed in reply. The two then offered their hands for a handshake.

"I have both of your new custom armour sets here," Sol said proudly. First, he opened Darius' chest, revealing a black and gold chest plate with a lion's face engraved in the centre, along with a red- and gold-infused chainmail shirt.

"Thank you, my friend," Darius said, bowing his head in respect.

"Now for the young Lord Xavier," Sol said while opening his chest. "There's more in here for you, since it'll be your first time as commander."

Xavier turned in surprise towards his father, and Darius smiled and nodded in confirmation.

"I guess I wasn't to mention that yet," Sol said, shrugging. "Come, Xavier, look at your equipment."

Inside the chest was a similar chest plate to his father's, but Xavier's included a neck guard. There was also the same chainmail shirt with a hood attached, padded leather trousers, and, as Xavier took each item out, his eyes lit up like the brightest stars when he saw two swords that only kings should bear.

"Glad you like it, lad," Sol said, patting Xavier on the shoulder.

"I know you prefer to use two swords—a short sword for parry instead of a shield and the normal long sword," Darius explained, "So, I quickly asked Sol to forge you two new swords."

"Thank you, Father. Also, I'm grateful for your skill and hard work, Sol," Xavier said.

"It was my pleasure," Sol replied, while Darius smiled back in response.

Xavier examined both swords as he held them. The pommel featured a gold lion head and wrapped around the handle was magic-treated leather, offering improved grip strength. The cross guard, made from a fusion of steel and other metals, had pointed edges.

"The blade isn't the only dangerous part of the sword," Sol informed him.

Xavier nodded in response, continuing to inspect his new swords. The blades themselves were forged from steel and diamond, giving them an azure colour. Notably, Xavier discovered inscriptions on both blade fullers, each with its own meaning.

Starting with the short sword, he read aloud, "I will always protect the land and the weak." Then, he recited the inscription on the long sword, "With the purest of hearts, I will stay the path." Xavier placed both swords back in their white leather-wrapped scabbards.

"Sol, you've outdone yourself there, my friend. Mighty fine work," Darius said.

Sol, after bowing, replied, "I poured my heart into it, as they say. I wish I could stay longer, but Victor and I have to drop off new swords for the Graw brothers at the palace." Sol placed his hands on each of Xavier's shoulders. "One more thing. These swords have magic infused inside them. Call upon it when you're confronted by pure evil; they will help you." Sol's tone was serious and meaningful.

"I will," Xavier said quietly.

Then, Sol jumped backwards, burst back to life, and exclaimed, "Farewell, friends! Oh, and my daughter will be joining the mighty House of Leo on this scouting quest thing."

Victor and Sol climbed back onto their wagons and left the manor's courtyard.

*

As the sun began to set, Darius and Xavier walked towards the barracks located on the far side of the manor, both donned in their new armour. Xavier, curious, asked his father a question that had lingered in his mind.

"Father, why don't you wear full armour?"

Darius, adjusting his chest plate, explained. "Well, son, when you get as tall as I am, armour becomes too uncomfortable and restricts my movement, which isn't good with a two-handed sword."

"I can't imagine anyone wanting to fight you on a battlefield."

Darius chuckled, patting his thick bushy black and grey beard. "With the scars on my arms, standing over two metres tall, and wielding a claymore, I've already beaten my opponent."

"Beating your opponent mentally is most important," Xavier added.

Darius patted him on the head. "Right, son."

In front of the barracks stood two hundred Knights of Leo in a triple column formation, with Captain Artemis in the lead, accompanied by Tiberius, Saya, and Jupiter. The gigas lions wore custom-made leather armour to protect their necks and bodies. All the knights were clad in full black plate armour, complemented by crimson chainmail or padded leather underneath. They each wore an emerald cloak and carried a weapon of their choice, with many bearing the crimson shield and a sword.

"My Lord Darius, Commander Xavier, the knights are ready and able," announced Artemis, standing at attention.

Darius raised his arm across his chest in salute. "Knights of Leo, my brothers, we are summoned to investigate an unknown threat on Alice Island. Be ready, for the enemy is hiding like cowards. Trust in me, trust in your commander, and trust in your brothers. Together, we will make it through the day!"

In response, the knights raised their weapons in a salute to their lord and commander. The knights loaded into the wagons, while some mounted their own horses. Captain Artemis mounted his horse, ready for the journey.

"Ready, son?" asked Darius.

"Yes, Father," Xavier replied as he mounted Saya.

Darius saluted him and then mounted Tiberius.

"Move out!" Darius commanded, accompanied by Tiberius' mighty roar. The convoy began its journey towards the Iron Coast.

Chapter Three

Friends and Foes

Nearly two days had passed since the convoy departed the Emerald Meadows, reaching the grey, damp atmosphere of the Iron Coast. The convoy descended the muddy and uneven road that cut through the heart of the town, heading towards the docks. They passed old rundown buildings, soulless faces wandering the streets, broken animal pens, and peculiarly shaped holes in the walls.

"Father, what are those holes in the wall?" Xavier asked.

"Magical blasts from mages during the last war," Darius replied.

Xavier looked at them, a mixture of fear and awe in his expression.

"Don't underestimate mages, lad," Artemis added, "You must strike quickly. Also, a little tip for you: they have to pause for a few seconds between spells, and that will be your chance."

"Understood," Xavier replied.

The convoy reached the docks, a crowded assembly of various ships, some not seaworthy, and a clean, well-kept tavern nestled in the corner.

"We know where all the money goes," remarked one of the knights, drawing a few chuckles.

Stepping off one of the ships were Ginn and Gavel Graw.

"Welcome, Lords and Knights of Leo, to the Iron Coast," Ginn said with sarcasm.

"Not as pretty as the Emerald Meadows, but we make do," added Gavel, nonchalantly enjoying a meat pie.

"Shut up, pig," someone retorted, eliciting laughter from the wagons.

"Who said that?" said Gavel, his face reddened with rage.

A cloaked figure emerged from the tavern, flanked by twenty similarly cloaked figures. The figure removed their hood. "I said it, you fool," she replied.

"Well, well, if it isn't the cow, River Silverlight," Gavel sneered, taking another bite from his pie.

River looked at him in disgust before turning towards Darius and Xavier. "My lords, I come with my father's best wishes and twenty of my finest archers," she said, saluting them.

"More than welcome, my lady," Darius replied.

Ginn interjected. "Are we done with the greetings? We've got work to do."

The Knights of Leo, accompanied by fifty of Ginn's men, were loading onto the ships. Xavier, River, Artemis, and Gavel, along with River's archers, boarded the command ship. Meanwhile, Darius was preparing the three lions to board the boat when Ginn approached him.

"Darius, you and I won't be going on this mission, and your pet cats won't be needed," Ginn said.

Darius turned to face him, his voice rumbling through the air, making Ginn nervous. "Who are you to give me such a command?" he asked.

"The king requests our presence at the palace, and as the future king, I echo his words with authority," Ginn replied, attempting to size up to Darius.

Darius erupted in hearty laughter, tears forming in his eyes. Suddenly, he turned serious, seizing Ginn by his collar and lifting him in the air. "We better not keep the king waiting, and if you ever try that stunt with me again, I'll happily crush you with my bare hands, you runt," Darius threatened in a low, sinister tone, releasing his grip and letting Ginn fall to the ground.

"Is everything okay, Father?" Xavier asked, peering over the port side of the boat.

"The king has ordered me to the palace," Darius explained.

"What? Now?" River said, her face reflecting confusion.

Darius shrugged. "I'm taking the lions with me as well."

"I'll look after them," Artemis said as he put his arm around Xavier.

The horn sounded, and the ships began rowing out of the docks. Xavier and Darius exchanged nods before Darius and Ginn left, heading towards the palace.

Three hours later, Darius and Ginn arrived at the palace borders, riding side by side in silence. Saya and Jupiter followed closely, their jade green eyes watching Ginn's every move. Ginn occasionally glanced back, meeting the piercing gazes of the lions.

Breaking the silence, Ginn said, "Your lions don't trust easily."

"No, they can sense lies and the untrustworthy nature of people," Darius explained. "I guess you must be hiding something from everyone."

Ginn laughed nervously. "I have nothing to hide."

Darius looked straight at him, issuing a warning. "My face will be the last you see if anything happens to my son."

Ginn remained silent for the rest of the journey to the checkpoint before the palace outer walls.

They passed through the checkpoint, saluted by the guards, and preceded beyond the massive iron gates. Entering the common grounds, they moved past tents and small stalls selling food and token items. Onlookers gazed in awe at the lions, a rare sight for many who hadn't seen one in person before, as only a handful were alive today. Tiberius roared, and the crowds cheered.

"Showing off as usual, boy," Darius chuckled.

Ginn rolled his eyes in disdain.

Continuing, they reached the inner walls of the palace. The white ivory walls glistened in the sun, adorned with angelic pictures in many of the palace windows. The palace itself stood as tall as the silver mountains.

Ginn and Darius entered the palace courtyard after passing through various gates. The courtyard was a symphony of colours with flowers and well-trimmed bushes. The pathway leading to the palace steps was adorned with bright crystal lamps on both sides, each housing a never-ending flame.

Dismounting Tiberius, Darius was followed by Ginn, and they proceeded along the path, flanked by their majestic animals.

At the bottom of the stairs, two figures awaited them. General Brock, clad in the bright white and gold plate armour of the royal army, stood alongside King Theo, who wore his casual attire—a red outfit with golden-coloured boots.

The four men exchanged greetings, and then ascended the palace steps, leaving stable boys to attend to the lions and Ginn's horse. Reaching the top, they entered the palace.

Inside, General Brock addressed Darius, his posh deep voice echoing in the vast open halls. "What is the report from Alice Island?"

"Nothing yet. The others must be close to the island as we speak," Darius replied.

"Why are you here now, Darius?" the king asked.

"Your Majesty, you summoned me before the ships set sail," Darius explained, growing irritated due to the confusion.

The king turned to Ginn, muttered, "You fool," and slapped Ginn on the side of his head.

"What is going on?" Darius demanded, growing more furious by the second.

"Forgive me, my lord. You were meant to come *after* the scouting mission," General Brock explained, "But some fool gave you the wrong information."

"I'm sorry, my lords," Ginn said with no remorse in his voice.

This filled Darius with rage, and the king, sensing it, grabbed Darius' arm.

"He will be dealt with, my friend, but your son and your knights are the most capable warriors in the land," King Theo said, trying to defuse Darius' temper.

"Move from my sight," Darius said to Ginn, his stern voice rumbling throughout the halls.

Ginn smiled at Darius before walking off into one of the many hallways in the palace, further infuriating Darius.

"Walk with me, Darius," the king said, and the two parted from General Brock, leaving him to attend to palace business.

Darius and the king entered one of the palace's many rooms. "Deal with him, Theo, before I do," Darius said with frustration.

"Calm down, Darius. I will deal with him. Now, leave it," the king replied.

Darius banged his hands on the table, and then stroked his beard while contemplating his thoughts.

"Lord Darius, are you all right?" a soft voice asked as Princess Isabella entered the room.

"Princess Isabella, pardon my behaviour," Darius said, dropping his head in a bow.

"Greetings, Father," Isabella said, bowing her head.

"Daughter, where is your sister? We must plan her wedding, as it is next month," the king said.

"I'll go fetch her, Father."

A few moments later, Isabella returned with Arabella. The two sisters looked similar; both had their father's beige complexion. However, Arabella's hair was a bright blonde, not golden brown like Isabella's, and she was a bit taller despite being the younger sister.

"Ah, Darius, where does time go? Isabella is twenty-three, and Arabella turned eighteen. It makes me feel old," the king said.

"Xavier turned twenty this past spring. Time waits for no man," Darius replied.

The two started to reminisce and laugh about old times.

"Are the old men finished reliving the good old days?" Arabella said cheekily. "We've got my wedding to plan."

Isabella held in her sorrow but put on an act to keep anyone from noticing.

"Very well, let's begin," the king said.

Isabella observed her sister as she assertively directed the details of her wedding, with their father readily agreeing to every demand. Isabella couldn't help but reminisce about planning her own wedding— what should have been the happiest day of her life—and a smile played on her lips. Arabella, misinterpreting the smile, beamed back at her.

Turning her gaze towards Darius, who stood by the window, Isabella noticed him chiming into the planning occasionally. She understood Xavier and his men were occupying his thoughts. In her heart, she shared the same worry and longed to see Xavier one last time before the impending wedding.

Chapter Four

The Moments That Change You

The ships rocked side to side in the rough tides, and the sounds of men vomiting echoed as they experienced the sea for the first time. Below deck, Xavier, Artemis, Gavel, and River were going over the plan. Xavier placed a map of Alice Island on the wooden table.

"We're landing here on the south beach," Xavier said, pointing to the map. "We'll push through this forest and make our way to this hill."

"Very good, Commander," Artemis said, nodding at him proudly.

"Any suspicious people are likely to be here," River added, "It's an open area, so it will be easy to make camp along with the fresh water source."

"We'll take up positions on all sides of this area," Artemis said, pointing to each location. "I'll take the west side, and River will take the east side on top of the hill with your archers. Watch over us."

"Of course, my darlings," River replied.

"That leaves me to take the north side," Xavier said, "And Gavel to cover the south. Gavel, you'll have to cover our escape route and protect the ships."

"Not to worry, young commander. Me and my men have got you covered," Gavel said while adjusting his chainmail over his oversized belly.

"We're leaving our escape route and ship to this fool?" River said with distaste.

"Well, I am a part of this mission and the most important here," Gavel said.

"Stupid pig," River replied, and then stormed off topside.

"I guess it's settled," Artemis said, and went off to check on the men.

Xavier rolled up the map and ascended topside. There, he noticed River leaning on the ship's side, evidently feeling unwell.

"Excuse me, Xavier. I don't look very ladylike," she laughed.

He smiled and reached into his coat pocket. "Here," he said, offering her a slice of a white fruit resembling an apple.

River accepted it without hesitation and quickly devoured it.

"Wow, it's very sweet. What is it?" she asked.

"It's called angel fruit. It calms the stomach from any pain or discomfort," Xavier explained.

"Thank you, dear," she said, winking at Xavier. "I don't know if it's the rough waves of the sea or being that close to that pig Gavel."

"Maybe both," Xavier replied, laughing.

The two stood there, gazing out onto the waves.

"Heard you're marrying Arabella," River said, breaking the silence between them.

"Yeah."

"Arabella is all right. She's a pretty girl, just a bit misunderstood and perhaps a tad power-hungry," River added, "But I know your heart belongs to someone else."

"Yeah, you," he replied.

They exchanged a glance and burst into laughter.

"Why aren't you married yet?" Xavier asked.

River exhaled loudly. “I’ve always aspired to be a knight since a young age. Now, at twenty-eight, I’m still going strong. Besides, my father wasn’t pushy about marriage.”

Xavier nodded and saluted her.

“Anyway, I prefer fighting men over marrying them,” she chuckled, giving Xavier a friendly slap on the back.

“Land approaching, make ready!” shouted one of the soldiers.

Artemis ascended to the deck, followed by Gavel. He nodded at Xavier and River, who were preparing themselves. River’s attention was drawn to one of her men carrying her bow and two quivers. She took them from him, slinging both quivers onto her back and resting her bow on her shoulder.

“Two quivers?” Xavier asked.

“One for shooting idiots like Gavel, and this special one on my left is for when we’re in real trouble, young commander,” she replied with a more serious tone.

“Understood.”

As the ship neared the shore, it eventually made contact with the south beach of Alice Island. All the men disembarked, anticipating orders. The Knights of Leo gathered around Xavier and Artemis, dividing into two groups. River and her men seamlessly integrated into Xavier’s group. She winked at Xavier, offering thumbs up for encouragement.

Gavel’s men, the last to disembark, resembled more common thugs than professional soldiers or knights. Their armour was old, mismatched, and soiled— a stark contrast to the disciplined appearance of the Knights of Leo.

All groups marched towards their assigned staging points, as marked on the map. Upon reaching the hilltop, they were met with a startling sight—an expansive barbarian encampment, complete with stockpiles of weapons and armour. River and Artemis, leaving their men at the designated points, quickly approached Xavier.

"Well, this is more than I thought we would find," Xavier said as they reached his position.

"There must be at least five hundred of them," River replied, "And we don't even have three hundred men combined."

"That's the least of our troubles," Artemis added.

"What now?" River asked.

"That person in the black cloak and mask is a mage," Artemis said with concern.

"River, you have to take them down before any real damage is inflicted upon us," Xavier said.

"I've got your back," she replied, patting him on the head.

"I'll attack from my side first," Artemis said, "After I've drawn them towards me, Xavier will come up behind them."

"I'll signal Gavel to join the attack," Xavier added.

"Let's hope the fool leaves a few men to protect the ship," River replied.

"Good luck, everyone," Artemis said, hurrying back to his position.

"This is it. You've got this." River gave Xavier a hearty slap on the back, and then ran back to her archers.

Xavier took a deep breath, glancing back at his knights who saluted in return. Their task was clear: watch for Artemis and his men to initiate the first attack. The silence hung heavy, broken only by the sound of breath and the knights behind him. Xavier could hear his own heartbeat, causing his chest plate to vibrate. Closing his eyes, he gripped the hilt of his long sword, attempting to channel all his power and might, seeking calmness.

His focus shattered by the sudden sounds of battle, he drew his sword. "For glory and the protection of the innocents!" Xavier shouted, rallying his men before the charge.

The knights drew their swords in unison, letting out a war cry. Charging down the hill, with Xavier at the forefront, they collided with the enemy. Some foes turned to meet them, but most were engaged with Artemis' group.

Xavier and his knights crashed into the barbarians, knocking some to the ground. The air resonated with the sounds of swords clashing against shields and armour; arrows whistled overhead from River's archers, startling many barbarians. Xavier and his men applied pressure, squeezing the opposition.

Growing in confidence after defeating a few enemies, Xavier ordered his men to intensify the assault. Suddenly, several knights were sent flying through the air. As Xavier's view cleared, he spotted the mage they had identified earlier, accompanied by a deformed, brutish man. The brute looked more like a monster than a man.

Artemis made eye contact with Xavier and pointed towards the mage, indicating they needed to take it out. Xavier and Artemis charged through the fighting crowds towards the mage and brute. However, Artemis was suddenly blasted into the air by one of the mage's magical attacks, rendering him unconscious upon landing.

Xavier came face to face with the brute and mage, drawing his short sword for added protection. The mage laughed and waved his hands, creating a dome that trapped Xavier and the brute inside. River noticed the dome and attempted to shoot the mage with a special silver arrow, but he kept teleporting around the battlefield. Two of Xavier's knights tried to break through the dome, but their efforts were in vain as the energy repelled them.

Waving the knights away, Xavier shouted, "Signal Gavel and his men. We need support."

Xavier assumed a defensive stance, holding his short sword close to his body and extending his long sword slightly further away, levelled with his neck. The brute roared and mumbled, then hoisted a massive battle axe off his back. The axe loomed taller than Xavier. The brute laughed, dragging his weapon through the dirt and sand as he approached Xavier.

Realising he couldn't defeat the brute in a purely defensive stance, Xavier closed his eyes for a moment and took a deep breath, purging his body of fear and doubt. Gripping his swords tightly, he charged the brute, catching him off guard. However, the brute recovered swiftly, swinging his axe towards Xavier's head. Xavier sidestepped quickly, seizing the opportunity to slash down the brute's side. Yet, to his dismay, the brute's tough skin deflected his sword, the recoil jolting Xavier to the core.

The brute laughed, turned, and, with surprising speed, grabbed Xavier's lapel, hurling him against the dome. River, witnessing the brute overpowering Xavier within the dome, intensified her efforts. She fired a rapid volley of arrows, attempting to break the dome, but they rebounded off its surface.

"Damn it!" she shouted. Glancing at her second quiver, which held only two silver arrows, she pondered. She knew she had to save these for the mage or possibly to use on the dome, although there was no guarantee they would dismantle the structure.

The brute relentlessly swung his axe, targeting Xavier's head. Xavier rolled and leapt to evade the attacks, but with each manoeuvre, exhaustion set in. The brute showed no signs of tiring, prompting Xavier to realise conventional methods wouldn't secure victory.

Closing the gap, Xavier manoeuvred inside the brute's swinging range. As the brute swung his axe, Xavier executed a swift roll and stabbed his short sword into the brute's foot. The brute screamed in pain, stumbling backwards. Seizing the opportunity, Xavier grabbed a handful of sand, throwing it into the brute's eyes. Despite the confusion, the brute swung his free hand, connecting with Xavier's cheek and drawing blood. Stunned, Xavier recovered quickly, stabbing the brute's other foot. With his long sword, he thrust it through the brute's throat, and then kicked out his legs, causing him to collapse.

Exhausted, Xavier dropped to his knees, while the brute lay gasping for air. As the brute's life faded, so did the dome. The dissipating dome caught the mage's attention, causing a brief pause in their teleportation. River, seizing the opportunity, drew a silver arrow and whispered an enchantment. The arrow transformed into a blinding silver light as she locked it onto her bow, pulling back the string with all her might.

With a powerful release, the arrow shot through the sky like a bolt of lightning. The mage attempted to conjure a barrier for protection, but it was too late. The arrow struck the mage in the chest, knocking them to the ground. The mage's body vibrated and steamed before exploding into a red mist, kicking up sand and dirt.

Xavier stood slowly, the echoes of battle still resounding around him. Surveying the scene, he observed his knights scattered into small groups, engaged in combat. There was no sign of Artemis. Xavier reached for his small horn attached to his belt, blowing it three times in rapid succession. The familiar signal prompted his men to form a V-shaped formation.

Responding swiftly to the call, his knights disengaged from their individual skirmishes and rallied into the ordered formation. The timing was impeccable, trapping the remaining barbarians in the centre of the V. Xavier blew the horn once more, a single note signalling the commencement of the press. His knights closed in on the barbarians like a vice, executing the strategic manoeuvre with precision.

Xavier was about to join his knights when he noticed Artemis on the ground a few metres away. Concerned, he rushed to his aid, shaking Artemis, but there was no response. Xavier, growing more urgent, grabbed Artemis by his collar, lifting him into a seated position, and delivered a resounding slap across his face. Startled, Artemis sprang to life.

"By all things mighty, I'm alive, boy," he said, rubbing his cheek.

"Good, we're not finished yet," Xavier replied.

He helped Artemis to his feet, picked up his fallen sword, and placed it in his hand.

Artemis winced while holding his shoulder. "I think it's out of place," he groaned, "But I can still fight."

"Let's go, old man," Xavier said, and the two rushed off to rejoin the formation.

The battle persisted for a few more minutes. Despite being outnumbered, the Knights of Leo, highly trained and conditioned soldiers, combined with River's skilled archers, proved formidable. The remaining barbarians, realising the odds were against them, attempted to break ranks and flee. However, River and her archers unleashed a hail of arrows, preventing their escape. Soon, the sounds of battle faded into the soothing sounds of the sea.

River raised her bow in salute at Xavier, and he responded by lifting his sword in acknowledgment.

"Well done, boys," River said.

"Thank you, River, for dealing with the mage," Xavier replied.

"I told you I had your backs."

"All right, men, start gathering evidence!" Artemis shouted.

As the soldiers began collecting weapons and items from the defeated barbarians, Gavel and his men finally arrived. This triggered River's rage, and she stormed towards Gavel with undisguised hatred. Drawing her sword, she pointed it directly at Gavel's face.

"Where were you?" she asked calmly.

"I didn't see the signal," he replied, smirking at his men.

"You are a fat, useless man, unworthy of this world."

River's rage reached a boiling point, and she aimed her sword at Gavel's throat. However, Artemis intervened, grabbing her and pulling her away to calm down.

Xavier scrutinised Gavel, and then addressed him. "Don't interfere with the evidence gathering."

"No, we have to burn all of it," Gavel said, attempting to assert dominance.

Xavier, still recovering from the battle, sighed; his patience thin. "We have to show this to the king. This isn't a minor raiding party; they were setting up for an invasion."

Gavel pushed past Xavier. "Know your place," he sneered, then ordered his men to burn everything.

"We're leaving with the evidence we gathered, and if you want it, you'll have to take it by force. It won't end well for you or your men," Xavier warned, locking eyes with Gavel.

Gavel spat on the ground, opting not to reply.

Xavier, recognising the futility of further confrontation, ordered his men to return to the ships.

While on the ships back to the Iron Coast, Xavier and River sifted through the evidence.

"Where are the remains of the mage's cloak and mask?" Xavier asked.

"That fat pig must have burnt it before your men picked it up," River said, slamming her fist on the table. "Artemis, you should have let me kill him."

"Then your father and brother would be punished along with you," Xavier reminded her.

"His day will come." A sinister smile crossed her face. "And I will be the one to kill that pig."

Xavier couldn't blame her, knowing the tension between River and Gavel.

Artemis walked in with his arm in a bandage. "Don't worry about Gavel; the king will believe our evidence."

"I hope so, old man," River said.

After River's words, they sat in silence, appreciating each other's company after a hard-fought battle.

A few hours later, they arrived at the port, gathering all the equipment and evidence off the ship.

"Place all the evidence on that wagon," Xavier said, "I'm taking it to the palace now."

"I'm coming with you," Artemis insisted.

"No, you go back to the Emerald Meadows with the rest of the knights."

"Don't worry, old man," River said. "Rest your broken wing; I'll go with him."

Artemis took a deep breath. "Behave yourself, River."

River smiled at Artemis, then ordered her archers back to the Silver Hills to inform her father of what took place. She then jumped on Xavier's wagon, and they set off to the palace.

CHAPTER FIVE

THE TRUTH

Xavier and River arrived in the palace courtyard, where Darius, Saya, and Jupiter greeted them. Xavier jumped off the wagon, and the two lions rushed over to him, rubbing their bodies on him and licking his hands. Xavier stroked their backs, finding comfort in their soft fur.

"I'm glad you're still alive, son," Darius said.

"It wasn't easy, but River, Artemis, and the knights made sure we all made it back."

"Thank you, River," said Darius.

"No problem," she replied, joining them after jumping off the wagon.

"Have you got the reports, son?" Darius asked.

"Yes, Father," Xavier replied. "We collected what we could from the battle for evidence."

"We could have gotten the mage's cloak and mask, but that pig said he had orders to burn it," River added.

"You fought a mage?" Darius asked.

"Yes, and River killed him with enchanted silver arrows," Xavier replied.

"The three of us will present the reports to the king now," Darius said. "Men, unload the evidence and bring it to General Brock."

The three then made their way into the palace and Arabella greeted them.

"I'm so glad you made it back, Xavier," she said, "We have so much to talk about."

"We'll meet you in the war chamber, but don't take long," Darius said as he and River left, leaving Xavier alone with Arabella.

Xavier took her hand and kissed it.

"Such a gentleman," she remarked. She then began sharing details about the wedding plans.

As she spoke, Xavier's mind slowly drifted away still preoccupied with thoughts of the battle and the political manoeuvres of the Graw brothers. He snapped back from his daydream and smiled at Arabella. Taking both her hands, he said, "I have to go back; we will have time to talk soon."

"Okay and get that cut treated," she said, shooing him away.

Xavier bowed and went off to join the others.

Xavier pushed open the door and was greeted by chaos. River was berating Ginn, Darius paced up and down, and the king sat in the background.

"Your brother is a worm of a man!" River shouted at Ginn.

"Is that so? You have no place among us, scum," Ginn replied.

"Greetings, Xavier," King Theo said, trying to interject over the heated argument.

"My brother sent his report by crow about what happened," Ginn said, "You and the Knights of Leo were looting the dead. On top of that, you threatened my brother at sword point."

The king stood up, took the report from Ginn, and Darius walked over to hand over their reports. After the king sat back down, he reviewed the reports.

Xavier approached River, asking, "What happened in here?"

"Well, we came inside, and Ginn was there. After what his brother did, I lost it again," she replied.

"You sure did," Darius remarked, shaking his head. He stood behind both of them, placing his hands on their shoulders. "The Graw brothers are nothing more than paid thugs. Since their father died, all the honour that house had died with him. The king pays them to keep the Iron Coast well-guarded and looked after to protect Malsdon's coast."

"From what I saw, that coin is going somewhere else," River added.

The king stood up and laid the reports on the table. "Xavier, well done on your first command. I'm sure your father is proud; however, I'm not." The king turned to River. "You bring shame to your house, threaten the life of a lord, and lie about the mage."

"There was a mage," said Xavier, "Everyone who was present on the field saw the mage."

"I'm going to let that slide, Xavier, because you're Darius' son, but don't ever interrupt me," the king warned him.

"Where's the evidence?" Ginn said, "My brother said it was someone with powerful enchantment skills who created that dome."

"My king, Xavier and River have no reason to lie," Darius said.

"She has hated me and my brother ever since we killed her stupid bear in self-defence. She has every reason to lie, and she has corrupted your son's mind as well," Ginn replied.

This was the breaking point for River. She leant over the table, grabbed Gavel's report, and laughed sarcastically for a moment.

"River, know your place," the king said, "Remove yourself from this room and calm down."

She turned and cut her eye at the king; a stunned look came across his face.

"This report is a load of lies and full of muck from the pig pen you and your brother crawled out from," she said. "A small camp with only a hundred men… River pointing a sword, well that's true, and burnt the bodies as they began to rot straight after death," she read from some of the report. She then turned to the king. "The Graw brothers will be your downfall. Mark my words."

"River Silverlight, remove yourself from my sight," the king replied sternly.

"We saw a camp of five hundred barbarians and a mage," she continued, "This was a battle group, and their purpose was to take and hold the Iron Coast for an invasion."

"Rubbish! No one can take the Iron Coast," Ginn adamantly declared.

"Unless you let them in. They're likely spies or an advanced scouting party already in Malsdon," she argued.

"My king, I'll remove her from the palace," Ginn said.

River got into a fighting stance, directing her posture towards Ginn.

"River, that is enough, you've said enough," King Theo said, "For your father's sake, I will not punish you, but you're not welcome at the palace until further notice. Return home to the Silver Hills."

In one last act of defiance, River grabbed the reports and threw them into the air. With an enchantment, she set them on fire and walked out of the room. Xavier followed her to see if she was okay.

"I'll take my leave, my lords, and look for these spies," Ginn said, mocking, as he exited the room.

"Darius, my friend, have I turned weak or too trusting?" the king said.

"Theo, you're not weak. Just many things are at play right now."

"Do I double the patrols and increase the garrison at the palace?" the king asked.

"My lord, once the word gets out, it will set things in motion. You must decide in what way the wind blows," Darius replied.

*

River stormed through the halls, tears forming in her eyes from the overwhelming emotions. Xavier caught up with her and pulled her by the arm.

"River, are you okay?" he asked.

"I'm fine," she said, wiping the tears from her eyes.

"We'll sort it out, don't worry."

"You saw what I saw. Things are only going to get worse from now on. I'm going back to the Silver Hills to muster the garrison," she told him.

"What happened to your bear?" Xavier asked. "I never knew you had bonded with a gigas animal."

Her head dropped in response to the question. "It was eighteen years ago. Me, my father, the king, the Graw brothers, and their father, we were hunting for the blue vultures," she said, struggling to continue telling the story. "The vultures were spawned from magic, and with the mages gone at that time, they were more out of control, attacking villages and livestock. So, the king and I brought along our gigas bears. I'd only been bonded to Silver for under a year, and they killed her."

Xavier smiled. "Your family loves all things silver."

River broke into light laughter. "Yeah, we do have an obsession."

"How did they kill her?"

"They lied, said she went crazy, and they had no choice but to kill her using the silver-forged spear we gave them to kill the vultures," she replied. Tears started forming in her eyes again. "She was fine; I sensed it. She was tracking the scent of the vultures' nest."

Xavier felt the emotions coming from River as she told the story, then something caught his attention. "Was the nest never found?" he asked.

River caught onto the same thought as Xavier. "No, the hunt stopped, and the king's bear fell ill," she said. "The bears were the only ones who could lead us to the nest."

Xavier looked at River and said, "I have a feeling there's a plot to take over Malsdon."

River nodded in response. "The Graw brothers are at the centre of this plot."

"Stockpile supplies and arms. We'll do the same," Xavier told her.

River nodded and hugged Xavier. "I'll be in the Silver Hills; call upon me when you're ready to fight," she said, before walking down the palace halls and out of sight.

Xavier wandered the vast halls of the palace, contemplating the events that had transpired and those that loomed in the future. His armour felt unusually burdensome, the wound on his cheek an irritating reminder. Lost in his thoughts, he entered a trance, standing motionless in the middle of the hall.

Darius was passing by and noticed his son standing there, his light brown eyes devoid of their usual vitality. Concerned, Darius rushed over and shook Xavier. "Son, are you all right?"

Xavier snapped back, blinking his eyes. "Something bad is going to happen, and I know you see it coming."

"Let me worry about that, son. You go to the kitchens, get some food, and have someone dress that wound."

"We're not going back to the Meadows tonight?" Xavier asked.

"No, you need a good night's rest, and the king has allowed us to stay."

"All right, Father," Xavier said and slowly set off in search of the kitchen.

Approaching midnight, most of the palace was asleep or had retired to their chambers. However, Xavier found himself in the kitchen, sitting alone for a while before deciding to search for food. He gathered bread, dried meat, and some freshly picked wild berries before settling down.

As he began to eat slowly, a voice from the door said, "Do you want some company?"

A smile appeared on his face. "Your presence is always welcome," he said, and Isabella stepped out of the shadow of the doorway.

The two sat together as Xavier finished eating.

"Your father told me to check on you; he's worried," she said.

"I'm okay, just a lot of things occupying my mind."

"Tell me what troubles you."

"I think we're all in danger, Isabella."

"Your father told me what happened, and I hope my father believes your report," she replied. Isabella stood up and took Xavier's hand. "Let's get you out of that armour and take care of that wound."

Xavier smiled, following her to one of the palace's guest chambers. Isabella led Xavier into the chamber, shutting the door behind them.

Unbeknownst to them, Arabella lurked in the shadows of the hall.

Consumed by rage and jealousy, Ginn whispered to her, "See, Arabella, he's not honourable, and neither is your sister."

"What are you going to do about her?" she asked.

"I just want to be king, and I have a plan," he replied.

"I want to be queen. I hate her," she said angrily.

"Your father knew about Isabella cavorting with Xavier and did nothing," he said, attempting to turn Arabella against her father.

"Father wants me to marry him," she said, trying to hold back tears of anger. "Tell me about your plan, Ginn."

Ginn smiled, knowing he had Arabella on his side. "Let's go somewhere more private, and I'll tell you everything, my future queen."

*

Inside the guest chambers, Xavier began the process of removing his armour. He started with his overcoat, a gift from Victor, and then moved on to his chest plate. Struggling with the last buckle, he found himself unable to reach it. Observing his difficulty, Isabella stepped forwards and skilfully undid the last buckle. With a relieved sigh, the chest plate dropped to the floor, and Xavier proceeded to remove his chainmail, eventually settling on a wood bench in front of the fireplace.

Isabella fetched a water bucket from the corner of the room and brought it over. "Let me clean your wound properly."

Xavier nodded, and Isabella reached into the bucket, drawing out a wet rag to tend to his wound.

After Isabella finished, the two remained seated in front of the fireplace, reminiscing about old times. However, time was ticking away, and Isabella was aware that being seen with Xavier could have disastrous consequences.

"Xavier, it's time for me to go, perhaps for good," she said.

Xavier, understanding the changing times for both of them, replied, "I know, Isabella. I know."

They both stood up, and Xavier gently took both of her hands before kissing them. "As long as I live, you'll always have my protection," he said, looking straight into her vale green eyes.

"I know," she whispered. A lump formed in Isabella's throat, and tears welled up. She tightly embraced Xavier, saying, "I didn't lose you in battle, but now I fear losing you to my sister, who doesn't deserve you."

Before Xavier could respond, she rushed out through the chamber's door.

*

The morning sun rose as Darius and General Brock conversed in the courtyard, overseeing the preparation of wagons for the journey back to the Emerald Meadows. Meanwhile, Xavier descended the palace steps alongside Arabella and the king.

Darius and Brock exchanged salutes before Brock proceeded towards the palace steps.

"Farewell, my friend," the king said.

"Farewell, my king," Darius replied.

Arabella beamed at Xavier. "My love, only a month until our wedding."

"Yes, it will be a joyful day," he replied.

"Also, my love, we'll be hosting a grand party two days before the wedding," she informed him.

Xavier looked at her, wondering if this was part of the plot or if he was being paranoid. "I'm sure it will be grand," he said.

CHAPTER SIX

HIDDEN DAGGER

The day of Arabella's grand party had arrived. The palace bustled with life as maids set up tables with food and drink, and music echoed throughout the halls. Arabella, with Isabella's assistance, tried on dresses.

"I heard Ginn has gifted you hundreds of the finest warriors from all over the lands," Isabella said.

"Yes, he has. They'll be stationed all around the palace," Arabella replied.

"Why do we need them when we have the royal guards?"

"I've given the night off to all the married guards."

"That seems a bit dangerous, being short on guards while hosting a party."

"Father said it's fine," Arabella replied sharply.

"I heard Xavier is bringing fifty knights with him," Isabella added.

"Xavier has been paranoid ever since that day at Alice Island," Arabella said. "Anyway, I'll be the one to comfort him as his future wife," she added, testing Isabella for a reaction.

"Well, sister, I must leave you now and prepare your gift," Isabella said.

Arabella was filled with excitement. "Thank you, Isabella. Now, go get my gift ready."

The sun began to set, and Princess Arabella's grand party was coming to life. People from all over Malsdon had gathered to partake in the festivities. Xavier and Darius arrived at the party fashionably late. Before entering the palace, Xavier discreetly stowed his swords on Saya and placed two spare ones on Jupiter.

"I understand your distrust in the Graw brothers, but our knights serve as bodyguards, and they are permitted to bear arms," Darius said.

Xavier remained silent, focusing on Saya and Jupiter. "I'll need your assistance if anything goes awry."

The two lions quietly withdrew, finding a secluded spot in the palace gardens to wait out of sight. Tiberius looked to Darius for instructions, receiving a nod of approval before trailing Saya and Jupiter.

Xavier and Darius entered the ballroom where the party was at its peak. Guests were drinking, and many were dancing. They were introduced to the room by one of the palace guards.

"Presenting Lord Darius and Lord Xavier of the House of Leo."

They mingled with the guests, exchanging small talk, and were approached by Sol Silverlight.

"Young commander," Sol said, raising his glass to Xavier.

"Good to see you, Sol," Darius said, nodding.

"Thank you for the swords and armour, Lord Sol," Xavier replied humbly.

Sol nodded and leant in close to Xavier, whispering, "River has mustered a thousand knights at the Silver Hills."

Xavier was surprised and thought, *She actually did it.*

"She waits for your signal," Sol added.

"Tell her she has my thanks," Xavier replied.

"Anyway, gentlemen, people to meet and such," said Sol as he wandered off into the crowd.

"He's a weird one," Xavier said.

"Don't let his character fool you," Darius replied, "He's the deadliest archer in all of Malsdon. He's only ever missed the target once."

"Who was the target?" Xavier asked.

"Someone we wished he landed the killing blow on," Darius replied.

Xavier didn't ask any more questions, sensing an uneasy feeling from his father about the matter.

Xavier reached for a goblet of wine when a voice warned, from over his shoulder, "Careful, it might be poisoned."

Startled, he turned, only to find Isabella standing there in a shiny cream dress.

"That wouldn't be great, would it?" he replied.

"No, it wouldn't," she said, taking the goblet from his hand.

"Ah, a princess shouldn't be drinking from the common wine table," he teased.

"I'm not too bothered; there are more important things to worry about," she replied, looking directly into Xavier's eyes.

He wondered what had happened since they last spoke.

"What do you know, Isabella?" he asked.

"My spies have observed numerous shipments arriving at the Iron Coast without inspection."

Xavier looked at her in surprise.

"I trusted you, so I instructed my spies to investigate Ginn and Gavel as well," she added.

"You're amazing."

"Also, Gavel has been seen in the Vermillion Sands for the past month. I've been told he might be bribing many of the smaller houses."

"Thank you, Isabella. You're the queen Malsdon deserves."

She laughed nervously and downed the goblet of wine she took from him. "Dance with me?"

Before Xavier could respond, he was dragged onto the dance floor.

"What's this about, Isabella?" he asked as they danced.

"This will be the last time we'll be able to do this."

Xavier absorbed her words, realising that if Arabella discovered his closeness to Isabella, it would endanger her life.

Meanwhile, at the top end of the ballroom, where the royal table was positioned, sat the king, Darius, Arabella, and Ginn.

"Quite the celebration," Darius said to Arabella.

"Indeed," she replied.

"It's heartening to witness the people of Malsdon gathered here," added the king.

As they conversed, a hooded lady approached the table. Darius stood up, ready to defend the king.

"Settle down, Darius," Arabella said. "This is the famous bard Delilah. She's here to enchant us with her wonderful songs."

Delilah smiled at Darius, who cautiously returned to his seat, still watchful of her movements.

The king and Arabella rose from their seats, and as the music ceased, all eyes turned to them.

"Lords and ladies of Malsdon," the king announced, "My daughter Princess Arabella has a gift for everyone."

"Behold Delilah, whose songs are known to warm the heart and relax the soul," Arabella said.

Delilah removed her hooded cloak, letting it drop to the floor, revealing her long golden hair and a white dress that gleamed in the ballroom lights like fresh snow under the moonlight. The crowd fell into awe. Delilah signalled to the musicians, and they began to play a slow, sombre melody.

As she sang, the lyrics had an unsettling effect. Darius and the king exchanged uneasy glances, observing others in the room as if entranced by the music. Meanwhile, Sol rushed over to Xavier and Isabella, who were seemingly captivated by the performance.

"Xavier, something doesn't feel right about that woman," Sol said, attempting to get his attention. Poking Xavier in the throat, Sol finally broke his trance.

"Sol?" Xavier asked in confusion.

Sol directed Xavier's gaze towards his father. Darius locked eyes with Xavier, subtly signalling danger. Xavier paused, gathering himself. Suddenly, the music stopped, and the room erupted in applause for Delilah.

"What's wrong, Xavier? And when did Sol get here?" Isabella asked.

"That bard, she feels too familiar," Sol said.

Ginn rose and Arabella joined him.

"Thank you, everyone, for attending the party before the wedding," Arabella said, "The night is still young and full of surprises."

The room erupted in cheers. Delilah strolled over to the royal table, catching Darius' gaze. She winked at him, brushing her hair back, revealing a scar on her neck from a sword slash. Darius, taken aback, moved back and was about to whisper something to the king.

Ginn noticed Darius' reaction and leapt over the table, causing a scene. He took Delilah's hand and addressed the crowd. "My fair people, this is a celebration of love." He looked straight at Isabella and Xavier.

Arabella jumped on the table, adding, "Yes, the wonderful Delilah. However, my sister Isabella isn't the wonderful princess you all think. She's been unfaithful to her husband and spends her time with another man. Father isn't the fair king; he's forcing me to marry that man."

The crowd gasped, turning their attention to Isabella and Xavier.

"That's enough, Arabella. You're drunk and talking nonsense," the king said.

An uneasy silence fell over the room.

Ginn then announced, "I declare my marriage with Isabella Lucius void, and I'll be taking Arabella as my wife," followed by a kiss with Arabella.

Isabella and Xavier stood in shock.

"Guards, remove this man and place him in the stockades," the king demanded, but the guards did nothing.

"They're not your men," Delilah revealed.

Darius jumped up to confront Delilah, but she pushed him away with a magical blast.

"Matriarch Delilah," the king acknowledged.

She let out a sinister laugh as her appearance transformed, her hair turning jet black, and her eyes becoming crimson. Delilah grabbed the king's head, whispering into his ear, "Long live the king."

The king went numb and lifeless before dropping to the floor.

"He isn't dead; we will save him for a public execution," Ginn said to Arabella, who nodded in approval.

"How dare you!" Isabella shouted.

Ginn, unfazed, looked at her and then shouted to the crowd, "Those who wish to live, leave now!"

The guests fled the ballroom, screaming and crashing into tables, leaving chaos in their wake. Only Xavier, Isabella, Sol, and ten Knights of Leo remained on the dance floor. Darius walked over to join them, but they were quickly surrounded by fifty barbarians, a surprise gift from Ginn. More barbarians lurked in the courtyard and around the palace.

Delilah and Ginn descended to the dance floor. A barbarian soldier rushed over, presenting them with two swords. Delilah waved her hand over the blades, engulfing them in fire. Just as Ginn was about to order the attack, the sounds of screams and bodies hitting the floor caught his attention.

Breaking down the door were the three lions—Saya, Jupiter, and Tiberius—their faces covered in blood. They ran over to Xavier and Darius, ready to protect their partners. Xavier reached into the armour of Saya and then Jupiter, retrieving his swords and two spare swords. He threw the spare swords to his father and Sol.

Isabella looked at Xavier, wondering where her weapon was.

He smiled and handed her his short sword, ensuring she could defend herself without becoming a burden to the others.

Tiberius and Jupiter charged at Ginn and Delilah, forcing her to conjure a wall of magic that blocked the lions off.

"I thought the lions were dealt with," Delilah said.

"We tried, but they were hidden; we couldn't locate them," Ginn replied.

"I don't care about any of that," Arabella said, "I want my sister and Xavier dead."

"Fight back to back!" Darius shouted as they fended off the charging barbarians.

"More are coming through the doors!" Sol added.

"Saya, clear the doors!" Xavier ordered.

"We can't stay here!" Darius said over the clamour of clashing steel.

"We can escape through the king's private baths," Isabella suggested.

"Lead the way, please," Sol said calmly.

The group ran through the doors, with Saya clearing a path in front of them.

"Don't let them escape!" Arabella demanded.

"Unless you want your throat inside a lion's mouth, we'll stay behind the wall," Delilah warned.

Tiberius and Jupiter slowly backed off then ran to catch up with the others.

"Don't worry, my love, they won't escape," Ginn said.

The group sprinted down the halls towards the baths, passing the lifeless bodies of palace staff and guards. However, their path was abruptly blocked by twenty barbarians standing between them and the private baths' entrance. A high-pitched cry tore through the air, accompanied by the swift movement of something slicing through the air—it was Hera. She swooped down, talons bared, crashing into the barbarians and dispatching most of them.

"Sir, we'll hold them off," said one of the knights.

Darius saluted what remained of his knights.

"One moment," Isabella said, "We need to ensure we hold the courtyard, as the exit leads behind the gardens and courtyard."

"I'll go," Sol volunteered.

"Tiberius will keep you alive," Darius said.

"Go through the window in the room to our right, and Hera will go with you," Isabella told Sol.

The trio rushed into the room, and the sound of shattering glass echoed down the hall.

Xavier and the others made their way into the private baths; the path led them through dimly lit, narrow corridors with low ceilings. The room was enveloped in steam, and two large bathing pools occupied the space; however, the steam made it difficult for them to see the way out. Saya and Jupiter used their powerful eyesight to locate the door.

Darius paused and looked back at the path they had just taken. "Hurry, they're coming," he whispered.

They quickly followed the lions through the exit; the sound of approaching footsteps grew louder and closer behind them.

"Quickly, they're on our path," Isabella said, fear increasing in her tone.

"I can see the exit!" Xavier shouted as he glanced back at her.

Saya smashed the door open and landed in the garden; the others hurried through the door after her. However, as Isabella was about to go through the door, a barbarian grabbed her arm, trying to pull her back in.

"Help me!" she shouted as she swung her sword to strike the barbarian.

Darius turned and pulled her through the door along with the barbarian who was holding her. Isabella seized the opportunity, driving her sword straight through the barbarian's gut as Darius and Xavier blocked the door behind them. The sound of banging and shouting echoed from the other side.

"That won't hold for long!" Darius shouted.

"We have to make it to the main gate and into the common area," Isabella said.

Saya and Jupiter led the way through the neatly trimmed gardens and into the courtyard. However, they stopped short and started to growl as Darius and the others caught up. Everyone saw what had caused the lions to stop.

The ground was littered with the bodies of barbarians, palace guards, and Knights of Leo. In the midst of it all, an injured Hera and Sol. He leant on the eagle, both bearing injuries of their own. Tiberius stood tall, undeterred by his injuries. Darius watched in anguish. Sol noticed them and gestured for them to leave.

Xavier approached his father, fully aware that Darius wouldn't abandon Sol and Tiberius.

"Xavier," Darius began.

"Father, I will come back with an army and avenge you."

Darius squeezed his shoulder in a final goodbye, stepping away from Xavier and towards the lions at the edge of the concealed bushes. He instructed Saya and Jupiter to go with Xavier and Isabella.

However, the lions were resolute in their decision to help Tiberius and were unwilling to leave him to die. Eventually, Saya joined Xavier and Isabella, but Jupiter stood beside Darius. Looking back at Xavier, he nodded, knowing he couldn't dissuade her despite their bond. Jupiter released a mighty roar that startled the barbarians and then charged at them alongside Darius. Tears streamed down Isabella's face as she witnessed Hera's injuries and Darius' selfless act of protecting his friends.

Xavier, Isabella, and Saya navigated through the courtyard, dealing with the few barbarians they encountered. The marauders were scouring the houses and storefronts in the common area.

"We're not going to make it out," Isabella said, in a defeated tone.

Xavier scanned the surroundings for a place to hide. Just then, a voice from one of the houses called out, "Hide in here, princess."

They rushed over and entered the house. A woman near the door hurried them inside and was startled by Saya following them.

"Hide under here; you'll all be safe until they leave," she said, lifting the hidden hatch on the floor.

Saya and Isabella descended first, followed by Xavier.

"Thank you. What is your name?" he asked before going down.

"My name is Grace Sommer, my lord," she answered, then closed the hatch behind him.

CHAPTER SEVEN

UNKNOWN SKIES

As the chaos unfolded at the palace, Artemis and the remaining knights were at the Emerald Meadows, checking equipment and performing various tasks around the manor. Artemis inspected the perimeter fence and noticed a strange orange hue flowing into the sky.

"Captain!" he shouted, and a soldier came running over, saluting as he arrived.

"Sir?" he replied.

"Ready the men," Artemis commanded.

Simultaneously, a rider rushed down the trail towards the manor gates.

"Artemis, the villages are under attack," the rider reported, "And the villagers are fleeing this way but are being chased."

"Catch your breath, boy," Artemis said. "How far behind are the barbarians, and how many?"

"At least three hundred and they're burning every village on their way here. They are five minutes behind the village group," the rider said, still trying to catch his breath.

Artemis quickly formulated a plan. "Captain, take fifty riders and ride to the villages. Whoever is still alive, take them to the Silver Hills and go along the eastern cliffs—it's the safer route."

"Yes, sir," the captain replied, and he went off to rally the riders.

Artemis set off with the remaining knights and met up with the villagers heading to the manor. The villagers shouted, "We're saved," as Artemis and the knights ran towards them.

"You're not safe here in the Meadows," he shouted.

The villagers stood confused then were ordered to hurry up and move out.

"Some of the knights will take you all to the Silver Hills."

The knights hurried them down a path in the forest which led to the eastern cliffs.

Artemis ordered his men to form a double line, creating a half-circle with the ends facing the approaching barbarians. The sounds of marching echoed through the forest.

"Make ready," Artemis commanded, getting into a defensive stance.

"Captain, the sky!" shouted a knight.

Artemis looked up at the sky as the bright stars and moon-light were covered by a black blanket moving towards them. The black blanket descended lower and lower. Suddenly, high-pitched screeches stunned Artemis and the knights.

"Shields up, men!" Artemis commanded, anticipating what was coming.

Several vultures descended onto the knights, crashing into them and lifting some knights into the air before dropping them from great heights.

"Shell formation!" Artemis commanded.

The knights quickly got into formation while fending off the vultures.

"Barbarians to the front!" a knight shouted.

While in formation, the knights and Artemis were vulnerable to close-range and flanking attacks. The barbarians seized this opportunity, swarming the knights and dealing significant damage to their numbers. Artemis and the knights tried to hold their ground but were unable to defend against both vultures and barbarians.

"Fall back to the manor!" Artemis ordered, grabbing the rally horn from his belt and blowing on it.

The remaining knights broke contact and ran for the manor, still harassed and attacked by the vultures.

"Captain, half of the barbarians broke off to the right, trying to flank us," a knight shouted.

Artemis looked to the right through the trees and saw the barbarians moving fast, almost keeping up with them.

"Watch out!" someone shouted.

A vulture dive-bombed Artemis and five other knights, throwing them into the air.

Artemis woke up in the manor's courtyard. The surrounding forests were engulfed in flames.

"Sir," a knight said, helping Artemis to his feet.

"How many of us are left?" Artemis asked the knight, holding his head.

"Only thirty," the knight replied, dropping his head. "The vultures have moved off towards the eastern cliffs."

"I hope they're ready for them," Artemis said, picking up his sword and preparing for the fight.

"They've broken through the gate!" a knight shouted from the other side of the courtyard.

The knights rallied to Artemis, forming a shield wall. However, the barbarians didn't charge; instead, they formed a formation twenty yards in front of the shield wall and waited for orders. Then, a familiar figure walked through the barbarian line.

"The mighty House of Leo has fallen at last," Gavel said with a smug smile.

"Your father is turning in his grave from what you have done here," Artemis retorted, looking down at Gavel.

"That old fool settled for scraps after the mage war. The Graw brothers will rule all of Malsdon now," Gavel declared.

"Are you running a high fever, man?" Artemis asked sarcastically.

Gavel laughed. “Right now, Darius and Xavier are probably dead, along with the king.”

Artemis walked forwards, pointing his sword at Gavel.

“No, sir, you’re injured from the fall,” a knight said.

“Yeah, we took the palace with the help of the barbarian tribes and Matriarch Delilah,” Gavel said, “So, I’m here to burn this place down and then kill that brat River and her brother.”

He stepped towards Artemis, noticing the injuries and feeling he could defeat him. “Old man, fight me in single combat and retain some honour for this house,” Gavel mocked.

Without hesitation, Artemis closed the distance between himself and Gavel, adopting a high ready stance despite his back injury from the fall.

Gavel smiled, fancying his chances against the injured Artemis, keeping his sword in one hand with a loose grip. Artemis lunged for Gavel, but his timing was off. Gavel countered with a kick to Artemis’ stomach, knocking him to the ground. The barbarian soldiers cheered, howling and banging their shields against their thin plate armour.

Artemis rose slowly, turning to look at his men. He saw the worry on their faces, understanding that losing was not an option. Circling Gavel, Artemis used his footwork to unbalance him. He threw a feint, and Gavel fell for it, swinging wildly and leaving his neck and chest open. Artemis seized the opportunity, aiming for Gavel’s neck, but the cut wasn’t deep enough to cause significant harm. Enraged, Gavel started swinging wildly with great force. Each dodge by Artemis was met with the wind from the swing hitting his face, and each block rattled his arms.

Artemis’ back prevented him from taking advantage of Gavel’s undisciplined fighting. He knew he couldn’t let this continue, with his back causing more pain with each passing minute. Gavel, spurred on by the cheers of his men, made a costly mistake. He threw a massive overhead strike, but Artemis sidestepped and kicked Gavel’s legs out from under him.

Artemis stood over Gavel, who was begging for his life. Kicking Gavel's sword away, Artemis placed the tip of his sword against Gavel's neck. "You deserve a slow, painful death, but we have no time, and your men will attack me the second you're dead," Artemis said, while trying to hold in the pain caused by his injury.

The barbarians started to get rowdy, stepping closer and closer to Artemis and Gavel. What was left of the Knights of Leo prepared to charge the barbarians, even though they were heavily outnumbered. Artemis pulled his sword back while lining up the tip to Gavel's neck. As he went to deliver the killing thrust, Artemis stopped halfway, dropped his sword, and then fell to his knees.

Looking down, he saw a javelin, thrown by one of the barbarians, stuck in his abdomen. This enraged the remaining knights, and they charged the barbarians. However, most were met with the same fate as Artemis or were cut down.

The barbarians surrounded the dying Artemis, and Gavel got up from the ground with a smug look on his face. "How the tables have turned," Gavel said, laughing as he stepped over the dead bodies of knights.

"You have no honour," said a knight in a faint voice.

"Kill him," Gavel ordered.

A barbarian soldier stood over the dying knight and drove his sword into his heart.

"I was told to take high-ranking people back to the palace for some reason, but I think I'll let you die here," Gavel said, looking down at Artemis. "You there, tell the rest to go through the eastern cliffs to reach the Silver Hills. We might be able to catch more Emerald Meadow peasants."

A barbarian nodded and ran off to fulfil the task.

"The rest of you, loot the manor and then burn it to the ground."

The barbarians cheered and rushed into the manor. They began smashing windows, throwing objects out the windows, taking clothes and other items, then placing them in a pile outside. Gavel stood there as a barbarian handed him a torch.

"The mighty lions have fallen," he declared, then threw the torch into the window.

Artemis could only look on with sadness as he watched the manor catch ablaze, along with the barbarians throwing things into the air. Gavel looked down at him, smiling. Artemis looked back at him, with smoke and fire filling the background and the sound of wood crackling amidst the cheers of barbarians.

"Your death will not satisfy the lands; only your pain and suffering will," Artemis said, trying to catch his breath with each word.

CHAPTER EIGHT

DEEP WOUNDS

Two days after the revolt, barbarians now masquerading as palace guards filled the grounds and the common area. The walls were plastered with wanted posters, bearing the descriptions of Xavier and Isabella, labelling them as wanted for high treason.

Darius awoke in the cells located behind the barracks. Slowly scanning his surroundings, he took in the damp and cold floor littered with hay that made little difference. The cast-iron bars ensured escape was impossible. The cell was dimly lit with no windows, intentionally designed to make prisoners lose track of time. The unpleasant smell, exacerbated by guards leaving waste buckets inside the cells, turned Darius' stomach.

"I see you're awake now," Sol said.

"Good to see you alive, friend," Darius replied, slowly trying to get up from the floor.

"You lost a lot of blood. Take your time, Darius," Sol said, going over to help him up.

A mumbling sound came from the only bed in the cell.

"Who's that?" Darius asked.

"It's what's left of the king. That witch did something to his mind."

Darius looked at what the king had become. He was curled up in a ball on the bed, whimpering and mumbling, his pupils dilated with his eyes wide open. Darius felt sadness for his friend. Then his mind suddenly shifted.

"What happened to Tiberius and Jupiter?" he asked.

"As you passed out from blood loss in the fight, Jupiter was gravely wounded, and Tiberius was captured," Sol said. "They're both alive, trapped inside cages, but I'm not sure if Jupiter will recover anytime soon."

The two sat there in silence; only the mumblings of the king could be heard. Footsteps echoed down the stairs, and two figures approached the cell. As they got closer, their faces became more visible.

"My lords, I hope you love your new surroundings," Ginn said, hitting his sword against the iron bars.

"You're never leaving here, but the king will be gone this afternoon," Delilah added.

"Try and take him," Darius challenged as he faced Delilah, only the iron bars separating them.

"There's nothing you can do; the king will be put to death by the axe," Delilah declared, with Ginn nodding next to her.

"By the way, Darius," Ginn said, mockingly, "My brother took a little visit to your manor. Let's just say some parts are not so green anymore."

Darius slammed the bars, causing Ginn to jump. "You're nothing but a worm."

"I don't need to take any more insults from you," Ginn replied, driving his sword into Darius' arm.

However, Darius didn't flinch or cry out in pain. He stood there with a straight face, glaring into Ginn's eyes. "I hope you know who you are dealing with."

"Enough of this," Delilah interjected, hitting Darius and Sol with an energy wave, knocking them onto the floor. "Go grab the king," she ordered Ginn.

Ginn walked into the cell, smiling at the dazed Darius and Sol on the floor. He then grabbed the king by his hair and dragged him out. The king was screaming nonsense as he was being pulled away.

"See you two at the party," Ginn said, laughing as he ascended the stairs, dragging the king behind.

*

The tower bells were ringing, and a huge crowd was gathering in the square of the common area.

"The bells are ringing," Xavier said as he got out of bed.

"Something major is happening," Isabella replied.

She got out of the tiny bed she was sharing with Xavier. They barely had room to move in the hidden cellar, but the two found comfort within each other in this difficult time.

Knocking from the cellar door caught their attention. "My lord, my lady, may I enter?" Grace said.

"Of course, you must call us by our first names, Grace. We owe you so much," Isabella said as she helped Grace down the steps.

"What's happening outside?" Xavier asked.

Grace looked at both of them, and then took Isabella's hand. Isabella looked at her, confused and worried.

"They're going to execute your father," Grace told her while squeezing her hand, offering comfort.

Isabella fell to her knees, tears filling her eyes. Xavier quickly knelt beside her and hugged her tight.

"Any news on my father or Sol?" Xavier asked.

"Nothing about them," Grace replied.

"I'm going to the square," Isabella said, breaking out of Xavier's hug and standing up. "I need to see my sister's face."

"If you are serious about going, I have spare clothes for you. It will help you blend in," Grace said.

Isabella nodded in response, and Grace made her way upstairs.

Xavier turned and looked at Isabella. "I will make things right and return you to your rightful place," Xavier promised.

"As queen?" she asked.

"Yes," he replied.

"Only if you're by my side as king, I want that and need that to happen," Isabella said as her vale green eyes looked straight into Xavier's brown eyes.

Xavier took her hand and kissed it. Grace returned with worn-out leather boots, dark brown trousers, a black long-sleeve top, and a black cape. She passed them down to Isabella. "This isn't much, but it'll help you blend in," Grace said.

"Thank you, Grace. Make sure you hide my clothes in case they find them and hurt you for information," Isabella replied.

Xavier turned around as Isabella was getting changed. He too took off his chainmail and covered his swords with cloth. He was now just wearing his padded cloth shirt and trousers along with the overcoat Victor made for him.

Isabella turned towards Xavier. "I'm ready," she said.

"You look good," he replied.

Isabella smiled and moved towards the steps. "Grace, we're ready."

*

The square was packed with nervous onlookers and whispers about what happened to Princess Isabella. The crowd erupted into loud boos and curses as the barbarian guards made their way from the courtyard, pulling a weak Tiberius and Jupiter, who were chained up and had their mouths bound, with untreated open wounds.

Xavier and Isabella made their way into the middle of the crowd, close enough to see the elevated platform in the centre of the square, but hidden well enough to avoid notice. Xavier looked on as they paraded Jupiter and Tiberius on the platform, whipping and kicking them. His hand reached for his sword, ready to intervene. However, Isabella grabbed his hand.

"Not here. We will save them, but not now," she whispered.

Xavier understood. He had promised to return her to her home and the throne that was rightfully hers, but seeing Jupiter and Tiberius treated like that hurt him deeply.

The royal horn sounded as Arabella and Ginn made their way to the square, accompanied by Delilah, who was pulling the king by a rope tied around his neck. The crowd went silent at the sight of the king's state as he was dragged onto the stage and pushed to his knees.

"Here is the former king, Theo Lucius!" Delilah shouted.

Ginn walked over and grabbed the king by his hair. "Isabella, I know you're here!" he shouted, yanking the king's head back and forth.

Arabella walked over to Ginn and handed him an axe she had taken from one of the guards. "I want you to kill him for us," Arabella said.

Ginn smiled and pushed the king to the ground.

"One moment, the main guests are arriving," Delilah said, pointing towards Darius and Sol. They too were placed onto the platform.

Xavier had mixed feelings when he saw his father. He was happy to see he was still alive, but would this be the last time he saw him breathing?

"Isabella, whatever happens, you must not react," he whispered as he held her hand tight.

"I don't know if I can," she whimpered and placed her head on Xavier's shoulder.

Darius was scanning the crowd for anyone he knew and caught eyes with Xavier. He was shocked, as was Xavier. Darius mouthed the words, "Your aunt."

Ginn ordered two men to place the king on the chopping block. They strapped his neck down and left his hands tied behind his back.

"Now witness the new era of Malsdon!" Arabella shouted.

"Any last words?" Delilah said as she lifted the spell.

The king woke and was in a state of panic. "What is going on?" he asked.

"Don't speak, you deserve this," Arabella said, stabbing the king in his back with a hidden dagger.

The king screamed out in pain. Isabella hid her face in Xavier's chest.

"Do not look, Isabella," he said.

Ginn brought the axe over his head.

"Kill him now!" Arabella screamed.

"I'm glad you're awake for this," Ginn whispered, then slammed the axe through the king's neck.

Isabella trembled and sobbed.

"I'm so sorry," Xavier whispered, and then kissed her on the forehead.

"I give you the new king and queen of Malsdon!" Delilah shouted, pointing to Arabella and Ginn.

"My first order as queen is that if anyone is helping or providing shelter to Isabella and Xavier, they will be put to death," Arabella said, her tone absolute. "The prisoner Darius Leo shall be locked in a cage with his two lions outside on this very square until further notice. With little food or water, maybe you'll see the lions eat their master."

"For Sol Silverlight," Ginn added, "He is to be locked in a pitch-black cell with his hands and feet tied."

"Madness will surely take his mind," Delilah said.

"Now bow to your new king and queen!" Arabella shouted to the crowd.

However, the crowd turned against them, shouting and throwing objects. This angered Delilah greatly, and she let out a blast of energy, knocking most people off their feet.

"It's time to go, Isabella," Xavier said as the crowd started turning into a mob. Xavier caught eyes with his father and placed his hand on his heart, mouthing the words, "Have hope, Father," before he and Isabella slipped through the crowd back towards Grace's house.

Grace was waiting outside with a horse as the two arrived. "This is for you; get help and save the land," she said, handing the reins to Xavier.

"Thank you so much; we will not forget you," Isabella said.

"When you're ready to take back the palace, some of us here will start a riot," Grace said.

Xavier was surprised by that statement.

"King Theo was a fair man, and what happened here needs justice," Grace added, "I know you two will be back with an army."

"That will help a lot. We'll send someone in to help you when the time comes," Xavier said. "Where's Saya?"

"She is waiting outside the outer walls. I showed her a safe way out," Grace replied, "But you two will get out fine, with most of the guards heading to the square."

"Thank you," Xavier said and gave her a hug before mounting the horse.

"Where are we going?" Isabella asked as Xavier helped her onto the horse.

"To the House of Panthera in the Vermillion Sands, to ask my aunt for help."

Chapter Nine

Blood and Silver

The peaks of the silver mountains were a breathtaking sight, yet Captain Lawson and the villagers found little solace. They remained relentlessly pursued by Gavel and his troops, with vultures circling overhead, eager to pick them off. Despite running through the night and into the day, the group, exhausted and on the brink of collapse, pressed on.

"Sir, the vultures are preparing to attack!" a knight reported to Lawson. Most of the men were dead on their feet, barely able to run, and several horses had succumbed to exhaustion.

"Keep the majority of the men to the rear," Lawson said.

The harsh sun drained their energy further, exposed on the cliffside to the elements. Through the heat mirage, Lawson discerned blurry figures of silver closing in on them. Suddenly, he was lifted into the air by a vulture's dive.

"We won't make it!" some villagers cried out as the barbarians closed in.

Suddenly, silver streaks of light tore through the sky and exploded around the vultures, either killing them or forcing them to retreat. It was River, leading forty riders, all clad in full silver plate armour. They rode past the beleaguered group, unleashing a volley of arrows at the barbarian raiding party, sending them flying into the air and off the side of the cliff.

"Aim for the wall! Bring it down on them!" River shouted, as she, too, took aim at the stones.

A dozen arrows struck the wall, triggering a rockslide that crushed and temporarily halted Gavel and the barbarians' advance. The group then turned their attention skywards to eliminate the remaining vultures.

"Those who are elderly or children, climb onto a horse!" River instructed, pulling a child onto her own steed.

As Lawson approached River's horse, he asked, "Are you in charge?"

"Yes, I am. And who are you?" River asked, looking down at him.

"I'm Captain Gregg Lawson," he replied. "Thank you for the help."

"Everyone, follow my men back to the fortress," River commanded, pointing in the direction of travel. "Lawson, walk next to me. I have some questions. Where's Captain Artemis?"

Lawson's uncertainty hung in the air. "I'm not sure if he's still alive; he stayed to cover our escape," he told her.

Sorrow clouded River's eyes. "I hope he made it out. Who's leading their force?"

"Gavel Graw and we believe he has a mage with him," he said.

"That would explain the vultures," she replied. "We're going to destroy that army."

"I hope so," he replied.

They reached the Silverlight fortress, strategically positioned between two silver mountains. This natural bottleneck, combined with high walls and flanking defences, provided both advantages and challenges. The fortress' great forge, nestled into the mountain at the back, awaited them.

"Send all the villagers to the lower levels and position all archers on the walls!" River's urgent command echoed through the chaos as she directed one of her knights.

Adjusting his armour, Lawson asked, "Where do you need us?"

"Wait at the main gate; I have a plan for them," River replied.

Lawson, along with the remaining Knights of Leo, hurried to the main gate and joined the rest of River's knights. She nodded in approval before joining her archers.

The echoes of marching resonated through the narrow passage—Gavel and four hooded figures flanking him on each side came into view.

"Mages!" River shouted.

Gavel ordered his men to stop fifty metres away from the main gate. Pausing, he glanced up at the mountains on both sides, noticing cross marks, but he ignored them.

"River, throw down your arms and you will be spared!" Gavel shouted.

"Turn back and leave Malsdon or you will be killed today!" River replied, pointing her arrow towards him.

"I've had enough of you and the words you utter at me!" he retorted, then ordered his mages forwards to blast the gate with magic.

"Archers, silver arrows, and fire at will!" River commanded.

"Is everything okay?" Lawson shouted while looking up at the ramparts.

"Yes, don't worry; I have a surprise for them," she shouted back.

The mages blasted the gate repeatedly, but to no avail. With each blast, the mages were left vulnerable. River's archers took advantage and killed two mages, piercing them with a volley of silver arrows.

Gavel ordered the first column of his army forwards. River watched him closely as the last row of men passed the cross mark.

"Now," River ordered.

A volley of arrows hit the two cross marks, causing a massive explosion, sending fragments of sharp rock raining down on Gavel's army like they were trapped in a rainstorm. Large boulders blocked off the rear of his army.

With his mages and three-quarters of his army trapped or

killed, Gavel started to panic. The shockwave from the explosion still had him confused.

"Archers again!" River shouted.

Another volley hit the same mark, but this time there was no explosion. However, molten silver that ran throughout the mountains started pouring out from the mountainside down onto the trapped men of Gavel's army. Screams of help echoed around the mountain.

Gavel was now at the mercy of River and her archers.

"Lawson, now!" she shouted, "But keep Gavel alive."

As the gate opened, Lawson and the Knights of Leo charged what was left of Gavel's army. Fear rushed through them as they tried to flee, but they soon realised, as the dust settled behind them, they were trapped. Lawson and the knights made quick work of the barbarian splinter group, not losing a single man.

"There he is," a knight said, pointing at a cowardly Gavel hiding and pretending to be dead.

River descended from the ramparts with a sinister smile etched across her face. Passing through the gate, she spotted Lawson and a Knight of Leo holding Gavel in a kneeling position. Drawing her short sword from its scabbard, she walked towards them, her ivory-coloured skin turning red as she gripped the weapon tightly. Her face filled with anger as Gavel begged for his life.

"This is the end for you," she seethed through her teeth, driving the sword through Gavel's thigh.

His scream echoed, and as he fell, River kicked him in the face with her silver-plated boots, sending blood and teeth flying. Lawson and the other knights watched in silence as River unleashed her rage, her screams echoing through the silver hills.

"Please, no more," Gavel choked on his blood.

"River, I think you should show mercy and keep him imprisoned," Lawson suggested.

River turned to him, hands bloodied, boots stained, pupils dilated, and long silver hair covering her face.

"Stay out of this," she warned, pointing her sword at Lawson before returning her attention to Gavel. Standing over him, she continued to assault him. "Get me rope and take his plate armour off now!" she ordered two of the knights.

They ran over, removed his plate armour, and tied his hands together in front of him. River took her bow off her back and proceeded to strike Gavel on his back several times.

River ordered her men to tie him against the inner wall of the fortress.

"Please, help," Gavel pleaded as people walked past, witnessing his binding.

"No one here will ever help you," River declared, delivering another kick. "Your slow death will be justice for all those you have harmed and betrayed."

Gavel, now in tears, continued to beg, his pleas falling on deaf ears. River stood there, watching him.

"River, what do we do now?" Lawson asked.

"We wait for Xavier to come to us," she replied, clenching her fist tightly. "Guard, only give him water and food every three days. We want him alive for when Xavier gets here." She delivered a final kick to Gavel before leaving with Lawson.

Chapter Ten

Helping Hand

Xavier, Isabella, and Saya reached the border of the Vermillion Sands, a vast expanse of sand dunes broken up by pockets of lush greenery and fresh water. The magic in the ground here pulsed with an unparalleled strength compared to the rest of Malsdon.

"Xavier, the horse won't be able to go on. We need to find water soon," Isabella said, her hand gently patting the horse's flank.

Xavier glanced at Saya and instructed her to find a water source. Saya, with a nose to the ground and eyes closed, suddenly darted north.

Xavier and Isabella followed, mindful not to strain the horse to the point of collapse. The Vermillion Sands stretched before them, the shifting colours of the sand dunes creating an otherworldly landscape. Isabella's worried expression mirrored Xavier's concern for the horse, and they both pressed on, eager to reach the promised pockets of green and a freshwater oasis.

The desert air held a dry, earthy scent, and the heat intensified as they ventured further into the sands. Saya's instincts guided them, the magic in the ground resonating with her as she led the way to a hidden source of life in the arid expanse.

They finally caught up with Saya and found her waiting next to a well surrounded by trees and plants they hadn't seen before. Xavier dismounted the horse and approached the well. Pulling up the bucket, he discovered crystal-clear, ice-cold water. He placed the bucket on the ground for the horse and Saya to drink.

Isabella threw a stone at a coconut tree, knocking some of the coconuts to the ground.

"Nice throw," Xavier complimented as he walked over to the fallen coconuts. Drawing his sword, he skilfully cracked each one open.

Isabella and Xavier sat down, indulging in the refreshing coconut water, a much-welcome treat.

"Do you think Ginn and Gavel bribed your aunt's house?" Isabella asked cautiously.

"My aunt is a strong woman; even my father speaks carefully around her," he replied with a smile. "She wouldn't take a bribe, plus she has a gigas lion that would make the Graw brothers think twice. Rumours say he's over a hundred years old."

"She's the chief of the Vermillion Sands?"

"Yes, and hopefully, she remembers me. It's been around twelve years," he said.

"What?" Isabella replied, a worried look on her face.

"Don't worry. I carry my mother's and father's family token," he said confidently.

"I hope that's enough," she said.

As Xavier and Isabella prepared to leave, both Saya and the horse suddenly dropped to the ground.

Xavier rushed to Saya, checking her over. "A dart," Xavier exclaimed, frantically scanning the surroundings for the shooter.

"Xavier, help me," Isabella pleaded before collapsing to the ground.

Confusion and panic set in as Xavier tried to make sense of the situation. Suddenly, a dart struck his neck, and as he began to lose consciousness, a group of hooded figures approached.

The world blurred, and Xavier felt a sense of dread wash over him. Who were these hooded figures? Had they been caught by Ginn's men already? Darkness enveloped him as he succumbed to unconsciousness.

*

Xavier groggily awoke inside a massive tent, Isabella still unconscious beside him. Three men who had drugged and captured them were in conversation with a lady seated on a throne-like chair. Her hair, as dark as shadow, and her warm honey complexion matched Xavier's.

"My lady, I have two prisoners for you, and we caught a gigas lion," one of the men reported.

"We don't see many of her kind here," the lady in the chair replied, pointing at Isabella.

"I believe she's the wanted princess," the man continued.

"There's a high bounty for her and Xavier Leo," she replied.

Xavier, in a strained voice, warned, "I'll kill you all if you touch her."

The lady in the chair laughed and clicked her fingers twice. After a brief pause, a gigas lion emerged through the tent wall behind her. His coat was as black as the night sky, and his mane a dark crimson. The sheer size of him shocked Xavier to the core, snapping him fully awake.

"Belthazor, these men harmed my nephew, blood Panthera," she said to the lion.

The three men quickly dropped to their knees and begged for forgiveness. Belthazor stood in front of them, his eyes glowing jade green, and the three men dropped flat onto the ground. Xavier looked on in awe, feeling the powerful magic that surrounded Belthazor.

"Untie them," the lady said.

Two guards cut the rope that bound their hands.

"Aunt Sabrina?" Xavier asked as he stood up.

"You look too much like your father," she replied with a smile.

"My lady, the girl isn't waking up," one of the guards said as they tried to shake Isabella awake.

Belthazor walked over to Isabella and placed his paw on her head. His eyes glowed once more, and Isabella woke up, and then screamed due to the surprise of Belthazor.

"What happened?" Isabella asked.

"You were brought here by some bandits who tried to claim the bounty that has been placed on you," Sabrina replied.

"Aunt Sabrina, I need your help," Xavier said.

Isabella and Xavier joined Sabrina on a walk to a meeting she had set up with the other houses.

"Not all have been bribed, but be on guard; they'll know who you are," Sabrina said.

"Let's hope honour means more than coin," Isabella added.

As they walked through the centre of the grand bazaar, Xavier and Isabella remained cloaked, hiding their faces from the public.

"There's the meeting tent. Remember, convince them to join your cause," Sabrina said.

The grand bazaar bustled around them, the vibrant colours of the stalls and the distant hum of merchants and buyers creating a lively backdrop. Xavier and Isabella felt a mix of determination and anxiety as they exchanged glances.

"Convince them," Xavier whispered to Isabella.

She nodded, her eyes reflecting a shared understanding of the stakes.

Inside the tent, a palpable tension hung in the air. The leaders of the other houses awaited their arrival, their expressions a mix of curiosity and suspicion. Sabrina led the way, her every step echoing with authority, commanding attention from all present. The fate of Malsdon teetered on a precarious edge as they stepped into the meeting.

The scent of aged parchment and candle wax filled the air, the dim light casting shadows on the faces of the leaders. Sabrina's eyes scanned the room, assessing the alliances and loyalties at play. Each gaze met held potential danger or opportunity. Xavier and Isabella, still cloaked, moved with a careful stride, aware of the delicate dance they were about to perform.

As Sabrina approached the central table, flanked by the seated leaders, the gravity of the situation became palpable. Whispers hushed, and all eyes focused on the unfolding drama. The negotiation had begun; a delicate web of words and intentions that would determine the course of Malsdon's future. The room, now a battlefield of diplomacy, echoed with the weight of the choices to be made.

"Greetings, friends. My name is George, the lord of House Moon," George announced.

"My lord," Xavier replied with a salute.

"Thank you for meeting us," Isabella added. "Allow us to present our case to all of you."

Xavier and Isabella took their seats at the table while Sabrina positioned herself near the tent entrance.

"My lords, a great threat has returned and has already taken the throne of Malsdon," Xavier began.

"We are aware of that," one of the lords interrupted.

"However, did you know that the king is dead, and that Matriarch Delilah is at the centre of it?" Xavier continued, a hint of frustration creeping into his tone.

The lords exchanged uneasy glances, and a hushed murmur swept through the room. The gravity of Xavier's revelation settled over them, and the air thickened with anticipation.

"Ginn never mentioned Delilah being part of his plan," George said out loud.

"You snake!" Isabella shouted, pointing at George. "You took the bribe money from him to harm me and my family."

"Watch who you're speaking to, princess of nothing," he replied, standing up.

"We should just collect their bounties!" a few of the lords shouted.

George smiled and drew his sword.

"If you do this, all your properties will be seized!" Sabrina shouted, drawing her sword as well.

"I don't care. Ginn has promised me riches," George replied.

Suddenly, two lords, ready to capture Xavier and Isabella, fell to the ground, holding their backs.

"Sit down, George, if you know what's good for you," a man said as he stood behind George, wiping the blood off his dagger.

"Cain Lupus, I didn't notice you," Sabrina said.

"What is this, Sabrina? Are you not going to arrest him?" George said.

"You tried harming my nephew, and let's leave it at that," Sabrina replied.

Cain stood behind George. "If I were you, I would listen to what they have to say before the meeting ends."

"Those who pledge their knights to Xavier, you have until midday tomorrow to muster and meet at the southern border," Sabrina announced as the lords walked out of the tent.

Cain watched as the lords departed, then turned toward Sabrina. "I don't trust any of them," he said.

"I know most of them took bribes, and George has them all scared," she replied.

"So, none will help?" Isabella asked.

"You have my support," Cain said, "I am lord of House Lupus, the last of the Lupus bloodline."

"I've heard my father mention your house before," Xavier said.

"Yes, our fathers fought in the mage war together. Our house was heavily hit by the mages during the first wave," Cain replied.

"Cain has the finest knights in this region," Sabrina added.

"Only a hundred, but we are capable," Cain replied.

"We'll see you at the border," Xavier said as he shook Cain's hand.

"Cain is right. The other houses have no honour left, only the lust for coin," Sabrina said with a heavy sigh. "He and his knights have helped me keep them in check up to now, but we cannot stay at my mansion tonight; it's too dangerous if they try to attack."

"Where can we stay?" Xavier asked, his brow furrowed.

"I have an outpost close to the southern border where my main force is camped. We'll head there now," Sabrina replied, her eyes scanning the surroundings for any signs of treachery.

As they spoke, the air seemed charged with uncertainty. The landscape, usually serene, now carried the weight of their predicament. Xavier and Isabella exchanged a glance, realising the gravity of the situation. The journey to the outpost would be fraught with danger, but it was a risk they had to take.

*

"Welcome to the first outpost of the Vermillion Sands. I have three hundred men here and another two hundred more on the way."

"Five hundred won't be enough to save Malsdon," Isabella said with a furrowed brow.

"More will meet us tomorrow," Sabrina replied as she patted Isabella's shoulder reassuringly.

Belthazor approached them as they entered the camp, his eyes glowing bright in the darkness of the night. He stared straight into Xavier's eyes, creating an uneasy feeling within him.

"Xavier, Isabella, the guard will show you to your tent," Sabrina said. "Saya is there waiting outside."

"Thank you for everything," Xavier said.

"You're family, and we always protect family," Sabrina replied with a warm smile.

As they walked through the outpost, the air was charged with a mixture of tension and determination. Saya waited outside the tent, her presence a comforting sight in the midst of uncertainty.

*

Xavier woke in the middle of the night from a haunting dream. He rose from the bed, draped his overcoat over his shoulders, and ventured outside. The camp slept peacefully, only by the vigilant night watch who saluted Xavier as he passed.

An irresistible spiritual energy pulled Xavier beyond the camp walls, leading him to a mysterious cave. Surrendering to the magic, he entered the darkness. Drips of water echoed through the cavern as he delved deeper.

In the heart of the cave, Xavier found Belthazor seated beside a pool of misty turquoise water. The ethereal glow cast an otherworldly ambiance.

"You came…"

Xavier hesitated before responding, the magical energy weaving around him. "Why did you summon me here?"

Belthazor's eyes, gleaming with an enigmatic light, held Xavier's gaze. "Malsdon is at a tipping point. Your fate is intricately woven with the destiny of this land."

*

Isabella awoke to an empty space beside her. Fear gripped her heart as she rushed outside, fearing something had happened to Xavier.

Sabrina intercepted her path, offering reassurance. "He's fine. He has something important to complete."

"Why didn't he tell me?"

"Not by choice. He was summoned," Sabrina explained, leading Isabella to her tent. "Come with me; the nights are cold here."

Seated by the warmth of the fire, Isabella couldn't shake off the thoughts and feelings that clouded her mind.

Sabrina, sensing her inner turmoil, engaged her in conversation. "How are you feeling about all of this?"

"Tired, confused, and angry," Isabella replied, her gaze fixed on the dancing flames.

"Matriarch Delilah is an evil and envious woman."

"I've noticed," Isabella replied, her curiosity piqued.

"Yes, she started the mage war, but her plot wasn't discovered until a year had passed," Sabrina said. "As you know, each house had a mage advisor, and all were female, as the male mages were more suited for combat. They found it hard to control their magic and emotions."

Isabella listened intently as Sabrina continued, unveiling a dark truth.

"The mages were kind and just; however, jealousy is powerful and can corrupt any mind," Sabrina explained. "Of wives that became mothers."

Isabella's confusion deepened. "What?"

"As the female mages discovered they couldn't bear any children of their own, they cursed each mother. If they tried for another child, they would die before the child was born," Sabrina disclosed.

"That's the reason why Mother died?" Isabella gasped, tears streaming down her face.

"I'm so sorry," Sabrina said, offering comfort.

Suddenly the tent door pulled swiftly open. "My lady, men are approaching," a man said, standing before them.

"Friendly?" Sabrina asked

"Our scouts haven't returned," he replied, raising the stakes of the impending encounter.

*

"Who said that?" Xavier asked, glancing around the cave, but only Belthazor was present.

"It was I," Belthazor's voice echoed in Xavier's mind. "My power is beyond your comprehension. You were summoned by the deep power that flows through Malsdon and me."

"I am no mage."

"No mage will ever be granted the power that awaits you," Belthazor affirmed. "A great threat, like the war before, is present here, and a protector who is pure of heart is needed."

"Can't you do it alone?" Xavier asked.

"I had your mother's father by my side, but I was unable to save him. So, I vowed to protect his bloodline to the end of time,"

Belthazor explained.

The gravity of the responsibility settled on Xavier. "I'm ready," he declared with newfound confidence.

"Just a warning: with the power that will be given upon you, something must be given in return. For this is the law of equivalent exchange," Belthazor cautioned.

"What was the price my grandfather paid?" Xavier asked with hesitation.

"One of his daughters, your mother."

Xavier's head fell as he came to terms with why he grew up without a mother. "It's a heavy price."

"You must enter the pool, and you will exit with the power to save this land," Belthazor said.

Xavier took a deep breath. "Forgive me," he said as he entered the pool. The water bubbled up, and steam began to rise.

"Repeat these words with all your might," Belthazor instructed.

"I'm ready," Xavier replied, drawing his sword. Kneeling in the waist-high water, he planted his sword in the ground, holding it with both hands.

"I am the light to break all darkness, I am the light to heal all wounds, the light to protect all life," Belthazor said, and Xavier echoed the words. "I accept these powers from the soul of Malsdon, and I give my love in return."

With the final words, Xavier's sword erupted in a radiant glow, illuminating the entire cave. The energy surged from the sword into his body, a sensation both electrifying and profound. As the power coursed through him, Xavier felt a profound connection to the very essence of Malsdon.

Exiting the pool, Xavier found his clothes as dry as when he entered. Before he could utter a word, Belthazor's ears twitched, and he turned towards the cave entrance.

"Your aunt is in danger," he declared. "Climb on now; we must make haste."

CHAPTER ELEVEN

WINDS OF CHANGE

The sounds of metal clashing and the cries of battle echoed in and around the outpost. Sabrina quickly took charge, handing Isabella a chainmail shirt. "Stay close to me and put this on," Sabrina ordered.

"But what about you? Your night robe won't protect you," Isabella protested.

"My skill will, and Xavier can't afford to lose you. You know it would destroy him," Sabrina replied, grabbing her sword and shield.

Two soldiers stormed into the tent, their faces twisted in malicious glee.

"There they are," one of them sneered.

Charging at Isabella first, the soldiers were met with Sabrina's swift intervention. She smashed the first soldier with her shield, sending him sprawling to the ground. The other soldier attempted to stab her in the side, but Sabrina parried the attack and retaliated by chopping off his hand, leaving him writhing in pain.

"Grab his sword!" Sabrina shouted to Isabella.

While Isabella seized the fallen soldier's weapon, Sabrina turned her attention to the unconscious man on the ground. "Go and finish him off while I talk to this one," Sabrina said.

Stepping on the wounded soldier's limb, Sabrina placed the tip of her sword to his throat. "You know who I am, so I'll only ask once. Who sent this group to attack us?"

"Lord George Moon and the other lords. They attacked Lord Lupus as well. Please don't kill me," the soldier pleaded.

Sabrina nodded, then swiftly drove her sword through his throat. Isabella, witnessing the scene, quickly dispatched the unconscious soldier to avoid any potential conflict with Sabrina.

"Good. We need to push them out of the camp. Stay close by my side," Sabrina told Isabella, her eyes sharp and focused on the ongoing battle.

*

Belthazor and Xavier emerged from the cave, stopping on top of the hill that overlooked the outpost. The night was alive with the flickering light of torches and the ominous glow of burning tents.

"Sabrina's men are pushing them back," Xavier said.

"Yes, it's true, but on open ground, the fight won't be in their favour," Belthazor replied, pointing his head towards additional forces waiting outside the gates.

"Let's go now."

"No, wait for them to engage, or we will be cut down," Belthazor advised.

As they stood on the hill, the sounds of battle reached their ears—the clash of swords, the shouts of warriors, and the crackling of flames. The air was thick with tension, and Xavier's gaze remained fixed on the unfolding chaos below.

"We must choose our moment carefully," Belthazor added, his eyes gleaming with a mixture of concern and determination.

*

Sabrina and her men fought fiercely, pushing the enemy forces back, but their triumph was short-lived as George and his three hundred men emerged, blocking their path.

"Oh, Sabrina, you've seen better days," George taunted. "Don't count on the rest of your men and Cain showing up in the morning."

"Why are you doing this? You think Ginn will let you rule here?" Isabella shouted.

"When I deliver you to him, he will," George said, ordering his men forwards.

"We're outnumbered, Sabrina," Isabella said.

"I'll take skill over paid thugs," Sabrina replied sharply, giving the order for her men to charge.

The clash was swift and brutal, with men falling on both sides.

"Fight to the last man!" Sabrina commanded.

In the midst of the chaos, Sabrina was pulled to the ground by her long black hair. Before her attacker could strike, Isabella tackled him, swiftly dispatching him with her sword. Pulling Sabrina back up, Isabella nodded and smiled before they re-engaged the enemy.

As the battle raged on, a thunderous roar vibrated the ground. Belthazor charged down the hill with Xavier on his back, sword raised and glowing azure blue. Knocking down enemy soldiers with a powerful energy wave, Belthazor unleashed Xavier into the air. With a mighty slam of his sword into the ground, Xavier created a massive explosive wave, cutting down a significant portion of George's men.

"He did it," Sabrina whispered. With George's men scattering in retreat, Sabrina shouted, "Let them run, but capture George!"

The chaos of the battle settled, and the dawn began to break. Sabrina had George Moon on his knees with his hands bound.

"Xavier," Isabella whispered as he approached with Belthazor. She and Xavier embraced, but Isabella winced in pain.

"What's wrong?" Xavier asked, concern etched on his face.

"I'm fine, just a little cut," she said, lifting the chainmail to reveal a stab wound on her hip.

"Please get that treated."

Belthazor looked at Xavier and said, "You can heal her."

Xavier looked back at Belthazor and then at Isabella. "Trust me, my love," he said as he placed his hand over the wound. The wound began to heal.

"What power," George mumbled.

"Be silent," Sabrina snapped, delivering a sharp blow to the side of George's head.

"How is that possible?" Isabella wondered as Xavier removed his hand.

"I'll tell you everything in time," Xavier replied, his eyes holding a mysterious glint.

The battlefield remained silent, and the rising sun cast an eerie light over the aftermath. Smoke curled from the smouldering tents, and the air was thick with the scent of blood and victory.

"Xavier, Isabella, good to see both of you alive," Cain said, bowing his head, "My Lady Panthera, sorry for the delay and lack of troops."

"Don't worry, Cain. As you see, the cause of all our troubles is kneeling before us," Sabrina said, a triumphant smile on her face.

George, still on his knees, spoke up. "Sabrina, I'm so sorry. If I knew what power that boy possessed, I would have pledged my loyalty to him."

"You and your men are driven by coin; you know nothing of honour and sacrifice," Sabrina retorted.

The atmosphere was tense, a silent acknowledgment of the shifting dynamics after the battle. Xavier and Isabella exchanged glances, their minds processing the events that had unfolded.

Cain grabbed George, pressing a dagger against his throat. "You will tell us everything you know, and you will walk away alive."

"You're lucky Cain is merciful," Sabrina added with a stern gaze.

George, beads of sweat forming on his forehead, stammered, "I'll tell you everything. Ginn has fortified the inner walls of the palace and has four thousand men, with hundreds more arriving from the Iron Coast every few days."

"Four thousand men," Isabella murmured her head dropping.

"Keep hope, my dear," Sabrina said, placing a reassuring hand on Isabella's shoulder. "We may not have many, but we will make things right."

Xavier clenched his fist. "We must make haste to the Silver Hills."

"I'll be coming with you," Sabrina declared.

"What about the Vermillion Sands?" Isabella asked.

"That's why I'm coming—to make sure it's there when I come back," Sabrina replied.

Cain, still holding George, spoke up. "Well, I'm ready. But what about that worm?"

"We can't let him go. He'll warn Ginn," Isabella said.

Xavier, thoughtful, responded. "It doesn't matter. Ginn knows we have to face him. Let George go."

A guard approached, cut George loose, and kicked him to the ground.

"You better leave now," Isabella warned as George stumbled away.

CHAPTER TWELVE

TURNING OF THE TIDE

It was late afternoon, and the rhythmic clang of hammers striking metal echoed through the forge. Victor, a young and exceptionally skilled craftsman, worked tirelessly alongside his fellow artisans. The flickering light of the forge danced on his face, emphasising the sweat and soot that marked his hard work.

River, Victor's sister and a commanding figure, entered the bustling forge. The heat and smell of molten metal greeted her as she navigated through the workshop.

"Victor, is everything okay?" River asked, her eyes scanning the busy scene.

"Yes, sister, all the troops' armour is completed," Victor replied, his focus unwavering as he continued to meticulously shape the plate armour on the anvil. The glow from the forge accentuated the determined set of his jaw and the intensity in his eyes.

"I just have yours, Xavier's, and Isabella's to make," he added, the clinks of the hammer against metal punctuating his words.

"Good boy. I'll check on you later," River said, a smile playing on her lips. Despite his prowess, Victor's occasional bossy tone never failed to amuse her.

As River exited the forge, the clamour behind her gradually faded. She headed towards the war room, her mind already strategizing for the challenges that lay ahead.

River entered the war room, where Lawson and two of her captains were going over battle plans. "Any news?" she asked.

"More troops are still arriving at the Iron Coast every other day," one of the captains said.

"There was a battle at one of the borders of the Vermillion Sands," Lawson said.

"Xavier?" River asked.

Lawson shrugged. "The main problem is retaking the palace, with four thousand plus troops," he said.

"We have to draw them out from the palace," River said as she pointed to the map. "Here!"

"Correct," Lawson said and pointed to a place on the map. "It's a marsh near the Emerald Meadows, where the land is unforgiving."

"What's there?" one of the captains asked.

"It's a strategic location. If we can lure them there, nature and the terrain will work in our favour," River said.

"On the border of the Emerald Meadows and the palace," one of the captains confirmed.

As River was about to reveal the plan for the reinforcements coming from the coast, a guard rushed in with news.

"Sorry, my lady, a convoy approaches," the guard said.

"Friendly?" she asked.

"Unknown."

River grabbed Lawson by the arm and pulled him with her to confront the unknown convoy.

*

"The mountains are beautiful," Sabrina said as they navigated the narrow passages of the Silver Hills. The sunlight bathed the mountains, causing them to sparkle.

"Riders approaching," Cain said.

The six riders halted in front of the convoy, prompting it to stop.

Isabella smiled. "I'm pleased you're still alive, River," she said.

"Likewise, princess," River replied.

Lawson rode up to Xavier. "Commander Leo, I'm Lawson of the Knights of Leo."

"The manor fell?" Xavier asked.

Lawson's head dropped. "Yes, my lord. We tried to hold as long as we could to let the villagers escape."

"You got them out safe; that's the main goal," Xavier said. "Where's Artemis?"

"I've got a surprise for you, Xavier," River said. "We'll lead you into the fortress."

The convoy made it through the gates; many were delighted but weary from the battle and journey.

"Everyone, we have food and water in the grand hall," River announced.

"My men are grateful," Sabrina replied.

River's gaze fell on a majestic lion. "Whose lion is that?" she asked, marvelling at its grand size.

"He is called Belthazor," Xavier replied.

"You bonded with a third lion?" she asked.

"It's a long story, River," he replied. Xavier turned towards two guards dragging a person out of a room. "Gavel Graw."

"Yes, I kept the pig alive," River said proudly. "He led a force to attack us but failed."

Xavier approached Gavel, looking straight into his eyes. "Killing you is too easy."

"Everyone you love will die; Artemis was first," Gavel mumbled.

"You can't even do that right," Artemis said, limping towards them.

Xavier turned to Artemis, embracing him in a hug.

"Careful, lad," Artemis groaned, "I'm still healing."

"You're up already," River remarked.

"He has to die," Artemis insisted.

"Artemis is right; the lives he's taken, their souls will finally rest," Isabella added.

"Kill me and you'll be just like me," Gavel laughed.

"I'll kill him," Cain said, pulling out his dagger.

Xavier turned and looked at River for her approval; she nodded back at him with a smile.

Xavier closed his eyes, then opened them. A deep growl vibrated their chests as Saya approached slowly from behind, walking straight to Gavel. All of Gavel's mocking and bravado left him as Saya's warm breath hit his face.

"Please don't," Gavel cried.

Xavier paused, then gave Saya the command. As quick as lightning, Saya swiped her paw across Gavel's face, cutting his face and breaking his neck simultaneously.

"That was quick," River remarked, disappointment evident in her voice.

"It's over now; we have more pressing matters to deal with," Xavier said as he stroked Saya's back.

River and Xavier stood on the ramparts, the sun setting, casting the mountains in a fiery glow.

"This place is magical," Xavier remarked, extending his hand towards the descending sun.

"Yeah, it is. I'm sorry about the Meadows," River said.

"I haven't seen the damage yet," Xavier replied.

"Not a pretty sight, I've been told by those who saved Artemis. But look, your princess isn't holding back, training with your aunt," River commented as she observed Sabrina training with Isabella. "Anyway, what happened to you at the Vermillion Sands?"

"The short version: I was given powers by Malsdon, and that lion has powers as well," Xavier explained.

River looked at him, then laughed and patted him on his arm. However, Xavier's facial expression revealed he wasn't joking. Noticing a cut on her hand, he placed his hand over hers and began to heal it.

"How did you obtain this power?" River asked, watching the magic heal her hand.

"Like I said, Malsdon gave it to me, but at a cost," Xavier replied.

"Everything has a price," River acknowledged.

Xavier nodded, staring into the sunset, aware that the price would be paid before the end.

*

It was two hours before midnight; the war room was filled with paper reports and people discussing the next best move for their campaign. Xavier entered the room and stumbled into an argument between Cain and River.

"What is going on?" Xavier asked them.

"The two fools are arguing over who gets to handle a mission," Artemis said.

"What's the mission?" Xavier asked.

"Blow up the docks in the Iron Coast," River replied, her gaze fixed on Cain.

"I and my ten men can easily handle this, and no one knows what we look like," Cain stated.

"He has a point," Xavier acknowledged.

"It's settled then. Cain and his knights will travel to the Iron Coast," Artemis declared sternly looking at River, dismissing further discussion on the matter.

"What about the main army?" Sabrina asked.

"We are almost two thousand in total," Lawson replied.

"Yes, many villagers from the Emerald Meadows and Silver Hills wanted to join us," Artemis added.

Xavier nodded and focused on the reports. "Strange creature sighted?" he asked.

"Yes, scouts reported something large with red eyes patrolling the palace borders," River replied.

"Belthazor and Saya will have to deal with that," Xavier said, concern etched across his face.

"Don't worry; that thing is no match for the mighty lions,"

Sabrina reassured.

"Vultures patrol the skies, and Delilah can see everything they do, so drawing their army out is no problem," River explained.

"General Artemis, Lawson, and Lady Panthera will lead the army," Xavier said.

"General?" Artemis asked.

Xavier nodded with a smile, and Artemis placed his hand over his heart, silently mouthing the words "thank you".

"Last thing: Isabella, River, and I will lead twenty men inside to free our fathers and others who were captured," Xavier said.

"With only that few men?" Sabrina asked.

"We have someone inside to start a little chaos as we arrive," Xavier replied.

"If those are all the major details, let's call it a night and get some rest," River suggested.

Everyone nodded and headed for the exit. Xavier reviewed the plans one last time.

"It'll be a day to remember," Cain said to Xavier before walking out.

"Cain!" Artemis shouted, trying to catch up with him.

"Yes, sir?" Cain replied.

"The wagon is loaded with explosive barrels disguised as wine," Artemis told him.

"Understood, sir. I'm getting my men and leaving now."

"Very good, lad," Artemis said.

"Until we meet again," Cain said as he shook hands with Artemis and then walked off to collect his men.

"Artemis, are you ready for this?" Xavier asked as he approached.

"Yes, lad. I'll be ready," Artemis replied.

"Your wound is saying otherwise."

"Xavier?" Artemis asked with a bewildered look on his face as Xavier placed his hand on the wound. Artemis looked to where his wound was and kept touching it. He felt no pain and was able to move his torso freely without discomfort.

"My dear boy, how is this possible?" Artemis asked.

"The light finds a way to remove the darkness," Xavier replied.

Artemis looked at Xavier, awaiting a more meaningful answer, but was left with the vague reply. Deciding not to press the matter, he said, "Get some rest, lad. History beckons," as he went to retire for the night.

Xavier was returning to his room, eager to get some much-needed rest.

Boy, I have something for you, Belthazor's voice echoed.

"Where are you?" Xavier asked.

I'm outside the fortress gates, Belthazor replied.

"I'm coming with you," Isabella said, peeking through the half-opened door. "I know you're going to wander off somewhere. You're not leaving me this time, Xavier."

They walked down the hallway leading towards the exit of the main building.

"There he is," Isabella said.

"You want her with you for this?" Belthazor asked.

Xavier nodded as they stood in front of the lion.

"Kneel down and let your minds go," Belthazor told them, his eyes glowing, and a vibrating sensation enveloped their bodies.

"Where are we?" Isabella asked as she looked around.

"Emerald Meadows? But some of these plants and trees haven't been seen in many years and the sky isn't the normal," Xavier replied as he studied their surroundings.

"This isn't real?" Isabella asked as she looked up at the golden sky.

"Not sure," Xavier said as he felt the dirt.

A hooded figure emerged from the forest, walking towards them. Her long black hair cascaded down to her stomach like vines on a wall.

"Who are you?" Xavier asked, adopting a defensive stance.

The hooded lady said nothing but pointed to her heart and stomach.

"Show me your face now."

She removed her hood, revealing her face.

"You look similar to her," Isabella remarked.

"I am your mother, Layla Leo, formerly Panthera," the lady replied.

"You're alive?" Xavier asked.

"My soul and body reside within the heart of Malsdon," Layla explained.

"Have you been here all this time?" Isabella asked.

"Yes, my dear. I've been watching," Layla replied. "I must go now, my son."

"Mother, don't leave me!" Xavier shouted. "How can I save you?"

"There is a way to save me, but what is the true value of a person's soul?" Layla said as she faded into the forest.

Chapter Thirteen

The Board Is Set

Xavier and Isabella were woken up by knocking on the door. "My lord, it's time," a guard said.

"All right, all right," Xavier replied.

"How did we get here?" Isabella asked.

"Nothing makes sense anymore," Xavier sighed as he rubbed his tired eyes.

"One thing at a time," Isabella said as she kissed him on the forehead.

Xavier and Isabella were getting ready, donning their padded garments when the wooden door banged again, irritating Xavier. "We're coming!" he shouted.

"Easy, Xavier," Victor said, giggling. "May I enter?"

"Of course," Xavier replied.

Victor pushed open the door, saluted, then gestured for someone to enter. Two blacksmiths followed him into the room, pulling two large chests. Their faces were tired and covered in soot. "Try not to lose this set of armour," Victor teased.

"He's a cheeky one," Isabella chuckled.

"Runs in the family," Victor replied.

They all broke into laughter. The two blacksmiths opened the chests, revealing the two sets of armour. Isabella was stunned by the craftsmanship coming from such a young boy.

"You do amazing work, Victor," Isabella complimented.

"Team effort," Victor replied, pointing to the other smiths, and hastily left the room with them.

"Black, gold, and red," Xavier remarked.

"Your house colours."

Xavier laughed. "That boy..."

Isabella wondered what thought had crossed his mind.

"He kept saying we're the new king and queen," Xavier explained. "Well, he just put my house colours on our new armour. Let's get ready."

"I guess mine is the one with a skirt," Isabella said.

"It's not a skirt. It's armour for the lower body. The Silver Hills knights wore it long ago," Xavier explained as he put on his chest plate.

Fully armoured and armed, Xavier and Isabella made their way into the courtyard, where they were met by River, Belthazor, Saya, and twenty knights on horseback, all wearing variations of their armour.

"The main army led by Artemis has gone to the marshes," River said.

"What else?" Xavier asked.

"Scouts reported that the palace is sealed, and the entire enemy army has left, marching," she said with a smile.

"That's great news," Isabella said.

"Yes and no," River added.

"I hope Grace is ready for us," Isabella remarked.

Xavier looked at Isabella, nodded, then climbed onto Belthazor's back. Saya approached Isabella, allowing her to mount her back.

"Any fancy words?" River chuckled.

"It won't be easy, but stay alive," Xavier said, winking at her.

River smiled and gave the signal to move out.

*

The main army marched determinedly down the coast and into Emerald Meadows, vultures circled overhead, tracking their movements.

"They know we're coming," Artemis said, gazing up at the circling vultures.

"General!" Lawson shouted as he rode towards Artemis.

"Report," Artemis said.

"They're avoiding the swamp area and holding in the middle of the field west of the forest."

"Smart. Forcing an open-field battle will give them the advantage," Sabrina said.

"What's the plan, General?" Lawson asked, pacing up and down on his horse.

"Split the force; half go on the attack, and half into the forest," Artemis ordered.

"We'll feign a retreat and lure them into a hasty ambush," Sabrina added.

"Yes, they'll have orders to leave none alive, and that will work to our advantage," Artemis replied.

"Lawson, you'll lead the ambush, and we'll engage the main force," Sabrina directed.

Lawson saluted and rejoined the formation as the signal for double time was given.

They reached the forest, and the triple canopy concealed their movements from prying eyes above. Before breaking through the tree line, Artemis signalled for Lawson and half the force to break formation to set up the ambush. Sabrina, Artemis, and the remaining army broke through the tree line, only to be stunned by the sheer size of the barbarian army.

"At least five thousand strong," Artemis whispered.

They continued marching further into the open, arranging the men in a double line formation.

The two armies stood at least three hundred metres apart from each other.

"A white flag. They wish to agree to terms," Artemis said.

"Let's go," Sabrina said, and the two of them, along with a knight, rode to the other party waiting for them.

"I am King Rex, and this is Queen Mara. We've been promised great riches and land," King Rex said.

"What are your terms?" Sabrina asked.

"We offer no terms; you must all be killed," Queen Mara declared.

"Looking at your tiny army, this should be easy," King Rex laughed.

"This is a waste of time," Artemis said, gazing into the king's eyes. "The next time we meet, your head will be in the dirt."

King Rex roared and threw his riding crop at Artemis. Artemis winked at the king, then turned his head towards the barbarian queen, blowing a kiss at her, further enraging King Rex.

After that exchange, the king and queen rode back, cursing in their native tongue.

"Well, that's done the trick," Sabrina laughed.

"They will chase us when we retreat," Artemis predicted as they rode back. He made his way slowly up the line, his sword raised high in the air. "People of Malsdon, heroes in arms! This is where the balance shifts; this is where we cleanse the land of their evil. We will take back Malsdon with the fires of liberation!"

"Sound the charge!" Sabrina commanded, and the horns bellowed a heart pounding tune across the fields as they began to march.

CHAPTER FOURTEEN

BY ANY MEANS

"Sir, more ships are docking," a knight reported, peering through the tavern window.

"You better get your wine to the dock before those barbarians take it," the bartender warned.

Cain swiftly downed his pint and extracted ten gold coins from his wallet, placing them on the bar. "For your troubles," he said, nodding as he and his men got up and left.

"Thank you!" the bartender shouted, hastily collecting the coins.

"Slowly bring the wagon to the docks, then release the horses," Cain ordered.

Three men led the wagon into the docks.

"Sir, we have eyes on us," a knight reported.

"Act normal," Cain whispered.

He and the other seven knights stood at the top of the ramp leading into the dock. The three knights sent the horses galloping back up the ramp, then unloaded the barrels and placed them at each end of the dock.

"Hurry!" Cain shouted, pointing to the approaching ships.

"What's going on here?" a guard asked Cain as he approached them.

"Just unloaded some of the finest wine from the Vermillion Sands," Cain replied.

"No shipments were scheduled today. As you can see, the docks are being used for troop movements," the guard said.

Cain began to sweat, realising it was too late to knock the guard out, as the approaching ships would see and start shooting at them.

"Move it now!" the guard ordered, pointing at the barrels.

Cain looked around at each of his knights, and they all gave him a nod, signalling they were ready to finish the mission by any means. Cain smiled at the guard then stabbed him in the stomach with his dagger. The guard screamed, alerting other guards who sounded the alarm. Cain and the knights at the top of the ramp drew their swords, holding off the incoming guards as the knights on the docks finished setting up the fuses.

"Let the ships dock, then blow it," Cain shouted as he fought off the guards.

The ships began to dock and opened fire on Cain's men.

"The fuse won't light!" one of the knights shouted, then was struck by an arrow.

"Cover me!" Cain shouted as he ran towards the barrels.

The remaining knights followed him, forming a protective circle as he tried to fix the fuse. They picked up broken boards of wood for cover against the arrows.

Cain looked up as the ships crashed into the docks. Panic set in as barbarian reinforcements scrambled over the sides, rushing towards them. Cain realised the fuse wasn't going to work. He glanced at his men holding off the barbarians, the echoes of splintering wood resonating through the chaos.

"By any means," he said, and the knights replied in kind. Cain placed his hand on the barrel and began an enchantment.

*

Horns signalling retreat muffled the sounds of battle; Sabrina rode her way through to Artemis, cutting down barbarians who wandered into her path.

"Artemis, we must retreat now, or you'll be cut off," Sabrina urged.

"I don't think the plan is going to work," Artemis replied.

Sabrina was dragged off her horse and was about to be executed until Artemis shoulder-charged the barbarian to the ground, driving his sword into the assailant's chest.

"We have to kill the king and queen," Sabrina said as she lifted herself up.

Artemis blew his horn, signalling the men to rally. "We push through the centre."

Lawson and the rest of the men emerged from the forest, attacking the right flank of the barbarian army. "Break through them, men! We have to help the general," Lawson commanded.

Sabrina and Artemis effortlessly pushed through the barbarian lines, exploiting the lack of training among the enemy forces that relied on overwhelming numbers and brute strength. The king and queen observed as Sabrina and Artemis, accompanied by their knights, cut down their men to reach them.

"I want his head," Rex gritted his teeth, expressing his desire.

"Make the dark-haired woman our slave," Mara added.

They both dismounted and approached Sabrina and Artemis.

"Stop now," King Rex commanded, lifting his hand, and the barbarians ceased fighting. "General, you wish to fight me and my queen?"

"Yes, and after you're dead, she will become my wife," Artemis teased, looking Queen Mara up and down.

King Rex roared in rage and charged Artemis, raising his sword high over his head. Artemis laughed and skilfully evaded the massive overhead swing.

The king and Artemis began to circle each other, and Queen Mara was about to join in when the king signalled her to stand back.

"I'm going to kill this worm by myself," King Rex declared, launching a barrage of heavy blows.

Artemis skilfully blocked the attacks, their clash characterised by raw power versus technique. However, both warriors began to fatigue under the relentless assault.

"Kill him, you fool!" Queen Mara shouted as she paced back and forth.

As King Rex charged Artemis, Queen Mara attempted to flank him but was stopped by Sabrina.

"Where do you think you're going?" Sabrina questioned, pointing her swords towards Queen Mara's neck.

Queen Mara, filled with hatred, spat at Sabrina and attempted to stab her in the stomach. However, Sabrina deftly sidestepped the lunge, leaving the queen's entire body exposed.

"Too easy," Sabrina whispered as she brought her sword up, swiftly chopping off Queen Mara's hands.

The queen let out a banshee-like scream, falling to the floor in agony. This broke the king's focus on Artemis, who seized the opportunity to deliver a pommel strike to the king's face, dropping him to the ground in a dazed state.

Artemis towered over the king. "Disband your army and leave Malsdon."

King Rex responded with a defiant spit, earning himself a swift kick in the stomach from Artemis.

"Look at your queen," Artemis said, gesturing towards the fallen queen, Sabrina's sword pressed against her throat.

She lay there, sobbing as she clutched the raw stumps that used to be her hands.

"Leave now. What the Graw brothers promised you is no more," Sabrina declared.

"We will never surrender," King Rex defiantly replied, shouting something in their native language.

Suddenly, the barbarian troops began to drop dead.

"What's going on?" Lawson asked as the enemy crumbled around him.

"It's something in their mouth," Artemis explained.

King Rex was about to bite down, but Artemis halted him with a punch to the jaw.

"You will not stop this," the king struggled to say.

"Sabrina, a few of them did not kill themselves," Lawson pointed out.

"Capture them at once," she replied.

"Stop struggling. I'm giving you a chance to go home," Artemis insisted.

"I'm not returning home." With one last act of defiance, the king pushed Artemis off and scrambled towards a rock.

"Stop him," Artemis ordered.

"The wrath of my spawn will find you and the fallen will rise against you," the king declared before smashing his head against the rock.

"Damn it," Lawson cursed as he didn't reach in time.

Laughter erupted from the queen. "My daughter will come for all your hearts," Queen Mara declared.

"Why wasn't she here?" Lawson asked.

"It wasn't her time. However, with the death of her parents and fellow countrymen, it's all the reason she needs," Queen Mara explained. "Malsdon will burn."

Artemis exchanged glances with Sabrina and Lawson. "We can't tell Xavier yet," he said.

Sabrina raised her boot and drove it straight into Mara's face, knocking her out. "She talked too much."

"Lawson, take the prisoners and wounded to the villages in the Meadows. Take a hundred men with you," Artemis commanded. "Everyone else, we move out in five minutes. We must make it to the palace in time."

"The men are tired. Give them more time. I will ride ahead with my mounted bodyguards," Sabrina suggested.

"Very well, we'll see you at the palace," Artemis agreed.

Sabrina signalled for her horse and her bodyguards. "Don't keep a lady waiting," she said to Artemis as she mounted her horse.

He bowed his head in response as Sabrina and her guards galloped off towards the palace.

CHAPTER FIFTEEN

ALL OF EVIL'S MIGHT

The sound of galloping echoed through the forest, shaking loose dirt from the ground. Xavier's group raced through the vast lands of the Emerald Meadows.

"Border ahead!" Xavier shouted.

"I don't see any guards," River added.

The group stormed through the empty checkpoint and entered the palace lands.

"We've made good time," Xavier said to the group.

"Look, smoke coming from the Iron Coast," Isabella said.

Their heads dropped for a brief moment, acknowledging that Cain had completed an impossible task.

"Xavier, stop," Belthazor commanded.

Xavier looked at Belthazor, confused. "Why?"

"Use your mind and tell Grace to start the chaos. We won't have time in a few moments," Belthazor explained.

The others looked at Xavier, wondering why he had stopped. Xavier placed his hand over his face and focused his power.

Grace, it's Xavier, he communicated.

Grace, walking back to her house, froze when she heard Xavier's voice. "How are you speaking to me?" she asked.

It's a long story, but I'll explain later. Right now, I need you and your friends to start the riot, then release my father. He will help you, Xavier instructed.

"Okay, Xavier, it will be done," she replied and ran off to gather the others.

Xavier shook his head. "Let's move," he commanded.

They moved deeper into the palace lands, traversing a thick forest that stood before the palace outer walls. Saya and Belthazor began to growl, and the horses grew nervous and frightful. Standing before them was Delilah, her sword drawn, dressed in full black robes and chainmail.

"Young Xavier, I've been waiting for your return," Delilah's voice echoed through the forest, sending a chill down their spines.

"Dismount and form up," Xavier commanded.

"Xavier, I sense other vessels of evil hiding here," Belthazor warned.

"I sense it too," Xavier replied, signalling River to keep her eyes up.

She nodded and readied an arrow on her bow.

As they approached Delilah, close enough to see the details of her face, she taunted him. "Oh, Xavier, we're not fighting here. I'm going to kill you in front of everyone, but my friends will keep you busy for now." Delilah then teleported away, laughing.

Loud screeches bellowed around them.

"Make ready," River ordered.

Two large figures appeared in front of them.

"What are they?" Isabella asked, her hands shaking.

"I believe they're called the Blighted Ones. Last seen during the mage war. She must have brought these foul creatures back to life by the looks of them," Xavier explained, as he studied their pale form, resembling more beast than man.

"Xavier, be careful. I sense great power from them," Belthazor warned.

"Saya and Belthazor will take one, and we'll attack the other one," Xavier commanded.

They all lined up opposite their chosen target. Saya and Belthazor let out a thunderous roar, shaking branches loose from the trees. The Blighted Ones stepped forward, beating their muscular chests with a force that sent vibrations through the groups' armour.

"They're powerful," River said.

The creatures charged, and Belthazor and Saya roared before launching their own attack.

"Archers, fire at will!" River shouted.

Arrows were unleashed on both targets, but they seemed impervious, holding their charge with arrows stuck in their lean and long bodies.

Belthazor collided with one of the Blighted Ones, sending both creatures crashing to the ground. Saya went in for the kill bite, but the Blighted recovered quickly, kicking her away.

The other creature ploughed into Xavier's group, knocking down soldiers.

"Circle that thing!" Xavier shouted.

Those still on their feet formed a circle around the creature.

"Keep shooting at it!" River commanded.

The Blighted creature locked eyes with Isabella and charged. Knights tried to block its path, but it threw them aside. Isabella got into a defensive stance, but it was too powerful.

At the last second before impact, River kicked Isabella out of the way and shot the creature in the face, stunning it. However, the Blighted creature grabbed River by the neck, resisting attempts from knights to save her.

Xavier rushed over, channelling power into his sword. With its large and deformed head, the creature head-butted River twice and the sound of her skull cracking shocked Xavier to his core. It threw River's body to the ground and turned towards Isabella.

The creature grabbed Isabella's leg as she tried to crawl away, lifting her in the air. It was about to grab her neck, intent on tearing her apart. Xavier slid across the ground, mustering all his strength and a bit of magic, to sever the Blighted legs.

Isabella, still clutched in its grasp, landed on top of it. Ignoring the pain, the creature tried to bite Isabella's stomach. Xavier acted swiftly, jumping up and driving his sword through the creature's mouth, ending its life instantly.

Three knights were tending to River.

"Isabella, check on River," Xavier said as he ran off into the woods.

"Stop, you need to heal her," Isabella urged.

Xavier stopped and turned towards River, but the roars and growls of Saya and Belthazor kept pulling his attention. He ran over and knelt next to River, placing his hands over her head, and began to heal her. He could feel the broken part of her skull slowly forming back together.

"She's not waking up," Isabella said, holding River's hand.

"She will wake; her brain is still recovering," Xavier reassured. He then ran off towards the lions.

The roars grew louder as he approached Saya and Belthazor, who were still engaged in the battle.

Belthazor and Saya had the Blighted One cornered against a tree, all three covered in bite and claw marks. Saya slowly moved to the right side of the creature, and Belthazor began to move head-on towards it. The Blighted roared and then charged Belthazor.

It tackled him to the ground wrapping its long limbs around the lion, but this was part of the plan. Belthazor used his hind legs to flip the creature over him to the ground. As this happened, Saya pounced on the Blighted, aiming for the kill bite. However, the creature protected its neck and punched Saya in the ribs, causing her to back off in pain.

Belthazor took this chance while the creature was still on the ground. He bit down on its head and yanked it across the ground with force, attempting to break its neck. However, only a kill bite would end this battle, as the Blighted One continued to fight back.

Saya slowly got back to her feet and prepared to pounce on the creature again when a voice in her head told her to move aside. It was Xavier, running towards them. He jumped high into the air and slammed his sword across the creature's neck, severing its head and killing it instantly.

Belthazor and Saya fell to the ground in exhaustion as the bells from the palace rang.

"It has begun," Belthazor said.

Xavier approached to heal Belthazor and Saya.

"No, boy, you must save your energy," Belthazor insisted, pushing Xavier's hand away.

Xavier prioritised Saya's more severe injuries before turning his attention to Belthazor. The lion was being stubborn, so Xavier slapped him on the nose.

"Stop being stubborn. I'm going to need you before the end," Xavier said as he began to heal him.

Belthazor growled, still surprised by the slap, but eventually, he gave in and relaxed. The bonds between them strengthened, a silent understanding passing between the healer and his companions as they prepared for what lay ahead.

Xavier walked back to the others along with the two lions.

"Xavier, you're alive," Sabrina said.

"Where are the others?" Xavier asked as he walked over to the awakening River.

"I thought you'd need help for the final push. The rest of the army isn't far behind," Sabrina explained.

Xavier nodded and checked on River. "You have to stay here with the other wounded," he said.

"No, I can fight," River said as she slowly got to her feet.

Xavier admired River's strength and pride, but her stubbornness would put her and others at risk. With one hand, Xavier gently pushed her, causing her to fall onto her behind. River's eyes popped out in surprise at Xavier's actions.

"Xavier, what is wrong with you?" Isabella shouted.

"I'm sorry, but she's not ready to fight. You know it as well, River. There is no shame in this," Xavier said calmly.

"Fine," River said, slamming her bow into the dirt.

CHAPTER SIXTEEN

PUNISHMENT

Market stalls burnt, their flames casting an eerie glow on the chaos below. The streets were littered with food, clothing, and bodies of guards and citizens who once inhabited the common area.

"Xavier, push towards the palace. I'll free your father and any others we find," Sabrina shouted over the tumult.

"Keep him safe," Xavier replied with determination in his eyes as he ran off towards the palace, Isabella and Belthazor at his side.

The air was thick with the acrid scent of burning debris and the sounds of destruction. Xavier, Isabella, and Belthazor manoeuvred through the mayhem, their hearts racing with a sense of urgency. The common area, once bustling with life, was now a battleground of despair.

Sabrina, Saya, and her bodyguards fought their way through towards the barracks. To Sabrina's delight, she saw Darius, Sol, and the two lions fighting to free the palace guards who were locked away in the cells. The fighting settled for a brief moment, and Sol set the guards free.

Tiberius and Jupiter ran over to Saya, and the three lions embraced after being apart for weeks.

"Darius Leo," Sabrina said with a smile.

"Sabrina Panthera," Darius replied with a chuckle.

"I'm glad to see you alive," Sabrina said.

"Barely. I feel my life force is slowly fading away," Darius replied.

Sabrina said nothing in reply, understanding the reasons behind his condition.

"Where is my daughter?" Sol asked.

"She was injured in a fight, but she's resting outside the outer walls," Sabrina said.

"I will go to her," Sol said, walking off before anyone else could say anything.

"Darius, go catch up with your son. We'll try to secure the commons," Sabrina said.

Darius climbed on Tiberius' back. "Saya and Jupiter, stay and help Sabrina," Darius said in a stern tone.

The two lions moaned and growled at Darius, expressing their desire to help Xavier, but eventually accepted the command.

Xavier and Isabella reached the palace steps along with Belthazor after overcoming a few guards in their way. They were about to climb the stairs when Xavier stopped and turned around to the sight of his father and Tiberius making their way to them.

"Well done, my son," Darius said.

"Father," Xavier said, a lump in his throat, but he held back the overwhelming emotions he was feeling.

They both smiled and embraced each other before climbing the stairs. Isabella looked on with joy, but her heart held sorrow, knowing she would never see her father again.

Tiberius and Belthazor gazed at each other, growling, despite being magical creatures. The overwhelming animal instinct of two alphas meeting filled the air.

"Enough!" Xavier shouted, but he was ignored.

Darius laughed, then pulled Tiberius away by his ear.

"Let's go, boy," Darius said.

They entered the palace, the air thick with tension and the once grand halls now silent and still, bearing the scars of the recent conflict.

"You ready for this?" Xavier asked Isabella.

"I have to make this right," Isabella replied.

"I'll find that rat Ginn," Darius declared as he went off with Tiberius to track him down.

Xavier and Isabella, accompanied by Belthazor, set out to find Delilah and Arabella.

"I can sense Delilah; she's in the throne room," Belthazor said.

"Lead the way," Xavier replied.

The palace, once a symbol of grandeur, now echoed with an eerie quiet, broken only by the determined footsteps of the trio as they moved towards the inevitable confrontation.

Tiberius and Darius separated from the others, made their way to the king's private chambers. Darius booted down the door, revealing Ginn packing trunks full of gold and valuable jewels. Ginn froze at the sight of Tiberius and Darius.

"Darius, there's enough for both of us if you let me go," Ginn said with a nervous smile.

Darius pointed to the door, and Tiberius sat in the doorway. Ginn closed the trunk nervously.

"You're not going to let me go?" Ginn asked.

Darius stepped forwards, drawing his sword. "You killed my friend and tried to kill my son," Darius said.

"I am the new king; you will do as I say and move," Ginn said, picking up the king's sword.

"I'm going to enjoy this," Darius said, charging Ginn.

Ginn blocked the attack but got pushed back against the wall. "You're struggling, old man," Ginn said, noticing Darius was tired already.

Ginn pushed Darius back and swung his sword at the same time. Darius sidestepped the strike and punched Ginn in the jaw, knocking him to the floor.

"You're a worm of a man," Darius said.

Ginn moaned in pain from the punch and slowly got back onto his feet.

"All the trouble you've caused, and you can't even fight," Darius said.

Darius performed a barrage of overhead strikes, each one forcing Ginn to his knees.

"Please don't kill me," Ginn pleaded while on his knees.

Darius knocked the sword out of Ginn's hands and raised his sword over his head, ready to execute Ginn. As he brought the sword down with great force, Darius lost all feeling in his arms and dropped the sword. Seizing the opportunity, Ginn pulled a hidden dagger from his trousers and stabbed Darius twice in the stomach.

Ginn got on top of Darius, ready to deliver a fatal blow with the dagger aimed at his neck. Darius, weakened and struggling, managed to grab Ginn's wrist with both hands. Tiberius, pacing anxiously by the door, was ready to pounce but held back as instructed prior to the attack.

Darius clung on with the last remnants of his strength, the dagger inching closer to his neck. Ginn, with a sinister smile, believed he was moments away from claiming victory over one of the mightiest knights in Malsdon. Darius, in the midst of the struggle, questioned if he was cursed. How had he become so weak? Yet, with each passing second, he knew he had to act swiftly as he bled profusely.

Summoning a final burst of strength and will, Darius released his grip on Ginn's wrist. Simultaneously, he moved his neck, causing the dagger to graze the side rather than strike true. With a swift motion, Darius pinned Ginn's arm against his chest and rolled him over, reversing their positions. Now, Darius was on top, his determined gaze meeting Ginn's desperate eyes.

Darius wasted no time, delivering three brutal punches to Ginn's throat. Ginn gagged and choked, gasping for breath. However, Darius, weakened and exhausted, couldn't go on any longer. He fell to the side, both men lying on their backs, gasping for energy and life.

Tiberius watched, witnessing Darius clinging to life. Unable to bear it any longer, the lion pounced onto Ginn. With a damaged windpipe preventing him from screaming, Ginn cried, futilely attempting to push the lion off. But there would be no mercy from Tiberius.

The lion pressed down onto Ginn's chest with his two front legs. Each rib cracked under the increasing pressure, rendering Ginn unable to make a sound or breathe properly. His diaphragm struggled against the relentless force, leaving him gasping for air in agonising silence.

Darius looked on in shock as Tiberius, acting on his emotions, didn't let up the pressure. Blood started spewing from Ginn's mouth.

"Tiberius, end this now." Darius strained to get the words out.

Tiberius heard his master's call. With a nod to his loyalty, he went onto his back legs and then slammed his front legs down with all his weight and power onto Ginn's chest, crushing every bone and organ in his torso.

Ginn lay there lifeless as Tiberius went to Darius. The lion started plucking fur from his body, placing it down on Darius' wounds. Then, he lay down next to Darius and placed his head on him.

In this silent moment, the bond between Darius and Tiberius was palpable. It wasn't just the physical wounds that were being tended to; it was a display of loyalty, understanding, and an unspoken connection between a knight and his loyal companion.

A sharp pain hit Xavier, causing him to stop in his tracks and fall on one knee. Isabella looked concerned and grabbed his hand.

"Were you injured in the fight before?" she asked.

"Doesn't feel like a battle wound," he said as he slowly got back to his feet.

Belthazor looked on, knowing that the price was almost paid. "I sense someone in that room over there," Belthazor said to Xavier.

"Who is there?" Xavier asked.

"Not the one you must face, but someone who has to be dealt with," Belthazor said, turning towards Isabella.

Xavier saw the hint from Belthazor and went to inform Isabella.

"Isabella, I believe your sister is hiding in there," Xavier said as he pointed to the door.

Emotions overwhelmed Isabella as her face turned red, and she held the grip of her sword so tight he could hear the leather wrap torque under the pressure.

"Xavier, I must deal with her alone," Isabella said quietly.

"I'll respect your wish," Xavier replied and gave her a hug.

"Stay alive," she said as she walked away towards the door.

"Xavier, she's still in the throne room," Belthazor said and ran off, leading the way.

Xavier paused for a second, looking at the door Isabella just went through, then ran to catch up with Belthazor.

Isabella entered the room, her mother's old chamber where important guests were once received. Sat on her mother's old chair was Arabella, adorned with their mother's crown and golden robes.

"How dare you wear that crown," Isabella said sternly, drawing her sword.

"I am the queen; that's why," Arabella replied with a smile on her face.

"You sided with a woman whose kind killed many mothers, including ours," Isabella said, stepping closer to Arabella.

"You got Father killed!" Arabella shouted, standing up from the chair. "You were with Xavier when Ginn was your husband, and Father knew. Father wanted me to marry Xavier when he knew you've been with him," Arabella shouted again, getting within arm's length of Isabella.

"What you did is unforgettable, and killing you quickly isn't going to bring justice to Mother and Father," Isabella said softly as she threw her sword onto the ground.

The room echoed with the weight of their shared history and the burden of their family legacy. The crown, once a symbol of authority, now stood as a silent witness to the unravelling of their familial bonds.

Isabella, fuelled by rage, removed her chest plate and threw it to the floor before tackling Arabella. The two sisters traded punches on the floor, their faces bloodied and swollen. Isabella gained the upper hand, getting on top of Arabella and delivering a powerful strike with her forehead that shattered her sister's nose. Arabella pushed Isabella away, and they both stood up, continuing their brutal exchange.

The hatred between them intensified with each punch. Isabella, consumed by rage, screamed and landed a vicious kick to Arabella's knee, forcing her to drop onto her other knee. Another kick to the face sent Arabella sprawling backwards.

"I hate you!" Arabella shouted, blood dripping from her nose and mouth.

"I don't care; you're not my sister anymore," Isabella replied.

The two sisters locked eyes; their gaze filled with mutual animosity. Arabella charged, but Isabella skilfully used her sister's momentum against her, throwing Arabella over her shoulder. Arabella crashed hard into the floor.

Isabella, standing over her fallen sister, retrieved her sword, and stared at Arabella's broken will.

"Mother and Father are crying in the great beyond because of this," Isabella said, her voice heavy with a mix of sorrow and anger.

Arabella looked up at her sister, hatred still filling her eyes as she spat blood onto Isabella's leg. "Kill me!" she said as a last act of defiance.

Isabella seized Arabella's hair, pulling her head towards her own. "You're going to live with everything you've done for the rest of your life," Isabella declared.

Arabella attempted to wiggle out of Isabella's grip, but this only made Isabella tighten her hold.

"You're going to live with a deaf mute where no one can hear your cries," Isabella continued through gritted teeth.

"If you don't kill me, you'll regret it dearly," Arabella said bluntly.

Isabella responded by hitting Arabella in the head with the guard of her sword, knocking her back. Isabella then looked up at the ceiling, took a deep breath, wiped the blood from her face, and began to tie Arabella's hands and legs with pieces of torn robes.

In this moment of restraint, the room echoed with the weight of their shared past and the consequences Arabella now had to face.

CHAPTER SEVENTEEN

A LION'S HEART

Xavier and Belthazor were in hot pursuit of Delilah, weaving through the palace corridors as she teleported ahead, taunting them with laughter.

"This is getting old," Xavier said as they raced down the hall.

"She's trying to frustrate you, get you off balance," Belthazor replied.

As they turned a corner, a large window at the end of the corridor caught Xavier's attention. Recognising the opportunity, he focused his thoughts. *She's enjoying this game too much. Time to end it.*

Delilah teleported once more, appearing right in front of the window. Xavier seized the moment, his eyes glowing with magic. With a swift motion, he drew his sword, unleashing a shockwave that tore through the air, hitting Delilah before she could teleport again. She crashed through the window.

Belthazor, ever agile, sped up and leapt through the shattered window after Delilah. Xavier, putting his sword away while running, took a leap out of the window too. As he descended, he focused his magic, unleashing a shockwave that cushioned his fall, allowing him to land gracefully on the ground below.

On the ground, Belthazor circled Delilah as she continued her eerie laughter. Xavier, drawing both his long and short swords, approached with determination.

"I said everyone will be watching you fall," Delilah said as knights from Xavier's army, along with Artemis and Sabrina, entered the courtyard.

Drawing a long sword as black as the night sky, black smoke oozing from the blade, Delilah awaited Xavier's move. In response, Xavier channelled his power, and his swords glowed with the azure hue once again. He took a fighting stance, advancing towards Delilah with Belthazor at his side.

"I must do this alone," Xavier said, determination in his eyes.

As they walked towards Delilah, the tension thickened. Delilah stood still, a sinister smile on her face.

Don't let your pride and your honour blind you, Belthazor's voice echoed in Xavier's mind.

"You're right. There will be no honour in this fight. She deserves nothing but death." Xavier grappled with the weight of Belthazor's words.

Belthazor stepped alongside him. "We'll do this together."

The courtyard held its breath as the confrontation between Xavier, Belthazor, and Delilah unfolded.

The two warriors split, each taking a side of Delilah, attempting to gain an advantage in the two-on-one confrontation.

"One or both of us are going to die soon," Delilah said, her ominous words hanging in the air.

She unleashed a shockwave of dark energy, and Xavier swiftly raised his sword to block it. Reacting with quick thinking, he redirected the force towards the palace. The resulting explosion sent debris flying into the air, raining down like a storm of destruction. Many sought cover, shields raised, or fled the area. Xavier, however, had no shield. In a moment of peril, Belthazor created a protective bubble just in time.

"Watch out," Xavier said, but Delilah seized the opportunity.

Exploiting the distraction, she sent two energy blasts at Belthazor. The first seared the lion's side, burning fur and flesh. Unfazed, Belthazor prepared to retaliate, but the second blast, concealed by the first, struck him in the head, knocking the mighty lion unconscious, leaving Xavier to face Delilah alone.

The clash of their swords created a dazzling display of sparks that scattered in every direction. Delilah, despite being a mage, displayed exceptional skill with the sword, making it challenging for Xavier to find an opening. Their strikes, blocks, and parries unfolded in a mesmerising dance, captivating the growing crowd.

"Everyone will see your downfall," Delilah taunted with a smirk.

In response, Xavier unleashed an energy wave, but Delilah skilfully absorbed the energy and returned it with double the force. The impact sent Xavier soaring into the air before crashing into a group of onlookers. Delilah, seizing the opportunity, teleported above Xavier, poised to deliver the final blow.

Before the decisive strike could land, Belthazor intervened with a deafening roar. The sound froze Delilah for a brief moment, granting Xavier the precious seconds he needed to regain his bearings amidst the chaos. Xavier regained his footing with Delilah dangerously close.

She taunted him with a sinister smile, her words cutting through the air. "You see everyone whispering?" she asked, revelling in the reactions of the crowd.

Xavier swiftly scanned the onlookers, catching glimpses of uncertain whispers rippling through the assembly.

"If you don't defeat me by yourself, they will always question your abilities," Delilah declared, punctuating her statement with a chilling, high-pitched laugh.

Xavier, feeling the weight of the crowd's judgement, shifted into a high-ready stance. "Enough talk," he said, his tone firm and resolute.

The clash of swords resumed, but as both combatants grew fatigued, each swing carried less conviction. Belthazor circled them, conflicted by the growing dilemma within him. Memories of failing to save Xavier's grandfather haunted him, and the pressure to please the crowd intensified.

Boy, you have to end it now, Belthazor's voice resonated in Xavier's mind.

With a nod, Xavier prepared for a decisive move. He seized Delilah's wrist and delivered a powerful shoulder strike, causing her to stumble backwards. But just as victory seemed within reach, Delilah unleashed a black mist into Xavier's face, blinding him. Xavier fell to the ground, desperately rubbing his eyes and losing his grip on his swords.

Standing over him, Delilah revelled in her apparent triumph. "You put up a good fight, little Leo," she taunted with hubris.

Meanwhile, Belthazor, angered by the crowd's demands, roared thunderously, making the ground tremble. Sabrina and Artemis, also disgusted by the crowd's response, voiced their frustration.

The internal conflict within Belthazor deepened, torn between loyalty and the expectations of the crowd. Xavier, on his knees and blinded, felt the weight of the impending doom. The crowd, indifferent to his plight, shouted for him to submit to Delilah's command. Delilah's laughter echoed through the courtyard as she swung Xavier's sword towards his head.

With a determined resolve, Xavier rolled beneath the blade and leapt up, seizing both of Delilah's wrists. In a low, menacing tone, he whispered in her ear, "Your time is done."

A high-pitched scream erupted from Delilah, causing people in the crowd to cover their ears in pain. Blood trickled from Xavier's ears, evidence of the deafening assault on his senses. Unbeknownst to him, his grip tightened, and he began burning Delilah's wrists. The acrid scent of burning flesh filled the air, intensifying the brutality of the moment.

Delilah, now on her knees, continued to scream, though with diminishing potency. As Xavier reached the bone, she began to beg for mercy. However, Xavier, still blinded and now deaf, remained oblivious to her pleas, consumed by the need for retribution.

Within the crowd, reactions varied. Some were horrified,

others enthralled by the spectacle unfolding before them. The atmosphere was charged with tension as Xavier pressed forwards, his determination unwavering

Tears of black liquid streamed down Delilah's face, a macabre display of suffering that begged for mercy. "Please, make him stop," she pleaded towards the crowd, her voice a desperate whisper.

In response to Delilah's plea, the crowd trembled, caught between fear and curiosity. Some exchanged uneasy glances, while others turned away, unable to witness the brutality unfolding before them. Sabrina and Artemis, standing as guardians of order, watched with stoic expressions, their thoughts and emotions hidden beneath the surface.

Xavier finally stopped, but it wasn't an act of mercy. Delilah's pleas went unanswered as he had burnt through her wrists, severing both her hands. The courtyard fell into a heavy silence, the air thick with the weight of justice served and the consequences of merciless retribution.

Xavier then grabbed her by the hair with one hand, trying to find his sword with the other.

"Please, Xavier, we only did what we thought was right," Delilah said.

"The only mercy you will get is a quick death," Isabella said as she approached them.

Isabella picked up Xavier's sword, then saw the state Xavier was in. She put her hand over Xavier's and he let go of Delilah as he recognised Isabella's touch.

"Heal him," Isabella said to Belthazor.

Belthazor rushed over and began to heal Xavier. Delilah attempted to crawl away, but Isabella kicked her onto her back. Without uttering a word, Isabella thrust the sword into Delilah's heart, twisting it a few times.

"This is for my mother and all the other mothers your kind killed," Isabella said as she pulled the sword out.

Delilah gasped, discoloured blood pouring from the wound. "This is just the beginning," she whispered.

Ignoring the dying mage's words, Isabella continued. "This is for my father." She drove the sword through Delilah's face.

A few members of the crowd cheered and shouted, "The true queen of Malsdon!"

"I can feel a shift within the land," Xavier said to Belthazor.

"You're the reason everyone and the land are safe again," Belthazor replied, lowering his head in respect.

"I didn't do it alone," Xavier said, glancing around at all his allies before placing his hand on Belthazor's head.

"What now?" Isabella asked, as she stood before Xavier.

"A long sleep," Xavier said, hugging her.

"It's Tiberius," Artemis said.

Xavier turned towards the lion and saw his father draped on his back. "Father?" Xavier whispered, then sprinted over to them, the others following behind.

"Father, can you hear me?" Xavier asked.

"I take it you killed that witch," Darius said softly, trying to save energy.

"Yes, Father. Isabella killed her," Xavier replied, looking at his father's wounds.

"Xavier, you must heal him," Artemis urged.

Xavier dropped his head. "I can't."

"What about your new lion?" Artemis asked.

"It can't be done," Xavier said softly, then walked off.

"Don't walk away, boy. Your father needs you," Artemis said, moving to drag him back.

"Let it be," Sabrina said, pushing Artemis back.

"Stop all this noise; I just need rest," Darius whispered.

"We'll make you comfortable, and the royal physicians will tend to you," Isabella said.

Xavier looked on with tears in his eyes as Tiberius carried his father back inside, with the others following.

CHAPTER EIGHTEEN

EXALTED PLAINS

Three hours had passed since the fall of Delilah and many actions had been ordered by Princess Isabella. Search and destroy missions led by River for any remaining barbarians still on Malsdon, the capture and arrest of any Delilah sympathisers, and the seizure of all their property.

In the palace courtyard, Isabella stood next to a blacked-out wagon. Inside, Arabella was accompanied by another lady, the deaf mute whom Isabella had promised to Arabella after their fight.

"In all honesty, my sister, I should kill you," Isabella said, tapping her nails against the wooden door.

"Now, I will always be a threat to your throne," Arabella replied, gazing into Isabella's eyes. The conviction in her sister's voice and eyes made Isabella feel uneasy.

"Driver, do you know where to go?" Isabella asked.

"Yes, my lady," the driver replied.

"Off you go. An escort will meet you outside the outer walls."

She watched as the wagon set off, fully aware that Arabella would spend the rest of her life contemplating her actions.

Isabella retraced her steps towards the palace when a stranger, dressed in black, approached her with intent. The bodyguard, who now accompanied Isabella everywhere, swiftly threw the stranger to the ground and restrained them. The guard, upon removing the hood, revealed one of Arabella's maids.

"What's in her cloak?" Isabella asked.

One of the guards retrieved a black rose.

"It's for you, from your sister," the maid explained.

Isabella took the rose and disdainfully threw it to the ground.

"Your end will come," the maid added.

"Arrest her and catch up with the wagon. My sister plans to escape," Isabella told the bodyguard, then stormed up the palace steps.

*

Xavier sat in the war room with Saya and Jupiter, reflecting on everything that had happened. "It all started on Alice Island," he said to Saya and Jupiter.

They glanced up, sensing the pain and stress he had endured.

"Thank you for being there, girls," he added, patting both of them on the head.

Isabella pushed the door open and saw Xavier's head slowly rise to make eye contact with her. She noticed Xavier was still feeling down, so she decided to keep the black rose message to herself for now. Walking over, she sat on Xavier's lap and gave him a hug.

"Thank you for everything you've done for me," Isabella said, then kissed him on the cheek.

"I will always protect you," Xavier replied in a low tone.

"Your father will be fine; he's the strongest man I know on this island," Isabella reassured him.

Xavier's head fell onto Isabella's shoulder. "Can we just sit here and enjoy the quiet?" he asked softly.

*

It was late evening when Belthazor entered the war room and discovered Isabella and Xavier sleeping on the floor next to the two lions. Belthazor lightly vibrated the floor to wake them up. Isabella's eyes opened, and she was startled by Belthazor, who then roused Xavier and the two lions.

"We slept for a long time. I hope no one was looking for us," Isabella said as she stood up.

"It's fine; we earned this," Xavier replied.

"We've been called," Belthazor informed Xavier.

Isabella looked at Belthazor and then at Xavier, asking, "Everything okay?"

Xavier nodded and smiled at her.

"Okay," she said and walked towards the door with Saya and Jupiter giving Xavier the room. She looked back and he gave her another reassuring smile.

"Are we going to the same place I saw my mother?" Xaiver asked.

"Yes, that astral realm is known as the Exalted Plains," Belthazor replied.

Xavier and Belthazor entered the Exalted Plains. They didn't wander far before a cloaked lady appeared from within the trees and stood before them, all in white, her face covered by a radiant white light. A bit uneasy, Xavier looked at Belthazor for clarity.

"Don't be alarmed, young Xavier Leo," said the lady.

"Who are you?" he asked.

The lady removed her hood to reveal her face; her skin was as pale as snow, and her eyes and hair were golden in colour.

"She is the divine deity, the soul of Malsdon," Belthazor said.

"You've done a great deal for Malsdon," the deity acknowledged.

"I will protect the land from all threats, as promised," he replied.

"You are noble, and the price you paid will not be in vain," the deity assured.

Belthazor growled at her response. Xavier looked at Belthazor, wondering why he was getting agitated.

"If Delilah had won, her corrupt magic would have killed you!" Belthazor shouted.

"But she did not win," the deity said calmly.

"You owe this boy your life!" Belthazor continued to shout.

The deity ignored him and smiled at Xavier, which angered Belthazor, causing him to jump in front of the deity.

"I am invoking an exchange: my powers for the father's life," Belthazor declared.

The deity grew angry. "I won't allow it," she said.

"What do you mean you won't?" Xavier asked.

"She has to; it's an equivalent exchange," Belthazor explained.

The deity knew what Belthazor said was true, and she had no choice but to carry out his wishes. Her golden eyes radiated vibrantly as she pointed one hand at Belthazor and the other into the fawn-coloured sky.

"It's done," the deity said with a displeased look.

"Thank you, Belthazor," Xavier said, bowing his head.

"There is one more thing I must do," Belthazor replied as he looked back at Xavier.

Xavier glanced at the lion, wondering what else he planned to do.

"I invoke one more exchange," he said to the deity.

"Exchange with whom?" the deity asked.

"I, Belthazor, lord of the gigas lions, last of the divine creatures of Malsdon, exchange my life force for the resurrection of Layla Panthera," Belthazor declared, his voice thundering through the air.

The deity was stunned by this exchange. "Why, Belthazor?" she asked.

"Something I have to do," Belthazor replied.

The deity nodded and began the exchange. Belthazor turned and walked back to Xavier; his body slowly began to fade into the air.

"I failed to protect your grandfather many years ago, and your mother was still taken. I hope I have repaid him," Belthazor said.

Tears filled Xavier's eyes as he placed his hand on Belthazor's head. "What you've done for me and my family, I have no words, my friend," Xavier said. Before he could say more, Belthazor faded into the air.

"Your mother will be in the Meadows where the grass is forever green," the deity said before she vanished, sending Xavier back to Malsdon.

Xavier woke up and looked around the room for Belthazor, but he was truly gone. Xavier dropped his head briefly out of respect, then rushed towards the door.

Isabella, along with the two lions, was waiting outside when Xavier crashed through the door.

"I must go quickly!" he shouted.

"What happened? Where's Belthazor?" Isabella asked.

"No time to explain," he replied.

He jumped on Saya's back and pointed at Jupiter while looking at Isabella, suggesting for her to jump on and follow. So, Isabella did just that.

Saya and Jupiter raced through the palace, weaving around people and fallen objects. After a few minutes, they made it to the main door. Sabrina was standing there, looking at the moon, and her face lit up when she saw Xavier.

"Xavier, stop for a moment," Sabrina said.

"With respect, I have little time to talk," he replied.

Sabrina could see the anxiety within Xavier; he kept shuffling back and forth on Saya's back, waiting for her to speak.

"Your father has made a full recovery," she said with a joyous tone.

"It actually worked," Xavier replied.

Isabella and Sabrina looked at each other, then at Xavier.

"What happened?" Sabrina asked.

"No time to explain," he replied, then pulled her onto Saya's back.

CHAPTER NINETEEN

THE LIGHT IN THE MEADOWS

The Emerald Meadows glistened against the light of the full moon, and the gentle breeze made the leaves dance as if they were welcoming Xavier back to his home.

"Where are we going?" Sabrina asked.

"To the centre of the Meadows, where the grass never dies, and the light never leaves," Xavier replied.

"Sounds magical," Isabella said, then turned her head to look around at the glistening meadows.

"Do you know where you're going?" Sabrina asked.

"Yes, it's where I found Saya and Jupiter," Xavier replied. "This place is etched into my soul."

They were deep into the forest, the triple canopy blocking the moon's light, making it impossible to see their hands in front of their faces.

"Don't worry, Saya and Jupiter have perfect vision in the dark," Xavier told the others.

The two lions tread carefully through the forest floor; Xavier felt the magic getting stronger the closer they got.

"We're here," Xavier whispered as he pointed at the wide opening ahead.

They all dismounted and approached slowly. Saya and Jupiter led the way, sniffing the air, and caught the scent of someone or something. Their attention was drawn to a large rock covered in emerald-green moss.

The two lions stood fast and started growling. Suddenly a grey panther jumped from behind the rock and growled back, however, it didn't attack. The panther was acting defensively as if it were protecting someone.

Sabrina drew her sword, ready to fight. However, Xavier waved his hand down as a signal for her to lower her weapon. He walked towards the panther, removing his scabbard and tossing it to the floor as a gesture of peace. Xavier extended his hand, displaying that he meant no harm. In response, the panther sat down in front of him.

I know of you, the panther communicated telepathically.

Xavier was shocked, causing him to take a step back. *How are you speaking into my mind? Belthazor was the last divine creature*, Xavier said.

Belthazor was a name the humans gave him, the panther explained. *Belthazor created me with a part of his life force and made a pact that those with the blood of the Panthera line would be forever protected.*

"What do I call you?" Xavier asked aloud.

"Her name is Luna," a voice said.

Sabrina stepped forwards and stood next to Xavier. "That voice…"

Xavier looked at her; she was trembling, her eyes fixated on the rock. A hooded and cloaked figure emerged from behind the rock and stood before them. Isabella watched anxiously with the lions at the back, waiting for the climax of this encounter.

"Who are you?" Sabrina shouted, overwhelmed with emotions.

"Your little sister," Layla said as she removed her hood.

Xavier smiled and approached his mother to give her a hug.

Sabrina gazed at Layla, her eyes full of tears. "How is this possible?" she asked.

"The power within Malsdon is beyond our comprehension," Layla explained as she hugged Xavier.

"I have decades of stories to tell you," Xavier said.

"I can't wait to hear all of them," Layla replied. She gently took Sabrina's hands and held them tight. "It's truly me."

Sabrina started sobbing, and Layla smiled, pulling her into a warm hug.

"I've missed you so much," Sabrina wept.

Xavier took Isabella's hand. "I'm glad you're here with me," he said to her.

"I'm happy you dragged me along for the ride," Isabella replied teasingly.

"So, this is what the future will look like," Layla remarked as she looked at Xavier and Isabella holding hands.

"We should head back to the palace; it's still not safe here," Sabrina said.

"Agreed. I know one more person who will be stunned," Xavier said.

*

Darius stood in the forest outside the palace walls with Tiberius, both engrossed in stargazing and soaking in the tranquil surroundings.

"What a journey, my friend," Darius remarked.

Tiberius glanced at Darius and offered a slight nod in response. Darius continued to gaze at the stars, contemplating how he had become so weak and yet had fully recovered.

The peaceful quiet was abruptly shattered by the sound of approaching riders, much to Darius' annoyance. "What is the matter now?" he shouted.

"It's me, Father!" Xavier's voice rang out. Xavier dismounted from Saya and rushed over to give his father a hug. "I'm sorry I wasn't there."

"I am okay, son. You've done more than enough for this island," Darius reassured him. His attention turned to the person dismounting from Luna's back. "Who is that behind Sabrina?"

"Someone we found in the Meadows," Xavier explained.

Sabrina and Isabella both smiled at Darius before stepping aside, revealing Layla to him.

Darius' face was filled with joy. "How is this possible?" Darius asked.

"Your son is the main reason I'm here in front of you," Layla replied.

Darius laughed and slapped Xavier on his shoulder. He slowly walked over to Layla, studying her face still amazed on how she was standing before him. "I'm never letting you go," Darius said as he held her tight.

CHAPTER TWENTY

THE LINE IN THE SAND

Two months had passed since that day, and the scars were nearly healed for all involved. Under the decree of the new king and queen, significant changes had unfolded across the land. An outpost was erected on Alice Island, serving as an early warning system. All wealth and properties belonging to the Graw family were distributed among the people of the Iron Coast. Those who had supported the rebellion found themselves either imprisoned or facing execution. Meanwhile, the bounty for the fugitive princess Arabella had surged to ten thousand gold coins.

It was a calm and pleasant day, with the skies as blue as the oceans around Malsdon. Xavier walked through the woods with his two lions, enjoying the tranquillity outside the palace walls. In the two months since the incident, his appearance had undergone significant changes. A thick but short beard adorned his face, and his frame had become more muscular.

Nothing like the Meadows, but it'll do, Xavier thought as he continued his walk through the woods.

"My king, your monthly report," said a guard approaching him, handing Xavier the report.

Xavier scanned through it. "Good, the fishing boats have been upgraded," he remarked aloud. Xavier paused on the last two lines of the report. "Is the prisoner ready for transport?"

"Yes, my lord. Lady Sabrina is waiting at the Iron Coast with her," the guard replied.

"Very well," Xavier responded.

The guard then handed over another report, sealed within a black envelope. Xavier opened it and took out a hand-drawn map and a written report.

To High Command,

Barbarian forces number in the tens of thousands. Ravana has conjured foul beasts from deceased animals using dark magic. No formal training observed; weaponry includes a mix of blunt objects, swords, and axes. Coastal defences are non-existent. An invasion fleet is under construction on the far side of the island, estimated completion in three months (see circled area on the map). Arabella has been sighted with Ravana and a corrupted gigas eagle, possibly Hera. Will continue scouting and await further instructions.

General River Silverlight.

Xavier burnt the report after reading it. "Have the other generals received their reports?" he asked.

"Yes, my lord," the guard replied.

"Get this map enlarged and tell the generals to meet at the Leo Manor at midnight," Xavier instructed.

"Right away, my lord," the guard replied, hurrying off.

Xavier mounted Saya's back and rode to the Iron Coast to handle the prisoner hand-off in person.

Xavier arrived at the Iron Coast and made his way to the docks, passing through the redesigned streets and houses. He dropped his head in respect towards the sign that read "Lupus Dock".

"King Xavier!" Sabrina shouted, waving him onto the ship.

"Lady Sabrina," Xavier replied as he boarded the ship, flanked by Saya and Jupiter. "Where is she?"

"In the cage below deck," Sabrina replied. "The meeting point?"

"At sea, ship-to-ship transfer."

"Sorry to interrupt, we're ready to set sail," the ship captain said.

The ship pushed away from the makeshift docks, embarking on the journey to the meeting point. Xavier stayed on deck with Saya and Jupiter, relishing the ocean breeze. Meanwhile, Sabrina descended below deck to check on the prisoner. The barbarian queen, her eyes fixed on Sabrina, couldn't forget what had been done to her.

"Your death will be slow," Queen Mara declared.

"It won't be at your hands," Sabrina laughed.

Queen Mara's face turned bright red as she furiously banged against the iron cage. "My daughter will make you suffer!" she shouted.

Sabrina smiled and returned to the top deck.

"Ship sighted!" the captain shouted.

The two vessels closed in on each other and came alongside, throwing ropes across to secure their positions. A walkway plank was then laid down between the ships.

Two mutated men walked across first. Xavier placed his hand on the pommel of his sword and observed the two brutes carefully. He remembered how challenging it was to kill just one of them, and now there were two standing in front of him. Suddenly, Xavier felt pressure all around him, squeezing his arms and chest. The pressure persisted as Ravana walked across. Her matted black and brown hair reached down to her waist, and her dark eyes contrasted against her beige-coloured skin.

"Bring me my mother!" Ravana shouted.

"She's coming up now," Xavier replied.

Sabrina pulled Mara upstairs by a chain around her neck. This enraged Ravana, and she exerted more pressure on everyone on the ship, causing a few to drop to their knees. Sabrina dropped the chain to hold her head, and Mara ran to her daughter. However, Ravana didn't embrace her; instead, she completely ignored her. Xavier saw the pain on the crew's faces, so he clapped his hands once.

"Enough!" Xavier shouted. The power of Xavier's clap negated Ravana's magic. "Take your mother and go!"

Ravana stared at Xavier, and then clicked her fingers; one of the mutant men picked up Mara. She was surprised at first then began to panic as the brute leant over the side of the ship and threw her into the ocean. Splashes and screams for help were ignored by her own daughter, whose gaze was fixed on Xavier.

"There will be no peace!" Ravana shouted. "You killed my mother and father."

"Are you mad?" Sabrina shouted back.

Xavier waved his hand, signalling Sabrina to stop. "We offered your mother back in good faith."

"That wasn't my mother. You took everything from her. Your bloodline will stain the ground for your actions," Ravana said as she gazed into Xavier's eyes.

Saya and Jupiter went to sit beside Xavier as the two mutant brutes gazed at him before leaving across the plank. The two ships pulled apart, creating some distance as both headed back to their respected lands.

"Sounds like war, but on whose terms?" Sabrina said.

Xavier was about to reply then turned suddenly facing the direction of Ravana's ship when a loud whistling sound tore through the air, and before he could react, he hit the ground hard.

"No, Jupiter!" Sabrina shouted.

Dazed from the fall, Xavier turned slowly and saw a large iron arrow lodged in Jupiter's side. Crawling over to her, he began to heal her as Saya attempted to pull the arrow out. Despite Xavier's efforts, he felt Jupiter's heart rate slowly decrease, and his healing powers couldn't bring her back.

"Jupiter, stay with me, girl," Xavier whispered, pouring more power into the healing process, but it was in vain.

Jupiter looked into Xavier's eyes, then took her last breath. Saya roared into the sky.

"Chase that ship!" Xavier shouted.

"We can't, my lord. We don't have the manpower," the captain said.

Xavier jumped up and headed straight for the captain. Sabrina stepped in front and wrestled Xavier to the ground. The young king roared out in sorrow.

"Let it out, Xavier," Sabrina said as she comforted him.

Xavier's eyes glowed brightly like a roaring fire as he looked over at Saya, who had curled up next to Jupiter's lifeless body. Sorrow, anger, and hatred filled his raging heart, burning a hole within him.

*

Xavier and Saya stood before the burning pyre; the flames cast a deep reflection in Xavier's tearful eyes. The death of Jupiter had left a permanent scar on his heart. Sabrina and Layla watched from the manor.

"I'm worried about him," Sabrina said.

"I will talk to him before he goes to the meeting," Layla replied.

Sabrina squeezed her sister's arm, then made her way inside to join the meeting.

Layla could see Xavier walking back towards her, with Saya following closely behind. Xavier's head was down, walking with purpose. Not even the gentle night breeze from the meadows could calm him.

"Xavier?" Layla called.

Xavier stopped in front of her and looked up, his eyes red and cheeks wet from tears. "Mother…"

She hugged him tight. "Jupiter did what she needed to do, and that is to protect you no matter the cost."

Xavier didn't respond, just took in a deep breath.

"Don't lose who you are," she added.

"They're all going to pay for that cowardly act," Xavier said.

Layla released the hug and looked straight into his eyes. "Careful what path you take, as many won't be able to follow you," Layla said before kissing him on the forehead.

"My path isn't revenge; it's punishment," Xavier said, then walked off into the manor.

Before Xavier entered the war room, a whistle from the shadows caught his attention. The person stepped out and smiled.

"River, you are a sight for sore eyes," Xavier said, his mood lifting slightly.

"I came straight here. Excuse the smell," River said.

"Good, I'm going to need your help."

"I've always got your back."

Xavier nodded and pushed open the war room door. All the lords from each region were present and saluted Xavier as he entered.

"We have a plan. General Artemis will explain," Darius said.

"Lords, the information gathered from reports by Lady Silverlight has led us to the decision to set up defences along the coast and destroy their ships as they approach," Artemis explained.

"Then we will seize their lands and materials," Sol declared.

Xavier looked at everyone in the room, pausing at each person for a few seconds. "We will not sit and wait to be attacked. They're not setting foot on Malsdon again," Xavier declared as he leant on the table.

River banged the table in support.

"I understand, Lord King, but they outnumber us," General Brock pointed out.

"There is only one way to end this," Xavier stated.

"Invasion," River said, finishing Xavier's sentence.

"Are you sure, son?" Darius asked.

"I'm not doing this out of anger; it has to be done," Xavier insisted.

"He has a point. Ravana is unstable and needs to be dealt with," Sabrina added.

Xavier laid out his invasion plan to his generals, every step carefully planned.

"A bold strategy," Sol remarked.

"Bold, more like a revengeful mission for Jupiter," Artemis said.

Darius was about to reprimand the general for his words, but Xavier signalled him not to. "First of all, don't you ever mention her name; secondly, don't ever question my motives."

"Don't worry about that fossil," River added, "He's upset that he has to leave Malsdon."

"This plan will work," Darius said, handing the drawn-out plan to Xavier. "Son, all we have to do is sign, and things will be set in motion."

Xavier placed the document on the table and signed his signature. Darius followed suit, as did the other lords and generals.

"All right, we've got work to do," Sol declared as he left the manor for the Silver Hills.

"I'll see you at the palace, Lord King," General Brock said, following Sol out the door.

Artemis was leaving, but Xavier grabbed his arm. "Do we have a problem?" Xavier asked.

"No problem," Artemis replied.

Xavier looked into his eyes, squeezing his arm tighter. "Now is the only time to address the issue."

"No," Artemis said, then pulled his arm out of Xavier's grip and slammed the door behind him.

"Now that it's just us, what are you up to?" River asked.

Sabrina and Darius looked at Xavier, awaiting his full plan.

"River, I need you to destroy their ships and dry docks just before they're seaworthy because our invasion army won't be ready in three months," Xavier said.

"It'll be done," River replied.

"Father, you will lead the army as planned, but I won't be with you," Xavier said.

"You're going straight for Ravana?" Darius asked.

"Yes, I'm taking two hundred Knights of Leo. Sabrina, I will need you to find me three hundred extra capable bodies and turn them into soldiers to join me."

"I'll find men and women who were greatly affected by the barbarian invasion," Sabrina said.

"We have six months, as was said in the plan," Xavier added.

*

Xavier stood outside, taking in the sounds of the Meadows at night. Everyone had left to start the preparations. His mother waved him goodbye as she retired to the manor, and Darius quickly came over to talk to his son before retiring to bed.

"Your plan to chase Ravana is risky with no heir to carry on after you," Darius said.

"I do have an heir; Isabella is pregnant. I sensed it," Xavier replied. "Mother knows, too. Isabella went to her first."

"Well, we both know without being told," Darius chuckled.

Xavier smiled and extended his hand towards his father. Darius grabbed his hand to complete the handshake.

"Goodnight, son," Darius said and walked off into the manor.

Xavier walked through the meadows with Saya, enjoying them and Saya's warm but silent company.

"So, Xavier, it will be on the Forgotten Lands where the fate of your time will be decided," Belthazor spoke to him through the meadow winds.

"Yes, it will be," Xavier replied.

"Be careful of the deity; she will try to offer you a deal you can't refuse," Belthazor warned.

"Old friend, the deity will want no part of what's to come. All things will end by my judgement."

Part Two

War's Dark Embrace

CHAPTER TWENTY-ONE

THE SPARK THAT IGNITES ALL

In the six months following Xavier's declaration of war, each region in Malsdon prepared its soldiers and knights to join the invasion force. General River Silverlight and her scouts were on the Forgotten Lands, mapping and reporting every detail to ensure a smooth invasion for Xavier. Sol and Victor Silverlight worked night and day in the silver forges, creating weapons and armour suitable for the harsh climate of the Forgotten Lands. General Brock and Artemis trained the current men and recruited more for the army. Darius Leo and Sabrina Panthera trained the three hundred men and women to join Xavier's new personal army, known as Jupiter's Moon. Layla Leo moved into the palace to help her daughter-in-law, Queen Isabella Lucius Leo, with the last three months of her pregnancy.

The clouds hung overhead like thick, black tar, and the relentless rain stung the skin. The weather in the Forgotten Lands was as rough and unforgiving as the history that had shaped it. River and her scouts were well-acquainted with these harsh conditions as they closed in on their ultimate targets.

A scout returned to the group's position with news. "General, there are over a hundred guards and workers in the dry dock," the scout reported.

"Twenty against a hundred, and even more if the alarm is sounded," River declared aloud.

"This is suicide," a few voices murmured in the background.

"No, we can make it work," River said, signalling for them to gather around.

They huddled as River drew out her plan in the dirt.

"Five archers on the cliff just above us will provide overwatch and destroy any support structures for the ships, using the explosive tips," River instructed. "Another five will break into the stables on the far side and steal enough horses for our escape. The rest of us will blend in, sabotage what we can before getting caught, and target the bigger ships and any flammable materials."

After the briefing, everyone went off to their starting positions.

"Captain Lynch, wait a moment," River called.

"General?" Captain Lynch replied.

River handed a copy of the final report in a black envelope to her. "If I'm captured, make sure Xavier gets this letter."

"See you on the other side," Captain Lynch replied, walking off to join her splinter group.

River and her ten scouts seamlessly blended in with the workers, their stolen clothes from the mission's outset proving invaluable. Passing by each ship, they discreetly injected a special acid into the wooden hulls, eroding the fibres within.

The heavy rain played to River and her scouts' advantage, allowing them to move undetected in their cloaked attire without arousing suspicion. The rain also served to conceal their distinctive silver and black hair, a trait none of the barbarians shared.

"General, look over there," a scout whispered, pointing towards a massive stockpile of oil, enough to level the entire dry dock.

"Gather the men and prepare to signal Captain Lynch," River commanded as she made her way towards the barrels.

Approaching the vast stockpile, she began creating a trail of explosive silver powder away from the barrels. Once she had covered at least fifty feet, she signalled the scouts.

The scouts swiftly drew their bows and swords, and a signal flare was shot into the sky, alerting the other two groups. River ignited the fuse just as chaos erupted. Guards and workers charged them with hammers and clubs upon spotting the flare. River raced back to her scouts, forming a defensive circle to hold off the barbarian attackers.

On the cliff, the archers protected the fuse, eliminating any barbarians who approached and targeting the remaining ships that River's group couldn't reach. Explosions echoed through the air, and the heavy rain and smoke obscured the view of oncoming waves of enemies.

"General!" a scout shouted, pulling her shoulder back.

River turned to see Captain Lynch's group returning with horses for their escape.

"Double line formation!" River commanded.

Her group formed a double line, stepping backwards through the thick, wet mud towards the horses. They finally reached the horses, some pairing up due to the shortage. River mounted her horse and used the last rally signal for the archers on the cliff.

Seeing the signal, the archers began making their way to the rally point when something in the sky caught their attention. A loud, deafening screech halted everyone.

It was Arabella on the back of Hera, accompanied by several vultures, some with riders.

"Run!" River shouted.

Everyone on horseback galloped away, but the five archers on the cliff were not fast enough. They were caught by diving vultures, who threw them into the air, and left to fall to their deaths.

River and the remaining scouts raced towards the beach on the south side of the island, with Arabella and the vultures relentlessly pursuing them, systematically picking off scouts one by one.

"We have to do something!" Captain Lynch said to River.

She turned to glance behind and noted that only eight scouts remained. River swiftly reached for an arrow, whispering an enchantment before releasing it into the sky. The air exploded, casting a blinding light that startled the vultures. However, the sudden disturbance caused one vulture to spiral out of control, crashing into River's and Lynch's horses, sending them tumbling to the ground.

River awoke to the sounds of Lynch fending off barbarians and vultures, firing at anything that drew near. Slowly rising to her feet, River joined the fray, targeting the diving vultures.

Suddenly, a lone rider returned to assist them, ploughing through a few barbarians before circling back to pick up Lynch and River. They galloped away, but Hera was right on their heels.

"Get her!" Arabella's voice echoed.

Hera descended, her massive talons snatching River off the horse.

"Stop now!" Lynch ordered the scout, as River dangled above them.

"No, Mona, make sure Xavier gets that report!" River shouted as Hera carried her further away.

CHAPTER TWENTY-TWO

THE HARD MARCH

The season of autumn had spread its grace across Malsdon, with cool air and the sun still shining brightly in the sky. Xavier stood on the balcony, observing Saya and Luna playing in the newly cultivated fields behind the palace. The peaceful moment was shattered by a loud knock on the chamber doors.

"My queen, is the king in here?" the guard asked.

"Xavier!" Isabella's voice rang out.

Xavier took a deep breath and made his way to the door. "What's the matter?" he asked.

"My lord, a scout by the name of Captain Mona Lynch is downstairs in the war room," the guard said.

Xavier exchanged a worried glance with Isabella.

"Don't assume the worst, my dear," Isabella said, attempting to reassure him.

Xavier followed the guard to the war room, and Isabella trailed behind slowly, concerned about how he would handle any potential bad news.

The guard opened the doors, and Captain Lynch stood to attention as Xavier entered the room. "Lord King."

"Captain, you have news for me," Xavier said.

"Sir, here's a copy of River's final map and report," Lynch said, handing it over to Xavier.

Xavier carefully reviewed the report and map, listing points of entry for the army and key locations to capture in the Forgotten Lands.

"Where's General Silverlight?" Xavier asked, his heart pounding in his chest.

Captain Lynch's head dropped, and she remained silent for a few seconds. "She was taken by Hera and Arabella as we were fleeing."

"What?" Isabella shouted from the doorway.

Xavier slammed the table, leaving a burning handprint on the surface. This startled Captain Lynch, causing her to back off.

"Xavier!" Isabella shouted as she walked over to calm him down. Isabella grabbed his hand, and though Xavier tried to pull it away, Isabella didn't let go. "Calm down; you won't save River like this."

Xavier heeded his wife's words and took a moment to calm down. "I'm sorry, Izzy," Xavier said.

Isabella smiled. "You haven't called me that in a while."

Xavier took her hands and said, "I love you; I'll be back before dinner."

Xavier marched into the front courtyard of the palace, with Captain Lynch following behind. "Lawson!" Xavier shouted.

Lawson turned and ran towards Xavier. "My lord?"

"Sabrina and Jupiter's Moon are training in the Vermillion Sands. Bring these muster orders to them. I'll be waiting at first light in the Iron Coast," Xavier instructed.

"It will be done, my lord," Lawson said, rushing off towards the stables to fetch his horse.

"Follow me," Xavier said to Captain Lynch as he led her to the barracks. "General Brock!"

"My lord?" General Brock replied.

"You must send a rider to my father and tell him to muster the army, and you must assemble the royal guards."

"My lord, we still need another week for the rest of the armour to arrive. Why such haste?"

"River was captured, and with sensitive information about our landing zones and routes, we must rescue her."

"The best I can do is keep the soldiers without the armour upgrades on Alice Island with General Artemis," General Brock suggested.

"That's good enough, General. I'm leaving at first light."

"Me and your father with the main army won't be more than a day behind you, my lord," General Brock assured and went off to set the plan in motion.

"Captain Lynch, someone will show you to the guest chambers. Get some rest; we leave tonight," Xavier said.

*

The night sky was clear as crystal, showcasing the moon and stars. Xavier found himself in the royal chamber with Isabella and Saya. Isabella assisted Xavier in putting on his armour. The plates covering his chest, shoulders, and thighs were full black with crimson trim, and the chainmail underneath was gold and white. Isabella handed Xavier his two swords to attach to his belt, and finally, she placed the overcoat over his shoulders—a creation made by Victor months ago.

"Xavier, look at your long sword," Isabella said.

Confused, he pulled the sword from the scabbard and placed it in front of her.

"With the purest of hearts, I will stay the path," Isabella said, as she recited the engraved message on the fuller.

Xavier sighed and gently touched Isabella's stomach. "I will stay the path and make sure I return to see my three ladies," Xavier said with a smile.

"What three ladies?" Isabella asked.

"You and my two daughters," he replied, rubbing her belly.

"We're having twins?" Isabella shouted and hugged Xavier tightly.

"I love you. Make sure to tell my mother the surprise," Xavier said before kissing her goodbye.

"Xavier, wait, Please be safe, my love," Isabella said as she ran over and held his hands, trying to hold back her tears.

Xavier made his way to the courtyard with Saya following right beside him. Captain Lynch was waiting there in her scout attire which was just a dark brown cloak with an olive-green leather top and trousers, along with gold chainmail she borrowed to wear underneath.

"You ready?" Xavier asked as he climbed on to Saya's back.

"Yes, my lord," she replied as she pulled her hood over her silver and black hair.

Xavier and Captain Lynch reached the Iron Coast at first light. Just outside the town, Sabrina stood with the knights of Jupiter's Moon, their armour similar to Xavier's except for the emerald-green chainmail. The knights stood at attention as Xavier rode to the front of the column.

"Aunt Sabrina, this is Captain Lynch from River's scouts," Xavier said.

"Greetings, nephew, and to you as well, Captain. They are ready and await your command," Sabrina replied.

Xavier marched with his knights through the town and to the docks. The townspeople looked on in awe at the well-drilled and equipped company. However, a familiar figure stood at the entrance to the docks with four guards flanking him on each side.

"I'm sorry, Lord King, but you are not allowed to enter the docks with any sizeable force," the guard said, looking at Artemis for approval.

"We are the advanced force on a time-sensitive mission," Sabrina replied.

"No means no. The king put me in charge of the Iron Coast and the docks," Artemis said, dismissing everything Sabrina said.

"Artemis, I am the king. I don't know what happened to you or between us," said Xavier with a stern tone, "But I'm telling you my patience has limits."

"You're the problem. You almost let your father die, and you're on a revenge mission over your dead lion, putting everyone at risk!" Artemis shouted.

The soldiers in Jupiter's Moon looked shocked at the way Xavier was spoken to. Xavier closed his eyes, took a deep breath, and the guards next to Artemis took a step back from him.

"General Artemis, we're going to rescue River, a person who saved your life. If your delay has affected me saving her, I will kill you with my bare hands," Xavier said in a calm voice.

"You see, everyone, he's mad, threatening to kill one of his generals and old mentor!" Artemis shouted.

Xavier seethed with anger but kept it in check. He could easily push past Artemis and the guards, but he didn't want to be seen as a king who abused his power and people.

"Enough of this," Sabrina said, pushing Artemis out of the way.

In retaliation, Artemis drew his sword on her.

"Enough!" Xavier shouted. His voice echoed through the town and docks. "Board the ships now! General Artemis, make sure you're ready when my father arrives with the main army, and don't delay them."

The two men gazed at each other with hate in their eyes.

CHAPTER TWENTY-THREE

ETCHING ON A LOST HEART

The sounds of voices and animals resonated outside. River's eyes slowly opened, revealing her surroundings—animal skins and skulls adorned the walls of the hut. She then realised her hands and legs were bound by rope, securing her against the wall. Two figures entered the hut: one was Arabella, and the other a tall man with markings across his face and chest.

"River Silverlight, it's been almost three days, and no one has come back for you," Arabella said as she picked up a wooden stick from the table.

"If you plan to torture me, good luck," River said defiantly.

Arabella smiled and struck River in the stomach three times. River coughed, then winked at Arabella.

"My little brother hits harder than you," she said, smiling.

"You're going to tell us everything you know," Arabella replied before handing the wooden stick to the tall man who had entered with her. "Make sure she feels everything," Arabella instructed before leaving the hut.

*

The five long ships passed Alice Island in the afternoon. Xavier was below deck in the king's quarters when a familiar voice spoke to him.

"Xavier, where you go is a dangerous place for you," Belthazor said.

"I know what to do, old friend," Xavier replied.

"Your skill with a blade is not in question, but your emotions when you use your magic will be. That place will consume you if your magic is drawn from hate or pain."

"I'm afraid of where this path will take me, Belthazor. In the moment, I can lose myself and come back."

"On Malsdon, yes, but over there, the dark magic will take over."

"With the purest of hearts," Xavier said quietly to himself.

"Be careful, young one," Belthazor added as his voice faded away.

The ships arrived at the south beach in the evening. Everyone was making final weapons checks and sorting out their gear and rations. Xavier and his knights made their way off the discoloured sand beach and onto the mainland. Xavier placed his hand on the dirt, trying to sense where River was being held, but a sharp pain travelled through his body, and a sinister voice followed. "You're not welcome here."

The pain caused Xavier to jump up.

"Are you all right?" Sabrina asked.

"It's nothing. We'll find River a different way," Xavier replied. He walked over to Saya and Captain Lynch. "Captain, do you still have River's scent on you?"

"It's the same cloak I'm wearing from when she got taken," Captain Lynch replied.

Xavier knelt down in front of Saya. "Find River," Xavier said as he pointed at Captain Lynch.

Saya sniffed Lynch's cloak for a few seconds, then turned her nose into the air and suddenly walked off.

"She's got it," Xavier said.

"Follow Saya, stay in a loose formation," Sabrina commanded.

The sky began to darken as Saya led them to a well-guarded

village, a mix of farmers and soldiers. This was where River's scent ended. Xavier ordered Sabrina and Jupiter's Moon to stay out of sight and set up a circle around the village a few hundred metres out so no one could escape or if Xavier needed back-up.

"Captain Lynch, I'll follow your lead," Xavier said, drawing his short sword.

Captain Lynch nodded.

Xavier knew Lynch's infiltration skills were greater than his, reducing the chances of getting caught.

Lynch slowly led Xavier through the many bends and huts inside the village, passing guards and sleeping dog-like creatures. Finally, they reached a hut located in the centre of the village with two guards outside.

"This must be the place," Xavier whispered.

Xavier was about to use his powers to knock out the guards when Captain Lynch stopped him.

"Wait," she whispered.

The tall man who had been torturing River exited the hut.

"Let's go now," Xavier whispered through gritted teeth.

Lynch led Xavier to the back of the tent, where she cut out a piece of the material so they could fit through. Xavier entered the tent, and his heart sank at the condition River was in. Lynch followed behind and ran over to release her.

"Xavier, Mona, you came for me," River said, her voice weak and trembling.

"We're here for you," Captain Lynch said as she helped River down to the ground.

Xavier stood there, speechless, just looking at River's wounds—her eyes almost swollen shut, her body covered in bruises and cuts.

"Xavier?" River whispered.

Xavier walked over and held River. He briefly looked at Lynch, who mouthed the words, "She won't make it back to Malsdon."

"I'm going to heal you the best I can," Xavier said as he placed his hand on her head.

River slowly moved Xavier's hand away. "It's not going to work; they cursed me with their magic," River whispered.

Tears filled Lynch's eyes as she walked off towards the exit. Xavier tried again, but it was in vain.

"River, it won't work," Xavier said.

"It's okay, Xavier. Just make sure you win this," she said as she grew weaker.

Xavier felt her heart beat slower with each passing second.

"I didn't tell them anything," she said.

"I know," he replied as he held her tighter.

"I love you, Xavier, my brother, my king," she said quietly as her eyes started to close.

Xavier hugged her tight. "I love you too, my friend." He stood up; his body became tense, and his dark brown eyes turned a bright sapphire. "Mona, stay with her."

Captain Lynch quickly went to River's body and held her in her lap.

Xavier channelled all his power within his body and drew his long sword, then slowly stepped out of the hut. The two guards were shocked by his presence but didn't react in time as Xavier punched one in the face, and the other he cut down with his sword.

Xavier slowly made his way through the village, killing everyone in sight. The alarm sounded, and the remaining guards approached Xavier, while what was left of the farmers tried to escape.

Xavier was confronted by six guards who attempted to surround him, but he engaged them before they could close in. He threw his short sword with such force that, upon impact, it sent one of the guards crashing into huts and other objects. Two other guards rushed Xavier simultaneously, swinging their axes. Xavier sidestepped gracefully, causing them to miss, and, using their momentum, he cut them in half from the hip.

As the other two guards ran off, one remaining guard challenged Xavier to a one-on-one duel. The guard swung wildly in an attempt to hit Xavier, who skilfully stepped from side to side, evading the attacks. Growing impatient, Xavier grabbed the guard's sword by the blade, cutting his hand in the process. He then began to melt the sword. The guard's face filled with fear, and before he could react, Xavier chopped his head off.

Xavier walked back to the hut and carried River's body to the others, with Captain Lynch following behind, stepping over the bodies left by Xavier's wrath. Sabrina and the soldiers rounded up all the prisoners as they awaited Xavier's arrival.

"Oh no," Sabrina said as she saw Xavier carrying River.

He placed her body down to the side, and Captain Lynch stayed with her. Xavier turned to the ten villagers they had captured.

"Who's the chief?" he shouted as he pulled his sword out, his eyes still glowing sapphire blue.

No one said a word.

Xavier clicked his fingers, and Saya came out from the bushes, biting one villager on the neck, causing them to bleed out.

"Who is the chief?" Xavier asked again.

No one replied, so Xavier clicked his fingers twice, and Saya killed two more villagers.

"These are the last people from your village. Speak now, and they'll be spared," Xavier said.

"What do you mean?" Sabrina asked, but got no reply.

Xavier was about to click his fingers again until the tall man shouted out, "Please, no more death!"

Xavier marched over to him and grabbed his hair with his bloodied hands.

"You will lift this curse that you put upon her!" Xavier shouted in his face.

"I will. Please, don't kill us," the chief replied.

Captain Lynch carried River's body and placed it in front of the chief. "Do it now!" she shouted.

The chief began to lift the curse, chanting in a language foreign to those who lived on Malsdon. Xavier watched closely, gripping his sword tighter each second.

"It's done," the chief said.

Xavier kicked the chief away from River and began to heal her. Placing his hand on her heart, he pooled all his strength to get her heart beating again.

A deep breath was followed by coughing. "Xavier?" she said softly as she slowly opened her eyes.

"Welcome back," he said with a smile.

"Let the prisoners go," Sabrina commanded.

"Not the chief," Xavier said.

The soldiers released the rest of the villagers and held down the chief.

"Get him, Saya!" Xavier shouted as he helped River slowly to her feet.

Saya grabbed the chief by his shoulder and dragged him into the darkness. Muffled screams could be heard, then a still silence.

"Captain Lynch, take River back to Malsdon. Stay at the palace and stay with her," Xavier said.

Captain Lynch nodded as a soldier brought them a stolen horse from the village and helped River onto the horse's back. Captain Lynch saluted, and River mouthed the words "thank you" before they rode off back to the ships.

A few minutes after Captain Lynch and River left the group, a strange thumping noise travelled through the ground.

"Magic or earthquake," a few voices muttered.

Sabrina looked at Xavier to see if he knew. Xavier put his hand to the ground, but this time, he overpowered the dark magic of the land and felt what was coming.

"Not an earthquake. Battle formations," Xavier said.

"She's coming?" Sabrina asked.

Xavier nodded and said, "Burn the village; we'll use the smoke as cover from the vultures."

A few soldiers ran into the village to set it ablaze.

"We have to hold them in this area until my father arrives," Xavier said.

"We won't last long on open ground," Sabrina said.

"Leave that to me. Get them into a double line," Xavier said before walking off.

*

Halfway between Malsdon and Alice Island, a fleet carrying four thousand soldiers led by Darius was on their way to the forgotten land.

"Make sure all the men are ready to move out when we land on the beach," Darius said.

"Yes, my lord," a soldier replied as he went to pass on the message to all the ship captains.

"Darius, what of General Artemis? He's not himself," General Brock said.

"I've put Captain Lawson with him."

"I hope that's enough, Darius. He's in control of the right flank."

"One of our ships is ahead!" the ship captain shouted.

It was River and Captain Lynch who passed them, giving them the urgent signal.

"Captain, signal the fleet, full speed!" Darius shouted.

The signal flag was raised, and all ships increased their speed.

"Final checks!" General Brock shouted, "When we land, join your battle group, and it's double time towards the smoke!"

The beach landing was successful, and all battle groups formed up and marched on towards the smoke. The sound of battle intensified as they got closer, and then the sight of war. Xavier and his company were fighting off a small group of Ravana's army.

"At least three to one down there," General Brock said.

"Not to mention the vultures," Lawson added.

"Cavalry, support their left flank on the double!" Darius commanded.

The three hundred riders set off to support Xavier and his troops.

"All groups to the centre, forward march!" Darius shouted.

"A show of force might scare them away," General Brock said out loud, agreeing with the plan.

The riders reached Xavier's position to find various deep holes in the ground filled with dead barbarians.

"Are you all right, my lord?" the cavalry commander shouted.

"Yes, Commander. Push their left flank; it will send them running!" Xavier replied as he blocked incoming swings.

The main battle horn bellowed thunderously across the plains as the main army marched towards Xavier's position. The barbarians began to flee at the sight of the army and the pressure put on by Xavier's knights.

"Commander, put a loose follow on them!" Xavier shouted.

The commander nodded and took three riders to follow the fleeing barbarians.

The battle settled, and his father greeted him with a firm handshake.

"Good work, son, but torching the village?" Darius said.

"No one was inside, and it was the best way to cover our position and signal you."

"Very well, get some rest; they're setting up camp as we speak."

"Make sure nothing crazy happens," Xavier added as he walked off towards the encampment.

Sabrina approached Darius as Xaiver walked towards the camp. "I need to speak with you," she said.

Darius ordered Tiberius and Saya to patrol the encampment area as he set off with Sabrina to talk.

"We can speak freely here," Darius said. The area they went to was a few hundred metres away from any foot traffic.

"Your son, my nephew, is a great king and warrior, but he's growing unstable," Sabrina said with great worry in her tone.

"How did you rescue River?" he asked.

"He did it with Captain Lynch, but when it seemed River was beyond saving, he killed everyone in the village… by himself."

"The failed assassination attempt that led to Jupiter's death, then almost losing his dearest friend for a second time," Darius said as he put his head into his hands.

"It's a lot for someone so young, plus ruling a kingdom."

"I'll talk to him later," Darius said before walking back to the encampment.

*

Midnight fell upon the Forgotten Lands. Xavier sat on his bed inside the tent, thoughts racing through his head, and conflict grew within him.

"My king, Lord Darius wishes to enter," the guard said, pulling back the tent door.

"Of course," Xavier replied as he slapped his head, trying to focus.

"Are you all right, son?" Darius asked as he entered the tent.

"Yes, Father, I'm okay," he replied.

Darius walked over and sat next to Xavier, looking at the various furs on the floor and walls. "Nice tent."

"Father, I did a villainous act," Xavier said as he looked down at the floor.

"I know, son. Tell me what happened." He put his arm over Xavier's shoulders.

"I lost control. I felt so much pain and injustice."

"You let your body and instincts take over?" Darius asked.

Xavier nodded in response and picked up his long sword.

Darius looked at the engravings. "The path isn't always clear and straight; many obstacles will be there, and it's up to you if you'll let them take you off the path." Darius squeezed Xavier's shoulder and got up to leave the tent.

"I won't let this control me or change me," Xavier said, looking down at his sword.

"I'm here if you need me, King Xavier the Lion," Darius said with a smile, then exited the tent.

Chapter Twenty-Four

Unforgivable

Three days later, Xavier and his generals were having a meeting in the command tent. They gathered around a makeshift table placed in the centre with a large map of the Forgotten Lands.

"Sorry I am late, my lords," the cavalry commander said.

"We were just starting," Xavier replied.

"Son, his name is Commander Williams, a great horseman," Darius informed.

Xavier nodded as a sign of recognition. "You have news for us?" he asked.

"Yes, my lord, if I may?" Commander Williams asked as he approached the map.

"Proceed, Commander," Xavier said, holding his hand out towards the map.

"The main enemy force is staging in the west behind these mountains, but they have to move through this valley to come south towards us. This was the way we took back, and it's the quickest," Commander Williams explained.

"The vultures will tear us apart in that narrow valley if we fight in there," Darius said.

"What about that open land close to the valley?" General Brock asked.

"Yes, we can use that," Commander Williams said.

"Explain, Commander," Xavier said.

"The ground is really soft mud. If we waterlog different areas, we can create a bog," he explained.

"Very good, Commander," General Brock replied, "Their force will move very slowly through that giving us easy openings for flanking."

"We divide the men into three sections," Darius said, "I'll control the centre, General Brock, you have the left flank, and General Artemis with Captain Lawson will control the right flank."

"Commander Williams, I'll be joining you and your men," Xavier said.

"We break camp at midnight," Darius said and ended the meeting.

*

Xavier's army marched hard, reaching the valley in two days, and used what water they could spare to create the bog. Xavier and Darius were overseeing the operation taking place.

"My lords!" a scout shouted.

"Speak quickly, son," Darius said.

"Ravana and her full force are less than a day away," he replied.

"Very good, pass the message on to the generals."

The scout quickly ran to tell the others.

"Father, I'm going to use myself and the cavalry to lure Ravana out. The flanks have to hold," Xavier said.

"You're not worried about the centre?" Darius asked.

"No, Father."

The army was ready and waiting for Ravana's army. Xavier hid the cavalry behind the right flank section and left Jupiter's Moon in the centre under his father's command. Xavier patted the horse he was on, then threw a piece of meat to Saya, who stood next to him. A few soldiers pointed to the sky, alerting everyone to the vultures approaching. A few moments later, the barbarian army was in sight.

The barbarian army stopped just before the bog they created, which was five hundred metres wide and long.

"We just have to get them to charge us," Darius said.

"No sign of terms as well," Sabrina replied with a smile.

"What are you thinking about?"

"I need Tiberius to help me."

Darius nodded, and Tiberius stood next to Sabrina. She then pulled out a pair of hands from her sachet bag and climbed onto Tiberius' back.

"Are those their queen's hands?" Darius asked with a bewildered look on his face.

"No... just some random hands I chopped from a body," she laughed, then rode out towards the barbarians.

General Brock looked across at Darius, who looked back and tapped his head, making General Brock laugh. He then looked towards the right flank; Lawson nodded with his sword drawn, and he saw Xavier was readying the cavalry. However, Artemis was emotionless, just gazing forwards.

Sabrina rode within a hundred metres of the barbarian army and waved the two chopped hands in front of them. There was a dead silence as Ravana stepped to the front line and she looked straight into Sabrina's eyes.

Sabrina smiled and winked. "I believe your mother left these behind."

Ravana grabbed her hair tightly and started pacing, then let out a deafening scream which triggered her army into a charge. Sabrina dropped the hands and Tiberius turned sharply and ran back to the army. As Tiberius ran through the bog, Sabrina made sure he didn't trigger any traps gently guiding him through.

The Malsdon army's battle horn sounded and echoed into the valley. Darius signalled with his hand, and each section got into defensive formations.

"You're crazy!" Darius shouted to Sabrina as she rode past.

The barbarians entered the bog, which slowed their pace, and then screams filtered through the air as they fell into the spike pits.

"Forward march!" Darius shouted.

The enemy clashed with the front lines of the Malsdon army as Xavier rode far right with the cavalry, trying to draw Ravana out. The fighting was brutal, as both sides fought hard, each having their own reasons to see the other side dead.

"My lord, she's not taking the bait!" Commander Williams shouted.

"Look, her left flank is ahead of the rest of her army. We go in there!" Xavier shouted and signalled the cavalry.

"Push hard, men!" General Brock shouted. His flank was getting pushed the hardest, but he knew how to manage his troops. "Skirmishers, now!"

Lightly armoured men jumped through the defensive line and attacked the barbarians to ease the pressure. They created enough space for the line to push forwards to match the centre.

"General Brock is doing well!" Sabrina shouted as she shot arrows into the barbarian army.

"Artemis is stretching his line too thin!" Darius replied. He then signalled to Jupiter's Moon to move to Artemis, but it would take them time as they were engaged.

Xavier and the cavalry smashed into the barbarian left flank, forcing their way to Ravana. Xavier could see Ravana gazing at him.

"Push, men!" Xavier shouted.

They hacked and slashed their way through, getting closer to Ravana. Suddenly, Xavier was pulled off his horse. However, Saya tackled the two barbarians before they could cause any harm. Xavier was within fifty metres of her. He disarmed a barbarian who charged him, knocked them out, and then took their poorly made spear. He channelled his magic and threw the spear at Ravana; however, she pulled a barbarian in front of her at the last moment.

Realising how close to death she was, she let out a scream in anger and then gazed at Xavier once more. One of Ravana's personal guards whispered in her ear, which caused Ravana to look around sharply at the battle. She whispered back, and then she and her personal guards started to flee, leaving her army behind.

Xavier jumped back on his horse, and with his cavalry, they started to pursue Ravana. They were a few hundred metres away from the battle when a rider came up from behind them.

"Xavier, stop!" Lawson shouted.

Xavier turned sharply. "What are you doing here?" he shouted as he saw Ravana go further into the distance.

"Our flank is folding. Artemis spread the line too thin."

"Ravana is right over there; we can end this now!"

"Chase her, and you lose your army and father," Lawson replied frantically.

Xavier let out a loud shout that travelled across the land. Ravana stopped and turned sharply in the distance. Even though they were so far away, their eyes met, and the hatred grew stronger.

"Move out!" Xavier shouted with a voice full of anger.

Xavier and his cavalry made it back to the battle.

"They're still fighting hard even though their leader is gone," Commander Williams said.

Xavier looked at him, then signalled the men to support Artemis' collapsing flank.

"What a mess!" Xavier shouted at Artemis as he rode past.

Xavier dismounted, drew both of his swords, then let the magic fill his body before he started carving a path through the barbarians with no mercy or thought.

"The enemy is wavering; push them back," Darius ordered.

One final push back and a few more dead bodies of their fellow tribesmen were the final nail in the coffin, causing the barbarian army to flee the battlefield.

"Hold fast!" Xavier shouted.

"My lord, I'll send scouts to follow," Commander Williams said.

Xavier nodded and watched the fleeing barbarians. "Gather the dead and wounded!" Xavier shouted as he cleaned his swords.

"Set a patrol and bring the wagons forward!" Darius said to his men as he stepped through the minefield of bodies.

"Xavier, your men did well," Sabrina said, as she patted him on the back.

"When the camp is set, I want a meeting with all the senior officers," Xavier said bluntly, looking towards Artemis.

Sabrina could see Xavier wasn't pleased with the whole outcome, and any light-hearted jokes wouldn't make him feel better. "It will be done," she said and saluted Xavier before walking off.

CHAPTER TWENTY-FIVE

WHO ARE YOU?

A dead silence took over the command tent. The generals felt uncomfortable as Xavier gazed at Artemis; his eyes flickered between the brown colour he was born with and the magically charged blue.

Lawson entered the tent, breaking the silence. "My lords, the battlefield report," he said as he placed it on the table.

"Captain Lawson, explain to me what happened on your flank?" Xavier asked.

Lawson looked at Artemis, who was showing no emotion, then back at Xavier. "He stretched the line too thin."

Xavier's anger grew greater, and everyone could see the young king struggling to hold it within. "Was it you or Artemis who decided you needed help?" Xavier asked.

Lawson remained quiet for Artemis' sake.

"The silence is your answer," Xavier said angrily. He walked over to Artemis. "Explain why a veteran knight and leader would do something like that?"

Artemis said nothing and looked down at his hands.

"Artemis, you must be reasonable!" Darius shouted.

"Artemis, you are not fit to command," Xavier said, "Therefore, you are relieved from your position as general and will be escorted back to Malsdon."

Artemis stood up and went to exit the tent.

"What has happened to you?" Darius asked as he grabbed his arm.

Artemis pulled his arm away. "Nothing is wrong with me," he replied, then walked out of the tent.

Xavier sighed and ordered Commander Williams to escort Artemis back to Malsdon.

*

It was now midnight, and the men of Malsdon were getting much-needed rest.

"What a day," Sabrina said.

"Yes, I'm worried about the vultures. They never attacked, just circling overhead as if someone was watching us," Lawson said as the two sat by the fire eating their dinner.

"You have a point there."

Xavier was walking through the camp with Saya next to him.

"Lord Xavier!" Lawson shouted.

Xavier waved to them and was going to carry on past them until Sabrina waved him over.

"Xavier, if the only person who controlled the vultures and corrupted Hera died, would they turn back into wild gigas animals?" Sabrina asked.

"Yes, that would happen," Xavier replied with concern growing across his face.

"But Isabella killed her; we all saw that," Lawson whispered.

"Evil like that never dies. Like a rat, they find a way to survive," Xavier said. "I must go and catch up with Commander Williams."

"You can't leave. I'll go for you," Lawson said.

"Very well. Saya will go with you," Xavier said.

Lawson quickly went to get his horse from the temporary stables and weapons from his tent.

Xavier watched as Saya and Lawson disappeared into the darkness of the night.

"Sit down and have some food," Sabrina ordered, patting the wooden bench.

Xavier sat beside her and received a plate with dried beef and golden-coloured vegetables. "You brought golden peppers and carrots with you?" Xavier asked.

"Of course, a month's supply," Sabrina replied with a smile.

"You always were my favourite aunt."

"I'm your only aunt," she replied with a chuckle, and they both continued eating.

"I long for Isabella, and I don't want to miss the birth of my children," Xavier said.

"I know. You could always go back; your father and I can lead the army."

"But you'll be no match for her. I alone must face Ravana."

"Well, we better finish this in two months."

"Yes, we could have ended this war already. Searching for her across this whole land will take more than two months. I'm going to retire to my tent," Xavier announced as he got up leaving the unfinished plate where he sat.

"Sleep well, nephew," Sabrina said not trying to push anything as Xavier walked away.

"Xavier?" Darius said, getting his son's attention before he entered his tent.

"Yes, Father?"

"Where did you send Saya and Lawson?"

"To help Commander Williams before it's too late."

"What is going on, son?"

Xavier kicked a bucket outside his tent in frustration. "Ravana got away, which might take months to find her, and Delilah is still alive."

"How is that possible? Xavier?"

Xavier didn't respond to the question. "Ready a meeting at dawn," Xavier replied, then went into his tent.

He sat on the edge of his bed, unable to sleep throughout the night. He channelled all his magic to reach out to Isabella's mind. *Are you awake?*

I am, dear. I miss you so much, Isabella replied.

A few tears fell down Xavier's cheeks. *I was so close to ending it and coming back to you*, Xavier confessed.

It's okay, Xavier. I'll still be here no matter how long it takes.

Xavier smiled. *I love you.*

I love you too, Isabella replied.

Struggling to maintain the connection, Xavier left her mind quicker than he wanted to, but briefly communicating with her filled him with a renewed purpose. He was ready for what would come next.

Chapter Twenty-Six

Tainted Minds and Lonely Hearts

The sun began to rise as Saya and Lawson caught up with the soldiers escorting Artemis. The two had to hide behind nearby bushes along the path as vultures landed around Artemis and Commander Williams, who was on the ground, holding his injured arm alongside his dead men. Hera landed with Arabella in front of Artemis, her eyes pitch black and her face pale as corrupted magic flowed through her.

"You did well, Artemis. Delilah will be pleased," Arabella said, stroking Artemis' arm.

Artemis said nothing; he stood there like a brainwashed drone.

Suddenly, a vulture bigger and darker than the others landed heavily in front of them. The creature looked around, then started shifting, the sound of bones cracking into different shapes until it reached its final form.

"She's still alive," Lawson whispered.

Delilah grabbed Artemis' head and looked into his mind. "Ah, I see the young king is losing control."

"He will fall right into our trap," Arabella laughed.

Delilah's face turned serious, then a huge smile appeared across her face. "We must take them."

"Take who?" Arabella asked.

"The children of the king," Delilah said with a smile.

"Leave that to me. I'll rip them away from their dead mother's hands," Arabella said, anger and jealousy filled her tone.

"You must wait for when she has just given birth; she will be at her weakest," Delilah said, "I still have followers in Malsdon; they will help you."

Delilah went up to Commander Williams and put a mind control spell on him, the same spell as Artemis. The spell only entered the person if they were injured, as the mind was weaker at that stage.

"I must go; I have things to set in motion," Delilah said and then vanished without a trace.

Arabella took armour from a dead soldier to disguise herself and ordered Hera to fly high above them as they started to set off towards the boats.

"Saya, you must go and show Xavier everything you saw," Lawson said, "And I'll follow them back to Malsdon."

Saya nodded and jumped out of the bush, then let out a mighty roar, grabbing the attention of Arabella.

"Quick, kill that lion," she ordered the vultures.

Lawson waited until Saya was out of sight with the vultures in pursuit before he began to trail Arabella back to the ships.

Saya ran hard back to the camp. However, she had a lot of ground and time to cover with eight vultures on her back. Saya tried calling out to Xavier, but the corrupt magic of the Forgotten Lands was too much for her to overcome while she was already stressed.

Meanwhile, back at the camp, Xavier and what was left of the senior leadership were discussing the new plan.

"I like your plan, Lord King, but we all will be isolated until the final point," General Brock said.

"I can communicate with all of you," Xavier replied.

"True, but it will leave you weak and vulnerable to the dark magic," Sabrina added.

"This is the best way to get her, and she can't escape," Xavier said.

"A sound strategy sweeping the land in a line," Darius said, "It will reduce the time we spend here. But be careful when you corner a wounded animal."

"Is something wrong, Father?"

"No, son. If the plan works, we will have her trapped in that mountain fortress in the north, and according to River's reports, there is only one way in and out."

"Very well. I and Jupiter's Moon will go straight through the middle of this land, clearing each village. Father, you and General Brock will go down the east and west coastline doing the same. Sabrina, you'll be less than a day behind us, protecting the rear routes and making sure supplies get to all of us."

They all nodded in response to Xavier's final order.

"We leave at noon; ready the men," Xavier added and exited the tent before them.

He stood at the edge of camp next to Tiberius, both trying to reach out to Saya, when Darius joined them.

"Still nothing?" he asked.

"The corrupt magic is blocking my connection to her, and I won't channel the dark magic into me."

"Okay, son," Darius replied.

"Make sure you—" Before Xavier could finish what he was saying, a loud, familiar roar echoed through the air.

Tiberius wasted no time and charged towards the roar.

"It's Saya," Xavier said out loud and jumped off the barrel he was sitting on, then began sprinting.

Darius watched as Xavier focused his inner power, enabling him to run faster than a normal man.

*

Saya was surrounded by vultures, her paw pads bloodied, and her legs trembling from fatigue. She was only two miles from camp;

however, she didn't have two miles left in her legs. She stood her ground, ready to fight and hoping her roar was heard.

The first vulture charged Saya head-on, but it only led to its demise as Saya swiped her paw down, hitting it with such force that it broke the vulture's neck, killing it instantly. The other vultures screeched, and three attacked her simultaneously. Two vultures dug their talons deep into Saya's back, then tried to lift her into the air. However, Saya rolled into the ground, causing them to lose their hold. Then she pounced on the third vulture, who was going to strike her, and clawed its throat out.

The other vultures who were watching began to charge, but a deep, thundering roar froze them, and the sight of Tiberius soaring through the air drove fear into them. However, they couldn't flee as Tiberius was in the air. He caught four of them and crashed into the ground with them. One vulture began to fly away but was suddenly split in half as Xavier cut through its body, then used one half to break his fall.

Tiberius was making quick work of the vultures he attacked; Xavier went straight to Saya, who was struggling to fight off the two who attacked her. Xavier walked over to Saya; the magical pressure he exerted filled the air and caught the attention of the vultures, causing them to stumble away from Saya. Xavier lunged, using magic to aid him, and with an overhead swing of his sword, he cut one vulture in half. Then he used his magic to force the other vulture's head into the ground, causing the creature to suffocate.

Saya slowly walked over to Xavier, limping from her wounds and panting from exhaustion.

"You did well, Saya," Xavier said as he rubbed her head and side.

Saya stood on her hind legs, putting her front paws on Xavier's shoulders, then pressed her forehead against his forehead. Xavier felt the anxious energy begin to flow through Saya, so he channelled his magic to look into Saya's mind, and all was revealed.

CHAPTER TWENTY-SEVEN

THE DARKEST NIGHT

"How are you feeling?" River asked as she caught up to Isabella.

"Heavy and hungry," she laughed as she stopped to wait for River.

The two continued to walk through the palace gardens under the bright afternoon sun.

"Anything from Xavier?" River asked.

"I felt him, as if he was trying to warn me about something but nothing after that, and it's been two months," Isabella said with a hint of worry in her voice.

"The dark magic is strong there; it must be blocking him."

"Well, he has under a month to finish everything off and come home to his girls."

"If he's late, I'll kick him right in the bum," River said as they both broke into laughter.

"River, thank you for staying with me. Layla is great, but she babies me. I know she means well."

"You want someone to see you as Isabella, not the pregnant queen."

"Yes, and I would want their godmother present for their birth."

River paused, then gave Isabella a hug and a kiss on the cheek, showing her admiration for such news. "Let's get you some food," River said smiling and took Isabella's hand.

The two women walked back towards the palace kitchens, laughing and remembering good times. However, Isabella stopped suddenly and jerked River's arm. They both looked at each other, then at the puddle of water below Isabella.

"It doesn't feel right; it's too early," Isabella panicked.

River placed Isabella's arm over her shoulders, then with her free hand, she placed it on Isabella's side to further support her. "You're okay; let's get you inside and into bed."

*

Isabella went into labour for twelve hours then gave birth to twin girls, Artoria and Liliana. The bells rang, breaking the deep quiet of the night, signalling the birth of the new princesses.

Isabella watched her newborn daughters being taken away by the physician and nanny.

"Don't worry, Isabella," Layla said, "They'll be right back, and you'll hold them again. In the meantime, be sure to finish the tonic the physician left for you. It will help restore your strength and speed up your recovery."

Isabella smiled, then tilted her head to the side, taking long sips of the tonic as she watched them leave the room.

"Well done, Isabella," River said as she held her hand.

"Seems like Artemis and Commander Williams want to congratulate you as well," Captain Lynch said, catching everyone's attention, "They're making their way up the palace steps."

"That's a lot of personal guards for a general inside the palace," Layla said as she looked out the window.

"Well, he has grown incompetent," River replied.

"That wasn't nice, River," Layla chided.

"When I spoke to Artemis, he didn't give a good reason for their return. It doesn't make sense when you think about it," River explained.

"You're worrying Isabella, and in this state, she needs rest," Layla advised.

"I know you mean well, my lady. I wouldn't say anything without reason," River said, and both said nothing else as the sound of footsteps echoed down the hall.

Artemis and Commander Williams entered the room, followed by a disguised Arabella and her men. They surrounded the bed, blocking off the door, with Arabella standing in the doorway. Captain Lynch looked at River and nodded, then they both stood on each side of Isabella. They all bowed but didn't say a word.

Arabella spoke, disguising her voice. "Congratulations, my queen."

"Who are you to speak before the generals?" Layla asked, looking her up and down.

"Forgive me, my lady. I forget my place," Arabella said mockingly.

Isabella sat up slowly, resting her back against the bedhead. "Who are you?"

"No need," Artemis groaned.

"Show yourself now!" River shouted as she drew her sword. This caused everyone in the room to react in kind.

"How dare you draw your swords against the queen?" Layla shouted as she pulled out her dagger.

"I'm the rightful queen of Malsdon!" Arabella shouted as she removed her helmet.

"I should have killed you," Isabella said as she got out of bed.

"Yes, you should have. Now, I'm going to take my nieces on a nice trip," Arabella said. "Kill them but leave the queen for me."

Isabella screamed and charged towards the door; the men, along with Artemis and Williams, charged with the intention of killing them all.

River cut down the two imposters closest to her and Isabella. "There's your opening; go save your daughters!" she shouted as she held off the third attacker.

Isabella nodded and grabbed a sword from the ground as she made her way through the door.

Screams echoed down the hall as Isabella ran with all her might to reach the nursery. Her blood dripped from her white-stained gown, leaving a trail behind. Isabella charged through the wooden door, breaking it down from the hinges. The bodies of the nurses and nanny littered the floor. Grace Sommer was backed into a corner, holding the twins with a defiance radiating from her. Standing a few feet from her was Arabella, her sword and hands covered in blood.

"You're just in time, sister," Arabella said as she kept her gaze and sword towards Grace and the twins.

Out of breath, Isabella charged towards Arabella; however, still weak and tired from the birth, she was moving slower than usual. This gave Arabella time to counter with a kick in the stomach, causing Isabella to fall on the floor. She dropped her sword to hold her stomach as the pain travelled through her body, causing tears to fall.

"I'm going to use my hands to kill you in front of your daughters. Let it burn into their memory," Arabella said as she stood over Isabella.

Arabella went to kick Isabella in the stomach again, but Isabella grabbed her leg, which only irritated Arabella. She pulled her leg away and then kicked Isabella in the face, cutting open her cheek. Isabella tried crawling away to create space but was met with continuous attacks from Arabella.

"Look at your worthless mother, unable to protect you!" Arabella shouted as she looked towards Grace and the twins.

Isabella slowly stood up; blood fell from the gash on her cheek. "I should have killed you, but like a fool, I showed you mercy," Isabella said as she wiped the blood from her face.

"You had your chance."

The two sisters began trading punches, but after a few seconds, Arabella started overpowering Isabella and gained the upper hand. Sensing this would be her last chance, Isabella poked Arabella in the eye, throwing her off balance. She followed it up with a punch to the throat, causing Arabella to bend forwards, gasping for air. Isabella, with what little energy she had left, didn't stop; she tackled her sister to the ground, wrapping both hands around her neck.

"You deserve a slow death, but I'm not giving you the chance to come back," Isabella said as she looked into Arabella's eyes, choking her.

Arabella was struggling to break free, trying everything she could to loosen her sister's grip. However, Isabella only squeezed tighter. Isabella stared straight into Arabella's soulless eyes, watching the life fade away as blood dripped from her face, staining Arabella's pale cheeks.

"I hope you find forgiveness in the afterlife," Isabella said to her sister as her life faded. Isabella released her hands from her sister's neck, revealing the deep red hand marks from all the pressure she applied.

Suddenly, Lawson and River came rushing in.

"Isabella, are you okay?" River shouted.

"My babies, are they okay?" Isabella said as she lay flat on the ground.

"They're okay, my queen," Grace said as she comforted the crying babies.

"Everyone else is okay, a few scars, nothing that won't heal," River said.

"Lawson, where did you come from?" Grace asked.

"He followed them back here," River replied as she walked over to help Isabella off the floor.

"I should have acted sooner, but Arabella and her men were well hidden, and I couldn't just attack two senior officers without being hanged," Lawson explained.

Isabella smiled at them all, then sat on the rocking chair on the far side of the room. Sounds of soldiers searching the palace grounds filtered into the room as Grace walked over with the twins and placed both of them into Isabella's arms.

"What happened to Artemis and Commander Williams?" Isabella asked as she held her daughters tight against her chest.

"Sadly, they gave us no choice," Lawson replied, "After all, they're not themselves. Honourable men such as themselves didn't deserve such an end."

"Too few ever get what they deserve," Isabella said softly as she looked down at her daughters.

*

The crackling sound of wood burning filled the background, and thick clouds of smoke filled the air.

Did I do the right thing? Xavier thought as he watched the final village burning to the ground.

"Son, they gave us no choice," Darius said.

"I didn't say anything."

"I can see it in your eyes, son."

"He's right, young king," General Brock said, "Also, the scouts reported that the fortress is less than a day away."

"This was the buffer before the fortress. Most of the people here were soldiers and willing to die for their queen," Darius said as he tapped Xavier on the shoulder before walking off.

"Very well, make camp and move at daybreak," Xavier ordered.

The fire from the burning village lit up the night sky over the camp. The men were quiet as they longed for home comforts and the familiar landscapes of Malsdon. A few men were singing songs around the campfires scattered throughout the encampment. Xavier watched from outside his tent as he drank his cider.

Sabrina walked towards Xavier, smiling. "Well, this is it, and just in time to get back to see the birth of your daughters."

Xavier nodded and took a sip of his drink.

"What's the matter?" Sabrina asked as she sat next to him.

"For a brief moment, I felt great joy from Isabella, and then great pain. It's getting almost impossible to reach out to her,"

Xavier said as he looked into his cup.

She put her arm around him. "I'm sure she's fine, and your daughters as well. They have all the help and protection they need."

"I don't see the fuss of cider and ales; they're disgusting," Xavier said with a smile.

"Something different other than water, I guess," Sabrina replied as she took the cup from Xavier and had a sip. "Before I forget, all the supplies we could fit onto the wagons from the ships, we will keep here."

"Like a supply base. Hopefully, it's not a long siege," Xavier said.

CHAPTER TWENTY-EIGHT

THE WALK AMONG THE DARKNESS

The sun rose slowly as the army of Malsdon marched towards their final objective. All with razor-sharp focus, knowing that failure in the first few hours would mean they would have to stay longer in this forsaken place. Out of the thousands of men, no one said a word; only the sound of marching and armour coming together.

"Stop, Xavier," a faint voice said.

Xavier turned his head sharply, trying to see who spoke.

The voice appeared again.

"Father, take control and secure the fortress. I must go," Xavier said.

"To the other place again?" Darius asked.

"Yes, Saya will keep my body safe."

"I'll keep some of Jupiter's Moon with you as well."

Xavier nodded, his eyes closed, and he drifted to the Exalted Plains.

Xavier's eyes glowed blue, ready to unleash his magic as he slowly walked around. "What happened here?"

The Exalted Plains were dark and decaying, as if someone had drained everything from within. Xavier froze and looked hard into the distance, trying to make out the object on the floor. The closer he got, the clearer it became.

"Oh no," he said to himself and ran over.

Belthazor was lying there lifeless on top of the divine deity. He rolled Belthazor to the side, and a gasp of air broke the dead silence.

"Xavier, is that you?" the deity asked.

"What happened here?"

"She came with the darkness. The Exalted Plains became vulnerable when you left Malsdon."

Xavier helped her up to her feet and then looked at Belthazor.

"I'll take care of him," the deity said, "You must go back and withdraw your army; it's a trap. She's planned this from the moment you killed her. Ravana is her puppet, a mind slave. Everything from Jupiter's death was planned to get you to the far side of the Forgotten Lands."

Xavier felt defeated, knowing Delilah played him from the very start. "Where is she?"

"I'm not sure, but you must get back to Malsdon before she drains the life force from the land."

Xavier took one last look at Belthazor, then at the deity who gave him a nod as he left the Exalted Plains.

Xavier's eyes slowly opened, making out his father's outline.

"Xavier, you're awake," Darius said.

"What's the situation?" Xavier asked, still groggy.

"Little to no resistance. Most of her army wasn't here, and we have her trapped in a room within the fortress."

"Father, we've walked into a trap," Xavier whispered.

"We'll keep the main army outside the fortress, and you take Jupiter's Moon inside and take full control."

"Signal Sabrina to bring the wagons to us. Not knowing what trap she has for us, it's best to bring everything here and keep everyone close."

Xavier signalled Jupiter's Moon to secure the castle, and the main army set up defensive positions around the fortress, as Darius sent a rider to inform Sabrina of the situation.

Xavier approached the room where Ravana was hiding,

flanked by a handful of knights. They stacked up against the door, and one knight kicked it down, allowing Xavier and the others to flow into the room. A dense, suffocating darkness filled the space, making it impossible to see his hand in front of his face. Xavier clapped his hands, causing the room to vibrate, and most of the darkness dissipated.

To their surprise, they found Ravana tucked into a corner, shaking and bleeding.

"Keep her alive," Xavier ordered, looking down at her.

A knight applied pressure to her wound. "Looks self-inflicted," he observed as he packed the wound.

"Ravana, can you hear me?" Xavier asked, still holding his sword towards her.

Ravana's eyes rolled back and forth. "The king with the lions?" she replied.

"One lion. What happened?" Xavier asked bluntly.

She coughed repeatedly, bringing up blood.

Xavier glanced at the knight treating her, who shook his head as a sign that she hadn't got long left.

"Ravana, you're dying from a stab wound. Tell me what happened," Xavier demanded, the gravity of his tone catching Ravana's attention.

"Do you know what it feels like to be a passenger in your own body, your own mind?" she asked.

"What are you talking about? You had no control over your actions?"

"Yes, she said she would grant me powers, enough to defeat you, but I would have to agree through a blood pact, and that's how she infected me through an open wound."

Xavier sighed and knelt down next to her, looking straight into her eyes. "Where is the rest of your army?"

Ravana started crying, followed by deep coughing. "She used my body to kill my mother and ordered my army to kill themselves."

Xavier stood up suddenly.

"My lord?" a knight asked.

Xavier then grabbed Ravana and violently lifted her up, causing her to cry out in pain. "What did she say before your men sacrificed themselves?"

"Your souls will rest, but your bodies will be put to greater use. You will pillage the night, and the old will rule the day. When the ground is beaten by darkness, the fallen will rise," she said while sobbing.

Xavier dropped her to the ground. "This isn't happening..."

Ravana's body started shaking uncontrollably, startling the knights. "Xavier Leo, we will meet again," Delilah said through Ravana, "And I will bring to bear nothing you have ever seen before. But first, I will destroy everything you hold dear to your heart."

"Kill me, please," Ravana whimpered as she crawled towards Xavier's feet.

"Lord King, what is happening?" a knight asked frantically.

"Burn all the dead bodies and reinforce all windows and doors," Xavier commanded.

Ravana, still bleeding out and pulling at Xavier's legs, prompted Xavier to place the point of his sword on her chest. He pressed it through, easing her pain. "Find peace in the company of your family," he said as he pulled his sword out.

*

The thundering hoofs and the squeaking of wagon wheels echoed as Sabrina's convoy stormed down the paths towards the fortress.

"This darkness came out of nowhere; I can't see a thing," the driver complained.

"We can't use the lamps; it will make us easy targets. Trust the horses," Sabrina said sharply.

Suddenly, the horses grew uneasy, and the drivers struggled to gain control, causing a few to crash into the bushes on the side of the narrow road.

"We have no choice now, my lady," the driver said.

"Halt the convoy, dismount, help settle the horses, and bring the wagons back on the path!" Sabrina ordered as she lit a lamp.

"I want full security around the convoy!" a knight shouted.

Sabrina wandered through the convoy and up to a knight who was flashing his lamp into the bushes. "Anything out there?" Sabrina asked.

"Nothing, my lady," the knight replied.

Rain started to pour down as they struggled to calm the horses.

"They've gone mad, my lady," a knight said as they tried pulling the horses away from the bushes.

"The rain feels weird," a few men mumbled.

Sabrina made her way to the physicians' wagon.

"My lady, our horse ran away, and our lamp won't work," a physician said as he wiped the rain from his face.

Sabrina shone the lamp towards his face. "Black rain," she whispered.

A scream came from the front of the convoy followed by Darius' rally horn in the distance. Sabrina ran towards the front of the convoy, followed by a few men.

"The dead rise," a panicked driver said as she pointed her lamp towards a creature eating a loose horse.

Parts of the ground began to cave in, and what rose from below were long-forgotten skeletons, decaying bodies of humans, and animals of the fallen.

"Protect the wagons at all costs!" Sabrina shouted as she drew her sword.

The sound of screams and bones breaking brought the darkness alive.

*

"They won't stop coming, my lord," a knight said to Darius.

"We have to hold the entrance!" Darius shouted.

The army formed a half-circle around the ramp leading into the fortress, waiting for the convoy to arrive.

"Father, the fortress is secured. They can't get in through anything!" Xavier shouted as he ran down the ramp, followed by half of Jupiter's Moon.

"No sign of the convoy, my king!" General Brock shouted.

Darius sounded his horn three times in rapid succession. "They must be trapped," Darius said.

"We won't survive two weeks without those supplies," General Brock added.

"I'm going to them," Xavier said.

"You won't be going alone," Darius declared.

Xavier smiled, then called Saya and Tiberius over.

"General Brock, you must hold the line," Darius ordered with great importance.

"Make it quick, lads. We won't last long out here," he replied.

*

"Lady Sabrina, we have to go now!" a knight said.

"We have to wait for the physicians to collect their medicines!" she replied.

Fighting was almost futile; as one undead dropped, two more took its place, and each soldier killed joined their ranks as soon as they fell. The four physicians ran through the convoy, their bottles clinking inside their bags as they weaved in and out of the broken wagons, dodging the grabbing hands of the dead.

"My lady, we gathered everything we could carry," a physician said.

"Good, jump on the first wagon," Sabrina said.

"Watch out, my lady!" the physician screamed.

Sabrina jumped back, dodging the grabbing hands of the

rotten human, then cross-chopped it in half. "We have to move now!" she shouted to the men on the perimeter.

"We can't push them back!" a knight shouted.

"We're trapped," someone cried out.

More of the waking dead surrounded the convoy, tightening the noose around the living. Sabrina and the remaining men held the last bit of ground, protecting the last wagons and horses.

"Fight to the last man, fight for your lives!" Sabrina shouted as the dead broke through the perimeter.

A deep roar caught their attention, followed by a shockwave that stormed through the convoy, knocking down everyone in its path.

"Sorry about the entrance," Darius said as he pulled Sabrina to her feet.

"Just in the nick of time," Sabrina said.

"Xavier, keep them off us!" Darius shouted.

Xavier nodded and formed a wind barrier around the convoy, knocking down any of the dead trying to get through. "I can't hold it for long!"

"What's the situation?" Darius asked, trying to make his voice heard over the wind barrier.

"We have four wagons remaining: one for food, two for water, and the last for weapons!" Sabrina replied.

"What kind of food is inside that wagon?" Darius asked.

"Normal food rations, but that broken wagon has seeds, grain, and beans," she replied.

"Xavier, how long can you give us?" Darius asked.

"I can try to hold the barrier for five minutes!" Xavier replied.

"Every free hand, grab a sack of grain from that wagon and place it on the lions and in the weapons wagon!" Darius shouted. He began clearing most of the weapons from the wagon to make space for the sacks. "Quickly now!"

Sabrina attached makeshift saddles to Saya and Tiberius, so the leftover sacks could be attached to them.

Darius nodded at Xavier, who nodded back and then unleashed the wind barrier, knocking down all the dead trying to get through.

"There's your opening!" Xavier shouted.

Each driver whipped their reins, and the horses took off in a hurry, pulling the beaten wagons behind them. Xavier quickly jumped on the last wagon to keep their backs clear. Saya and Tiberius were ordered to run ahead, ensuring that some of the grain and seeds made it to the fortress.

Darius looked back at the convoy as they stormed down the beaten path towards the fortress. A whistle, followed by the deep boom of Xavier's shockwaves, reminded everyone they were not safe yet. Darius sounded his horn as they exited the bushy path and entered the open plains with a clear view of the fortress. The convoy went into a line formation as they crossed the dirt plains.

"This rain won't let up, and more dead keep rising!" the driver shouted to Darius.

Before Darius could reply, a loud bang and the sound of wood breaking apart caught his attention. He turned his head to the right and saw Xavier and his driver flying through the air along with barrels of water, crashing hard into the ground. To their misfortune, a nine-foot giant appeared from the ground, with most of its body exposed as a skeleton. Darius signalled to the other wagons to keep going as he jumped off his moving wagon and ran to Xavier.

Xavier crawled over to check if the driver was still alive. "Damn it."

"Son, are you all right?" Darius shouted as he came closer.

"We've got that thing to deal with!" Xavier replied as he slowly got up.

"Is he dead?" Darius asked, looking at the driver.

"Broke his neck on the landing," Xavier replied as he picked up his long sword and drew his short sword.

Darius gripped his claymore tighter as the giant grew closer. The black rain pelted their chainmail hoods and plate armour. The giant stopped within five feet of them.

"Father, shield and sword?" Xavier asked.

"Might be the only way, son."

Darius charged the giant, drawing its attention towards him and blocking each swing from its rusty sword. As Darius blocked each attack, Xavier attacked the giant from the flanks or behind using their sword and shield technique.

"Father, the rain is bringing up more creatures!" Xavier shouted as dog-like skeletons rose from the ground.

"Keep them off me; I'll deal with the giant!"

Xavier did his best to crush the skeletons before they could interfere. However, as one fell, two more took its place. Darius continued pushing the giant back, but each blow that would kill a mortal man had no effect on the giant creature.

"Oh no," Darius said as the rain clouds covered the half-moon. Darius stood still and listened for the movement of the giant, but it was hard to cancel out the heavy rain beating his armour and the ground open.

Moonlight peeked through the clouds, and Darius froze as from both sides of him skeleton dogs were ready to jump for his throat, and the giant was mid-way through an overhead swing. Darius closed his eyes as a force knocked him to the ground, losing all feeling.

CHAPTER TWENTY-NINE

THE PAST AND THE FUTURE

Isabella sat alone in her bedchamber, near the window, cradling her twins in her arms. Moonlight beamed into the room, giving it a celestial glow.

"I hope you're okay, Xavier," she whispered.

A knock echoed on the heavy oak door of her chamber.

"You may enter," she called.

River and Captain Lynch entered the room.

"My lady, we have to move you and your family to a secure location," Captain Lynch said.

Isabella smiled, her gaze shifting from Artoria and Liliana to River with confusion and worry. "My family?"

"Isabella, I'm not going to lie to you," River said, "There's a strange storm crossing the sea. It has already hit the Iron Coast and will be here before we know it."

"We're moving my newborn babies from a fortified palace because of a storm?" Isabella remarked with a hint of sarcasm. She locked eyes with River and sensed something was being kept from her.

Banging on the door drew their attention.

"Captain, the wagon is ready, also the chainmail," Lawson informed.

Captain Lynch walked over and collected the chainmail.

Isabella observed, and her heart sank. "For my babies?" she asked.

"The danger is real. Reports say the barbarians used the storm as cover and are planning another invasion," River disclosed.

Captain Lynch approached Isabella with the chainmail. "Let's get them ready, my queen."

The royal wagon, ready to move out, was accompanied by ten mounted escorts, with Lawson among them. The wagon itself was crafted from magically infused oak sourced deep within the Emerald Meadows. It featured thick chainmail-lined curtains all around, painted black with crimson trim to make it less noticeable when travelling at night. Inside, Isabella, Layla, and the twins sat on cushioned benches, preparing for the journey ahead. Isabella looked through the window at Grace who waved her final goodbye from the steps as she volunteered to stay behind and be Isabella's decoy.

"Move out!" River shouted.

The mounted escort and Lawson led the way out of the palace grounds with Luna following from behind.

River opened the driver's hatch, which led to the sheltered part of the wagon, and stuck her head through. "We're heading to the Silver Hills. It will be safer there."

Isabella smiled back as she cradled Liliana.

"Very well," Layla said, gently rocking Artoria to sleep.

River smiled, then shut the hatch.

They made it into the Meadows when the black rain caught up with them.

"Driver, stay on the paved path," River said, "This rain is strange; don't want to get caught in the mud."

Luna, on the edge, kept looking to the side and behind her, followed by the horses becoming stressed.

"Something is spooking the animals," Captain Lynch mentioned to a royal guard.

"It's nothing, just the rain," he replied in a way to cut off any further discussion.

The animals grew more restless, eventually slowing the wagon down to a crawl.

"River, what's going on?" a voice from inside the wagon said.

Luna started growling and backed up in front of the wagon door.

Captain Lynch looked back towards River with a confused expression.

River swiftly pulled a pouch from her pocket and threw the dust into the air, which illuminated the area around them. "We have contact!"

"Protect the wagon!" Captain Lynch commanded.

The escorts attempted to force their horses around the wagon. However, most were thrown off by their startled horses and succumbed to the undead.

"Go, you stupid animal!" the driver shouted as he violently whipped the reins.

Undead creatures started climbing onto the wagon, attempting to break in. River and Captain Lynch fought fiercely to protect the driver and the wagon. Unfortunately, the driver was pulled from his seat and killed by a skeleton.

"The wagon!" River shouted to Captain Lynch.

Captain Lynch leapt onto the roof of the passenger section of the wagon and began hacking and kicking the skeletons off the top. Luna and Lawson protected the horses from the undead, swiping down skeletons and decaying bodies. River scanned the surroundings as undead swarmed the wagon, ultimately killing the last of the royal escorts and pulling Lawson away into the night.

"Lawson, hang on!" Lynch shouted.

"No, leave me and get out of here. The little ones must live!" he replied.

"Hold on tight!" River shouted as she reached into her pocket.

River pulled out a different pouch of powder and threw it on her left side, where the main group of undead gathered. She then clapped her hands, causing a loud explosion that took down most of the skeletons and decaying bodies. However, the explosion had a more critical effect—it shocked the horses into action, and they sped off uncontrollably down the path with great speed. Captain Lynch held on for dear life at the top of the wagon as they ventured deeper into the unknown.

The night grew colder as the black rain drenched all things around them.

Captain Lynch sat next to River, who was driving the wagon. "More keep spawning from the ground!" Captain Lynch shouted as she looked from side to side.

"We'll be okay if we stay on the paved path!" River replied.

"What are they?" Isabella asked as she poked her head through the driver's window.

"The undead, and I'm guessing this rain is bringing them back like this!" River replied.

The heavy rain and the sound of galloping horses made it difficult to hear each other speak.

"The Fallen," Isabella muttered and closed the driver's window.

The four horses ran hard for many hours until early dawn, exhaustion starting to take hold of them. However, being royal transport horses, they were trained to run to the edge of collapse, which was approaching soon.

The morning fog lay thick in the Emerald Meadows, making it hard to see the path ahead. The black rain continued to fall, bringing up more of the Fallen.

"The horses won't last long!" Captain Lynch said as she steered the reins.

"The rain is the problem," River remarked.

"What did you say, River?"

River shook her stained silver hair. "This damn rain!" she replied.

River turned and opened the window to speak to Isabella and Layla. All were sleeping except for Isabella; the babies were curled up with Luna to keep them warm, and Layla was sleeping sitting up on the bench.

"My queen, are you okay?" River asked.

"I'm worried about the future," Isabella said in a docile tone.

"One step at a time, my queen," River replied with a smile.

Isabella looked down towards her daughters and smiled. "The future is in our hands, my friend."

River nodded and smiled again, then shifted the topic to the difficult situation they faced. "My queen, the horses won't make it to the Silver Hills fortress. We have two options: risk stopping at Leo Manor and hoping there are horses in the stables or continue until the horses collapse, which will most likely be at the edge of the border."

"The Meadows are pure forest with little villages scattered across; the Fallen will be many there," Isabella said.

"My thoughts as well, my queen," River replied. "I'll send up flares when we reach near the border and pray my people come to our aid."

"Your lands are of silver and stone; the Fallen will not rise there, but they will follow us in," Isabella said.

River nodded, acknowledging Isabella's statement.

Three bright red flares shot into the morning sky.

"Hopefully, the morning watch will see the signals," Captain Lynch said after she shot the flares.

They stopped on the border side of the Silver Hills and River unhooked the horses from the wagon; white foam had formed around their mouths, and they were hot to the touch. She slapped each one on the back, sending them running towards the Silver Fortress.

"If they don't see the flares, they'll see the horses at the gate," River said.

Layla and Isabella were strapping each of the twins to their chest, making sure the chainmail covered their tiny bodies. Isabella took in a deep breath and nodded to River.

"Let's go. Isabella and Layla, stay in the middle of us," River said as she led the group out, with Luna following behind.

Even on the dullest of days, the Silver Hills always shone brightly. The group moved through the narrow passages and cliff edges of the silver mountains. The closer they got, the more at ease they felt, especially since the black rain hadn't reached the Silver Hills.

"There's no rain or Fallen?" Layla asked.

"The pure silver in the mountains must have kept them away," Captain Lynch replied.

"Yeah, something like that," River added.

They continued walking through; all were tired from lack of sleep. Passing by two of the horses that had been let loose, lying dead against the rocks, River went over to check the bodies, followed by Captain Lynch.

"What happened?" Captain Lynch asked as she placed her hand on River's shoulder.

"Talon marks on their necks and back," River whispered.

Captain Lynch walked back towards the others to deliver the news when a high-pitched screech pierced their eardrums, causing them to cover their ears in pain.

River looked into the sky and saw Hera with three vultures diving down to attack Isabella and Layla. "Run. They're after you and the babies!" she shouted.

Isabella didn't hesitate and ran for her life, pulling Layla along with her. Luna stayed behind and attacked Hera; the two gigas beasts fought viciously.

Claws and fangs punctured flesh, leaving each other bloodied. The three vultures targeted River and Captain Lynch, whose swords had little effect against their airborne opponents. Each attempted a swing whenever the vultures dived down for an attack, but to no avail, resulting in wounds of their own.

"This is taking too long!" River shouted, growing more frustrated.

Captain Lynch picked up a rock from the ground and waited for one of the vultures to dive again.

"Now!" River shouted.

Lynch threw the rock at the vulture, striking it in the head and causing it to flop onto the ground. River quickly dashed over and removed its head with a swift swing of her sword.

"We have to catch up with Isabella!" River shouted to Captain Lynch.

"What about Luna?" Captain Lynch asked.

River looked over at Luna, still in battle with Hera but losing ground.

"We have to leave her," River replied, pointing in the direction the others had gone.

Captain Lynch led the way as River covered their rear, keeping a watchful eye on the last two circling vultures, waiting for another chance to attack. Roars and cries echoed throughout the valley as Hera and Luna sought to inflict killing blows on each other.

Luna leapt onto the front of Hera, biting into her neck in an attempt to land a fatal blow. However, Hera endured the pain, and the bite missed the main vein in the neck. Luna's attack from the front left her belly exposed to Hera's talons. Taking advantage of Luna's inexperience, Hera drove both talons deep into Luna's stomach, causing her to cry out in pain. Hera then took off into the air, with Luna hanging from her talons, attempting to bite herself free.

Ignoring the pain, Hera continued to climb until she reached a height she was satisfied with, then dropped Luna, sending her plummeting to her death. Hera let out a mighty cry of victory and redirected her attention to the fleeing Isabella and Layla.

Isabella and Layla stopped dead in their tracks as they saw a bloodied Hera blocking their path. They held the twins tightly against their bodies as Hera slowly walked towards them. Isabella extended her hand, attempting to reconnect with Hera, as they had been bonded before. However, Hera's mind had been twisted, and all the good memories had been washed away. The eagle let out a high-pitched screech as Isabella tried to connect with her again.

Startled by the screech, Isabella and Layla took a few steps back. However, Hera grew more aggressive, closing the space between them as she prepared to attack. Isabella picked up a rock and threw it, striking Hera's eye. Enraged, the beast fixated on Isabella.

"Run now!" Isabella shouted as Hera chased her.

Layla ran for her life, carrying Liliana, towards the Silver Fortress.

Isabella ran only a few metres before collapsing on her back. Fear and exhaustion took over her body, running on nothing but survival. Hera stood over her, pinning down Isabella's legs with her talons, then attempted to peck at Isabella's neck. Isabella screamed for help, dodging the fatal pecks aimed at her neck.

Suddenly, a violent burst of energy sent Hera crashing into the wall. Relief and shock filled Isabella as she looked around for her rescuer, but no one was there. Then she gingerly looked down at Artoria, lifting her chainmail cover, and saw a familiar blue glow in her eyes.

"You saved us, little one," she whispered.

Isabella stood up and ran for the passage. However, Hera quickly took flight and began her dive towards Isabella.

The ground shook, and the words of a familiar voice shouted, "Isabella, drop!"

Isabella fell limp to the ground as a silver arrow shot over her like a bolt of lightning, striking Hera in the chest and causing her to cry out in pain before falling to the ground.

Isabella turned her head to look upon her former gigas eagle as a second arrow struck her in the heart, ending the eagle's life instantly. "Hera," she whispered.

"My queen, are you okay?" Sol said from horseback.

"Are Layla and Liliana safe?" Isabella asked as she got back to her feet.

"She's on her way back with two of my personal guards," Sol replied.

Relief and joy filled Isabella's heart. She felt like she could relax as more Silver knights came towards them to secure the surrounding area.

"Father!" River shouted as she and Captain Lynch appeared around the corner.

Sol smiled at her, then signalled his men back to the fortress, and fresh horses were brought forwards for them to ride back. "Help the queen on her horse," he said.

"Father, we have to do something," River said as she mounted her horse.

"This isn't the time or place; let's go," he said dismissively, then began to ride off.

"When the time is right," River mumbled.

Isabella smiled at River and Captain Lynch. "Thank you, my dear friends, my sisters," she said, then trotted off behind Sol.

River and Captain Lynch followed closely behind, knowing life was about to change forever.

Part Three
The Journey

Chapter Thirty

One Way

The longer we stay here, the more I use my powers, the more I feel myself turning into the very thing I have to destroy. I feel so lost. I can't recall the sight of the emerald-green grass of the Meadows nor the sound of the forest as it awakes with the sunrise. Father and my aunt Sabrina have been running the fortress which has been a great help as anger still fills my mind when I'm troubled.

Today marks fifteen long years along with the fact it rained for ten of those years bringing up all the undead on this forsaken island. The men call them the Fallen, a fitting name. The skeletons are more active during the day, and at night the decaying bodies or ones who have just fallen recently reveal themselves. The decaying ones are much stronger and harder to kill as they still have muscle and fat which is hard to cut through with our dull weapons. We had to ration our food and water for a very long time. This was only possible as we saved the grain and planted our own food, but the main worry was keeping Saya and Tiberius fed, strong, and healthy. Father and I let them eat some of the bodies we were meant to burn without the others knowing.

Many have left the fortress and tried to make it to the ships, but they never made it. We saw their dead bodies returning to haunt us. As the rains stopped, no more Fallen have risen. However, we've noticed that if you are exposed to the black rain you join the Fallen when you die. Our numbers have fallen from the thousands to only two hundred with horses for only twenty. We're at breaking point; the last stores of food and water are about to empty, so this might be my last entry as we've decided to make a break for the ships in full force at daybreak.

Xavier closed his journal, tied it with a fine rope, and placed it in his saddlebag. Saya lay under the window, observing his every move as he paced around the room.

"It's okay, girl," he said.

She let out a loud yawn and returned to sleep.

Two knocks on the door were followed by a deep voice saying, "It's time."

Xavier opened the door, and there stood his father—an imposing figure, now adorned with a long grey beard and a scar on his bald head, making him even more intimidating in Xavier's eyes.

"Everyone is waiting in the hall," Darius said.

Xavier nodded and followed his father. The narrow hallway exuded coldness, its bland stone walls offering no warmth or sense of home.

"One moment, Father," Xavier said just before Darius opened the doors to the hall.

"Yes, my son?"

"With all my might, I will bring you back to see Mother again."

"My son, my king, I will bring you home to see your wife and daughters."

They exchanged smiles, followed by a tight embrace.

"You're getting weak, old man," Xavier chuckled.

Darius tensed his arms, showcasing his large biceps. "Old and mighty," he replied, then pushed open the doors.

The two entered the room, smiles on their faces, amidst the hum of conversation across the three large tables. Sabrina stood in the corner as Xavier and Darius made their way into the room.

"Be seated, men," Xavier said, gesturing as he headed towards the head of the central table.

All eyes turned to Xavier as he stood at the head, flanked by Sabrina and Darius.

"This was meant to be a brief invasion, but we've been here for fifteen years, and for that, I am sorry. I have failed you all," Xavier said, lowering his head.

"No, you haven't!" a soldier said.

"You're the reason my family survived the barbarian invasion!" another added.

"My lord king, we will follow you to whatever end," a knight from Jupiter's Moon declared.

"To whatever end!" echoed the unified chorus.

Darius and Sabrina exchanged smiles, moved by the heartfelt loyalty shown by the soldiers and knights.

"It's been a true honour, warriors of Malsdon!" Xavier declared.

The men erupted into a chant, and Xavier let it continue for a few moments before raising his hand for silence.

"At daybreak, we make for the ships," Xavier said, "The journey could take up to four days, but we must do it in two. We won't last four days out there, as we know from the attempts of our fallen friends. We can only make camp once we reach the old encampment on the south side of the island, and then the final push to the ships."

"Are there any questions?" Darius asked the men.

A brief silence ensued until one person raised their hand to speak. "It's almost a three-day march to the southern encampment. How do we plan to do it in one day?" a soldier asked.

"We're travelling light—no armour," Darius replied, "If your sword is sharp enough, bring it. If not, swap it out for a hammer or anything."

"The last of the cavalry will clear the path ahead and cover the flanks, along with Darius and Tiberius," Sabrina added.

Xavier drew his sword and raised it above his head. "Men, eat and drink your fill of water, for when the sun rises, we embark on the journey for our lives!"

The hall erupted with loud cheers and banging on the tables, men hugging each other and shaking hands. Xavier nodded at Sabrina and Darius before exiting the hall.

*

The sunlight broke through the gaps in the boarded-up windows, illuminating half of the room. Xavier sat at the end of the bed, gently stroking Saya's back as she sat beside him.

"Well, Saya, into the pits of hell we go," he said.

Saya rested her head on Xavier's lap. As he gazed over her body, he noticed the numerous battle scars she had acquired over the years of fighting.

"I've asked a lot of you over the years. In the end, I will not ask you to fight again," he said softly.

Saya turned, and her big green eyes met Xavier's.

"She'll never leave your side and will fight to the very end for you. You know this," Darius said, pushing open the half-opened door.

Xavier stood, already dressed in padded clothes and the jacket Victor had made for him.

Darius picked up Xavier's sword, leaning against a trunk. "For the journey home," he said, handing the sword to Xavier.

The journey back to Malsdon began. Darius and Sabrina led the twenty-man cavalry ahead of the main group to clear the path ahead the best they could, with Xavier leading the group out in a light jog setting a steady pace with Saya in front of them.

The group made steady progress, encountering minimal resistance which was swiftly handled by the cavalry. The soft land, a result of years of the black rain, made the extended run easier on the knee joints. Xavier glanced back at his men, noticing the group starting to break apart. Concern gnawed at him; they hadn't reached the halfway point to the encampment, and their pace needed to triple during the night.

Sabrina rode back to check on Xavier, doing so at regular intervals. "Your pace has slowed."

"We had to slow down; most are starting to fade," Xavier replied, sparing some breath for his words.

Sabrina looked towards the setting sun. "We can't wait for anyone when the night sky takes hold," she said before riding off.

Xavier ordered his men to a marching pace. "Catch your breath and take in water while you can!" he commanded.

Most of them inhaled deeply and splashed water on their faces, while others took small sips to conserve for the night.

CHAPTER THIRTY-ONE

THE DARKNESS AND THE SECRETS WITHIN

The sound of thundering hoofs and shouts from men fighting for their lives echoed deep into the night. The group navigated a stretch of dead forest, surrounded by lifeless trees and dry thorn bushes. The Fallen closed in on all sides, picking off soldiers one by one, making it increasingly difficult to push through.

Xavier, realising the severity of the situation, ordered his men into a box formation, hoping to limit casualties. He led them slowly through the dead forest, with Saya at his side, attempting to clear the path ahead.

"My king, get inside!" a soldier shouted.

Xavier surveyed the situation, recognising the risk of being cut off from the front of the formation and leaving them vulnerable to the Fallen. He took a deep breath, channelling his magic into his sword, turning it as hot as molten lava.

"Just follow me through until the cavalry comes back!" he shouted, forcefully hacking and chopping through the Fallen with newfound ease.

The cavalry returned to the main force, though five fewer men than before. Darius nodded at Xavier, signalling the path ahead was clear. The cavalry flushed the flanks of the box, trampling any Fallen in their path.

"Break formation and run!" Xavier said as the last horse passed him.

The men dispersed and sprinted with all their might towards the southern encampment, which lay a few miles away. The cavalry, with what men they had left, formed a protective circle around the fleeing soldiers.

As the group approached the abandoned encampment, the encounters with the Fallen became less frequent.

"Almost there, men!" Darius shouted, scanning the surrounding area.

"Weird. We haven't seen any more Fallen," Sabrina said to Xavier.

"Something doesn't feel right," he replied, sensing an unease in the air.

They reached a hilltop overlooking the encampment. Xavier and Sabrina crawled to the edge of the cliff as the men took a moment to rest.

"What can you see?" Xavier asked.

Sabrina searched her bag for something to help her observe the camp. "Well, the lights are on," she said as she continued searching. Pulling out a small glass tube, she placed it close to her eye.

"How is that so small?" Xavier asked curiously.

"Shhh." Sabrina focused on the camp and its perimeter. "Well, this is going to be interesting," she whispered, handing the glass tube to Xavier.

He looked through it at the camp. "How is that possible?"

The encampment was occupied by forty men dressed in black, each with a skeleton crown insignia on their chest plate. However, what caught their interest wasn't just the ominous attire; it was the fact that the Fallen were walking among them.

"By the look on your face, I'm guessing we've got trouble," Darius said as Xavier and Sabrina walked back to the group.

"Visitors from Malsdon and the Fallen are having dinner together," Sabrina replied with a hint of sarcasm.

Many heads turned towards her at the mention of people

from Malsdon.

"We need to take one of them alive," Darius said.

Xavier nodded. "Not a problem. There are only forty men and a handful of Fallen."

Xavier knelt down in the middle of his men, drawing a plan in the dirt to take the camp. He outlined the camp as a circle, with four squares representing units and a triangle for the cavalry, before explaining the plan.

The men collected themselves and slowly got into positions using the darkness as cover. Sabrina nodded at Xavier then charged the cavalry straight towards the front gate, the sight of torches flickering around and the sound of orders to chase down the cavalry bellowed into the air. The gate crashed open and most of the host gave chase to the cavalry on horseback or foot.

That was the signal for the others to rush the camp. Tiberius and Saya ran at full speed, crashing into the Fallen, with the rest of the group close behind, engaging the men dressed in black.

"We need a prisoner," Darius said as he fought his way to the centre of the camp.

Xavier was on the other side, clearing out the Fallen with his enhanced sword.

"It's almost cleared, my lord!" a knight shouted from the north side of the camp.

Xavier and his group finished clearing their side with few injuries sustained. Loud screams followed by bodies flying through the air, then bone-chilling words echoed through the camp. Xavier rushed towards the origin of the shouts and screams.

There stood a witch, hooded and cloaked in black, her red eyes the only visible feature. "You're the one we're after," she said with a sinister tone.

Xavier signalled his men to stand back. The witch smiled and shot a blast of lightning at Xavier, knocking him to the ground.

"Come on, Xavier!" a few men shouted.

Xavier slowly stood up, readying himself. The witch sent another blast of lightning, but this time, Xavier deflected it towards the ground.

The witch laughed. "Is this all the mighty king has to offer?"

Xavier looked towards his men. He sensed morale was low, and the witch gaining the upper hand on him would unsettle the troops further. He caught eyes with his father and he mouthed the words, "Don't do it." Xavier channelled the magic within, trying not to draw it from the land. His eyes glowed a dark blue instead of the light blue from before.

The witch smiled, revealing her black, fang-like teeth, and charged at Xavier with sound-bending speed. Xavier responded by sending an energy wave towards the ground, causing it to crumble and knocking the witch off balance mid-stride. Seizing the opportunity, Xavier followed up with another wave that violently lifted her into the air.

Stepping under where she would land, Xavier readied his sword. As she descended back towards the ground, with one swift swing, Xavier chopped off her legs from above the knees. Standing over her body, Xavier pointed his sword tip at her throat as the witch cried out and cursed in an unknown language. The men were silent for a few moments, shocked by the speed and violence that the combination of magic and a skilled fighter could unleash.

CHAPTER THIRTY-TWO

WHISPERS IN THE WIND

Xavier sat alone on the far side of the camp, attempting to clear his mind. The rotting magic from the Forgotten Lands was trying to take hold of him, and flashbacks of pain and suffering popped in and out of his mind. He placed his head in his hands, attempting to squeeze away the pain. Then, slender hands wrapped around his wrist and pulled his hands away.

"Izzy?" Xavier whispered, his head still bowed.

"No, dear, it's me," Sabrina said softly. "Are you okay?"

Xavier stood up, breaking her hold, and shook his head. "I'm fine. I won't let the darkness take me."

Sabrina nodded. "We'll need you before the end, my dear."

The light from the rising sun caught Xavier's attention. "It's time to go. Ready the men and put the wounded on the extra horses," he told Sabrina before walking away.

"Are you going to check on the prisoner?" Sabrina asked before he was out of sight.

Xavier raised his hand in response to her question. He walked through the middle of the camp towards the tent where the witch was being held. He passed his men as they prepared for the final push to the ships at the coast. He also noticed Saya and Tiberius fixated on the gate. Xavier called to Saya, but the only response was a flicker of her ear.

Suddenly, the deep boom of the warning horn sounded from

outside the gate. Darius came charging out of the tent with blood on his sword.

"What happened?" Xavier shouted.

"She was whispering a chant, so I killed her," Darius replied.

"How far did she get into her chant?"

"I'm not sure. Was that a call for help?"

Xavier nodded and ran towards the gate. He used the ladder hitched against the camp wall for people to see over. He saw the patrol running for their lives as the Fallen chased them.

"Xavier, how many?" Darius shouted.

"Too many. Order everyone out the back gate. I'll follow the last man out!"

The five-man patrol was taken down by Fallen beasts before they could reach the camp gate. The massive horde slammed against the gate and walls. Xavier made his way to the back gate, and Sabrina on horseback walked in circles, urging everyone to hurry out.

"Head straight for the ships!" Xavier said, "Clear anyone out and ready the ships!"

Sabrina was about to reply, but the crashing sound of the wooden gate failing under the pressure of the horde caught her attention.

"Go now!" he shouted.

Sabrina rode off, leading the cavalry to the ships.

Xavier slammed the gate shut as most of the Fallen horde flooded into the camp. He turned towards the direction of the ship and saw his men running scattered and filled with fear, but calmly waiting for him were Saya, Tiberius, and Darius.

"They won't make it running like that," Xavier said calmly as his eyes turned dark blue.

"Xavier, let's go now!" Darius shouted with a concerned look.

Xavier held his hands towards the encampment. "None of us will make it with all the Fallen on this godforsaken place chasing us!"

Xavier focused all his energy and gathered some from the land.

"Stop!" Darius shouted, but his words had no meaning to Xavier.

He let out a lion-like roar, and the encampment exploded into flames, sending some of the Fallen into the air and everything else into ash. Xavier turned to walk towards Darius, then collapsed.

"Damn it, Xavier," Darius said as he ran over to his son. He placed him on Saya's back.

More Fallen were mindlessly approaching them.

Darius climbed onto Tiberius. "Mighty lions, show me the meaning of haste!"

After a hard gallop and losing a few men, the cavalry made it to the beach. However, the ships they arrived in had rotted and decayed over the fifteen years they were stuck on the island. But to their fortune the hostile men from Malsdon had arrived in three ships.

"Clear the ship out—I don't want any surprises—and push them to the shallows!" Sabrina shouted.

Sabrina and what was left of her cavalry loaded onto the three ships and waited for the others to arrive. Slowly, the men trickled onto the beach and boarded the ships.

"Where is everyone?" Sabrina asked a soldier trying to catch his breath.

"All I saw was Fallen all around us, my lady," he replied.

"What about the king and Lord Darius?"

"I didn't see them."

Sabrina paced back and forth, scanning the bushes and pathways, waiting for them to arrive.

"My lady, we'll have to leave soon," a knight said.

"No, we have to wait for them!"

"The tide, my lady…"

"How long do we have?"

"Twenty minutes, then we'll lose the tide."

Sabrina thought, *I don't know how we're going to win this war, so few men left*, as the twenty-minute warning weighed heavily on her.

"Lower the ropes!" a knight shouted.

Sabrina's attention was caught, and she rushed over to the port side of the ship. There, Darius and Xavier were on the backs of their lions, breaking through the bushes. However, Xavier remained unconscious from burning down the camp.

Jumping through the shallows, Saya and Tiberius went along the side of the ship. Darius leapt off, then grabbed one of the ropes and proceeded to tie it around Xavier's limp body.

"Pull him up!" Darius started securing the rope as the Fallen rushed through the bushes, heading straight for the ships. "You two, climb now!" he shouted at the two lions.

The lions dug their claws into the boat and swiftly ascended to the top. The men began to pull Darius up as the Fallen poured into the shallows. Darius looked down at the Fallen at his feet and let out a sigh of relief, sensing the end was near. Then, he felt a jerk in the rope and the sound of tearing.

"Quickly, throw the other rope!" voices at the top shouted.

But it was too late; the rope snapped, and Darius began to fall. Suddenly, he let out a loud cry of pain. In the moment the rope snapped, Tiberius jumped over the ship, digging one paw into the side of the ship and the other into Darius' shoulder, then yanked him to the top of the ship.

Sabrina signalled the other ships to move out of the shallows and into open water. The creaking of old wood and the sound of oars hitting water echoed as the ships pushed out into deeper waters. The Fallen who tried to follow sank when they ventured into deeper waters.

Darius walked over to Sabrina, clutching his wrapped shoulder. "Well, how many men made it?" he asked.

"Hundred men and twenty horses," Sabrina replied. "Our army died the second we knew we were stuck in that place."

"I'm to blame," Xavier said as he gingerly walked over.

"You should be resting," Sabrina said.

"I will, but we need a plan for when we land at the Iron Coast," Xavier said.

"We'll need to make it to the Meadows or Silver Hills, then find whoever is still loyal to the true king and queen," Darius added.

"True," Sabrina said, "But how will we get past the likelihood that the docks will be heavily guarded by the enemy?"

"We dress like them," Xavier replied, "However, hiding Saya and Tiberius won't be easy."

"I'll deal with the lions. Sabrina, you ready the men. You, son, get some rest," Darius said before walking off below deck.

CHAPTER THIRTY-THREE

THE AGGRESSOR AND THE PROTECTOR

The sound of screams echoed deep within the forges of the Silver Hills, yet none of the smiths took notice and continued their work.

"Maybe this one will break quicker than the others!" a person shouted.

A few other men started laughing and began placing wagers on the time it would take.

In a room between the two large forge areas was where the screams came to life.

"Please, please no more. I had no choice; they would have turned my family into Fallen," the prisoner pleaded.

"You know, I've been tortured before, so I know what you're going through. Just tell us the true location of the spawning ground," River said as she waved a blood-stained hammer around.

"I thought it was a great honour being turned into one of the Fallen," a voice said from the doorway.

River turned her attention to the door and nodded at Artoria. Her tall and slender frame filled the doorway, and her warm beige skin glowed with sweat as her long jet-black hair stuck to her face.

She handed River a pouch of water, which River drank wildly in front of the prisoner. Her face and clothes were wet from the spillage, and the prisoner tried to look away, but his parched throat longed to be quenched.

"So, you're the one responsible for the death of my men," Artoria said, then grabbed the prisoner's face with one hand.

"Please, I just want to see my family again," he pleaded.

"Your family is dead, my men are dead, and you'll die slowly if you don't tell us!" Artoria shouted. Artoria's green eyes turned cyan and glowed brightly. "We don't have time for this."

She placed both her hands on the sides of the prisoner's head.

"Artoria, don't! You'll cook his brain," River said as she tried pulling Artoria's arm down.

Artoria resisted and began reading the prisoner's mind. Tears and screams for help filled the room. The longer she stayed in his mind, the more lifeless he became until his eyes glazed over.

Artoria released her grip, and the prisoner's lifeless body flopped to the floor.

"Your mother won't be pleased; they're still our people," River said as she checked the body.

"He was a worm of a man, selling out his own people. I saw everything," Artoria said defiantly, then kicked the prisoner's body.

River looked up at Artoria. "Where's the spawning ground?"

"Deep within the Emerald Meadows. They have chambers underground; that's why we never found it," Artoria replied.

"Very well. I'll give you sixty men and go find your sister. We'll need her," River replied. "This is a raid; quick in and out. Don't linger there for too long. Now go, princess."

Artoria rolled her eyes out of annoyance and left the room, but not before giving the body of the prisoner one last kick.

The upper courtyard of the Silver Hills fortress had been transformed into a market and living quarters for those seeking refuge from the witch queen's unjust and oppressive rule. People from all four regions of Malsdon gathered under one roof. With Sol incapacitated and bedridden, the responsibility of managing the fortress and maintaining peace fell upon River and Victor. Isabella and Layla assisted by overseeing the living quarters.

The midday sun shone brightly upon the silver mountains, making them gleam. Its warmth embraced the farmers tending to the harvest of various fruits and vegetables on a manmade plot at the far side of the courtyard, away from any human traffic.

"The harvest looks good, my lady," a farmer said.

"How you got the fruit from the Vermillion Sands to grow here is remarkable," another farmer added.

"A little bit of love with a drop of magic," Liliana said softly as she pulled out a sand pear from the plot.

"Here, my lady, try this apple," the farmer offered.

"I've never seen this type before," she said.

"It's a mix of two apples: one from the Meadows and the other from the Vermillion Sands. Try it, try it."

Liliana bit into the apple, then froze. Her face contorted, and she stuck her tongue out. "Mother's love, why is it so sour?" she said while coughing.

The farmer laughed. "If you ever feel tired or run down, have a bite of this apple, and you'll have more spring than a rabbit."

Liliana chuckled. "Let's finish the harvest and make sure those apples are in their own basket."

Liliana and the farmers carried the baskets of fruits and vegetables to the food stores inside the fortress, ready to be added to the weekly rations.

"My lady, you're needed," a soldier said.

Liliana looked at the farmers.

"We'll be okay. This is the easy part," they assured her.

"My lady," the soldier insisted, gesturing towards the barracks.

Liliana handed her basket to one of the farmers and followed the soldier.

Entering the main room of the barracks, Liliana found River and Captain Lynch briefing the men. Beside them stood Isabella and Artoria. Liliana's entrance caught Artoria's attention, who glared at her with disappointment.

"No plate armour, only chainmail and their black uniform,"

River said, "We want to get in and out of the chambers quickly. We don't know how tight the tunnels will be. Dismissed."

Artoria stormed over to Liliana with an annoyed look on her face. "What took you so long? Playing in the dirt again?"

"You mean helping the farmers grow food for everyone to eat, including you," Liliana replied.

"Girls, stop this now," Isabella said.

"She was late to our first mission in charge with River," Artoria complained.

"I'm sorry. I know you've been waiting for this moment," Liliana said as she put her arm around Artoria.

"Well, I can't and won't do it without you," Artoria replied.

The two sisters then hugged and started laughing.

"I don't like how nice you make," laughed Artoria.

"Girls, one last thing," Isabella said, waving over a guard carrying an object. "My sword. I want one of you to use it today."

Artoria took the sword and handed it to Liliana. "You're the best with a blade, and it'll be more useful in your hands than mine," Artoria said, her words filled with respect and love. Artoria went off to her table to prepare for the raid.

"Liliana, before you go, keep your sister safe. She's driven by passion, and that gets her into trouble more often than not," Isabella whispered.

"I'll always protect her, as I am the shield that covers the sword," Liliana replied and hugged her mother before heading to her table.

Isabella watched as her daughters led their men out of the barracks. She gave them a smile as they turned back to look upon her before the door slammed behind the last man. The slamming of the door sent chills up Isabella's spine, causing her body to shudder.

"Isabella, they'll be fine," River said.

"I wish you or Mona was with them," Isabella replied.

"They're ready for this. Trust in them. Also, their magical abilities will keep them safe. I believe their powers would have rivalled their father's."

Tears ran down Isabella's face as she tried to wipe them away. River squeezed her with a tight hug.

"I can't lose them. They're all I have left of him," Isabella sobbed.

CHAPTER THIRTY-FOUR

A DANGEROUS DANCE

"This place is our birthright," Liliana said.

Artoria looked around as they rode through the green meadows.

"It's slowly coming back to its past glory, and I wish we saw it before the black rain."

"We destroy this spawning ground, and then we can secure the Meadows."

The two sisters nodded and quickened the pace.

The raiding party stashed their horses a few hundred metres away from the location and travelled on foot.

"Keep an eye out for any Fallen," Artoria commanded.

With swords drawn, spears at the ready, and bows poised to fire, they marched towards the location Artoria had seen in the prisoner's mind.

"You five, watch the area. You know the drill. The rest of you, with me," Artoria said.

She smashed the muddy wooden hatch and jumped into the narrow tunnel. Liliana and the men followed her down. They ran through the tunnel for a few minutes before it split into two directions.

"I go right, and you go left?" Liliana asked.

The group split off down their selected paths.

Liliana's path was littered with Fallen. She ordered her group to push and force their way through the Fallen, the sound of skulls cracking against steel echoing as Liliana's group left pieces of rotten limbs and bones behind them.

"There's nothing here!" a soldier said.

Liliana jogged up to reach the front of the group. The soldiers were knelt down, searching for items on the ground.

"What have you found?" she asked.

A soldier stood up and handed her a necklace. "Personal items of the victims, my lady."

"You three, gather all you can. Maybe their loved ones are at the fortress. The rest of you, back through the tunnel," Liliana ordered.

Artoria stood over a pit of black rain, with human and Fallen bodies scattered on the ground around. "Liliana, look at that," Artoria said as her sister approached.

"The smell," Liliana replied, holding her nose.

Artoria nodded and looked around the pit.

"What are you thinking?" Liliana asked.

"Collapse everything," Artoria replied with a mischievous look.

The men trickled out of the tunnel and stood far back from the entrance. Artoria and Liliana climbed out last. Artoria signalled the men to step back even further. The two sisters channelled their magic, their eyes glowing cyan, ready to unleash their power.

Firstly, Artoria sent an intense blast of fire down the tunnel, destroying everything in its path. Then, she sent shockwaves down the tunnels, weakening their structure. Finally, Liliana placed her hand on the ground and pushed down, causing the chamber and tunnel system to collapse on itself, leaving a crater in the ground.

The men cheered and hugged each other.

"Well done, everyone!" Artoria said, "Not one death, only scars!"

"Are the drinks on you tonight?" a soldier shouted.

"Yes, of course!" she replied. Artoria walked around, patting and shaking the hands of her men.

However, Liliana stood off from the group, focusing her attention to the east.

"Sister, are you not happy?" Artoria asked, still filled with joy.

"Someone powerful is approaching us," Liliana said softly as she gripped her sword tightly.

"Lily, is it her?"

"I'm not sure. We'll confront them, and the men can ambush if needed."

*

The ground shook violently, unsettling the horses.

"What was that?" Darius exclaimed.

"My lord, should we release the lions?" a knight asked.

Darius was about to answer when Xavier interjected. "If they see the lions, our cover is blown," he said sternly.

"Do you sense something, Xavier?" Sabrina asked.

"There are two witches ahead of us," he replied.

The men began to grow uneasy, glancing aimlessly around them.

"Listen, we got through the docks with their uniform; leave the talking to me and my father," Xavier instructed.

They rode further ahead, and the two witches came into view.

"Son, cover your face," Darius whispered.

They rode further down the path and stopped in front of the two witches.

"We felt the ground shake. Is everything okay?" Xavier asked.

"That's the one I felt," Liliana whispered.

Xavier placed his hand on his hip close to his sword. Artoria noticed his movement and placed her hands on her hips.

"Everything is under control, sir," she answered.

"You and your men are not needed here," Liliana said

nervously.

"Are you sure?" Darius asked, his deep voice startling the two sisters.

"His powers are growing by the minute," Liliana whispered.

"Where are you heading?" Artoria asked.

"To reinforce the Meadows," Xavier replied as he looked straight into Artoria's eyes.

"Sister, we can't fight him; we'll let them pass," Liliana whispered.

Artoria nodded at her sister.

"I think they're letting us pass," Sabrina whispered to Darius.

"You may pass," Liliana said and lifted her arm as a gesture to pass.

As Liliana lifted her arm, her cloak lifted and exposed the hilt of Isabella's sword. This caught Xavier's eye, and he pulled hard on his horse's reins.

"That sword, how did you come by it?" he asked, his hand tightly gripped on his sword.

Darius was about to ask why Xavier stopped, then he saw the sword hilt as well.

"Sir, you and your men can pass," Liliana said as she took a step back.

"Answer me, witch!" Xavier shouted.

"Don't you dare shout at us," Artoria said firmly.

Xavier laughed and jumped off his horse. The others followed suit and stood closely behind him. "I'm not going to ask you again."

Artoria stood in front of her sister with her sword drawn and signalled the men to come out. They too stood behind the sisters.

"Well, I'm going to have to beat the answers out of you," Xavier said as he drew his sword.

Xavier's eyes turned a slightly deeper shade of blue, reminiscent of his time in the Forgotten Lands. Liliana and Artoria's eyes transformed into a vivid cyan, swords drawn on both sides, each waiting for the other to flinch.

"I'll draw them two away, wound the others. Don't kill them; we'll need answers," Xavier whispered to Darius.

As soon as he spoke those words, Xavier turned quickly and unleashed an energy wave that caught Artoria and Liliana off guard, sending them flying into the woods.

"Charge!" Darius shouted.

Xavier darted off towards the direction where the sisters had landed before finding himself caught in the middle of two charging units.

"Lily, my arm, I think it's broken," Artoria said, wincing as she stood up.

Liliana quickly examined her sister's arm. "I have to reset the arm before I can heal the bone."

"You'll have to fight him by yourself, and I'll try to knock him out when I have an opening," Artoria said.

Xavier walked down the uneven slope and reached the open ground where the sisters were standing. Liliana charged at Xavier before he could get set, but he still managed to send energy at Liliana. She deftly deflected it towards a tree, causing it to explode. Swords clashed, and close combat ensued. Artoria circled them closely, waiting for the opening.

The two were so evenly matched that they mirrored each other's moves.

"You're a good fighter, witch, but that changes nothing. I still want answers," Xavier said, pausing between words to catch his breath.

Liliana ignored him, applying more pressure and attempting to use her magic to unbalance him. However, Xavier countered. Liliana then executed a huge overhead swing, forcing Xavier to block, but she kept pushing down, bringing him to his knees. Feeling the blade of his sword touching his head, Xavier rolled to the left, causing Liliana to stumble forwards. He quickly jumped to his feet and kicked Liliana in the face, breaking her nose. Liliana fell to the floor, spitting out the blood that entered her mouth from her nose.

Xavier stood over Liliana, with the point of his sword pressed against her chest. However, he forgot about Artoria for a brief moment and was caught off guard by Artoria's energy wave, which sent him through the air, crashing into a tree.

Artoria quickly helped her sister to her feet. "Lily, you okay?"

"Damn, he's good with a blade. I can't find an opening," Liliana replied.

"I have an idea. If you can lift the fallen leaves up around him, I'll set them on fire, and that's your opening."

The two sisters nodded and watched Xavier making his way back to them, rolling his shoulders. Liliana charged him again, but this time she threw a feint, which Xavier fell for, and he jumped. Liliana then slapped the ground with her hand, causing the leaves to vortex around Xavier.

"Artoria, now!" she shouted.

Artoria summoned her most powerful blast of fire, knocking down Xavier and burning his clothes.

"Lily, finish this!" Artoria screamed.

Liliana ran hard, making sure she'd get there before Xavier could get to his feet. She saw him slowly beginning to stand as the burning leaves fell around him. Liliana stood over Xavier, who tried to swing at her, but she sidestepped and drove the hilt of her sword with a little magical force straight into Xavier's face, knocking him out and breaking his nose in the process.

Liliana fell to the ground; exhaustion took over, and she couldn't move. "Artoria, gag him and bind his hands," Liliana said.

"You did great, Lily. Give me a few moments, and I'll help you drag him back," Artoria said proudly.

Liliana and Artoria dragged Xavier back to the others. There was no sound of battle as they approached the position of their men. As they appeared through the bushes, Darius and Sabrina, along with their men, were on their knees, having surrendered.

"Why did they surrender?" Liliana asked, looking at Darius, who was gazing at the wagons at the back.

"They surrendered when we took control of the wagons," one soldier said.

"We heard breathing from inside these black crates, so we threatened to drive our spears through," another soldier added.

"Kill whatever is inside," Artoria commanded.

The soldiers were about to stab the crates with their spears; the shouts from Darius and some others fell on deaf ears.

"Stop!" Liliana said, "We take all of them back to the fortress. We need answers and to see what is inside those crates."

"Liliana, don't be silly. We might put the whole fortress at risk," Artoria whispered.

"Whatever is inside would have broken out and killed our men, and that old bald man seems very concerned about what's inside," Liliana replied.

Artoria nodded in agreement and ordered the men to bind and blindfold Darius and the others, then they began their journey back to the Silver Hills.

*

The horn sounded as Artoria and Liliana returned through the fortress gates. The prisoners were taken to the courtyard and seated in a group, still blindfolded with sacks over their heads and gagged to prevent them from seeing the fortress. Xavier was dragged to the front of the group, with Darius and Sabrina beside him. River, Captain Lynch, and Isabella approached the sisters, who stood proudly next to some of their men in front of the prisoners.

"Girls, you outdid yourselves," River said proudly.

The sisters smiled at each other.

Isabella rushed over to them. "You're both hurt, what happened?" she asked.

"That one, their leader, put up a damn good fight," Artoria

said, then turned around and kicked Xavier, causing him to fall on his back.

"How many did we lose?" River asked.

"Five of theirs and ten of ours, but we got them to surrender when we threatened to kill whatever is inside these crates," Artoria said, pointing at the wagons at the end of the courtyard.

"They're very fond of whatever is inside," Liliana added.

"The leader has magical powers?" River asked.

Liliana and Artoria nodded.

"I wonder if their leader is Delilah's head mage," River said.

"He's pale and has black eyes. Did you see his face?" Captain Lynch asked.

"No, they were covered and still are," Liliana said.

"Let's see who tried to kill my daughters," Isabella said, grabbing Xavier and pulling him back on his knees.

Artoria and Liliana drew their swords, as did everyone else around them.

"Be careful, Mother," Liliana warned.

Isabella pulled out her dagger and placed it against Xavier's throat, then grabbed the sack and pulled it off his head. Isabella froze, dropping her dagger, and stumbled back, falling on her bottom.

"For all things pure, it can't be," River said softly.

"Release them!" Captain Lynch shouted.

Passersby began to kneel before Xavier. Isabella was crying uncontrollably as she pulled off Xavier's blindfold and hugged him tightly.

Artoria and Liliana looked around, confused and lost for words.

"What is going on? You're releasing them?" Artoria shouted.

"Artoria, that is our father, the lost king," Liliana said softly.

River ran over and hugged Darius.

"No, it can't be. They all died," Artoria said as she looked around at people cheering and hugging each other.

Both sisters were startled when Saya and Tiberius were released.

"A living gigas lion," Liliana said.

Overwhelmed by emotions, Artoria threw up, then ran off inside the barracks. Liliana followed her in. The cheers continued as long-lost friends and loved ones rejoiced.

Evening fell over Malsdon as the drinking and parties began all over the Silver Hills fortress. Songs of joy and happiness filled the evening air. Xavier and Isabella sat next to each other on the ramparts, both smiling but yet to speak a word. Saya lay down next to them, waiting for the ice to break.

"You look even more beautiful than I remember," Xavier said softly.

"You look tired and a lot like your dad; let your hair grow back," Isabella replied, teasing Xavier.

"I thought of you every day and night. I tried to reach out to you."

"It's okay, Xavier. You're here back by my side."

"I'm sorry for leaving you."

"Xavier, stop apologising."

Xavier sighed and grabbed Isabella's hand. "I saw the hilt of your sword. I thought they killed you, but I was trying to kill my own daughters instead."

"You didn't know. I'm not happy about it, but you didn't know."

Xavier hugged Isabella tightly, then kissed her on the forehead. "I won't go far next time."

Saya sat up and watched closely as someone approached them.

"Mother, may I join?" Liliana asked.

Isabella patted the floor next to her. Liliana was a bit hesitant to sit with Saya watching her movements.

"She won't hurt you," Xavier said with a smile.

Liliana smiled back, still a bit shy and embarrassed to talk to Xavier.

Isabella smiled from ear to ear. "King Xavier Leo, I would like you to properly meet Princess Liliana Lucius Leo, your daughter."

"I'm sorry about your nose," Xavier said.

"I'm sorry about yours and burning you. Well, the burning part was Artoria's doing."

"I don't want to know," Isabella said, shaking her head.

Xavier stood up, then knelt in front of Liliana and held his hand out in front of her face, causing Liliana to flinch.

"It's okay," Xavier said as he began to heal her nose.

Liliana felt the warm healing powers fixing her nose. She slowly held her hand out towards Xavier's nose and began to heal him as well.

Isabella began to cry.

"Mother, what's the matter?" Liliana asked.

Before Isabella could speak, Liliana hugged her tightly.

"I'm so happy we're all back together," Isabella sobbed.

"So am I," Xavier said.

Isabella wiped her tears and fixed her top. "Right, show your father around," Isabella said as she pushed both of them to their feet.

Liliana looked nervous and glared at her mother.

"Saya and I would really appreciate it," Xavier said while patting Saya's head.

Liliana walked off, then waved Xavier over to follow her.

"Find your sister as well!" Isabella shouted before they walked down the stairs.

Liliana led Xavier and Saya to the new locations, from the new barracks to the camps. Each passerby bowed or offered their blessings to Xavier.

"The people really love you," Liliana said.

Xavier said nothing and just smiled as they walked towards the tavern.

"River had this built about five years ago," Liliana said as they stood outside the window.

"Built it into the rock," Xavier said as he touched the stone wall.

Shouts from inside caught their attention. Suddenly, the tavern door crashed open, hitting the stone wall.

"Liliana and Xavier Leo, join us!" River shouted, slurring her words as she spoke.

Xavier poked his head through the doorway, and everyone inside cheered, including his mother and aunt.

"Maybe later," he said, then patted River on the shoulder, causing her to spill some of her ale on the floor.

"Ahhh, you better. You owe me a drink now," River said before stumbling inside.

Liliana laughed and watched River through the tavern window. "This is the happiest I've seen her in years."

"I'm happy for all of them," Xavier said sincerely.

"Come on, we've got more to see. Also, Victor will want to see you," Liliana said and pulled her father further into the courtyard.

Chapter Thirty-Five

The Time We Lost

Conversations between nurses and physicians leaked into the hallway where Darius was pacing up and down, awaiting news about his dying friend. After a few more minutes, the door opened, and a physician walked over to Darius.

"How long has he got?" Darius asked.

"A day or two," the physician replied. "It was like he was waiting for you. Those who were greatly exposed to the rain died years ago."

"Why was he exposed like that?"

"Maybe you should go ask him," the physician replied, showing Darius the open door.

Sol sighed angrily as the door opened. "No more physicians, leave me be; I know my fate."

"What about an old friend?"

"Is that you, Darius?" Sol asked as he slowly sat up.

"You look terrible," Darius said as he came into view.

Sol laughed then broke into a mild coughing fit. "Come closer, my friend; you won't catch it."

Darius sat beside Sol's bed and gave him a firm handshake. "Sol, what happened to you?"

"Building all the new things you see while the black rain fell was a bad idea," Sol said, gesturing to his frail body.

"But how did you live longer than the others?"

"Your granddaughter Liliana gave me a few more years."

"How did she do that?"

"Well, we found out that healing the infected organs had no effect. That black rain was the ultimate weapon."

"Sol, how?"

"Sorry, she gave me fruits that were grown in soil fused with silver and bone dust from a gigas animal."

Darius took a moment to take in all that Sol said. "How old was she when she thought of that?"

"No older than nine." He grabbed Darius' hand tightly and whispered, "Liliana is the future. Keep her safe and watch Artoria carefully; she can easily fall down the wrong path."

Darius nodded and squeezed Sol's shoulder, showing he understood the delicate position the future was in.

Sol coughed and called for his servant. "We'll need wine and food please, dear."

The servant looked at Darius with a look of concern.

"Sol, are you meant to have wine?" Darius asked.

"I'm dying, and my friend came back from the dead. I want to drink and hear all about his time on the Forgotten Lands," Sol said defiantly.

Darius nodded at the servant, and she left to gather the requested items. Sol gestured with his hands for Darius to start talking.

*

Victor and the other smiths were hard at work in the forge area, crafting new weapons, equipment, and parts for various things around the fortress. As Xavier and Liliana entered the forge, the smiths all bowed then continued with their work.

"There he is," Liliana said, pointing at Victor.

His face was covered in sweat, his tied-up silver hair stained with dirt and other things. Victor looked to grab his larger hammer, then he smiled when he caught eyes with Xavier.

"You took your time," Victor said.

Xavier chuckled and walked over to shake Victor's hand. "You've grown."

"I'm not that quirky little kid that made you that coat."

"No, you're not. Speaking of that coat…"

Victor chuckled. "As long as it served you well, don't worry about it. I can make more."

Xavier nodded and squeezed Victor's broad shoulders.

"Victor, have you seen my sister?" Liliana asked.

Victor rolled his eyes and pointed to the small room, then continued with his work. Liliana sighed and led Xavier off to the room.

"I'll see you around, Victor!" Xavier shouted as he walked off.

Victor raised his hammer in salute and continued his work.

Xavier paused and surveyed the room's exterior; its dullness and exposed raw materials gave it an uneasy atmosphere. The echoing clangs from the anvil behind him revealed the purpose of the room.

"Father, are you okay?" Liliana asked.

"I'm fine; it's just a bit hot down here," Xavier replied.

Liliana smiled, then slowly opened the door. Artoria sat on the floor, her back against the corner of the room. Teary eyes looked up at Xavier and Liliana as they entered.

"What do you want?" she said.

"Father wanted to see you," Liliana replied.

Artoria turned her head towards the wall, ignoring the question.

"Arty, I know how you're feeling. I felt the same until I saw mother with him. That made me feel at ease," Liliana explained.

"Mother's favourite and now the favourite of this man called Father," Artoria mumbled.

Xavier stepped forwards and knelt down close to Artoria, giving enough space to make her comfortable. "What can I do?" he asked.

"Let me read your mind," Artoria said, turning to look straight into his eyes.

"No, you're not doing that!" Liliana interjected.

Xavier raised his hand, signalling her to stop. "My mind is unlocked. It's up to you how you open it," he calmly said, dropping his head to meet hers.

Liliana observed Artoria with a displeased look, aware of what usually transpired after Artoria delved into someone's thoughts. Artoria stood up, and with sweaty hands, she seized Xavier's head. Her eyes glowed as she concentrated, attempting to enter her father's mind. Xavier remained calm, despite the room's oppressive heat making it feel like an oven. Artoria, on the other hand, grew increasingly frustrated as she encountered resistance in reading Xavier.

"Why are you blocking me out?" she shouted into Xavier's face.

He calmly met Artoria's frustrated gaze and gently said, "You will not read my mind by overpowering me like your past victims. That is why you killed them."

"Listen to him!" Liliana shouted.

Filled with overwhelming emotions, Artoria redoubled her efforts to forcefully penetrate Xavier's mind. Xavier shook his head with disappointment, then abruptly stood and seized Artoria's head, transferring all his memories into her. Artoria fell silent as her eyes flickered violently, overwhelmed by the flood of information.

"You're hurting her," Liliana said softly.

"No, give it time. This was the only way; her stubbornness and anger wouldn't let her into my mind," Xavier replied.

After a few moments, Xavier released Artoria. She stumbled to the floor, crying uncontrollably. Liliana rushed over to comfort her. Artoria looked over Liliana's shoulder and straight at Xavier.

"How are you still alive?" she sobbed.

Xavier knelt down and hugged both his daughters. "You two and your mother are the reason I'm still alive," he said softly, his eyes beginning to water.

CHAPTER THIRTY-SIX

LIFE AND DEATH

A few days later, Lord Sol Silverlight passed away, leaving River Silverlight as the leader of the Silver Hills. His death had a profound impact on many, given Sol's reputation as a kind and gentle person. Sol was sent off on a grand pyre of fire, for he couldn't be buried like the lords of old. The poisonous black rain would have turned him into one of the Fallen.

The tavern was crowded with people raising their glasses to Sol's memory. Courtyard flags were lowered to half-mast under the full moon sky.

"The mountains are gleaming brightly tonight," Darius remarked to River as they stood outside the tavern.

"I'm glad the two of you got to see each other before the end," River replied.

"Where is your brother?" Darius asked.

"In the forge. Ever since Father fell ill, he spends all his time there. That's his comfort. Others find it at the bottom of a bottle." River paused, then took one more sip of her ale and poured the rest onto the ground. "I've let myself go."

Darius put his arm around her. "Don't feel ashamed. We all have the power to make things whole again and you kept everyone alive and safe in your father's place."

River nodded. "Tomorrow will be the new beginning, and the fires of liberation will rise again."

Nothing but the sound of wind moving creaky windows and doors could be heard, as everyone was either passed out drunk or tired from the long day and the passing of Sol.

Xavier woke suddenly in the night, looking around frantically.

"Go back to sleep," Isabella whispered as she rolled over.

"You didn't hear that?"

"No, go for a walk and let me sleep."

Xavier slowly got out of bed, grabbing his sword and wool jacket as he exited the room. He wandered down the hall as the same voice called his name.

"I must be going crazy," he said.

Xavier ended up in the courtyard and sat outside the barracks, still wondering where the voice was coming from.

"Who are you?" he asked the voice.

"I need your help," the voice replied.

"Father, you're here as well," Artoria said, leading a sleepy Liliana.

"You hear the voices?" he asked.

"Started a year ago, a deep voice asking for help," Liliana said, then let out a big yawn.

Xavier stood up sharply and paced around. "It can't be," he said out loud. He grabbed his daughters by the hand and led them outside of the fortress gates. "Soldier!" he shouted.

"Yes, sir?" the soldier replied.

"Watch over us!"

The soldier followed them to a little clearing to the side of the fortress.

"The magic has always been strong here," Xavier said as he stood in the middle of the clearing with Liliana and Artoria. "Focus your energy with mine."

Their eyes glowed, the dirt rumbled beneath their feet, and suddenly, their bodies turned limp. The soldier rushed over to stop their bodies from falling, but their limp forms braced each other up.

"Girls, wake up! It's not safe," Xavier shouted, shaking both of them.

Artoria slowly woke up, surveying her surroundings of dying trees and black-stained grass. She stood up, drawing her sword, while Xavier helped Liliana to her feet.

"I feel weird. What is this place?" Artoria asked.

"It's the Exalted Plains, the origin of all magic on Malsdon," Xavier replied.

"There's tainted magic everywhere," Liliana whispered, "And I sense two powerful energies, one getting closer than the other."

"Father, I'll lead us through the forest," Artoria said.

Xavier nodded and followed closely behind Artoria, with Liliana beside him.

"This place looks similar to the Meadows," Artoria said.

"The Emerald Meadows is the place with a lot of natural and organic magic," Xavier explained.

"What about the Silver Hills?" Artoria asked.

"Without the liquid silver flowing through the veins of the mountains, it would just be a normal place," Xavier replied.

They continued to walk through the endless forest of dying trees.

"Something is close," Liliana said, taking a defensive stance.

They got into a defensive posture, covering each other's backs.

"Could be Delilah or her head mage," Artoria whispered.

The dead silence weighed heavily on Artoria, prompting her to take a step forwards—a step too far. Suddenly, a creature leapt from the thick bushes, striking Liliana and causing her to fall into Xavier. The creature then pinned Artoria down, poised to kill her. However, Xavier unleashed a wild and powerful energy wave, propelling both the creature and Artoria into a nearby tree.

Xavier swiftly charged towards the creature before it could recover. Amidst the black-tainted ground, he struggled to discern its form. Just as Xavier closed in for a fatal blow, the creature locked eyes with him, causing a momentary pause. Seizing the opportunity, the creature swiped at Xavier's feet, sending him crashing to the ground and knocking his sword away.

Before the creature could rise, Liliana encased it in an energy bubble, shouting, "Quick, Father, kill it!"

Xavier slowly stood, coming face to face with the trapped creature. "Is that you, Belthazor?" he asked.

"Xavier, the road has been a lonely and difficult one," Belthazor replied.

"Are you okay, Father?" Liliana asked, watching as her father relaxed his posture.

"He's an old friend. Lower the bubble and help your sister."

Belthazor slowly sat up, his massive body covered in scars and open wounds.

"What happened here?" Xavier asked.

"Delilah sent her mages and Fallen to corrupt and control the Plains," Belthazor explained.

"I'm sorry I wasn't able to help you."

"We were all played by Delilah and the deity," Belthazor said.

"Where is she?"

"She's dead, and I feel no sorrow for her passing."

"You called us for help?" Liliana asked as she and Artoria listened from a distance.

"Yes, however, when I sensed your powers, they were in great flux," Belthazor replied.

"So, what's the plan?" Artoria said, cutting the conversation short.

"Yes, follow me," Belthazor instructed.

He led the group to the hollow glass throne hall, nestled at the end of the forest, where the head mage and Fallen awaited their arrival.

"This is it. Don't die here, for your soul will never return to your body," Belthazor said to Artoria and Liliana.

They nodded in response, their faces filled with concern.

"Trust in your abilities and each other, and you'll feel the sun's warm embrace again," Xavier added as he touched both their shoulders.

Belthazor nodded in agreement with Xavier's words. "Xavier, you and Liliana will take on the mage."

"Why is Liliana going with Father?" Artoria asked.

"You chase glory when there is more to winning a battle," Belthazor scolded her outburst. "You and I will draw the Fallen out and deal with them."

Belthazor let out a deep, booming roar, causing some of the Fallen to freeze in their sluggish movements, while others spun around towards him. The Fallen shuffled and limped towards Belthazor and Artoria, who wore a displeased expression on her face. They engaged the Fallen, cutting and ripping through each one in front of them.

Artoria glanced over at Xavier and Liliana, sneaking into the throne hall. Jealousy and rage overtook her, and she lost all composure. Her sword strokes became wild and overpowered, punctuated by random screams.

"Control yourself!" Belthazor shouted. His deep voice would send chills down any spine.

Artoria ignored him and yelled, "More coming from the forest!" She charged at the Fallen emerging from the forest, leaving Belthazor vulnerable.

CHAPTER THIRTY-SEVEN

THE BALANCE

Statues of crystal lined the wall path of the hall, leading to the glass throne elevated by three steps. At the end of the path, the head mage, clad in a long black cloak, stood before the throne.

"Show no fear," Xavier whispered to Liliana as they walked towards the mage.

The mage stood slightly taller than both of them but more slender in stature. With a flourish, the mage removed her cloak, revealing a female face and an armoured corset that exposed her pale legs and arms.

"A woman?" Liliana whispered.

The mage took a deep breath and smiled. "I can smell your magic," she said, taking another deep breath. "So powerful, the both of you."

Liliana pointed her sword towards the mage. "We've been looking for you."

The mage smiled, revealing broken teeth and black gums. "I know you have. Do you want me to be your new mother?"

Liliana gritted her teeth. "Abomination, I'll kill you."

The mage laughed, dismissing Liliana's threat. "What about you, King Xavier?"

"The easy or hard way, you're going to end up dead, and then I'll take your head," Xavier said with nerves of steel.

"If you're going to kill me, you have to earn it," the mage said, letting out a high-pitched laugh.

The mage's eyes turned black along with black veins that became visible on her pale skin. Xavier and Liliana channelled their magic getting ready for the fight ahead.

Bolts and waves of magical energy crashed around the hall, both sides not giving an edge. The mage smiled and laughed with each attack she struggled to deal with.

"We've almost broken through," Xavier said as he showed no sign of tiring.

Liliana's confidence grew with each magical attack she blocked.

"Wait!" the mage shouted.

Xavier and Liliana stood fast, expecting a trick from the mage.

"It is clear that we are evenly matched in our skill in magic," the mage continued.

"I don't think so," Liliana replied.

The mage looked straight into Liliana's eyes, ignoring the comment. "What about your skill with a blade? Accept the challenge?"

"This isn't a game," Xavier said sternly.

"Life is a game," the mage chuckled as she picked up her sword and bone club, resting on the steps to the throne. "I want single combat!"

Xavier gripped his sword tightly and was about to step forwards when Liliana tucked his arm back. With a determined look and her mother's sword in hand, she wasn't taking no for an answer.

"Watch out for the club when you parry her sword, and don't cross over the same path," Xavier advised Liliana.

She nodded and stepped in front of Xavier.

"You, sheathe your sword!" the mage ordered Xavier.

He walked back, sat down on a broken statue, and held his sword with both hands, the tip pressed into the ground. Then he winked at the mage, trying to torment her.

Sparks, sweat, and blood littered the crystal glass floor. Xavier watched, gripping his sword tightly each time the mage got the upper hand. Liliana fought fiercely, blood trickling down from her forehead, blocking her left eye at times. The endless back and forth made them grow more tired and prone to mistakes.

Liliana smashed the hilt of her sword into the mage's face, ripping open her cheek. Discoloured blood sprayed everywhere, into Liliana's mouth, causing her to gag and take a few steps back.

Artoria rushed into the hall like a violent wind. "Liliana!" she shouted.

Liliana turned suddenly towards Artoria, leaving her back exposed to the mage. The mage clubbed her in the head, then with a blast of magic sent her through the air like a spear into Artoria, crashing into a statue.

The mage dashed over to both of them, her sword ready to deal the final blow. However, when the mage went to stab Liliana, a faint energy bubble blocked the strike. Liliana's flickering eyes defiantly stared into the mage's from within the bubble with each strike that followed. Suddenly, the mage was violently thrown to the floor by her hair.

The mage quickly got to her feet as Xavier threw the matted hair which got caught in his hands on the floor.

"How dare you interfere!" she shouted, spit and blood pouring from her mouth.

Xavier said nothing as he walked towards the mage, his sword glowing, and his eyes bright blue.

Tired and wounded, the mage stood no chance against the skill and power of Xavier. Each strike carried purpose, causing the mage to crumble under the relentless assault. Her bone club shattered, sending splinters of bone everywhere.

The mage dropped to her knees, then threw her sword away. "Mercy, please?"

"You're too dangerous to be left alive," Xavier declared.

The mage let out a deafening scream and lunged up to stab Xavier with a concealed dagger. However, the king, undeterred, lunged backwards and swung his sword, cutting the mage in half from the waist. Xavier didn't flinch at the spraying blood or the dying screams of the mage. He knelt down and set her ablaze.

"Are you okay, Father?" Artoria asked gingerly as she helped her sister walk.

Xavier wiped his sword and returned it to its scabbard, then walked over to his daughters. Ignoring Artoria's question, he took Liliana's arm and pulled her away from Artoria, beginning to heal her head wound.

"Your lust for glory and recognition almost got your sister killed," Xavier said, barely acknowledging Artoria.

"Why was she fighting on her own?" Artoria shouted.

"This is sacred ground, and anything said or agreed must be honoured," Belthazor explained as he limped into the hall.

"I want out of this place," Artoria said, dismissing what was said.

She stormed outside the hall and Liliana followed gingerly to talk with her sister.

"Xavier, I must speak with you," Belthazor said.

After ten minutes passed, Xavier exited the hall. Belthazor watched on as Xavier joined his daughters.

"Father, is everything okay?" Liliana asked.

"Things are now set in motion," he replied vaguely.

Belthazor let out a booming roar charging up the magic to send them back, their celestial bodies slowly fading from the Exalted Plains.

CHAPTER THIRTY-EIGHT

LESSONS

Three days passed from the death of Delilah's head mage in the Exalted Plains, and Xavier and the knights of Malsdon took full advantage of this vital moment. Darius and Artoria led a few men to sweep and lockdown the Emerald Meadows, while Xavier and Liliana were making final preparations before heading to the Vermillion Sands to destroy Delilah's main spawning grounds.

"I still think you should bring more people with you," Isabella said adamantly.

Liliana sighed as she finished packing her saddlebag.

"Excuse me, Xavier," Isabella said, glaring at him.

"The two of us will have a better chance of getting in unseen," he replied as he fed Saya.

Isabella stormed over to Xavier and stood beside him. "Keep her safe," she said.

"With my life," he replied.

"Both of you come back to me," she added, squeezing Xavier's hand.

"We will," he said as he brushed her hair to the side to kiss her on the cheek.

Liliana mounted her horse, followed by Xavier getting onto Saya's back.

"Keep an eye on Grandmother," Liliana chuckled.

"I will," Isabella replied with a smile.

Xavier looked back and forth at both of them with confusion.

"It's a long story," Liliana smirked, then whipped the reins to move her horse.

"One more step, my dear," Xavier said to Isabella before he moved off.

*

The ground shook, trees exploded, and body parts soared through the air like birds of prey as Artoria unleashed her full power against the last isolated pockets of Fallen throughout the Emerald Meadows. The soldiers looked on in awe at her display of destructive power. However, Darius sensed great anger and frustration from his granddaughter.

"Lady Artoria, that was great!" a few men shouted as they walked past her.

Artoria smiled and then rolled her eyes.

"You won't make many friends with that attitude," Darius said.

"So, this old village was under your rule?" she asked, changing the subject.

Darius knew better than to press her on her actions and emotions. "It was a wonderful village, full of life, and the villagers threw great parties," he replied.

"You joined in?"

"Yes, and your father came along a few times," he added as he drifted towards the memories of the past.

"Grandfather, are you okay?" she asked.

"My dear, you must empower your people, respect all, and share the bounties of the land, and only then will you be loved and respected by your people," Darius said.

"Grandfather, I—"

"My lord, the village is secured, and barriers have been placed," a soldier interrupted.

"Very good. Loan me five men. I'm going to check the manor," Darius replied.

The soldiers nodded and ran to collect the men.

"Can I come along?" Artoria asked.

Darius smiled and put his arm around Artoria. "Tiberius is waiting for us."

*

"Father, what will happen when this is all over?" Liliana asked as they rode along the outskirts of the Emerald Meadows.

"With all my might and strength, I'll make sure that my daughters and my wife are safe," he said.

Liliana looked at her father's face after he spoke, noticing an expression of sadness.

"Father, what aren't you telling me?" she asked.

"Nothing. Let's pick up the pace," he replied before Saya accelerated.

Xavier's comment lingered with her for a few moments, and she gripped the reins tightly as her horse picked up speed.

*

"The Leo manor," Darius said as they approached the vine-infested gate.

Overgrown bushes covered the paths towards the manor, and wildflowers grew between the cracks of the stone ground in the courtyard.

Artoria observed the joy the rundown manor brought to Darius. She sensed the flood of memories returning to him.

"It will take some work, but we'll get it back to its former glory," she said, attempting to connect emotionally with Darius.

Darius turned his head and smiled. "Yes, we will. This manor, the Emerald Meadows, and the whole of Malsdon will return to its former glory."

Darius froze as they stood in front of the worn oak doors. Artoria could sense the overwhelming emotions flowing through Darius, wondering why he couldn't open the door. "Should I open it for you?" she asked.

Darius shook his head, took in a deep breath, and pushed open the doors. They creaked and groaned as they swung open; the echo of nothing and the sweeping dust hit them at the door.

"Make sure there are no surprises," Darius commanded the men as they flooded in.

The men shouted "clear" as the last room was checked. Artoria started to wander around the manor, taking in all the history soaked into the walls. She ended up stumbling into the war room where Darius was seated at the table.

"This room was the start of many battles and wars," Darius said as he patted the tabletop.

"A round table, but you're the head of the house?" Artoria asked as she took a seat.

"Everyone who sat at this table, I saw them as my equals. When we die, we all end up in the ground together; only a title makes us different."

"Grandfather, would you teach me the ways?"

"Of course. Why not your father?"

"He favours Liliana. That's why he took her to the Vermillion Sands and not me."

"There will be a lot of sick and injured people trapped there. Don't you think your sister is more suited to deal with that?" he asked.

Artoria went quiet and dropped her head. "I'm useless."

"No, you're not. Do you think I could fight a mage on my own?"

Artoria shook her head.

"But you can, and that's why you're here with us. Everyone has a purpose, my dear," Darius said.

CHAPTER THIRTY-NINE

ONE OF MANY

Deep pits of black rain littered the ground where the famous bazaar of the Vermillion Sands used to be. Tents made from torn fabric were scattered in the distance, surrounded by an iron fence.

"This would destroy Sabrina," Xavier whispered as he continued looking through his telescopic looking glass.

"Father, I sense many low-level mages down there."

Xavier nodded and started to detach his swords and other items that could identify him then placed them on Saya, instructing Liliana to do the same.

"If things turn bad, Saya will come for us. Until then, we have our magic and wit to protect us."

Liliana started to rub dirt and other foul things onto her clothes.

"One step ahead, I see," Xavier said as he began doing the same.

The two slowly made their way into the camp; conditions were terrible, with food left out in the open exposed to direct sunlight, and water kept next to the waste pit.

"Old man, what happened here?" Xavier asked.

"You must be new here," he replied.

"I was knocked on the head and lost all memory," Xavier explained.

"That would do it," the old man chuckled. "Well, every afternoon they take people to the pits and turn them into those creatures."

"The Fallen," Liliana whispered.

"Yes, but now they're taking more people than usual. I heard their other pit in the Meadows got destroyed."

"Where do they take them?" Xavier asked.

"To the palace, where Delilah is massing her army," the old man said.

"You have my thanks, old man," Xavier said as he offered his hand.

The old man shook his hand firmly. "I knew you would come for us."

Xavier paused for a moment.

"Don't worry," the man said, "I won't tell a soul. Just get this filth out of Malsdon for good."

*

It was late afternoon when the enemy circled the camp, collecting people for the process.

"Make sure those who are able to fight are ready and watch for my signal," Xavier explained.

"Wait, what signal?" Liliana asked.

"You'll know it when you see it."

Xavier staggered into the path of an incoming mage, knocking them to the ground. The other mage rushed over and restrained him.

"Big and strong, he'll go first," the mage declared as he stood up, delivering a punch to Xavier's gut.

Liliana watched as they took her father and many others away. She clenched her fist and began spreading the word of revolt. She made her way to the back of the camp to a large tent. It looked cleaner and better made than the others.

"Be careful, young one. They're not to be trusted," an old lady said as she shuffled past.

Liliana turned back to find out more but the old lady was nowhere in sight. She took a deep breath and entered the tent. Inside, fur pelts covered the floor, and a massive circular table dominated the space. Seated at the table were five men, dressed in clean and well-maintained clothing in stark contrast to the rest of the camp. Women servants attended to their every command.

"You there, do you wish to have a better life?" one of the men shouted.

Liliana remained silent, surveying the surroundings.

"Little girl, I'm talking to you!" he shouted, abruptly standing and knocking his drink off the table.

The other four men rose with him. One of them snapped his fingers, signalling a servant to clean up the mess.

"As you were so rude, she will be punished because of you," one of them declared.

The leader of the group ordered the servant to lick the drink off the floor, and the men laughed, throwing bits of food at her.

"So, girl, I'll ask you again. What do you want?"

"I want a better life for me and everyone."

"What's your name?"

"Liliana, and it will be the last name you ever hear."

The men laughed and picked up various sharp items from the table.

"Let's kill this little rat!" one of the men shouted.

Liliana's eyes glowed brightly as tears of anger trickled down her face.

"She's a witch!" another man shouted.

Before they could reach Liliana, she hurled the table, crushing most of the men. Two of them tried crawling away but were stopped by the servant girls, who held them down and started beating them. Liliana walked past and grabbed the leader by the neck.

"I have three questions for you. Answer them, and I'll give you a quick death," she said through gritted teeth.

*

Xavier and a few others were led out into the open desert where the pits of black rain lay. The mage group talked and laughed among themselves, paying no notice to their captives, confident there was nowhere to run.

Xavier glanced back at his fellow men and saw emptiness in their eyes, their heads hanging low, and their feet dragging through the golden sand. Xavier knew he would have to dispatch their captors quickly to boost morale and start a chain reaction. To their right, more people were on their way to be processed.

"Eight in total," he mumbled to himself.

One of the prisoners behind him lifted their head. "Don't try anything; you're no match for magic."

"What was your profession?" Xavier asked, continuing to walk forwards.

"Sword for hire, before everything went sideways."

"Something is going to happen. I need you to lead the people back to camp and protect them."

"Hold on, don't do anything stupid, my friend," he cautioned Xavier.

Xavier chuckled as his eyes glowed, melting the metal bonds that bound him. "Run now!"

*

Liliana wandered around the camp with purpose, nodding at each person who crossed her path. They nodded back, awaiting the signal.

"When will it happen?" the servant girl asked her.

Suddenly, a loud bang echoed across the desert sand, followed by a breathtaking shockwave that knocked many off their feet.

"Now, the fight for Malsdon starts!" Liliana shouted as she

helped the servant girl to her feet.

Screams and cries of anger and rage bellowed as the people charged their captors, who were still stunned by what was taking place. A few of them were taken by surprise; bodies of camp members started flying through the sky as the mages gathered their bearings.

Liliana led the weak and vulnerable away from the fighting towards the direction of the Emerald Meadows.

"What about those left fighting in the camp?" a lady asked.

"I must get you close to safety first!" Liliana replied.

Her group didn't get far from the camp before they were stopped in their tracks by three mages and over two hundred Fallen.

"What are we going to do?" a few people muttered.

Liliana stepped three paces in front of the group, clenching both fists. Her eyes glowed brightly, ready for anything and willing to do whatever it took.

"Return to the camp now, you worthless things!" one of the mages shouted.

"They're leaving with me!" Liliana replied.

"Who do you think you are?" a different mage shouted, waving her sword at Liliana.

"I am Liliana Lucius Leo, daughter of the true king and queen of Malsdon, and you will be put to death for the treatment of my people."

The passion in her words uplifted the people behind her, and they began to shout and curse at the mages and the Fallen before them.

"Royalty or not, you will all die the same!" the mage shouted.

Liliana's group started moving forwards, ready to fight the Fallen and mages with their bare hands if needed. However, their progress was brought to a halt as a wave of lightning rushed towards them. Instinctively, Liliana threw up a protective barrier dome, shielding everyone within from a painful death.

The lightning continued to beat against the barrier like a drum, while explosions echoed in the desert, causing them to flinch.

"We're helpless!" many cried.

Liliana looked back at faces that were once filled with confidence, now filled with fear. She knew she had to hold the barrier up for as long as possible.

The mages nodded at each other, and one raised his free hand, signalling the Fallen to attack. Panic set in as many tried to flee, beating on the barrier from within.

"Stop, you're not helping matters," a lady shouted.

"We're going to die," many cried.

"Please stop," a tired Liliana said, rivers of sweat pouring from her face.

The group settled for a moment before the Fallen began to beat against the barrier. Deafening screams pierced the eardrums and the soul.

"Liliana, please hold on," an old lady said.

Liliana looked back at her. "We've met before, your voice…"

Before Liliana could finish her sentence, her mind went blank as she started to drift away, dropping to one knee, trying to fight the urge to give in.

A roar so deep and booming it could cause the heart to skip many beats bellowed towards them. This shook Liliana to her feet, and the sight of Saya crashing into the Fallen gave everyone inside the dome hope. Suddenly, the ground shook violently, tossing the three mages into the air and knocking others, including those in the dome, to their knees.

As the dust settled, Xavier stood in front of the three mages, while Saya fought off the Fallen.

"We have to help Saya!" Liliana shouted.

She dropped the barrier and sent a shockwave, knocking over the Fallen who were closest to the dome. Liliana charged out with all her strength towards Saya and grabbed her sword off the lion's back. The people followed, energetic and full of belief, as Liliana and Saya fought the Fallen beside them.

Screams, the roars of violence, and the cries of pain trickled into Xavier's ears, but his focus remained on the three standing before him. His long sword was tightly gripped in his right hand, and his stance was loose, inviting overconfidence from his opponents. The three mages drew their oddly shaped swords and began to walk slowly towards Xavier, their free hands ready to strike with magic at any moment.

Xavier started walking towards them, bringing his sword above his head, holding it with both hands. In doing so, he exposed his chest to them. One mage became bold and charged at Xavier while shooting lightning bolts at him. The lightning struck Xavier in the chest, but it had little to no effect. The other two tried to call their companion back, but it was too late.

Xavier and the mage engaged in close combat. Xavier quickly gained the upper hand, dominating the mage. The other two mages didn't watch idly by; they quickly moved over to help their fellow mage. Xavier held his ground, but the more they used their magic, the more the advantage tipped in their favour.

Xavier sent out a shockwave to push them back, gaining a momentary breather.

"Look, he's getting tired and scared!" one of them shouted.

They all laughed and increased the pressure with each sword swing and magical blast.

Liliana looked on at her father, desperate to help him. However, Xavier put his hand up to stop her. She was surprised, as he didn't look back at her, but he could sense her anxiety.

Xavier was slowly losing the fight, primarily on the defensive, and desperation started creeping in. He knew that if he fell now, his daughter and the others would be in great danger. Sensing this, the mages set a trap for Xavier.

One of the mages led the engagement and purposely allowed Xavier to strike him down with a violent but desperate swing.

This left Xavier's back open, and he was blind to who was on his left. The second mage swung wildly at Xavier's back, and without thinking, Xavier spun to the left to dodge the blow. Then came the sound of flesh being torn and blood staining the sand. Xavier looked down at the sword that had been rammed into his gut, then up at the mage, her rotting black teeth grinning.

Liliana looked on, screaming, as the mage pulled the sword out and kicked Xavier to the ground. She tried to push through the Fallen who blocked her path, but to no avail. However, that didn't stop Saya, who bounded over the group and charged the two mages who remained.

Bolts of lightning struck Saya many times as she charged in her rage-filled fury. The mages panicked as she approached, sending several more volleys before Saya abruptly stopped in her tracks.

Xavier looked on as he struggled to rise to one knee, attempting to heal his wound but to no avail. For his efforts, the mages blasted him with another bolt of lightning, knocking him flat on his back.

One of the mages walked then stood over Xavier with her sword pressed against his chest ready to end his life. Xavier tried kicking her legs out, but the other mage drove his sword into Xavier's leg.

The mage smiled again as she lifted her sword in the air to deliver a fatal blow. But she paused for a second as something caught her attention—a faint whistling. Then there was a high-pitched scream as the mage dropped to the ground, a silver arrow stuck in her chest.

The other mage panicked and stumbled about before a silver arrow brought him to the ground as well. Then came the sound of the Malsdon battle horn, bellowing from afar. Xavier looked up, and in the distance, he saw the glimmering silver armour of thirty riders heading towards him.

The last mage alive tried to pull the arrow out, but the pure silver burnt his hands with every attempt. He then saw Xavier attempting to get to his feet again, holding his wound shut with one hand. The mage grabbed Xavier's sword from the ground and dragged himself over to Xavier.

Another arrow whistled through the air, but the mage deflected it with a swing of the sword. "Now it's time for you to join the dead," the mage said as blood spat out from his mouth. He swung the sword, narrowly missing Xavier's head.

Screaming in pain and anger, Xavier jumped up and grabbed the mage from behind. He seized the sword on the blade with one hand and the other over the mage's hand. With all the strength he had left, he threw his body back as he pulled back on the blade. The mage was helpless as the blade passed through his body, cutting it in half.

Xavier hit the ground hard, unable to move due to blood loss and exhaustion. The sight of River's long silver hair was most comforting as she started to close in.

River jumped off her horse and ordered her men to continue on, to help Liliana and the others.

"You're a mess," River said as she packed Xavier's wound with cloth.

"It happens when everyone wants you dead," Xavier mumbled through the pain.

"Can't you heal yourself?"

Xavier shook his head in response, then looked towards Liliana.

River stopped one of the last riders before he entered the fight.

"Yes, Commander?" he asked.

"Bring Liliana here at once," she ordered.

The rider sped off towards the fight. However, before the rider made it halfway, through the dust emerged Saya with Liliana riding hard towards Xavier.

"Oh no, Father," Liliana said as she jumped off Saya.

"Quick, girl," River said.

"Don't panic the girl. It's fine," Xavier whispered.

Liliana knelt down beside Xavier and placed her hand over the wound.

"Calm your mind and breathing. I'm not dying, don't rush," Xavier said calmly as he looked up at Liliana's worried eyes.

Liliana took a deep breath and began to heal Xavier. The wound closed up quickly, and colour began to return to Xavier's face.

"Remarkable," River whispered as she watched Liliana's magic at work.

The battle horn sounded again as River and Liliana helped Xavier to his feet.

"Look, Father, the Fallen are running away," Liliana said as she pointed at them.

River and Xavier turned their attention to the Fallen.

"Not running. They're being ordered back," Xavier said.

"She's getting desperate," River chuckled.

"What's the plan, Father?" Liliana asked.

Xavier contemplated for a moment as he picked up his sword. "Time is against us. We have to end Delilah while she's weak, and she knows this as well."

"She's going to have a wall of Fallen in front of her," River added.

"I'm not worried about that; it's the Fallen on the Forgotten Island," Xavier said.

River was about to brush off Xavier's comment until she realised. "They're still in control of the Iron Coast."

"Ships and the followers of Delilah will easily get there and back with ships full of them," he added.

"We must go now," Liliana said.

"That mission is for others," Xavier replied, "We must rest, then push on to the palace with the main army."

"The main army will be staging in the Meadows," River said.

"Very well. Those unable to bear arms will be sent to the Silver Hills, and everyone else to the Meadows," Xavier ordered.

River nodded and went off to give out the orders.

"Who will take control of the docks?" Liliana asked.

"I'm going to inform them now," Xavier replied.

CHAPTER FORTY

THE WISDOM OF OTHERS

Artoria sat in the courtyard, petting Tiberius as the wind blew the leaves, making them dance under the sun. The creaking of the large oak doors as they opened caught their attention.

"We've got a job to do," Darius said.

"It's so peaceful here," Artoria replied.

Darius sat next to her and Tiberius, taking in a deep breath. "It cleanses the soul and mind."

"What's the mission?" she asked.

Darius waved over one of the guards. "Assemble fifty men and bring large shields."

"Tell me, Grandfather."

"We're to take control of the Iron Coast and stop Fallen reinforcements from landing," he said.

"Were there a lot of Fallen left on the island?"

"Too many," he whispered. Darius smiled as he patted Artoria on the back. "Let's go."

*

Darius stood in the middle of a circle formed by his men as they awaited the battle plan. Artoria stood in the centre as well, feeling nervous to stand next to Darius, whose aura was powerful and demanded respect.

"We know there is one main street that leads all the way to the docks," Darius said, "That's where the shields come into play.

Two lines of shield wall, and we force our way to the docks."

"What about the side alleys?" a soldier asked.

"Those not in the wall will have to cover the flanks and rear," Darius replied.

The soldier nodded, along with a few others.

"Finally, Artoria will be on the rooftops, covering us from above and keeping an eye out for mages. Any questions?"

The men remained silent and ready to go.

"Very well. Board the wagons and prepare to move out," he ordered.

The men broke the circle and boarded their respective wagons.

"Grandfather, I wanted to fight at the front," Artoria said.

Darius gave her a stern look, then said calmly, "Your eagerness to fight is both admirable and dangerous. The role you have been assigned is perfect for you. How could you use your powers or spot mages before they attack us if you're stuck in the shield wall?"

"I need to prove—"

"Prove what?" Darius cut her off. "You have nothing to prove to anyone, and you only have to see that because everyone else does. Keep your mind and feelings clear."

Artoria said nothing as she jumped on a different wagon from Darius.

Darius sighed and ordered the convoy to move out.

The convoy dashed along the beaten path as the sun began to set on the day where many lives would be in the hands of the few. Artoria sat there, deep in thought.

"I always get pushed aside with these pitiful assignments," she said to herself. Artoria looked around at the men with some smiling back at her with others checking their weapons, then at the wagon in front where Darius was. "They don't value my power."

"No, they don't, my dear," a voice said to her.

Startled, Artoria wildly looked around for the female voice, but she was one of four females on this mission, and the others were in the last wagon. "Who are you?" she asked.

"I've sensed your pain, my child," the voice replied.

Artoria said nothing back, feeling a bit scared and wary of what was happening.

"I'm like you: powerful, beautiful, and hated by many," the voice said.

"I'm not hated," Artoria replied defiantly.

"Let me tell you a story, my dear."

"Be quick about it."

"People like us were hunted down by men and gigas beasts over a mistake. We tried saving the queen during childbirth, but we failed and were framed for her death. Many were killed, including my husband," the voice said.

"The Mage Wars… you're Delilah," Artoria said sharply.

"I have to tell you my side of the story. You can't trust everything your family tells you," Delilah replied. "I have one more story to tell you, and it's about your parents."

"I already know what happened and what you did."

"Did they tell you everything?"

"No, I saw everything in my father's mind."

"Only the stuff he wanted you to see."

"You won't turn me against my mother," Artoria said, beginning to feel frustrated.

"Your father wasn't meant to marry your mother but her sister Arabella. Your mother was married to Ginn Graw, but your father was secretly seeing your mother and ruined everything. Darius and the king knew of this and did nothing," Delilah said.

"I never knew it was meant to be that way," Artoria said softly.

"Yes, my dear. So Ginn asked me for help to save the kingdom from the traitor Xavier, who only wanted the throne, and your mother who was already married. Ginn was meant to be your father, my dear."

"How did he die?" Artoria asked.

"Murdered by Darius and his fleabag lion."

"I don't know what to say."

"It's okay, my dear. I tried saving you and your sister with the help of your aunt Arabella, but she was killed by your mother."

"I can't hear any more."

"Think about everything I've told you. I'm too weak, and your father and sister will definitely destroy you for good. You can be the most powerful, but it's up to you," Delilah said as her voice faded.

"Artoria!" Darius shouted, "We're waiting for you!"

Artoria shook her head to see everyone was standing around the wagon, ready and waiting for her.

"Move out!" Darius ordered the men. "Are you okay?" he asked when everyone was out of earshot.

"I'll do what needs to be done," Artoria said bluntly.

"Remember, we all have a purpose in this war," Darius said, trying to appeal to Artoria's pride.

Artoria nodded at Darius and drew her sword as she walked away.

Fire from the torches reflected off their shields and armour as they marched in formation towards the town. Tiberius was on high alert, scanning the forest for any surprises. The men all felt at ease with the mighty lion with them, his bright emerald eyes piercing the pitch-black background.

"The town, straight ahead," a soldier whispered.

"The hard part is not over yet," Darius said, pointing to the entrance of town.

The entrance was littered with Fallen who were just standing there, not moving.

"It's strange they're not moving," a soldier said.

"Meat shields to slow us from the dock," Artoria said as she pushed through to the front.

"If you push them back, we can quickly get into a shield wall and begin the push to the docks," Darius said to Artoria.

"With pleasure," she replied with a sinister smile. Artoria let out a violent scream, and a powerful shockwave followed, throwing the Fallen in every direction.

"Let's go!" Darius shouted.

The men formed the shield wall, and the slow march began. However, Artoria was in front of the wall, not listening to Darius' calls to head to the rooftops. Instead, she used her magic to destroy anything in her path.

Picking off the scraps left behind from Artoria's path, Darius and the group followed closely behind.

"My lord, she's out of control, and she'll get tired keeping this up," a knight whispered to Darius.

"I know. We'll have to quickly grab her if she falls," Darius replied, the annoyance from Artoria's actions evident in his voice.

The group made good progress through the town, and Artoria showed no signs of tiring. However, randomly, a soldier would drop from exhaustion and be unable to move. Panic began to creep in as they thought a mage was hiding in one of the buildings, picking them off one by one.

Darius looked over at Tiberius, as the lion would be the first, other than Artoria, to sense a mage, but he was focused on the Fallen. Darius then looked towards Artoria. "She couldn't be…"

Suddenly, two more soldiers dropped, who were standing next to him.

"Artoria!" he shouted.

Artoria turned around, her eyes as black as a starless night, blending in with the darkness behind her. It was like looking into nothing.

Darius ordered his men to stop, and Tiberius quickly jumped next to him, sensing the new evil energy. "Artoria, what are you doing?" Darius asked calmly.

"Since my father has come back, I've been undermined. I'm the strongest, and yet I'm overlooked!"

The Fallen had grouped up behind her as if they were waiting for her orders.

"Look at what you're doing to your fellow men and look what

you're turning into."

"I know the whole truth. You and my father are traitors. Delilah told me everything!" she shouted again, but this time the ground shook ever so slightly.

"My lord, the ships are coming into view," a knight whispered to Darius.

"Artoria, she has poisoned your mind against us. Delilah started this war, and the one before, over jealousy," Darius explained calmly after feeling her anger.

"Mother, Father, and you are not innocent, and I wouldn't have had to grow up like this if it wasn't for the actions all of you set in motion."

"You would kill your own family?" Darius asked as he lowered his sword.

Silence fell upon the town. All that could be heard was the breathing of the living.

"If I must," Artoria said.

Artoria sent the Fallen charging into Darius and his men, turning what was a mission to secure the docks into a fight for their lives. She watched Darius and Tiberius carefully as the fighting took place, shadows of limbs being severed and blood spraying casting eerie silhouettes in the fire-lit street. Fully engulfed by hate and rage fuelled by Delilah's poisonous words, Artoria started picking off soldiers one by one, killing them instantly or throwing them into buildings.

"Sir, we have to stop her!" a knight shouted over the sound of battle.

Darius looked at Artoria, hesitating whether to order Tiberius to intervene.

"Sir, we must do something!" the knight shouted as he shook Darius by the shoulders.

"That's my granddaughter, my son's daughter. I can't kill her," Darius said.

Morale plummeted as the group was relentlessly pushed back

by the onslaught of the Fallen and Artoria's devastating magic. Suddenly, Tiberius was hurled through the air, crashing straight through a brick house. Artoria's twisted smile met Darius' gaze as shards of glass and brick rained down upon his men, injuring and disorienting them amidst the chaos and dust.

In the midst of the tumult, the Fallen swarmed in, mercilessly dispatching those who were injured or incapacitated. Panic gripped the survivors, and those who were still standing began to flee in a desperate attempt to escape the carnage.

But Artoria couldn't afford to leave any witnesses behind. With a grim determination, she unleashed her power once more, bringing down what remained of the building upon them, sealing their fate beneath a crushing avalanche of debris.

The aftermath of the battle left Artoria standing over the injured Darius, his body battered and broken but his spirit still defiant. Despite his grievous wounds, he faced Artoria with a steely resolve.

"You stand before me now with your newfound power and allies. What fate do you have in store for me?" he asked, his voice heavy with resignation.

"You have failed, and your time has come to an end," Artoria said, her tone cold and unwavering.

Amidst the rubble, a weak roar echoed, drawing Artoria's attention. She watched as Tiberius emerged from the debris, his body battered and broken, yet his loyalty to Darius unyielding. The injured lion limped over to his master, placing himself protectively in front of him.

"Tiberius, go, warn the others," Darius urged, attempting to push the loyal lion away.

Despite the fragments embedded in his flesh and blood staining his fur, Tiberius refused to leave Darius' side, demonstrating unwavering loyalty.

Artoria, unmoved by the display, advanced towards them, her sword poised for the final blow. However, in a sudden act of defiance, Tiberius lunged at Artoria, catching her off guard and pinning her to the ground. With a desperate act of sacrifice, Tiberius sank his teeth into Artoria's shoulder, momentarily incapacitating her.

But the respite was brief. As Artoria drove her dagger straight into his heart then shoved Tiberius off of her, Darius sank to his knees, watching in anguish as his faithful companion's lifeforce slowly faded.

"Dirty animal," Artoria spat, callously dismissing Tiberius' sacrifice.

Darius' voice, soft but filled with sorrow, pierced the air. "You tread a path from which there is no return. When the others learn of your deeds, they will seek your end," he said, his words a solemn prophecy of the inevitable consequences of her actions.

The chilling presence of Delilah interrupted the solemn aftermath of the battle, her voice like an ominous harbinger of darkness. Artoria's smile at the sight of her arrival hinted at a disturbing alliance, one that sent shivers down Darius' spine.

"I know that voice," Darius muttered, his gaze falling upon Delilah's frail form cloaked in darkness. Despite her weakened appearance, the malevolence in her eyes was unmistakable.

"The years haven't been kind to you." His voice was tinged with bitterness as he observed Delilah's deteriorated state.

Delilah's response was cryptic yet revealing. "All my powers have been passed on to my children, and my last gift bestowed upon my chosen one," she explained, her gaze shifting towards Artoria.

Darius' anger flared as he lashed out at Delilah, his futile attempt to stab her was met with swift retaliation from Artoria. With a merciless display of force, Artoria subdued Darius, leaving him vulnerable to Delilah's sinister intentions.

As Delilah knelt over Darius, her hand morphing into a lethal weapon, Darius braced himself for the inevitable. The sharp pain of betrayal pierced his heart as Delilah plunged her makeshift blade into his chest, injecting darkness into his veins.

Struggling against the encroaching darkness, Darius fought to resist Delilah's control, but her power was overwhelming. With a sense of resignation, he succumbed to the darkness, his once defiant spirit subdued into docility.

Delilah's laughter echoed through the night, a chilling testament to her triumph. Artoria, unsettled by the sight of Darius' transformation, questioned Delilah's intentions for him.

"I will put him to good use," Delilah said ominously, her eyes gleaming with malevolent purpose. With a final command to Artoria, she instructed her to maintain the illusion of an ambush, ensuring their enemies remained unaware of their true alliance.

Artoria watched Delilah and Darius fade into the wind. She looked around at the damage and dead bodies then towards the docks where one ship had made port and the captain was walking up the road to speak to her.

"My lady, I assume we're under your command," the captain said.

"Why would you think that?" she asked.

"We saw everything, and Delilah told us," he replied.

Artoria nodded, then stood pondering her next move. "You need to return to the Forgotten Lands."

"What? We just arrived, and the ships are laden with the Fallen."

"Listen to me. It must appear as though we completed the mission and you never made it ashore," Artoria replied.

"That wasn't the plan!" the captain shouted.

Artoria's expression hardened, and she seized the captain by his throat. "You must listen. Delilah's time is running out, and I will assume command. Return to the island and await my orders."

She threw the captain to the ground and pointed towards the ship. The captain scrambled back aboard, fearing Artoria's wrath, to allow her plan to proceed.

Artoria swiftly scanned the soldiers to confirm their demise, but some began to transform into the Fallen. She seized a sharp object and inflicted wounds upon herself, piercing her stomach and leg, before seeking refuge beneath the rubble of the collapsed building.

"Father, I need your aid," she whispered, reaching out to Xavier's mind.

*

"River, ensure the army is prepared to mobilise!" Xavier's voice echoed across the camp as he dragged a horse from the makeshift stables.

"Father, what's happening?" Liliana asked, rising to her feet and trailing behind him.

"Something is wrong. Your sister is in peril," Xavier replied, patting the horse's flank as a silent command for Liliana to mount.

Saya approached, awaiting Xavier's signal.

"River, if you don't hear from me at sunrise, proceed to the palace and rescue Malsdon!" Xavier ordered, swinging onto Saya's back.

River nodded, signalling for the rally horn to be blown.

CHAPTER FORTY-ONE

BLINDED BY THE DARK

Xavier and Liliana reached the edge of town, shrouded under the night sky, while torches scattered on the ground illuminated the lurking Fallen within.

"Father, look at all the men," Liliana said, gesturing towards the horde of Fallen.

"I can't spot my father or Artoria," Xavier replied, scanning the chaotic scene.

Liliana extended her hand, reaching out for her sister. "I found her!" she said, darting into town with Xavier close behind, clearing a path with precise shockwave energy shots.

Liliana's horse ploughed through the Fallen, kicking aside any who dared to grab her, while Liliana herself pointed towards the collapsed building. She leapt from her horse and swiftly dispatched any Fallen near the rubble.

"Liliana, create a protective barrier. Saya and I will extract her," Xavier commanded.

Artoria stirred, greeted by Saya's bright green eyes and dusty face. As Saya moved aside, Xavier's hand replaced paws.

"Take my hand!" he shouted.

Artoria slowly extended both hands through the opening.

"Close your eyes," Xavier said as he pulled her through the gap.

Artoria sat quietly as Liliana tended to her wounds.

"You could have bled out," Liliana admonished gently.

"Thank you for saving me," Artoria murmured.

Xavier knelt beside her, brushing the dirt and dust from her hair.

"Your hair looks like River's," Liliana said.

Artoria chuckled softly, then reached for her father's hand. "I did my best," she whispered.

"I know," he replied.

"I couldn't stop her."

"Stop who?"

"Delilah."

"What happened to Father and Tiberius?" he pressed.

Artoria's tears began to flow, and Xavier stood, scanning their surroundings anxiously. Saya growled as footsteps approached, but the Fallen did not attack.

"Why aren't they attacking us?" Artoria asked.

Liliana shook her head. "I don't know."

As the figure drew closer, Saya backed away, trembling with fear. Xavier reached out to calm the frightened creature, but his surprise turned to dread as a familiar deep roar echoed through the air.

"Oh no, Tiberius." Xavier's heart sank. "Get your sister and go back now!"

Tiberius continued his advance.

"We can help!" Artoria protested.

"No, we must obey Father," Liliana insisted, pulling her sister towards the horse.

"Both of you are the future. If I fall, you must kill Delilah!" Xavier shouted after them.

Liliana and Artoria raced past Tiberius on horseback, but the monstrous lion paid them no heed. Xavier moved to intervene, but Saya halted him, pressing her paw against his foot before stepping forwards to confront Tiberius. This was more than a mere skirmish for Saya—it was a battle for dominance, for the alpha position among them. However, the odds were stacked heavily against her. Tiberius was twice her size and now transformed into a Fallen beast, making him nearly impossible to defeat without severing his head.

With a deafening roar, Tiberius shook the rubble around them, but Saya responded with a deep, resonant roar of her own. Xavier felt a shiver run down his spine, understanding the significance of this primal exchange and the stakes involved. He knew what was about to unfold would be a brutal and horrific battle, driven by instinct and survival.

The two lions violently clashed, their heads shaking rigorously from side to side as each attempted to bite down on the other. Their golden fur was stained with both their own blood and that of their opponent. Despite Saya maintaining the upper hand against Tiberius, her blows and bites would have caused a living lion to crumble. However, Tiberius was no longer part of the living; although her attacks were damaging his body, he felt no pain. Xavier watched nervously as his lion fought on, recognising the great power and purpose behind her every move.

The fight continued unabated, neither lion showing any signs of backing down. Xavier could discern that Saya was losing energy, her strength waning as she bled profusely—a disadvantage that would affect her more than Tiberius.

"Saya, you have to immobilise him!"

The two lions faced each other, Saya panting heavily while Tiberius remained seemingly unfazed. With a determined charge, Saya lunged at Tiberius, pinning him to the ground in an attempt to deliver a fatal blow. Despite tearing into his neck, Tiberius persisted. Using his hind legs, he forcefully launched Saya off him, propelling her into a nearby building and causing the windows to shatter from the impact.

Tiberius turned his attention to Xavier, slowly advancing with bared teeth. Xavier braced himself, charging his sword with magic until it emitted an azure glow, illuminating the area around them. As Tiberius prepared to charge, Saya burst out through the shattered window with a bone-shattering roar, diverting Tiberius' focus back to her. The two lions resumed their ferocious battle, further staining the ground and their fur with blood.

Xavier's anxiety heightened as he observed Saya's visible exhaustion. "Finish it, Saya!"

Saya understood her fatal bites were proving ineffective against Tiberius, especially given her numerous wounds and substantial loss of blood at this stage of the fight.

The two lions squared off once more, Tiberius charging in for a fatal bite. Saya agilely dodged his attack, then reared up on her hind legs. Her eyes blazed with intensity as she raised her right paw and swiftly swiped down at Tiberius' hip, causing the lion to collapse. Another roar erupted from Saya as Tiberius dragged himself across the ground, his hip shattered by the force of the blow.

Saya swiftly pinned him down, one paw on his head and the other on his shoulder, and began tearing into his neck, ripping away chunks of flesh until she reached bone. Xavier turned away, unable to witness Tiberius being torn apart in such a brutal manner. With Tiberius' spinal column exposed, Saya tenderly pressed her forehead against his as a final gesture of love and respect before delivering the fatal bite.

Saya let out a deafening roar that echoed through the sky, the sound reverberating for a few moments before she limped towards Xavier and settled beside him. Together, they surveyed the devastation and the fallen Tiberius.

"It's strange how they just stop and disappear," Xavier said. He knelt down and picked up a torch. "Thank you for protecting us all until the very end. May you rest in the evergreen pastures," he whispered before igniting Tiberius' body.

As Tiberius' form began to be consumed by flames, Saya let out another mighty roar. A few tears trickled down their cheeks as they mourned their fallen companion.

"I have to find Father."

CHAPTER FORTY-TWO

THE LIGHT THAT REMAINS

"A rider is approaching!" a guard shouted.

River and Isabella hurried over to see who had returned.

"Mother, what are you doing here?" Liliana asked as the guards helped them off the horse.

"I'm glad you're both okay," River said.

"Where are Xavier and Darius?" Isabella questioned.

"I think Delilah took Darius," Artoria replied.

Liliana fixed her gaze sharply on her sister. "Wait, you said you didn't know what happened."

"Easy, Liliana," River intervened calmly. "Artoria senses that your grandfather was taken, and given Delilah's presence and her attempt on your life, it's likely she's involved."

"Father and Saya were fighting Tiberius as we left the Iron Coast," Artoria added, addressing Isabella's earlier inquiry.

Isabella's and River's expressions fell.

"He became one of the Fallen," Liliana murmured softly.

"No matter what, we march at sunrise and end this evil once and for all. We do it for everyone we lost," River declared, attempting to rally them.

Isabella meet Liliana's longing eyes as they both hoped Xavier and Saya would make it back to them.

*

The sun began to rise as the army of Malsdon made their final preparations. They were wearing new armour: black plates with red trim on the edges, white cloth clothing, silver chainmail, and a black cape or cloak. River and the other officers wore the same but had dark green chainmail and capes or cloaks. The royal family wore the same style of armour. However their plate armour had gold and red trim, gold chainmail, and their capes and cloaks were emerald green with gold and red trim.

"Father still isn't back yet," Liliana said as she and Artoria made their way towards the army.

Suddenly, loud cheering and the banging of shields brought the forest to life.

"I guess that's Father," Artoria replied, her voice lacking enthusiasm.

Liliana dashed off to see for herself, while Artoria rolled her eyes and followed her sister.

"The king returns!" a few soldiers shouted.

Xavier nodded and saluted his men as he walked through.

Isabella stepped into his path with a broad smile. "You both look terrible," she remarked, scanning them up and down.

Xavier chuckled and returned the smile.

Isabella grabbed his hand tightly and pulled him into a hug, eliciting cheers from the entire army. "I'm sorry for what you and Saya went through," she whispered to him.

"I don't know how to describe the feeling," he replied.

Isabella squeezed him tightly. "It's okay, we're going to end this."

"Father, you're okay!" Liliana shouted as she came crashing through the crowd.

Isabella stepped aside and smiled at both her daughters. Xavier opened his arms, and Liliana ran into them. Artoria slowly jogged over, doing the minimum to keep up appearances.

"Are you two ready to end this?" Xavier asked his daughters.

"Yes, Father," they replied in unison.

"King Xavier, you have time to rest and get ready. We can delay the march," Commander Lynch offered.

"No, there's no need. I'll get ready now," Xavier replied as he gave his daughters one last hug before heading towards his tent.

"We'll get Saya ready," Liliana said, leading Saya away towards the stables.

"Feels like yesterday we were getting ready to take the palace back," Isabella said as she watched Xavier put on new clothes.

"Feels like we get new armour every time something major happens," he replied with a chuckle. "The armour?"

Isabella gestured towards the oak chest in the corner of the tent.

Xavier walked over and opened it slowly. "Looks familiar."

"Similar to your previous set with a few small changes," Isabella said.

Xavier first donned the gold and white chainmail shirt, followed by the black leg plates with red trim.

"Still don't like the arm plates?" Isabella asked.

"Yeah, I can't move freely."

Isabella handed him leather wrist guards. "Take these."

"They're lovely."

"Thank you, I made them myself," Isabella said proudly.

With Isabella's assistance, Xavier then put on his chest plate, also black with red trim. At the bottom of the chest lay a black coat with a dagger.

"A gift from Victor and your mother," Isabella explained.

Xavier examined the dagger. "It has all the family crests engraved in the handle."

Isabella smiled. "You've protected everyone in Malsdon more than once and in more than one way."

Xavier squeezed Isabella's hand, his expression softening. "I don't want you to fight in this battle. If anything happens to me…"

Isabella shook her head defiantly. "You've told me this many times, and you know the outcome."

"Isabella—"

"No, this is my home. This country is my home, and I'll fight for it no matter what."

Xavier rolled his eyes playfully before smiling at her. "From helpless princess to warrior queen."

Saya popped her head through the tent door.

"What's that on your head?" Xavier asked.

"It's a helmet, like what the horses wear," Liliana said.

"Victor made it for her along with the body armour," River added as they both poked their heads through the entrance.

Xavier waved them into the tent. Saya's armour colour and pattern matched Xavier's. She sat down next to him and received a pat on the head.

"Are we ready, my lord?" River asked.

"Let's end this. We all deserve peace," Xavier replied solemnly.

"Very well. The army is waiting for you," River said before departing from the tent.

"Mother, Father, I love you both," Liliana said softly, then hurried out of the tent.

"She's nervous," Xavier said.

Isabella nodded. "We all are. It's your job to lift everyone for what comes next."

Artoria found herself grappling with inner turmoil on the other side of the camp, haunted by Delilah's voice and haunted by Darius' last words. "I don't know what to do anymore," she muttered to herself.

With a surge of frustration, she unleashed two shockwaves into an old oak tree, scattering bark and leaves in all directions.

"Artoria, what are you doing?" Liliana's voice cut through her thoughts.

Startled, Artoria turned abruptly, her uncertainty palpable.

"Target practice?" Liliana suggested, noticing Artoria's tense demeanour.

"Yeah, I just want to be ready," Artoria replied, her nerves evident in her voice.

"Let's go. Father is ready."

"I'm coming," Artoria replied, brushing the bark off her armour.

As they made their way towards their father, Delilah's voice whispered hauntingly to Artoria. "Remember, this is just the beginning for you."

"I know what to do!" Artoria shouted aloud, determination overriding her doubts.

"I know you do. It's okay to be nervous. I am too," Liliana replied softly as she turned to face her sister.

"Enough talking, let's go," Artoria said sharply, breaking into a brisk pace and leaving Liliana behind.

CHAPTER FORTY-THREE

FOR ALL WE HOLD DEAR

Xavier stood before the army, flanked by Saya and Isabella, their eager expressions reflecting their readiness to follow his lead. The intensity in their eyes mirrored the determination of the men gathered before them. Xavier glanced at Isabella; she nodded and offered a reassuring smile before directing her attention to the awaiting troops.

"What words can I offer to rally your spirits?" Xavier's voice rang out, filled with conviction. "The atrocities inflicted upon our homes, our families, and our cherished land are enough to fuel our vengeance. This conflict traces back to the mage wars, a legacy of bloodshed that predates many of us standing here. They slew our mothers out of jealousy, and Delilah's relentless return has only fuelled our resolve. But mark my words, this shall be her final reckoning. I swear upon my life to reduce her body and soul to naught but ash and dust."

A thunderous roar erupted from the assembled ranks, their shields clashing against their armour in a symphony of solidarity.

Liliana applauded enthusiastically, while Artoria stood beside her, her gaze fixed on Xavier.

"My daughters, make way for them!" Xavier's voice boomed over the clamour of banging shields.

The soldiers quickly parted, creating a path for the twins to join Xavier, their cheers resounding as they passed through.

Placing his hands firmly on their shoulders, Xavier's voice cut through the din. "They are the reason I never faltered, the reason I refuse to yield to death, and the reason my blade will never tire!" His words echoed amidst the cheers, stirring the men's fervour. "I have my purpose, and each of you must find yours and fight for it with all your heart!"

With a swift motion, Xavier drew his sword, raising it high, and in response, the soldiers mirrored his action, their weapons gleaming in the sunlight.

"For Malsdon!" Liliana's voice rang out above the growing roar of the crowd.

Xavier nodded in acknowledgement to Commander Lynch, who saluted him before leading her scout cavalry ahead of the main army. Then, turning his attention to River, he gave a subtle nod. River responded by blowing the rally horn, its haunting sound cutting through the air.

With renewed vigour, the army began to march, their cheers blending with the rhythmic beat of their footsteps and the stirring melodies of their songs.

"Xavier, we'll attempt to push them back past the common area," River said, "Then hold them in the courtyard."

"That would be the ideal plan. My daughters and I will utilise one of the hidden passages in the courtyard to infiltrate the palace," Xavier replied, his gaze steady and resolute.

River nodded in agreement, then clasped Xavier's hand firmly. "I'll see you on the other side, my friend," she said before riding off towards the front of the army.

Turning to his daughters, Xavier sought their readiness. "Are we prepared?"

Liliana and Artoria exchanged a determined glance before turning their attention back to their father.

"We'll follow you to the end," Liliana said.

"To the very end," Artoria echoed.

Two soldiers stepped forwards, leading three armoured horses towards the trio. The horses' coats gleamed white, reminiscent of freshly fallen snow.

"Beautiful creatures," Liliana said.

"Strong horses," Xavier agreed, his hand gently patting the flank of one of the steeds.

With practised ease, the twins and Isabella mounted their respective horses. While Xavier prepared to mount Saya, his keen eyes caught sight of a hooded figure lurking in the background, observing the scene.

"Join River at the front," Xavier said, his voice firm. "I will follow shortly."

As the tail end of the army began to depart from the camp, Xavier approached the hooded figure with cautious steps.

"My dear boy."

"Mother, what are you doing here without an escort?" Xavier asked, his concern evident in his tone.

"I needed to see you before you leave," Layla replied, her voice trembling slightly.

Xavier enveloped his mother in a tight embrace as tears welled up in her eyes.

"Please, be careful, and bring your father back to me," she pleaded between sobs. "I can't bear the thought of losing both of you again."

"We will return, Mother, I promise."

Layla reluctantly pulled away from the embrace, wiping away her tears with a determined gesture. "Keep him safe," she implored Saya, her gaze turning to the loyal companion by Xavier's side. "You've always been our guardian."

"Mother, I must go now," Xavier said gently. "There are still a few soldiers left to dismantle the camp. They will escort you back to the Silver Hills."

"No, I will wait for you and Darius here, in our home in the Meadows," Layla replied, her voice unwavering.

Xavier mounted Saya, his expression reflecting a mix of determination and affection. "Very well, Mother. We will return to you soon at the manor," he promised before urging Saya forwards, leaving his mother behind as the army moved out.

CHAPTER FORTY-FOUR

THE FIRST HURDLE

The army made good time, arriving at the checkpoint before the forest outside the palace by noon. Xavier swiftly moved to the front alongside the others, his gaze focused and determined. At the checkpoint stood Commander Lynch with her scouts, and River halted the army before riding forwards to confer with them, Xavier by her side.

"What's the situation?" River asked, her voice tense with urgency.

Commander Lynch's expression was grim as she responded. "The forest is swarming with Fallen, all the way up to the main gates, and likely more within."

"Damn it!"

"It's our only passage," Commander Lynch explained, her voice resigned. "The other gates are too narrow, leaving us vulnerable to ambush by the Fallen."

Xavier interjected, his voice calm yet determined. "We'll need to use brute force. My daughters and I will lead the way, clearing a path through the forest right up to the gates. Once inside, we'll assess the situation and proceed accordingly."

River and Lynch turned to Xavier, nodding in understanding.

"Should we have the cavalry on the flanks?" River asked.

"Yes. We clear the path, and you sweep in behind us."

With their plan in place, River gave the order for the army to advance into the woods, while the cavalry circled around to cover each flank, ready to provide support as needed.

The forest reverberated with the thunderous sound of marching feet and galloping horses, drowning out all other thoughts and feelings. The Fallen creatures stood poised, waiting like vigilant guard dogs protecting their territory, their eyes gleaming with malevolent intent.

"Girls, are you ready?" Xavier's voice cut through the din, his tone a mixture of determination and concern.

"Yes, Father," they replied in unison, their resolve evident.

Xavier dismounted from Saya's back, his eyes gleaming in the dim light of the forest. With a swift motion, he drew his blade and took a step forwards, his daughters following suit.

As they advanced, Xavier's sword began to glow with an ethereal light, his eyes mirroring the same intensity as he charged up a powerful shockwave. With a shout, he unleashed the energy, sending a wave of force rippling through the front rows of Fallen, scattering them like leaves in the wind.

"Let's get this done!" Xavier's voice boomed with determination, rallying his daughters and the army behind him.

Artoria surged ahead, unleashing a barrage of wild shockwaves that tore through the ranks of the Fallen, her movements fluid and precise. The army followed in her wake, cutting down the Fallen who had been weakened by the shockwaves.

Xavier kept a watchful eye on his daughter, shouting for her to stay close, but Artoria seemed consumed by her own fury, her attacks growing more reckless and wild with each passing moment. Xavier knew the danger she faced—not only from the Fallen, but from the influence of Delilah, who wielded control over these twisted creatures.

"Father, go with her! I'll stay at the front with Saya!" Liliana's voice pierced through the chaos, her own determination matching that of her father's.

Xavier hesitated for a moment, torn between protecting Artoria and leading the charge against the Fallen at the front. But with a nod of acknowledgement from Liliana, he knew. With a determined stride, he followed Artoria into the heart of the battle, trusting Liliana to hold the line with Saya by her side.

Artoria reached the gates, surrounded by the Fallen who cautiously approached her, feigning subservience. Xavier's voice boomed through the chaos, filled with urgency and concern, as he unleashed blasts of energy, scattering the Fallen.

"What are you doing?" Xavier's words cut through the tension, his eyes locking with Artoria's.

Artoria turned to face her father, her expression guarded, her eyes darker than usual.

Xavier's heart clenched with worry as he approached her, his voice soft but firm. "Artoria, this isn't the path to follow. Trust me."

Artoria's grip tightened on her sword, her panic evident. She believed she had been exposed, her fears consuming her. "Why do you say that, Father?"

Xavier continued to fend off the encroaching Fallen, his movements deliberate and controlled. "Channelling your anger into your magic will only lead to darkness."

Artoria's tension eased slightly, relief washing over her as she realised she hadn't been discovered. "But I'm angry, Father. Angry at everything Delilah has done."

"I understand, my daughter. But we will end this, once and for all," Xavier reassured her.

With renewed resolve, Artoria nodded, her determination mirrored by her father's. Together, they fought side by side, their blades flashing in the dim light, as they held the area in front of the gates, ready to confront their greatest enemy.

"That's the first part over with," River said, her gaze fixed on the imposing oak gates.

"We have to leave the wounded here; they'll be safe," Xavier replied, casting a glance back at the army.

"Father is right. The only enemies left are behind these gates," Artoria added.

Xavier and Artoria positioned themselves in front of the gates, poised for action.

"Artoria, we have to hit the gate at the same time," Xavier said, "Aim for the top so that it falls and crushes anything behind it."

Artoria nodded, preparing herself.

"Stand back!" River shouted.

Following River's command, Xavier and Artoria unleashed a vicious shockwave that devastated the wooden gates, sending splinters the size of daggers into the waiting crowd of Fallen.

"That'll do," Xavier said.

Artoria dashed into the crowd of Fallen, tossing them into the air and swiftly dispatching those who tried to evade her sword.

"Begin the charge!" River commanded.

The army swiftly closed the distance to support Artoria.

"That daughter of yours..." River remarked, rolling her eyes, before joining the charge.

Xavier and Liliana waited for the entire army to enter the walls before joining the rear with the cavalry.

"Izzy, stay with the cavalry," Xavier instructed.

Isabella was about to reply with a sharp comment but remembered the gravity of the situation. Understanding that Xavier needed to focus on the fight, she simply responded with, "Will do."

"We'll keep her safe," Lynch added.

Xavier nodded, then turned to Liliana. Her pupils were dilated, taking in all the carnage around her.

"This isn't our part of the battle. Stay close," he advised.

The army pushed the Fallen deep into the commons, nearing the inner palace gates. Artoria led the fight, her armour and sword stained with stale blood as she blasted through the last set of gates, urging the men forwards.

"Artoria, stop!" River's voice cut through the chaos as the men rushed past her.

Artoria turned sharply, her expression reflecting disdain at River's command.

"Slow down; you're spreading the army thin!" River shouted over the clamour.

"They need to keep up," Artoria snapped back.

"Not everyone has powers like yours," River retorted sharply.

The two locked gazes momentarily before River broke away, ordering the men to reform the line.

"Wait for your father," she instructed before joining the line herself.

The army steadily pushed the Fallen towards the inner gates, trapping them between a moving shield wall and the palace steps. Obstacles like bushes and statues in the courtyard provided cover for Xavier and his daughters to sneak off to the side. River ordered the men to tighten their formation and gradually cut down the Fallen, noticing that the rapid pace set by Artoria had drained most of the men of their energy.

Commander Lynch's voice cut through the chaos. "River, some of the men have dropped from exhaustion!"

River glanced over to the left flank and saw men collapsing to the ground, only to be slain by the Fallen. "They shouldn't be in that state!"

Commander Lynch rode up to her through the crowd of men. "I'll send the scouts over to reinforce the left flank."

"It doesn't make sense," River said.

"General!" Lynch called out, snapping River to attention.

"Go, go and pick up the shields from the dead and hold the line," she ordered firmly.

Lynch nodded and signalled the cavalry over to the left. The horsemen dismounted and rushed to their new position. Lynch then rode back towards their previous position.

"Stay close to me, my queen. We should be safe here," Lynch reassured Isabella.

Isabella slowly nodded, though secretly she longed to join the fight for her home as she watched the defining battle of good versus evil unfold before her eyes.

CHAPTER FORTY-FIVE

LIGHT AND DARK

Xavier and his daughters made their way cautiously through the hidden passages underneath the palace.

"Father, I can sense two powerful energies," Liliana whispered.

"Can you pinpoint them?" he asked.

Liliana halted and concentrated her energy. "They're in the centre of the palace."

"The throne room or the great hall."

Artoria remained silent, observing both of them from behind.

"Let's hurry," Xavier said as he turned back to his daughters.

The splinter group navigated through the narrow passages until they reached one of the guest bedrooms. They climbed out of a small door hidden inside the wardrobe. Artoria cautiously peeked through the slightly opened door.

"Any guards?" Liliana asked.

Artoria shook her head and proceeded through the door. "Quickly now," she said, beginning to jog.

"Wait, Artoria, you don't know the way," Liliana replied.

Artoria halted and gestured impatiently. "You lead the way and be quick about it."

Tension filled the air as they exchanged uneasy glances.

"Girls, stop this. I know it's a stressful situation, but we need each other," Xavier said, placing his hands on their shoulders.

"Yes, Father," they responded in unison, their previous hostility momentarily subdued.

With a nod from Xavier, Liliana took the lead with haste.

As they approached the throne room, the air grew thick and almost unbearable at moments.

"No guards? Not a single one?" Liliana asked.

"She's overconfident in her abilities to stop us," Xavier replied.

They halted outside the doors, prepared to confront their adversary once and for all.

"No matter what happens, make sure she doesn't escape alive," Xavier said firmly as he positioned himself in front of the doors.

Both Liliana and Artoria nodded in agreement before exchanging a determined look.

"I've got your back," Artoria reassured Liliana.

Xavier smiled at his daughters, then turned back to the door and blasted it off its hinges. With resolve, he marched into the throne room.

Sat on the gold and white throne was Delilah, wearing a black cape and chainmail dress and stood beside her was a tall, hooded figure. Their presence filled the air with an ominous energy.

"The king has returned for his kingdom," Delilah mocked.

Xavier smiled and pointed his sword at her. "We've come for your soul and your friend's as well."

Delilah chuckled, then descended the three steps from her throne, followed by the hooded figure. "My soul is here for the taking, but my friend's is already mine," she taunted with a teasing smile.

"You're looking a bit fragile," Xavier replied, eyeing her movements.

"I'm at my end, but my legacy and my will live on through my heir."

"All the mages you spawned are gone. You have no one left and little power remaining," Liliana said.

"Not even your friend next to you," Artoria added, locking eyes with Delilah, both understanding the impending fate.

"Enough talk," Xavier said, assuming a fighting stance, "Draw your sword and stand to be counted."

"Though, Xavier, you won't be fighting me. My friend here will give you a run for your money." Delilah laughed before drawing her sword.

The hooded figure obeyed Delilah's hand signal and removed their hood, revealing a corrupted Darius.

"Father, can you hear me?" Xavier shouted, his shock evident.

Delilah laughed and dashed for a hidden door behind the throne. Xavier froze as he stared into Darius' dead eyes.

"Father, she's escaping!" Liliana cried out.

"He's not moving," Artoria said.

"Artoria, chase her down. Don't let her escape."

Artoria nodded and followed Delilah through the hidden door.

"We don't have time for this," Liliana muttered to herself, attempting to break Xavier's trance. Failing, she reluctantly struck Xavier in the face.

He staggered back, finally snapping out of his daze. "Lily, go help your sister."

"But, Father..."

Xavier nodded, stepping aside to keep Darius in his sight.

"I'm sorry," Liliana whispered before sprinting after Artoria and Delilah.

Darius advanced towards Xavier, his sword drawn and ready for battle. Xavier assumed a defensive stance.

"Father, I know you're still in there. Fight it!" Xavier pleaded.

Darius pressed forwards, seemingly unaffected by Xavier's words. Xavier's heart sank as he realised his father's mind was lost to the corruption.

"Father, please hear me!" Xavier shouted one last time as Darius closed the distance between them. "So be it."

*

Artoria cornered Delilah against a large glass window at the end of a narrow corridor.

"Are you ready to take the next step?" Delilah asked, her voice carrying an air of anticipation.

Artoria looked down, closing her eyes briefly. "I am ready."

Delilah smiled and gestured for Artoria to come closer. "I'll give you the rest of my power."

"Will you be gone forever?"

Delilah nodded solemnly. "But my legend will live on, and you will continue my will." With arms raised and chanting complete, Delilah beckoned Artoria closer. "Straight into my heart, and my powers will be yours."

As Artoria readied her dagger, a sudden interruption came.

"Step back, Artoria!" Liliana's urgent voice echoed as she turned the corner.

"Quickly, child," Delilah urged in a whisper, her focus undeterred.

However, just as Artoria was about to strike, Liliana, noticing her sister dangerously close to Delilah. From pure love and desire to save her, Liliana's power erupted from within as she fazed into the air, teleporting herself right next to them. The shockwave of the teleportation blasted all three of them through the window.

"My queen, look up there!" a soldier shouted as the three fell through the air, struggling to maintain their balance.

"No, it's not complete!" Delilah exclaimed, her eyes widening as she glanced at Artoria.

In a desperate bid to survive, Liliana and Artoria propelled themselves towards Delilah, each grabbing onto her before they all crashed to the ground.

*

"Wake up, Lily!" Isabella's voice pierced the air as she shook her daughter.

Liliana groaned, her arm clenched tightly against her side.

"Feels like your arm's broken and ripped from your shoulder," Isabella murmured, assisting Liliana to her feet.

"What are you doing here? Where's Artoria?" Liliana's words tumbled out in a frantic rush.

Isabella gestured towards Artoria and Delilah, encased in a protective bubble with soldiers outside attempting to breach it.

"I split from the main group to come help you," Isabella explained.

Before Liliana could respond, a soldier's urgent cry reached them. "Delilah is crawling towards Artoria!"

Liliana shoved her mother aside and teleported inside the bubble, colliding with Delilah, who screamed, "Finish it!"

In a blur of motion, Artoria seized the dagger and plunged it into Delilah's heart. Liliana, unable to discern the assailant, seized Delilah's sword and, fuelled by magic and determination, swung it with all her might, beheading Delilah.

"What have you done?" Artoria's accusation rang out, but before Liliana could answer, a blinding light erupted from Delilah's torso, triggering an explosion that sent them hurtling in opposite directions.

Isabella stood frozen, a witness to the chaos unfolding before her. Soldiers rushed to aid Liliana and Artoria, their forms tossed like leaves in a violent gust.

*

As events aspired in the courtyard, Xavier and Darius had been in a heart-wrenching fight. Both carrying physical wounds, no one could get the upper hand for more than a few seconds as if they were fighting a copy of themselves.

As the fight dragged on, Xavier knew that the longer it lasted, the less likely he would be able to muster his full magical might. However, the thought of using his full power against his father didn't even enter his mind. Stepping back from Darius, Xavier took a few moments to gather himself.

Blows to the head haven't shaken the hold in his mind. Then, an idea struck him. With determination, his head dropped, and a bright glow emanated from him. Xavier re-engaged with his father, skilfully blocking each swing as he patiently awaited the perfect opportunity.

The skirmish continued, and Xavier grew increasingly frustrated as the ideal opening seemed elusive. Peering into his father's eyes, Xavier still detected no sign of recognition, indicating that someone or something else still held sway. Darius exhibited none of the minor errors a fully conscious person might make.

Realising he needed to disrupt Darius' balance, Xavier decided on a drastic course of action. With a sudden surge of energy, Xavier executed an attack to create distance between them, hoping to provoke a reaction from Darius.

"Perfect," Xavier muttered as Darius fell for the bait, lunging for an overhead strike.

Using his magic, Xavier swiftly pulled Darius' support leg, causing him to stumble forwards. Seizing the opportunity, Xavier swiftly struck, severing Darius' left hand. Then, with a powerful blast of energy, he propelled Darius into the wall opposite them, the impact reverberating through the air, followed by the sound of rubble cascading onto the marble floor.

With determination, Xavier tossed his sword aside and rushed to his father's side with urgency.

Xavier gently turned his father onto his side, supporting his head with care. "Can you hear me?" Xavier's voice was soft as he lightly shook Darius.

"Xavier, I'm so sorry," Darius murmured, tears welling in his eyes.

"Father, let me heal you," Xavier urged, his voice tinged with desperation.

Darius pushed Xavier's hand away. "It's too late, son. I can still feel the hold on me. The pain is keeping my mind clear for now."

"No, I can heal you, and your mind!"

Xavier attempted to lift the curse that bound Darius, but his efforts proved futile. In his frustration, Xavier punched the marble floor, breaking two fingers in the process.

"Son, you're the king. Don't fret over me. You'll have to let me go," Darius insisted, tears streaming down his cheeks.

"I can't!"

"You have to."

As Darius struggled, Xavier tried to hold him in his arms.

"Father, please, I can't…"

The scuffle brought both men to their feet, each fighting for control—Xavier to save his father, and Darius to take his son's life. As Darius reached for Xavier's dagger, Xavier forcefully pushed him back to the floor. In a desperate move, Darius seized a piece of rubble and hurled it at Xavier, striking him squarely in the face. Blood began to flow from Xavier's forehead as he staggered from the impact, sinking to his knees.

Seizing the opportunity, Darius charged at Xavier, intent on overpowering him.

"I love you," Xavier whispered as his father rushed towards him.

With practised skill, Xavier countered the charge with a swift hip toss, sending Darius crashing headfirst into the ground. Following through with the throw, Xavier pinned Darius down, tears mingling with blood on his father's face.

With a heavy heart and a moment's hesitation, Xavier reached for his dagger. In a swift motion, he drove it into his father's heart. The struggle ceased as Darius' eyes returned to their normal state.

"I love you too, son, for now and forever," Darius murmured, his voice fading with his last breath.

Xavier withdrew the dagger, casting it aside with a mixture of anguish and rage. A heart-wrenching cry tore from his lips, resonating through the hall like the roar of a wounded lion. The walls and floor cracked under the weight of Xavier's overwhelming emotions and magic, his sorrow transforming into seething anger.

Xavier remained motionless beside his father's lifeless form, his mind consumed by a whirlwind of thoughts. As the chaos of battle subsided, he found himself grappling with questions of what could have been and why it had come to this. Lost in introspection, he was abruptly drawn back to the present by the sense of an approaching presence.

Turning his gaze towards the door, Xavier felt a glimmer of hope stir within him. Despite the weight of grief and anger that hung heavy upon him, a smile slowly spread across his face as Saya limped into view. The lion, battered and weary from the fray, collapsed beside him, sharing in his exhaustion and pain.

Together, they sat in silence, a bond forged through battle and adversity, offering each other solace in their shared moment of vulnerability.

*

"General, just a few pockets of resistance left," a soldier reported.

"Very well, sweep the area again. I want no surprises," River replied.

The soldiers nodded and dispersed, intent on their task.

River turned her attention to another soldier nearby. "What was that explosion?" she demanded.

Before the soldier could respond, Lynch came charging in on horseback, her expression wrought with concern. "Something's happened. I can't find the queen."

"How did you lose her?"

"She must be on the other side, where the explosion occurred," the soldier interjected, offering an explanation.

"Let's go," Lynch said, reaching out to offer her arm to River, a sense of urgency palpable in her demeanour.

As they reached the other side of the palace, River and Lynch spotted Liliana and Isabella attempting to revive Artoria.

"What happened?" River asked, dismounting from her horse

to offer assistance.

"Liliana saved Artoria from Delilah," Isabella explained.

River and Lynch exchanged nods with Liliana.

"How are you feeling?" Lynch asked.

"I'm not sure. Father...?" Liliana's voice trailed off, her expression suddenly frantic as realisation struck her.

"Slow down, Liliana. Who was Xavier fighting?" River pressed, sensing her distress.

Attempting to teleport, Liliana found herself unfocused and in pain.

"Lily, tell us," Isabella urged, concern evident in her voice as she observed her daughter's panicked demeanour.

Closing her eyes, Liliana gathered her thoughts. "It was Darius," she confessed before teleporting away.

The revelation that Xavier had to face his own father left them stunned.

"Isabella," River said, "These men will assist you in transporting Artoria to the wagons we've prepared for the injured. Lynch and I will enter the palace through the main door."

Isabella nodded softly, her emotions swirling with the weight of the news and the harrowing events she had witnessed.

Liliana hurried into the throne room, her dislocated shoulder causing her to wince with every step.

"Lily, you're all right," Xavier exclaimed with relief as Liliana approached him, dropping to her knees in front of him.

"It's over. I killed her," Liliana said, trying to uplift his spirits.

"I'm proud of you, my child," Xavier replied softly, his voice filled with pride and exhaustion.

Liliana enveloped Xavier in a tight embrace, seeking solace in his presence. "Father, we can't stay here," she whispered urgently.

"I can't move. I have no strength left."

"We must bring Grandfather home to rest."

Xavier nodded. "I made a promise to Mother."

With Liliana's help, Xavier struggled to his feet, Saya rising slowly beside him, ready to lend support.

"Father, let me heal both of you."

"It's all right. Just help me lift Darius so we can carry him home," Xavier replied, his voice strained with pain and sorrow as he fought to maintain his composure.

CHAPTER FORTY-SIX

THE JOURNEY HOME

River, Lynch, and a handful of soldiers rushed up the palace stairs, urgency etched on their faces.

"Secure the palace and find the king!" River's command echoed through the corridors as the soldiers sprang into action.

As they moved forwards, the soldiers split into two groups, but their progress was abruptly halted as Xavier emerged, carrying his father on his shoulders. The soldiers stopped in their tracks and snapped to attention, saluting as Xavier passed. River and Lynch bowed their heads respectfully as Xavier approached.

Reaching the palace stairs, Xavier was met with a solemn honour guard formed by the onlooking soldiers.

"Get one of the wagons!" River's voice cut through the air.

"No, I'm carrying him all the way," Xavier said sharply, his determination evident.

"Father, you won't make it all the way in your condition," Liliana pleaded, her concern evident.

"I have to get him home."

"You will, Xavier. Let us help you," River said, her voice gentle yet resolute.

Darius was gently placed on the wagon, and the group gathered around to pay their final respects.

"I must go alone," Xavier announced as he prepared the horse for departure.

River nodded in understanding and signalled for everyone who wasn't family to step away from the wagon.

"No, Father," Liliana protested, her voice tinged with sadness.

Xavier shook his head, his expression resolute, and climbed onto the wagon. Artoria, who had been silent since waking up, kept her gaze fixed on her sister. Though Liliana smiled at her, Artoria's response remained distant.

"Will everyone be all right here?" Xavier asked, addressing the gathered group.

"Yes, my lord, we'll handle everything for your return," Commander Lynch assured him.

"I won't be coming back," Xavier declared, his tone sombre.

A heavy silence settled over the group.

"What do you mean?" Isabella demanded sharply.

"Please, Isabella, I can't explain," Xavier replied, his voice filled with regret.

Without hesitation, Isabella climbed onto the wagon, her expression defiant. "Let's go, and that's the end of it."

Liliana watched with a mixture of sadness and pride as the wagon began its journey, waving them off as they departed.

"Now, what's the problem between the two of you?" River asked.

"I don't have a problem," Liliana replied, her expression reflecting confusion.

Artoria remained silent for a moment before finally speaking up. "She ruined my moment again."

"I saw you in trouble, and I wasn't going to let my sister die," Liliana replied softly.

"No, I had her where I wanted her."

Tension mounted between the two sisters as Artoria felt slighted by Liliana's interference.

River intervened firmly, her tone brooking no further argument. "It doesn't matter who killed her. Delilah was a problem for everyone on Malsdon, and she's gone now, along with her followers."

"No… It was meant to be my glory, not hers," Artoria persisted defiantly, squaring off with her sister.

"That's enough!" River's voice boomed, cutting through the escalating tension. She motioned for a few soldiers to step in and escort Artoria away to calm down.

Artoria resisted, pushing the soldiers away. "Don't touch me!"

"Artoria, walk away now!" River commanded firmly.

As Artoria's eyes glowed with an unsettling darkness, both Liliana and River noticed the change.

"Artoria, please calm down," Liliana said, her own eyes beginning to glow in response.

Artoria offered a chilling smile before turning and walking away, her words hanging ominously in the air. "This isn't finished."

River exchanged a concerned glance with Lynch and Liliana. "Her eyes… they didn't glow like that before."

"Perhaps the explosion during Delilah's demise had some effect," Lynch suggested.

"I still feel the same," Liliana said.

"We'll keep an eye on her," River replied, "For now, let's secure the area and get some rest."

*

The journey to the Emerald Meadows was shrouded in silence, with Xavier scarcely uttering a word. Isabella respected his quietude, choosing instead to offer him silent support by holding his hand as they rode.

Suddenly, a light fog materialised ahead of them, causing the horse to skid to a halt.

"Xavier?" Isabella's voice cut through the mist as she strained to peer into the foggy veil.

Xavier focused on calming the spooked horse, his eyes flicking to Saya, who remained composed, showing no signs of alarm.

"The journey is nearly at its end," a familiar voice resonated through the fog, sending a shiver down Isabella's spine.

"Who's there?" she asked.

Xavier's gaze followed Isabella's as a large lion emerged from the swirling mist.

"Belthazor?" Isabella breathed softly, recognising the majestic creature from their past encounters.

The setting sun cast its warm rays across the flora of the Emerald Meadows, soothing the heart and calming the mind at the mere sight.

"What a view," Isabella remarked, breaking the silence between them.

"Xavier, what is your decision?" Belthazor's serious tone shattered the peaceful ambiance.

"What is he talking about?" Isabella asked, her gaze fixed on Xavier.

"My lady, my essence is fading by the day, and I can't protect the Exalted Plains much longer," Belthazor explained.

"I take it Xavier is meant to take your place?" Isabella's voice was filled with anger and sadness.

Belthazor nodded.

"I've done horrible things. I'll never be the same person again. I deserve exile," Xavier said softly.

"No, you don't run. You're not a coward!" Isabella's voice rose.

"I'm not a coward. I've killed loved ones and lost loved ones, and I failed to protect the kingdom."

"So have I. Have you forgotten how this all started?" Isabella's fury intensified. "You owe it to everyone to make this kingdom safe and great again."

"There is another way," Belthazor interjected.

"Go on," Isabella said.

"He must return to where he was given his powers and relinquish them. That's the only other way to keep the Exalted Plains safe," Belthazor explained.

"That's the plan," Isabella said, speaking for Xavier.

"How long do I have?" Xavier asked.

"No more than three days, and I'll meet you there," Belthazor replied.

They nodded to each other before the fog reappeared.

"I'm sorry for all you've been through, both of you. Magic is both a curse and a gift," Belthazor said before vanishing into the fog.

An awkward silence descended upon their journey once more as they treaded through the dark path, the moonlight struggling to penetrate the thick forest canopy.

"We're almost home," Xavier whispered.

"Xavier, why would you leave me again?" Isabella asked, her voice trembling with suppressed emotions.

"I'm not the person you need around."

She punched his arm lightly, then clasped his hand. "You're the right person for me and Malsdon! You never took the easy path, and you always did what was right, even if it meant risking your life."

"You're too kind," he replied softly.

"I love you, your daughters love you, and the kingdom does too," she said before resting her head on his shoulder.

The manor gates swung open, and the guards bowed their heads as they arrived. The wagon halted outside the steps, and Xavier ascended before standing at the entrance to the main door.

"Tell Lady Layla we have arrived," Isabella instructed a guard.

Saya walked around and settled next to Xavier.

"We made it home," he whispered to Saya as he gently rubbed her ears.

The manor doors creaked open slowly, and the guards snapped to attention as Layla emerged in her nightgown, torch in hand. She tried to maintain her composure at the sight of Darius' wrapped body in the wagon, but she stumbled on the last step.

Xavier caught her as tears began to flow.

"Thank you, my son, for bringing him home," she sobbed.

"I tried my best, Mother," he said, his voice cracking. Xavier held his mother tightly for a few moments. "We will stay here tonight."

"Okay, son. We'll have the funeral tomorrow," Layla said, wiping away her tears.

"Okay, Mother."

"I'll make the arrangements now and have them sent off," Isabella interjected, then bowed her head.

"Thank you, my dear," Layla replied.

The night fell silent as Darius' body was taken away by the guards, as if the Emerald Meadows knew they had lost their benefactor and protector.

Isabella and Layla watched through the window as the guards departed.

"We'll set the pyre behind the manor," Layla said, trying to hold back tears, "Where he and Tiberius would train and enjoy the meadows."

"That will be a fitting resting place for them. Their spirits will unite and watch over the Meadows," Isabella said as she squeezed Layla's hand.

CHAPTER FORTY-SEVEN

THE LITTLE THINGS

The clean-up from the battle stretched long into the night, with everyone pitching in. The damage was extensive, not only from the recent battle but also from the years of Delilah's grip on the palace and Malsdon. Liliana observed from one of the bedrooms that once belonged to her mother when she was growing up. Among the items she discovered were handmade jewellery, dresses that could be altered to fit her now, and a diary tucked away at the back of a wardrobe.

She opened the diary to the first few pages and smiled, tracing her mother's childhood through the entries. Her smile turned into a smirk as she read about her mother's feelings for Xavier. Liliana wrapped the diary in a green silk blanket and carried it out of the room, eager to read more. She clutched it tightly as she made her way down the brightly lit halls.

Liliana passed by the throne room but doubled back when she saw Artoria sitting on the throne, Xavier's sword in hand.

"Comfortable seat?" Liliana asked.

"Don't worry, it'll never be mine," Artoria replied. She stood up and stumbled down the steps, waving the sword at Liliana. "You're his favourite, you with no real powers!"

"Sister, you're a drunken mess. Go sleep this off."

"No, I will not take orders from you!" Artoria slurred, getting closer to her sister.

The sword came within striking range, and Liliana had to dodge several times.

"Stop this madness. Why do you hate me?"

"I hate you? Is that what you think? Or do you hate me and just projecting onto me?" Artoria dropped the sword and attempted to fight her sister with her fists.

Liliana easily avoided her blows. "Stop this now!"

"No, I will not listen to you!"

Liliana, unusually losing her patience, grabbed her sister's neck and delivered three punches to her face, knocking her out. "Guards!"

A group of footsteps rapidly approached them. "My lady?" a guard asked.

"Put her to bed and ensure she wakes in the morning."

"Very well, my lady," the guard acknowledged before he and the others carried Artoria away.

I need your help, Xavier whispered in her mind.

Liliana froze for a moment, then quickly composed herself. She focused her energy and teleported away.

Liliana landed outside the manor gates where Xavier was waiting for her.

"You've grown more powerful, my dear," Xavier said.

"I feel different after killing Delilah," she replied.

Xavier paused, studying her closely. "You still feel like yourself?"

"Yes, Father, but the power flows more easily now."

"It's possible that you and your sister absorbed Delilah's powers when she died."

Liliana looked stunned, pondering for a moment. "How is that possible? We've defeated mages before and never absorbed their powers."

"I don't know, dear. It's a mystery for another time," Xavier said with a smile. "I need you to take me to this place in the Vermillion Sands." He showed Liliana the location from the images in his mind.

"What is that place?" she asked, her expression filled with concern.

"I'll explain when we get there. We must hurry," he replied.

Liliana nodded and focused all her energy on teleporting both of them over a great distance.

They landed in the Vermillion Sands just outside the cave entrance.

Liliana took a moment to sit and rest, gazing up at the night sky. "This place is beautiful," she remarked, inhaling deeply.

"Yes, without the scars of war, beauty has a chance to shine," Xavier agreed, also admiring the moonlit sky.

They proceeded into the cave, making their way to the pool where Xavier had received his powers.

"I feel strange, Father," Liliana confessed.

"This place is pure energy, straight from the heart of Malsdon. The feeling will pass soon."

Liliana nodded, trusting her father's words, and followed him further into the cave.

"There it is," Xavier said, pointing to the small pool.

"Father, tell me why you are here."

"I need to return what was borrowed."

"Your powers, Father?" she said before dropping to her knees.

Xavier rushed over to Liliana and supported her. "What is happening?"

"She's been corrupted by dark energy," Belthazor said as he appeared from behind.

"When we killed Delilah?" Liliana whispered.

Belthazor nodded. "Xavier, you must take her into the pool with you."

"No, why are you taking Father's powers?"

"To protect Malsdon," Belthazor explained.

"Lily, it was me or the powers," Xavier said as he held his daughter's hand.

He helped Liliana to her feet, and they walked together into the pool.

"My part is over in this. You and your sister are the new protectors of Malsdon," Xavier said with a smile.

"Father, we have to get Artoria here to help her," Liliana said urgently.

"We will."

They both looked up to Belthazor, who began the enchantment. A soft light aura began to dissipate from Xavier's body.

"Father?" Liliana whispered, concern etched on her face.

"I'm okay, Lily."

As the enchantment concluded, Belthazor bowed his head to Xavier as he exited the pool. Turning his attention to Liliana, Belthazor initiated a different enchantment. Liliana began to groan, clutching her head.

"It'll be over soon!" Xavier shouted over Belthazor's chanting.

Dark aura rushed out of Liliana as she screamed, then she fell face first into the pool. Xavier moved to rush in and save her, but Belthazor stepped in front of them. The chanting intensified, becoming more aggressive and deeper. The dark aura circled above the pool, then suddenly, it exploded into a shower of light aura that rained down into the water.

The chanting ceased, and Xavier hurried over to the pool. Before he could enter, Liliana sprang out, gasping for air.

"Lily, are you okay?" Xavier asked, offering his hand and helping her up. "Were you able to change the dark aura, Belthazor?"

"It wasn't a lot, so I was able to transform it into light. However, even with a heart as pure as yours, it was enough to cause conflict within Liliana," Belthazor explained.

"Thank you," Liliana said.

Belthazor guided Xavier and Liliana out of the cave. Liliana walked with a newfound sense of pride and power, her posture reflecting her inner strength.

"She'll make a great leader," Belthazor said.

"Yes, she will. And what about her sister?" Xavier asked.

Belthazor halted, prompting Xavier to do the same, allowing Liliana to walk ahead.

"You must bring Artoria here, no matter what," Belthazor insisted. His serious and deep tone conveyed the gravity of the matter.

"What are you not telling me?" Xavier demanded, his tone stern.

"Energy is given, it cannot be forced out of oneself," Belthazor replied cryptically.

Xavier's shock and fear surged at the implication that Delilah might have given her powers to Artoria.

"Do not assume the worst, just bring her back here," Belthazor said.

Xavier nodded, his mind racing with worry, as he caught up with Liliana.

"Are you ready, Father?" Liliana asked.

"When we return, you must talk to your sister and bring her here," Xavier explained.

"She won't listen to me. I might have knocked her out before coming to you," Liliana admitted hesitantly.

Xavier shook his head in disbelief, then squeezed Liliana's hand in reassurance. With a nod from Belthazor, they teleported away.

CHAPTER FORTY-EIGHT

HOME AND AWAY

An honour guard lined the path to the pyre site on a cold and misty day, obscuring any sense of time. Layla stood solemnly, her face veiled in black, flanked by Sabrina, Artoria, and Isabella for support. Opposite them, Liliana stood with River by her side, their expressions etched with grief.

"How did this happen?" Liliana whispered, her voice barely audible amidst the solemn atmosphere.

"There was nothing you could have done," River replied softly, her gaze fixed ahead.

"It doesn't make sense. They were overwhelmed. Grandfather wouldn't have had such a flawed plan of attack," Liliana insisted, her tone tinged with frustration.

"Now is not the time for this, Liliana," River said firmly, placing a hand on her shoulder.

Liliana glanced down, her thoughts swirling, before meeting her sister's unwavering gaze. Neither sister looked away as the wind whistled through the trees, scattering leaves across the ground as if marking the path for Darius.

A man walked through the honour guard, blowing a rally horn as Darius' body came into view. Xavier, Victor, and two of Darius' personal guards carried the body towards to the pyre site.

"Our fathers will be drinking ale together again," Victor said softly, his voice heavy with sorrow.

"Great friends for many years," Xavier replied, a faint smile crossing his lips.

The honour guard drew their swords and saluted as the procession passed through. Layla's eyes filled with tears as Darius' body moved past her, her grief palpable.

The body was placed beside the pyre, and everyone looked up as the wind whistled once more, stirring the fallen leaves and sending them cascading onto Darius' wrapped body.

"The Meadows bid their final farewell to his earthly form and welcome his spirit," Layla said, her voice tinged with a glimmer of hope.

Xavier stood solemnly beside his father's body, facing the assembled crowd, ready to deliver his speech and bid his final farewell to his father. Isabella nodded softly, offering her support.

"A great person and father, the most trustworthy and reliable man I know," Xavier began, his voice steady but filled with emotion. Pausing briefly to compose himself, he glanced up and met his mother's proud gaze before continuing, "Darius' death was a tragic and unexpected loss. Yet, I find some comfort in knowing that his granddaughters have avenged him by vanquishing the bane that has plagued us for years."

The guards echoed their respect by banging the hilts of their swords against their plate armour.

"From a young age, my father protected Malsdon, alongside many others who are no longer with us, from numerous dangers, ensuring a future and a beautiful home for the children of Malsdon." He motioned for Liliana and Artoria to join him, their confusion evident as they approached. "I want both of you to place him on the pyre."

"Of course, Father," Liliana responded proudly, while Artoria simply nodded in agreement.

The two sisters lifted the body gently with their powers and slowly lowered it onto the pyre. Victor walked up to Xavier and handed him a torch. Bowing his head, Xavier slowly placed the torch into the pyre. As Xavier stepped back, the small torch ignited the pyre, turning it into a roaring fire. As everyone began to bid their final farewells, Xavier felt compelled to address the gathered crowd once more.

"Before we depart, there's one more matter I must address," Xavier announced, his gaze sweeping over the sombre faces before him.

Isabella shook her head, silently urging him not to broach certain subjects, but Xavier pressed on.

"I could have easily been the one on that pyre, but my father sacrificed his life so that I could live. If the situation were reversed, who would take my place?" Xavier's words hung heavy in the air as he looked around, finally resting his gaze upon his daughters. "Being blessed with twin daughters is a great joy, but only one can inherit the throne."

Liliana and Artoria stood before him, their expressions reflecting their divergent emotions—one smiling, the other stoic.

"From the moment we met and the time I've had to observe your characters, it became clear to me that you both possess the qualities of great leaders. However, different times call for different types of leadership. Malsdon is currently in mourning and in need of a supportive and healing presence," Xavier explained, his eyes fixed on Liliana.

As Xavier declared Liliana as his heir and announced the date of her coronation, Artoria's facade of acceptance masked a storm of conflicting emotions raging within her. She watched as the others embraced Liliana, offering words of praise, before they retreated to the manor. As the sisters locked eyes, the love they once shared seemed to vanish, replaced by a palpable sense of distrust and resentment.

CHAPTER FORTY-NINE

PEACE AND THE FUTURE

Two months had passed since the conclusion of the war, and Malsdon had begun to mend its wounds. Today marked a special occasion for the entire kingdom—a day of loyalty sworn and the acknowledgement of the heiress apparent.

From the woods outside the palace walls to the bustling courtyard, stalls laden with food and goods lined the streets, while people celebrated and recounted the dramatic events of the recent past. Amidst the festivities, Xavier and Saya moved through the crowds, exchanging greetings and sampling various delicacies from every corner of Malsdon.

The pair stood out from the throng, adorned in their ceremonial armour. Xavier donned white trousers and a long shirt beneath his red chainmail, topped with a gleaming gold chest plate with the image of a lion's head. Saya, likewise clad in white and gold plate armour, exuded an air of strength and regality as she moved gracefully through the crowd.

All around them, people paused to greet and express gratitude to the pair for their tireless efforts in service of the kingdom.

A young boy dashed up to Xavier and threw his arms around him.

"Son, you mustn't do that!" his father shouted, hurrying after him.

"It's all right," Xavier reassured with a smile.

"Forgive me, my lord," the father said as he gently pulled his son away.

Xavier knelt down to the boy's level. "What's your name?" he asked kindly.

The boy hesitated but received a little tap of encouragement from his father. "My name is Leo Greenford," he said softly.

"A strong name," Xavier remarked with a smile.

"My mother told me it means 'lion', and that's the name of your house," Leo said proudly.

His father rolled his eyes but couldn't hide his smile.

"What do you want to be when you're older?" Xavier asked.

"Well, I'm ten years old now. When can I become a knight?" Leo asked eagerly.

"When you're fifteen, come to the Emerald Meadows, and we'll train you to be one of the finest knights there," Xavier promised proudly.

"Like you and your father?" Leo questioned, glancing at Saya, who was watching them with interest.

"Leo!" his father reprimanded.

"It's all right," Xavier replied, "Yes, like me and my father."

The young boy's face lit up with joy, and he began to bounce with excitement.

Xavier stood up, addressing Saya. "She won't hurt you."

Xavier observed Leo interacting with Saya, a smile playing on his lips.

"I'm sorry you missed this stage with your daughters," the boy's father remarked, his tone tinged with regret.

"So am I," Xavier replied softly.

"Forgive my manners. My name is John Greenford," he said, extending his hand.

"A pleasure," Xavier responded, reciprocating the handshake.

The four of them strolled through the common area together, exchanging stories.

"So, you must have interacted with my father quite often?" Xavier asked.

"Yes, he would frequently visit the villages in the meadow, procuring supplies and recruiting future knights," John replied.

"You seem like a capable man. You weren't offered the chance?"

"I'm no fighter, but my wife… she became a knight just before the barbarian invasion. She lost her life fighting the Fallen here on Malsdon."

"I'm sorry."

"It's all right. I'm just one of many," John replied.

"I know."

"Life isn't fair sometimes. As long as my son outlives me, I'll be happy. No parent should have to bury their children," John said, his voice heavy with emotion.

His words resonated deeply with Xavier. "John, you and Leo will be my guests at today's ceremony."

"All right, I know it's wise not to turn down an invitation from the king," John replied with a smile.

As they entered the palace, the royal guards greeted them saluting Xavier and Saya before casting a discerning glance at John and Leo.

"They're with me. Show them around the palace, then bring them to the throne room for the ceremony," Xavier said, to which a guard nodded and led them away just as River arrived.

"Who are they?" River asked, her gaze shifting between Xavier and the newcomers.

"They're from the Meadows, and John knew my father."

"And you trust them?" River pressed, her tone cautious.

"My powers may be gone, but all my senses remain heightened. I trust them."

"All right, I'm just doing my job."

"I know, Lord General," Xavier responded with a friendly slap on her shoulder. "Start bringing in the guests. I'll check in on them."

Xavier left River to issue orders to the guards. He strode past the throne room where the afternoon events would take place. Peering inside, he spotted Victor seated amidst the palace staff, overseeing the final preparations.

"I like the new design of the throne," Xavier remarked, stepping closer.

Victor nodded in acknowledgement. "It was easy to modify."

The throne room boasted two thrones of equal size and quality, positioned side by side for the king and queen. Six steps led up to them, while at the base of the steps sat another, slightly lesser throne-like chair, reserved for the lord general.

"I've got the other two items as well," Victor announced with a smile.

"Perfect. I want you to walk down with them," Xavier said.

"Why?"

"I want you to witness the people acknowledging your marvellous work," Xavier explained.

"For you and your family, I'm always at your service," Victor responded warmly, extending his hand.

Xavier clasped it firmly, gratitude evident in his gaze.

*

"You look wonderful," Isabella remarked as she helped Liliana adjust her dress.

"Too bad that armour is going to spoil it," Layla chimed in with a teasing smile.

"It'll be fine, Grandmother," Liliana replied, smiling back at Layla.

"I just want the day to be perfect for you," Layla expressed, her tone softening with affection.

Liliana smiled and hugged Layla, then turned to embrace her mother. "I love the both of you very much."

A guard entered the room, whispering something to Isabella before swiftly exiting.

"Mother, what's the matter?" Liliana asked, noticing the

change in Isabella's demeanour.

"Your sister won't be coming," Isabella informed her, her expression troubled.

"It's not a matter of choice, it's mandatory," Layla interjected, her frustration evident.

"Where is she?" Liliana pressed, concern etching her features.

"In the palace, but don't worry about her. Focus on you," Isabella advised gently, attempting to ease Liliana's worry.

One of the maids approached, placing the chest armour on Liliana and securing the straps. The silver of the armour complemented the white dress with black trims elegantly.

"A true warrior princess." Xavier's voice echoed through the room.

"Hello, Father."

Xavier took both of her hands in his. "Are you ready for this?"

"I am, Father."

"Your hands say otherwise. It's okay to be nervous; you'll be fine," Xavier reassured her, kissing her hands gently.

The bells bellowed, signalling that the time had come.

"I'll see you soon," Xavier said before exiting the room.

"Mother, he forgot to bring back my sword," Liliana panicked.

"It'll be fine, trust me. We'll meet you in there," Isabella reassured her.

They exchanged hugs before Isabella and Layla left Liliana alone in the room.

Weird feelings swirled within her as the pressure built by the second. She took in a few deep breaths. "I'm ready," she declared aloud to herself.

Suddenly, a knock at the door startled her, causing her confidence to waver.

"Excuse me, but it's time," the guard announced from outside the door.

The horns blew at a medium tone as Liliana began her procession down the aisle towards the thrones, where her parents sat.

Saya occupied a spot at the base of the stairs next to River's seat. People rose from their seats as she passed by, their gazes filled with awe at her beauty and power.

She halted a few steps in front of the thrones, and as the horns ceased their sound, the crowd gradually resumed their seats, their murmurs of admiration filling the air.

Xavier descended the steps, gesturing for Liliana to come closer. "Liliana Lucius Leo, we are gathered here today as one people to witness history," he declared with solemnity.

Isabella beamed at Liliana, who managed a small smile in return, her nerves still evident.

"The past sixteen years have been unlike anything our great land has ever seen. Many loved ones have been taken from us by evil individuals. But it's up to us to honour their memory, rebuild this land, and usher in an era of peace," Xavier proclaimed passionately.

The crowd erupted in cheers, and the guards banged their shields in agreement. Xavier motioned for Victor, who stood at the back of the room, to join them. Victor approached, carrying two boxes—one long and the other small. As he walked by, the onlookers whispered in curiosity.

Handing the boxes to Xavier, Victor bowed respectfully before returning to his position. Isabella descended the stairs in her flowing cream dress, standing beside Xavier and accepting the small box from him.

Liliana watched, slightly confused by the unfolding events.

"My reign as king was troubled, marked by years of war and my absence," Xavier continued, his voice tinged with regret.

The crowd murmured in protest, but Xavier signalled for River to allow an elderly lady to speak.

"Before you ascended to the throne, you defended this land with your life. As king, you led us in, driving back the forces of evil. And in your absence, Princess Liliana and Princess Artoria protected us from further harm. We owe a debt of gratitude to your family," the lady proclaimed, bowing her head in respect.

The crowd erupted in applause, chanting "Leo" at the top of their lungs, honouring the bravery and sacrifice of the royal family.

Xavier raised his hand to silence the room. "I am deeply moved by your heartfelt words."

"We all are," Isabella added, her voice echoing his sentiment.

Xavier then gestured for Liliana to kneel before him. Opening the box, he withdrew a sword still sheathed in its scabbard.

"This sword was crafted from blades wielded by my father, your mother, and the former king, your grandfather, in battle," he explained.

The scabbard, adorned in full black with silver trimmings, held a silvery-grey hilt with intricate engravings and a white gem nestled within the pommel.

"Do you promise to protect and serve the people of Malsdon?" Xavier asked solemnly.

"I do," Liliana replied.

"Do you promise to set aside all selfish ambitions for the betterment of the land and its people?" Xavier continued.

"I do," Liliana affirmed, her voice unwavering.

Xavier handed her the sword but paused before she could rise. "One moment. Do you solemnly swear, with the purest of hearts, to rule and lead the people of Malsdon fairly and justly?" His tone was stern, catching Liliana off guard.

After a brief moment of contemplation, Liliana took a deep breath, fully understanding the gravity of her response. "With the purest of hearts, I will," she declared confidently, aware that this oath was not typical for a mere heir.

"You will forever have my love," Xavier whispered to her.

"I love you too, Father," Liliana replied, her voice filled with warmth and affection.

Turning to address the crowd, Xavier announced, "With this oath taken, Isabella and I will step down as king and queen."

The news stunned almost everyone present, leaving them speechless.

"It is time for a new regime, led by a better leader—a healer, a just soul," Xavier continued passionately. "I present to you the High Queen of Malsdon. Rise and be recognised, Queen Liliana Lucius Leo!"

The crowd erupted in cheers and applause, some still in disbelief but acknowledging Liliana's capability, having witnessed her growth into the queen she had become.

Isabella retrieved the crown from the box and placed it upon Liliana's head. Crafted in silvery-grey with a white band, the crown bore a rugged, ancient appearance, with spear-like points encircling the band.

"This crown symbolises your wisdom, resilience, pure heart, and your connection to the common folk," Isabella explained to Liliana, her words filled with pride and reverence.

Xavier looked at Liliana and gestured towards his throne. As Isabella finished attaching the belt and scabbard to her daughter, Liliana gracefully made her way to the high throne and seated herself. The entire assembly knelt before her, including Xavier and Isabella.

"Long live the queen!" River's voice rang out, breaking the reverent silence.

"Long live the queen!" echoed the crowd in unison, their voices thundering through the grand chamber.

As the applause and cheers resounded once more, Isabella's gaze met Artoria's at the open door. Artoria, dressed in sombre black attire, stood silently observing her sister. John Greenford noticed Artoria's presence and followed her gaze as she began leaving the room.

Liliana raised her hand, signalling for silence, and delivered her first speech as high queen before dismissing the assembly to attend the feast in the great hall.

*

John Greenford trailed Artoria to a forest just before the Iron Coast, stealthily hiding his horse before slipping into the cover of a bush. From his concealed vantage point, he observed Artoria meeting with a mysterious figure.

"Your ship is waiting, my queen," the man muttered.

"Good. Any trouble bringing it into dock?" Artoria asked, her tone composed.

"There was minimal resistance," the man chuckled. "We have temporary control of the town."

"Very well. Recall your men, and let's depart," Artoria instructed.

With a shrill blast from a high-pitched horn, the man summoned his men, who gradually emerged from the shadows, numbering twenty in total.

"What are you carrying?" Artoria asked one of them.

The man revealed two gigas wolf pups, one white and the other grey. Artoria's expression softened with interest as she approached him.

"Powerful magic courses through them. Where did you find them?" she asked.

"Deep in the forest," the man replied, somewhat cryptically.

"I know you found them in the forest, but where exactly?" Artoria pressed, her frustration mounting.

The man remained silent, either unable to comprehend the question or uncertain how to articulate his answer.

Sensing his hesitation, Artoria seized the opportunity, grabbing the white pup and forcing a bond with it. "You will grow strong and ruthless, more powerful than Saya, and you will be her downfall."

"And the other one?" the man asked.

Artoria's smile turned sinister as she swiftly dispatched the grey pup with a stab to its chest, causing it to collapse to the ground. The men watched in bewildered silence.

"Forcing a bond with one gigas beast and controlling it is no easy feat, so the other one is unnecessary," Artoria explained coolly.

Artoria whispered a command to one of her men, sending him off in a different direction while the rest headed towards the docks. With only the distant cries of the wounded wolf pup echoing through the forest, John rushed to its aid. He quickly tended to its wound, packing it with a torn piece of cloth from his shirt and securing it tightly.

"You'll make it, little one," he whispered reassuringly, casting a wary glance around before gently scooping up the pup and carrying it back to his horse.

Suddenly, a sharp pain pierced John's side, causing him to gasp for breath. He looked down to see a black dart protruding from his flesh, his vision blurring as he stumbled and collapsed to the ground. Through the haze, he watched the setting sun cast its golden light through the trees above.

"I'm afraid you won't live to see the moon rise tonight," Artoria's voice cut through the darkness as she loomed over him, her presence ominous and foreboding.

She knelt beside him, gripping his hair tightly and forcing his gaze to meet hers. "Who sent you to follow me?"

"I… didn't know it was you… watching your sister," John managed to mumble, his voice barely audible through his laboured breaths.

"So, you thought you'd play the hero and try to arrest me?" Artoria taunted, a cruel smirk twisting her lips.

"You've fallen from grace… the entire land will despise you," John muttered weakly, his strength waning with each passing moment.

"Since you're dying, I'll share my plan for Malsdon with you. I intend to drain the resources from the Forgotten Lands and raise an army unlike any seen before. I will accomplish what Delilah could not," Artoria proclaimed proudly, her eyes gleaming with malice.

John struggled to respond, his heartbeat slowing to a faint rhythm. Sensing his imminent demise, Artoria spoke to herself, her voice filled with dark ambition.

"A Fallen army fit for a true dark queen," she declared, before callously casting John's head to the ground and departing into the shadows, leaving his lifeless body behind.

Artoria strode through the war-torn streets towards the docks, where her men were pillaging the town and herding prisoners onto the waiting ships, while the Fallen patrolled the area.

"The mark Delilah gave you still grants you control over them?" Artoria asked a soldier.

"Yes, my queen, but it's your mark now, and they are your Fallen," the soldier replied proudly.

"Indeed," Artoria acknowledged with a smile.

The wolf pup at her side began to growl and bark at the townsfolk being rounded up, its loyalty to Artoria evident as her will imprinted upon it.

"I must think of a name for you," Artoria mused aloud as they navigated through the chaos. "I'll call you Alastor."

The pup responded with a series of enthusiastic licks to her face.

"It remains a mystery as to where you came from, little one," Artoria remarked.

"My lady, the prisoners are secured below deck, and we are ready to depart," the captain informed her.

"Very well, Captain. Are the charges set?" Artoria asked.

The captain nodded, a smile spreading across his face, before signalling to the crew to set sail.

The three ships departed from the docks and sailed into open waters.

"If you'll do the honours, my queen," the captain said, presenting Artoria with a bow and arrow.

Artoria gently placed Alastor on the floor and accepted the bow. With a flicker of her magic, she ignited the arrow and took aim at the docks, which were still visible in the distance. With a steady hand, she released the arrow, and it soared through the air.

A few moments later, a deafening explosion echoed across the sea. Then, three more explosions followed in quick succession, sending powerful shockwaves that rocked the ships side to side.

"Well, if that doesn't send a message…" the captain remarked, as they watched the Iron Coast collapse and burn under the night sky.

*

The great hall buzzed with joy and laughter as the people feasted and danced well into the night. Isabella and Liliana twirled gracefully alongside the townsfolk, their laughter mingling with the lively music.

Meanwhile, Xavier sat at the table, sharing a meal with his mother, Layla. Her words carried a touch of melancholy as she spoke.

"Xavier, I wish your father could see this," she murmured softly.

Xavier reached out, clasping her hand gently. "As do I, Mother," he replied, his voice filled with warmth and understanding.

As the setting sun cast a golden glow through the large painted windows, Layla's gaze drifted to Liliana, her expression softening. "What a beautiful sight," she remarked, a hint of pride in her voice.

Xavier glanced to his right, offering another turkey leg to Saya, who sat nearby.

Layla turned her attention back to her son. "What will you do now?"

Xavier met her gaze, contemplating his response. "I'll return to the manor in the Meadows with my wife and our little one here," he replied, a smile playing at his lips. "I don't wish to overshadow Liliana's reign, and as for Artoria, she's in need of assistance but stubbornly refuses to accept it."

"I'll stay for a while, then perhaps return to the Sands with Sabrina," Layla mused, her eyes distant for a moment.

"We would be delighted to have your company, Mother. Don't be a stranger," Xavier said warmly, reaching out to grasp her hands in his own.

Layla returned the gesture, her expression softening with affection. "Thank you, Xavier. I want you to know how grateful I am for everything you've done for Malsdon and for me. I love you very much, never forget that."

A smile touched Xavier's lips, his eyes reflecting his love for his mother. "I know, Mother. And I'm grateful to have you back in my life."

The celebrations showed no signs of slowing as the evening wore on, with laughter and merriment filling the air. Xavier found himself seated alone at the table, surrounded by the revelry of those close to him, who danced and indulged in copious amounts of ale.

Suddenly, a voice cut through the festivities. "Lord Leo, Lord Leo!"

Xavier's attention snapped towards the source of the voice, where he saw a guard blocking the path of a small boy attempting to approach the table.

"Let him through," Xavier commanded, his tone firm but gentle.

The guard nodded, stepping aside to allow the boy to pass.

"What's wrong, Leo?" Xavier asked, concern etching his features as he addressed the young boy.

"I don't know… My father left during the ceremony," Leo replied, his voice tinged with worry and confusion.

"He didn't say anything to you?" Xavier pressed, his brow furrowing with concern.

Leo shook his head dejectedly, his gaze falling to the ground.

Without hesitation, Xavier rose from his seat and crossed over to where Leo sat, offering him comfort and reassurance. "We'll find out what happened. Let's speak to the watch guard and see if they saw him leave," he said, his voice gentle but resolute.

Xavier guided Leo through the swirling mass of dancing bodies and spilt ale, gripping the boy's arm tightly to ensure he wouldn't be lost in the tumult. Suddenly, Xavier came to a halt, his gaze fixed intensely on a nearby window. A flash of light and a tremor followed, causing a hush to fall over the room.

Liliana and Xavier locked eyes, a silent exchange passing between them as they both sensed the impending danger. Then, the warning horn sounded from the guard tower, jolting the occupants of the hall into action.

The music ceased abruptly, replaced by a rising tide of murmurs and panicked whispers as people began to frantically make for the exits. However, their flight was halted by Saya's thunderous roar, which echoed through the hall, commanding attention.

"No need to panic! You're safe here. Return to your seats for now," Xavier's authoritative voice rang out above the chaos. He turned to River, issuing swift commands to secure the palace.

River nodded in understanding, swiftly directing the guards to their stations while the frightened crowd slowly began to settle back into their seats.

Meanwhile, Liliana stepped forwards to address the gathering, her voice steady and commanding, reassuring the people before exiting the room.

Xavier gently handed Leo over to Layla and Sabrina, his expression filled with determination. "I promise, I will find your father," he assured the boy before giving him a reassuring pat on the head.

With a nod to his mother and aunt, Xavier followed Liliana out of the hall, his senses alert and his resolve firm.

Liliana approached the waiting guards, who were mounted on

horseback at the gates. "What area was attacked?" she asked, her voice steady despite the underlying tension.

"The Iron Coast," Xavier replied, his expression grave.

The guards nodded in confirmation. "You see that glow?" one of them pointed out.

"That's where the Iron Coast is," Liliana remarked, her gaze fixed on the distant glow.

"The damage appears to be serious if we can see it from here," another guard observed grimly.

"We'll need more men," a third guard suggested, his tone urgent.

"It's just a recon mission," Xavier said, "If we encounter a large force, we break contact."

The guards nodded in understanding, making their final preparations as Liliana and Xavier mounted the horses provided for them.

"Let's move out!" Liliana ordered, her voice ringing out with determination.

With Saya leading the way, the riders charged out of the gate, their steeds thundering beneath them. However, before Xavier could join the pursuit, he paused, turning back to the gate guard.

"Did you stop a man named John pass through this gate?" he asked.

The gate guard shook his head, his expression apologetic. "I'm sorry, sir. I didn't see or stop any man called John."

They rode hard through the night, relying on Saya and their horses to guide them through the darkness of the forest where neither the moon nor the glow of the blaze could penetrate. As they approached the section of the forest nearest to the Iron Coast, Saya slowed down, sensing something amiss. Suddenly, she startled a hidden horse, causing it to crash into Xavier and two other guards.

"Father, are you all right?" Liliana shouted, concern etched in her voice as she dismounted from her horse to assist.

Xavier slowly rose to his feet, brushing himself off. "I'm okay," he reassured her, though his tone was tense.

"I've seen this horse before," a guard remarked, his brow furrowing in recognition.

"When and where?" Xavier demanded sharply, his focus intensifying.

"A man was riding it, as if he were running away or chasing someone," the guard replied, his voice tinged with uncertainty.

"If he was chasing someone, you would hide your horse like that," Xavier deduced, his senses sharpening as he prepared for potential conflict.

Liliana noticed her father's sudden shift in mood, his focus turning razor-sharp as if he were preparing for battle. Then, she too sensed it—a dark presence lurking nearby. "To arms!" she shouted, her voice cutting through the tense air.

"You sense it too?" Xavier asked, locking eyes with his daughter.

"Yes, Fallen… and something else on the other side of these bushes," Liliana confirmed, her senses heightened by the glow of the burning buildings nearby.

The group braced themselves for whatever lay ahead, the heat of the flames intensifying the urgency of their situation.

As the group waited, tension hung heavy in the air, anticipation mounting with each passing moment. But no attack came, leaving them to exchange puzzled glances, uncertainty clouding their expressions. Suddenly, a guard ventured closer to the bushes, only to emit a blood-curdling scream as he was violently dragged into the underbrush, the sickening sound of steel meeting flesh echoing through the night.

Then, with a sudden flurry of motion, a dozen Fallen emerged from the shadows, accompanied by five men who charged at the group without hesitation. The air crackled with the intensity of the impending battle as combat erupted.

Xavier ensured he stayed close to Liliana, their bond providing strength and resolve in the face of danger. With swift precision, Xavier commanded Saya to subdue one of the human assailants. The fierce creature leapt onto her target, pinning him to the ground before sinking her teeth into his shoulder and dragging him away. As a few Fallen gave chase, the guards rallied to cover Saya, recognising the importance of capturing a prisoner for interrogation.

"Not many remaining!" Liliana's voice cut through the chaos, her words a rallying cry amidst the clash of steel.

Xavier and Liliana fought side by side, seamlessly executing a well-practised sword and shield technique. Their movements flowed in perfect harmony, a testament to their shared sword skill and mutual trust. With each strike, they violently dismantled their adversaries with a ferocity akin to a raging river unleashed.

As the last of their enemies fell, the guards stood in awe of the duo's prowess, offering a salute of respect and admiration. Xavier and Liliana turned to face them, their expressions a blend of determination and resolve, united in their commitment to protect Malsdon at all costs.

They all regrouped around Saya who still had the prisoner clenched with her jaws.

"Who ordered you to ambush us?" Xavier asked.

The prisoner laughed and spat at Xavier's boots. Xavier smiled and ordered Saya to let go then ordered the guards to tie him to a tree.

"Father, I can still sense something and I'm going to check it out," Liliana said.

"Okay, take Saya with you. We'll have this guy singing soon," Xavier said.

Liliana and Saya followed the scent of the mysterious presence, pushing through the thick foliage with determination. Saya's instincts led her on, her pace swift and purposeful. Liliana, however, struggled to keep up, hindered by her ceremonial dress, more suited for appearance than mobility. Despite her efforts, she lagged behind, her breaths coming in quick gasps as she broke through the final barrier of bushes.

As Liliana emerged into the clearing, her eyes fell upon Saya, who lay next to a lifeless body.

"He's the source?" she asked, her mind racing with questions.

Approaching cautiously, she knelt beside the body, her gaze shifting to Saya for guidance.

"Do you know him?" Liliana asked softly.

Saya nodded, her expression solemn, before gently pulling at the body to reveal an injured wolf pup hidden beneath. Liliana's heart clenched at the sight, and without hesitation, she cradled it in her arms as she began to channel her healing magic.

As the pup stirred and regained strength, Liliana spoke to it softly, seeking answers. "What happened to you, and where did you come from?"

The pup's gaze met hers, and in that moment, a connection sparked between them. Their eyes locked, and Liliana felt a surge of energy pass between them, a bond forming in an instant. With a sudden rush, memories flooded Liliana's mind, a torrent of images revealing the pup's journey and struggles.

Overwhelmed by the flood of emotions, Liliana collapsed to the ground, tears streaming down her cheeks. The pup, sensing her distress, nuzzled against her, offering comfort in its own way. Saya, too, pressed close, her presence a silent reassurance.

"Why, Artoria?" Liliana's voice rang out, filled with anger and betrayal.

What had initially seemed like sibling rivalry now revealed a darker truth—an insidious plot unfolding, with Artoria at its centre, poised to assume the role of Delilah, the witch queen.

Liliana stood at the entrance of the Iron Coast, her resolve unshaken despite the fierce heat of the roaring flames. The pup cowered between Saya and her, its small frame trembling with fear.

"Liliana, what happened?" Xavier's voice broke through the

chaos, drawing her attention.

As she turned to face him, tears glistened in her glowing eyes, catching Xavier off guard.

Approaching her cautiously, Xavier's gaze lingered on the pup. "Where did you find it?" he asked, his tone laced with curiosity.

"Under a dead body. I believe it was the man you were looking for," Liliana replied.

Xavier reached out to grasp her arm, a silent plea for answers. "What happened? Tell me."

"You should deal with the body," Liliana deflected, her attention fixated on the devastation before them.

Nodding in understanding, Xavier signalled for the guards to attend to the fallen man. As they moved to carry out his orders, Liliana's emotions overwhelmed her, and she sobbed openly, the pup rushing to her side in a gesture of comfort.

"A gigas wolf pup," Xavier murmured, a flicker of recognition crossing his features as memories from the past resurfaced. "Who, Liliana? Tell me?"

"She is my sister, your daughter!" Liliana's voice rang out, filled with anguish and betrayal.

Xavier's heart sank at her words, grappling with the weight of the revelation. "We were too late to help her," he murmured, his voice heavy with sorrow.

"No, she didn't want our help. This is what she wanted!" Liliana's voice rose, her grief turning to anger as she recounted Artoria's betrayal.

As Liliana collapsed to her knees, consumed by anguish, Xavier knelt beside her, enfolding her in a tight embrace.

"I know she had something to do with Grandfather's demise. I just know it," Liliana sobbed, her words punctuated by her pain.

"First, you must help the people of Malsdon," Xavier urged gently, his own anguish evident.

"She has to pay for everything!" Liliana cried out, her fury uncontainable.

"You are the queen. We will follow you to whatever end, but you know what must be done first," Xavier reminded her, his voice a steady anchor in the tumult of emotions.

Part Four
Battle of the Queens

CHAPTER FIFTY

FULL CIRCLE

In the five years since Liliana's coronation, Malsdon underwent a profound transformation in preparation for the inevitable clash with Artoria and her Fallen army. The Iron Coast, once a site of destruction, was now fortified and repurposed into a formidable naval port. The displaced residents found refuge in the Vermillion Sands and Emerald Meadows, while patrols and watchtowers dotted the island's perimeter, ensuring constant vigilance against any incursion.

Ships patrolled Malsdon's waters ceaselessly, with a fortified outpost on Alice Island serving as an early warning system against potential threats from Artoria's fleet. Borders were rigorously patrolled day and night, and the populace underwent rigorous training, many transitioning into part-time or full-time soldiers to bolster Malsdon's defences.

Meanwhile, Xavier spearheaded the reformation of Jupiter's Moon, handpicking and training fifty elite swordsmen to join the esteemed order. Stationed at the Leo estate in the Emerald Meadows, these warriors honed their skills in preparation for the impending conflict.

As Malsdon fortified itself against external threats, the land began to heal from the ravages of the past. Flora and fauna flourished once more, as the remnants of the black rain were gradually cleansed from the island. With the return of abundance, the people of Malsdon found solace in the rejuvenation of their homeland, ready to defend it against any who dared to threaten its newfound prosperity.

It was the summer season across the island, and summer was particularly enchanting in the Emerald Meadows, where the local flora thrived with life. As midday approached, Xavier began to stir.

"No more late nights," he mumbled to himself.

"You're not as young as you used to be," Isabella said with a yawn.

Xavier chuckled softly before making his way to the bedroom window. "I will never tire of this view," he said as he gazed out.

He watched the grass and flowers sway gently in the light breeze, Saya, their faithful companion, napping peacefully in the midst of the fields, and some of his men training on the far side. Suddenly, a bellowing howl echoed from the forest in front of the manor, grabbing his attention.

Xavier observed a dozen hooded riders, accompanied by a wolf, emerging from the forest and onto the path leading to the gates. "We have a special guest."

"It must be urgent, given that we received no prior indication of their arrival," Isabella replied.

"I'll greet her; you get dressed," Xavier said as he pulled on his boots.

Xavier swung open the manor's doors to behold the riders in his courtyard. "Greetings, daughter."

She removed her hood and smiled. "It's been a while, Father."

The other riders followed suit, revealing themselves.

"It's been a long ride. We'll bring your horses over to the stables," Xavier offered.

"Most generous, my lord," Commander Aurelia replied.

Liliana dismounted her horse, allowing her guards to take charge. "I must speak with you, Father."

"Very well. We'll take a walk through the meadows," Xavier replied.

Commander Aurelia glanced back with concern.

"I'll be fine, Commander. Tend to the horses, and get some rest," Liliana reassured.

"Yes, my queen," Commander Aurelia replied.

Xavier frowned at the commander.

"What's the matter?" Liliana asked.

"Does he not think me capable of keeping my daughter safe?"

"He's just doing his job," Isabella interjected, "Ensuring our daughter's safety."

Liliana turned sharply at the sound of her mother's voice and rushed over, embracing Isabella tightly. "I've missed you, Mother," she said.

"So have I. Don't mind your father; he just woke up."

Xavier rolled his eyes. "When you're ready, I'll be in the fields to the left."

"My word, Shadow has really grown," Isabella said as they both sat on the steps.

"Yes, he has," Liliana agreed.

Isabella sighed and then took her daughter's hand. "I'm guessing you're not here to spend a few days with your parents."

"No, Mother, I'm afraid not," Liliana replied as she squeezed her mother's hands tightly.

*

"Make sure the horses drink plenty of water," Commander Aurelia ordered as he placed the queen's horse into the stables, while the others took on water just outside.

"Look who it is…" a voice said.

"Who's there?" the commander asked.

A woman emerged from one of the pens, with pale ivory skin and hair as dark as night, much like his own. Her clothes were covered in hay and mud.

"You've come to see how real knights act," she taunted.

"Captain Ursula Annora, it's always a pleasure," the commander replied.

Captain Annora spat on the ground as a sign of disrespect.

"Remember, I outrank you," Commander Aurelia added.

Captain Annora laughed uncontrollably, then started coughing. "I don't answer to you. I am captain of Jupiter's Moon, remember that," she said sternly. "Why don't you do what you do best and pine over the queen?"

"You forget your place!" he shouted as he reached for his sword.

"That's enough!" a deep voice boomed.

A group of knights entered the stables, clad in the black and crimson colours of Jupiter's Moon, led by a man whose deep ebony skin glistened with sweat as the sunlight streamed in through the stable windows.

"Henry, it's good to see you again," the man said.

"Likewise, Edward," Commander Aurelia replied.

"I expect better from you, Captain. Go and cool off," Edward said.

"Yes, Commander Grey," Captain Annora replied.

"Right, Commander, you and your men, come join us for lunch in the barracks," Commander Grey offered.

"We will. Thank you for the invitation," Commander Aurelia replied.

The new barracks stood three hundred metres to the right of the manor, two storeys high with living quarters upstairs. The hall, along with the kitchen, were on the ground floor. Inside, chatter and the clatter of utensils filled the hall.

"Apologies for Ursula's behaviour. It was her birthday last night, and she lost a wager with Xavier, so she had to clean the stables," Commander Grey explained.

"It's fine. I took no offense," Commander Aurelia replied.

"She's a formidable knight, fierce as a grey bear, one of the best with a sword," Commander Grey added.

"Yes, she is."

Captain Annora entered the hall with her head down, drawing a few chuckles from the knights as she approached the table where the commanders sat.

"Commander Grey, forgive me for my actions," Captain Annora said sincerely.

"Very well, Captain, but it's not me you need to apologise to," Commander Grey replied.

"I'm sorry, Aurelia," she said.

Commander Grey sighed as Captain Annora smirked, knowing that not addressing him as "Commander" might cause offense.

"Thank you, Captain. I hope you enjoyed your birthday," Commander Aurelia said, then waited a few moments to wink at her.

This irritated Captain Annora.

"Now that's settled, come take your seat and have lunch," Commander Grey said.

Captain Annora glanced at Aurelia and then at the queen's guard. "I'll eat alone; I'm not dressed for company," she said, then walked off.

Commander Grey placed his head in his hands and sighed loudly. "The chip on her shoulder will never go."

"What is she trying to prove?" Commander Aurelia asked.

"She was saved by Xavier and Liliana when they liberated the Vermillion Sands. She was weak and unable to defend herself or her mother, who was turned into a Fallen creature," Commander Grey explained.

"That's why she doesn't like me? Because she thinks she's the better person with a sword? She should be protecting our queen, not me," Commander Aurelia replied as he watched Captain Annora take her food and go outside.

"Her heart is always in the right place," Commander Grey smiled.

CHAPTER FIFTY-ONE

UNWANTED WORDS

The midday sun's rays danced through the leaves atop the trees, casting shifting shadows onto the path as Xavier and Liliana strolled along.

"Why is it so peaceful here?" Liliana mused, absently toying with Shadow's ear as the wolf trotted beside her.

"The land is at peace," Xavier replied serenely, drawing in a deep breath as the fresh breeze caressed his face.

"Father, I suppose you have an inkling of why I'm here," Liliana said, her tone shifting, imbuing the moment with gravity.

"What news do you have about your sister?"

For hours, Xavier and Liliana wandered through the forests of the Meadows, lost in conversation, before finally returning to the manor.

As early evening approached, Liliana and her guard saddled up the horses, preparing for their journey back to the palace. Isabella, Xavier, and Commander Grey accompanied them to the gate, exchanging final farewells. Xavier watched as they galloped off down the path, disappearing into the forest.

"Commander Grey, gather all the knights in the hall," Xavier ordered.

"My lord, is everything all right?" the commander asked.

"We've been activated."

The commander nodded, swiftly making his way towards the barracks.

"I'll wait for you in the manor," Isabella said, kissing him on the cheek.

"I need you to come as well," Xavier said.

"Are you sure?" she asked.

"Yes, you need to hear this too."

Xavier, Isabella, and Commander Grey stood at the front of the hall, facing Captain Annora and the assembled knights as they took their seats.

"Knights, you are the best at what you do, and few can challenge us!" Xavier declared.

The knights banged the table with their fists three times in unison.

"With the capabilities we possess, we will be tasked with missions that would be nearly impossible for most," Xavier continued.

Again, the knights banged the table in unison.

"The mission we've been selected for would be considered suicide for most, but not for us. We have less than a ten percent chance of returning home," Xavier explained, scanning the faces of each of his fifty knights. "I and three others will go on this mission."

"I'm with you, my lord," Captain Annora declared without hesitation.

"Commander Grey will stay behind and carry my authority," Xavier stated.

"Of course. We will all take our final orders from the lady of the manor," Commander Grey added in a formal tone.

"I will join you," a voice spoke up from the back.

"Stand and present yourself," the commander ordered.

Xavier saw who it was and shook his head. "You must stay."

"My lord, with all due respect, I'm coming with you," Leo Greenford said.

"There's a high chance your name ends with you, my boy."

"Those responsible for my father's death will meet my sword or my bare hands," Leo replied.

Commander Grey nudged Xavier. "Let the boy go. That drive will keep him alive."

"Or lead him to an early grave," Xavier countered.

Xavier looked Leo in the eyes and nodded.

"There is no shame in not raising your hand. Many of you have not seen real combat, nor do you have children of your own," Xavier addressed the hall.

The room remained silent after Xavier's words.

"Will we have Saya with us?" a knight asked.

"No, she'll stay here with the remaining knights," Xavier explained.

"The rest of you return to your quarters," Commander Grey ordered.

The knights slowly ascended the stairs, their minds filled with a mix of regret for not volunteering and apprehension about the unknown mission.

"Take a seat," Xavier instructed the volunteers.

They complied, settling in and awaiting the briefing on the mission ahead.

"We've been ordered to infiltrate the Forgotten Lands to sabotage military assets and, if possible, assassinate the leadership," Xavier explained.

"Is Artoria on that list?" Isabella asked.

Xavier nodded. "We must do as much as we can before our invasion fleet arrives."

"How long will we be in the country?" Captain Annora asked.

"I'm not sure, but we'll find out more during the final brief at the palace," Xavier replied.

"Any more questions?" Commander Grey interjected.

Xavier gazed at both of them intently. "Rest up. We leave in the morning."

Xavier and Commander Grey exchanged a few words before they both headed off.

"Ursula, wait a moment," Isabella called out.

Captain Annora paused and turned back, descending the few stairs she had taken.

"Yes, my lady?"

"I know you're very fond of my daughter and husband. Please keep him safe."

"I will protect him with my life."

"Don't throw your life away. I want all three of you to come back safely," Isabella said sincerely.

"You have my word. I'll bring him back, no matter what," Captain Annora replied, then bowed to Isabella.

Isabella and Xavier walked back to the manor, both unsure of what to say to each other. They entered the house and settled by the fireplace in their bedroom, with Saya curled up behind them.

"I don't like this, not one bit," Isabella said sternly.

"It's an order from the queen, our daughter," Xavier replied.

"I don't know, Xavier. I just don't."

"Izzy, there's always a reason for everything, and we'll find out at the palace."

"I'd feel slightly better if Saya were going with you."

"No matter what, I'll always find my way back to you," Xavier said, squeezing her hand.

"I know, my dear. You've turned me into such a worrier," she said, then kissed him on the cheek. "I still don't like it."

Xavier reached for a thick book on a side table. "Would you like me to read more?" he offered, trying to comfort his wife.

She smiled and leant her head on his shoulder, positioning herself to see the pages of the book. Xavier opened to the marked page as moonlight beamed through the window, and he began reading his diary from his time in the Forgotten Lands.

*

Morning arrived with a loud knock on the door, startling Xavier and Isabella, who had fallen asleep in front of the fireplace. Saya jumped to her feet and inspected the door.

"Who is it?" Xavier called out with a strained voice.

"My lord, it's Edward. The horses are ready and waiting," Commander Grey's voice said from the other side.

"Ride ahead. We'll meet you on the road," Xavier replied.

"See you soon, my lord," Edward said before the sound of retreating footsteps faded away.

"I think I'll stay in the palace for a few days after you go," Isabella said as she began to wash her face at the barrel in the corner of the room.

"That'll be good. Mother should be there as well."

"I long to see her," Isabella added, her voice muffled by the cloth she used to dry her face.

Xavier began to pace around the room as doubts surfaced in his mind. He started triple-checking all his gear. Saya nudged him with her body, and Xavier looked into her green eyes, sensing her worry.

"Xavier, try and relax. You're making her nervous, and me as well," Isabella said gently.

Xavier nodded. "I'm sorry, my dear. I guess I'm not as brave as I once was."

Isabella opened the door. "You're the bravest man I know, and you'd do anything for the people you care about. Now, let's go and be done with all this so we can sit under the stars."

"Yes, I'll make sure I'm back for that."

CHAPTER FIFTY-TWO

THE NEW

They arrived at the checkpoint in the forest outside the palace gates. Four guards manned the checkpoint, one of them positioned on a ballista with a giant iron arrow, ready to launch.

"Lord Xavier, Lady Isabella, welcome back," the guard said to them and waved them through.

The group slowly made their way through the forest and reached the main gates, where they were stopped again. This guard looked them up and down, his demeanour less welcoming than the previous one.

"The queen is expecting you," he said bluntly.

"Do you know who you're talking to?" Captain Annora challenged, leaning down from her horse.

Xavier tapped her on the shoulder.

"My lord, you should be addressed with respect," she insisted.

"It's fine. We can pass through. Just let it be," Xavier said, riding through the gate with the others.

Annora lingered for a moment, staring down the guard, who became uncomfortable under her gaze. She spat at his feet before riding off to catch up with the others.

"Ursula, I hope you didn't do something foolish," Grey said.

"Nothing he doesn't deserve," she replied with a smile.

Grey rolled his eyes, and Isabella chuckled.

"Am I not a nice person?" she asked.

"Of course, you are," they all said in unison, though with a hint of hesitation.

"Well, you can be a bit mean and harsh," Leo chimed in.

"Now you've done it," Grey muttered.

Ursula's smile turned sinister. "I'll deal with you later, little man."

The commons were bustling with activity, filled with the trading of various items, from exotic plants to butchered meat and crafted weapons. People noticed Xavier and his companions trotting past the stalls.

"My lord, it's good to see you again!" a man shouted.

Many ladies offered him fruits and flowers.

"Never knew you had so many lady friends," Isabella teased.

"No, it's not like that," Xavier said, his face becoming flustered.

"The mighty lion flustered by the lioness," Grey chuckled.

Isabella playfully slapped Xavier's arm. "I'll have to keep my eye on you."

Xavier turned back and blew her a kiss. "All right, everyone, let's pick up the pace. It's rude to keep people waiting," he said in a light tone, not wanting to end the fun abruptly.

Some of the queen's guards and General Silverlight greeted them.

"Well, isn't this a sight: the lord and lady of the Meadows," River smiled.

Xavier smiled and nodded as they came to a stop; the guards took their horses away as they dismounted.

"Xavier, you don't write or visit. Are we not friends anymore?" River teased.

"Well, I had to keep you away from Commander Grey," Xavier teased back.

"My lord?" Grey asked in a confused tone as he adjusted his armour.

River chuckled and winked. "Anyway, Lady Isabella, always happy to see your graceful face."

Isabella laughed. "I think palace life has turned you into someone else."

"Good to see you, Izzy. I hope you've been keeping Xavier happy and not turning his beard grey," River replied.

"That's better." Isabella smiled, and the two hugged.

"Right, now that all the soft stuff is out of the way, I'll take you to the war room," River said as she started to walk towards the steps.

The group followed River through the maze of hallways that crisscrossed the palace.

"Not much has changed," Xavier said, taking in the familiar surroundings.

"Liliana wanted to keep it the same without altering too much," River replied.

"Ballistae at each checkpoint, that's new," Grey added.

"Yes, they've recently been installed at all the main road checkpoints, and there are multiple ones at the palace checkpoints," she explained.

"It's a good idea," Grey replied, "Any large hostile group wouldn't stand a chance against that."

"Well, thank you, Edward," River said, then turned her head to wink at him.

Grey smiled shyly, then glanced around, attempting to conceal his embarrassment.

They stood before the two imposing iron doors, painted black with the royal crest in red at their centre.

"Open the doors," River commanded the two guards. As the doors swung open, River turned to Xavier and the others. "Are you ready?"

Liliana greeted them warmly as they entered the room, while the guards ushered them to their seats around the large, round table positioned in the centre. Each chair was identical except for the one designated for the ruler, slightly taller and of a different hue.

River gestured to the guards to secure the doors. With a resounding thud, the doors slammed shut, the locks clicking into place.

As everyone settled into their seats, anticipation hung thick in the air, awaiting the impending information.

"In recent years, Artoria and her Fallen army have expanded at an alarming rate," Liliana said, cutting straight to the chase, "It's evident to all of us that it's only a matter of time before she directs her attention back to us. I will now defer this part of the briefing to Commander Lynch."

"My queen." Lynch gave a respectful bow before rising from her seat. She signalled for a guard to bring over a board bearing a vast map, positioning it for all to see.

"Is that a map of Malsdon? It seems too large," Grey said.

"No, Commander. This is a map of the Forgotten Lands. Artoria has transformed it into an almost perfect replica," Lynch clarified.

"Is she attempting to recreate our homeland?" Sabrina asked.

"That's part of it, but ultimately, it's a bid to assert her capability to create a superior Malsdon and govern it more effectively than her sister," Xavier explained, his composed demeanour drawing everyone's attention.

"There are a few distinctions," Lynch said, "Where the Vermillion Sands lay, there's a desolate wasteland plagued by many unnatural events. Injured individuals incapable of fighting or labour are transformed into Fallen soldiers. The area resembling our Meadows serves as the living quarters for all workers. Artoria has also launched assaults on the northern islands, eliminating the tribal leaders. However, most of these tribes were mere barbarians, now regarding her as a deity."

"Has there been any aggressive action from Artoria?" Xavier

asked, his gaze fixed intently on the map.

"Some, but it's been costly," Lynch replied with hesitation.

"We lost many scouts gathering this information," River added.

"Also, the ship captains patrolling near Alice Island report that she's amassing a fleet and reacting aggressively to any approach," Commander Lynch continued.

"Wouldn't we do the same?" Xavier posed the question to the table. "What's the plan for me and my companions then?"

"Father, I understand some of this may not seem worthy of your involvement, but Artoria and her Fallen army could easily overrun Malsdon with their numbers, six thousand to our three thousand. We don't have the luxury of time to bolster our forces," Liliana said.

"I understand. Tell me what you need."

"Sabotage their military assets, cause as much destruction and chaos as possible," Liliana replied. "When things get dangerous, with only the three of us against a formidable force, Alice Island is a few hours away. We'll have the garrison from Alice Island aboard ship patrolling—"

"I want my knights aboard those ships," Annora said, her tone assertive.

"You dare interrupt the queen?" Commander Aurelia retorted sharply.

"Don't speak to me. Our lives will be on the line, and I want my fellow knights on board," Annora replied bluntly.

"You may be one of Xavier's knights, but you do not speak out of turn," River said. "You may continue, but mind your manners."

"My life, Leo's, and Xavier's will be in their hands the moment we set foot on the island. I'll speak when necessary," Annora said.

"Any other day, you'd face consequences for your actions," Aurelia replied.

"If you're so brave, try me now!" Annora said, drawing her sword.

The tension escalated as the guards encircled Annora, prompting Xavier and Commander Grey to draw their swords in reflex, their voices lost in the escalating commotion.

"That's enough!" Liliana's voice boomed, cutting through the chaos as she slammed her hand on the table, splitting it down the middle in the process. "The enemy is out there; in here, you're among brothers and sisters of Malsdon."

"Return your swords," Xavier said to Annora and Grey, setting an example as he sheathed his own.

As the situation diffused, Liliana's gaze softened, her eyes returning to their normal state. "Commander Grey will coordinate with General Silverlight to ensure Jupiter's Moon is aboard one of the ships to support you."

"Thank you," Xavier said.

"We will now hand it over to Lady Sabrina and Lady Layla to discuss the supply plan," Liliana added.

*

The meeting concluded as the stars emerged in the Malsdon sky, casting a serene glow over the departing attendees. Formal goodbyes were exchanged as people made their way out of the room.

"My lord, shall I ride back immediately to assemble the knights?" Grey asked.

"There's time tomorrow, my friend. Rest for the night," Xavier said.

"Hey, Commander, I heard you appreciate good ale," River said from across the hallway.

"Not tonight," Grey replied sharply, attempting to dissuade her.

"Pay no mind to him; he'll join you shortly," Xavier said.

"My lord, really?" Grey whispered.

"It's a wise move. Word will spread of what occurred, and if people see two high-ranking officers sharing a drink, it will mitigate any concerns," Xavier explained in a hushed tone.

Grey pondered Xavier's words, finding merit in the suggestion despite his initial reluctance. River smiled and beckoned Grey over, shooting a playful wink at Xavier.

"For a man of his stature, he's surprisingly shy," Annora remarked.

"Ursula, I appreciate your concern, but that's not the way," Xavier gently reprimanded.

"It just seems like an unnecessary risk for us to take," she replied.

"You volunteered for this mission," he reminded her.

"We can't dispatch the main army immediately," Liliana said, approaching with Aurelia and three guards in tow, "We'd risk losing half our men at sea and would be vastly outnumbered on land. What you're about to do will increase our chances of victory."

Annora froze, then swiftly knelt before Liliana. "Forgive me, my queen."

Liliana extended her hand, helping Annora to her feet. "All is forgiven. You're a good person, and you wouldn't have my father's blessing and care if you weren't."

"Thank you, my queen. If you'll excuse me, I should retire for the night," Annora replied.

"I'll see you at dawn," Xavier said as she departed.

"Father, before you retire, meet me in the throne room."

Xavier nodded in acknowledgement. "I will."

He lingered in the throne room, leaning against River's chair. The palace was enveloped in an airy silence, punctuated only by the sporadic footsteps of guards that echoed through the dimly lit hall. Despite the stillness, Xavier couldn't shake off his unease.

The door creaked open, and Liliana entered slowly. Xavier's apprehension melted away as he embraced his daughter tightly for a few moments.

"Liliana, are you all right?" he asked.

"No, Father."

"Let's sit down, all right?" Xavier said, guiding Liliana to the steps of the throne where they settled together.

"Ever since that day we found the Iron Coast burning and your friend dead in the forest, I've never been able to relax," Liliana confessed.

"We all feared that it could happen again, but to more places in Malsdon. The waiting is unbearable."

"Yes. Is she waiting for something to happen before attacking us, or has she left us in the past?"

"She's your twin sister and my daughter, but the atrocities she's committed leave death as the only outcome."

"I make no mistake in thinking she won't be a formidable opponent."

"You'll have to be the one to end her. Without my powers, I'll be no match," Xavier said, locking eyes with Liliana.

Liliana nodded solemnly, her gaze falling to her hands. "I will not hesitate, no matter what."

Xavier stepped off the steps and knelt before Liliana. "With all my might, I will ensure Malsdon has a future, even if it leads to my death. For my queen and country, I will not fail."

"And for your daughter and my mother, you will make it back alive, so you both can live out the rest of your days in peace," Liliana replied, her voice filled with determination and love.

CHAPTER FIFTY-THREE

FAMILIAR GOODBYES, RUDE WELCOMES

Xavier stood in the courtyard with Saya and Isabella next to the wagon that would take him and his two companions to the ship awaiting them at the docks. He knelt down in front of Saya and enveloped her in a big hug. "You look after Isabella for me," he said softly.

Rising, he turned to Isabella and embraced her. "My beautiful wife, I promise we'll have more nights in front of the fire and under the starry sky," he whispered.

"I like the sound of that," Isabella replied, trying to contain her emotions.

Xavier held her hand tightly until the others arrived.

A few minutes later, Leo and Ursula arrived accompanied by Grey and River. Leo nodded at Xavier, then climbed into the wagon. Ursula nodded at Grey and exchanged a glance with River before joining Leo.

"My lady, I'll make sure he behaves," Ursula said, attempting to ease Isabella's pain.

Isabella managed a grateful smile. She turned back to Xavier, locking eyes with him, and kissed him. "You make sure you do anything you have to, by any means, to get this done and get back safely."

Xavier nodded solemnly and hugged her one last time before jumping into the wagon.

"Whatever it takes," Isabella murmured as Xavier settled in.

With that, the wagon slowly began its journey.

The wagon sped down the main roads and forest trails, the passengers sitting in silence, absorbing the views Malsdon offered. Xavier took out his dagger and began shaving off his beard. Ursula and Leo observed as Xavier's hand remained steady despite the rough terrain.

"Impressive, my lord," Leo said.

Xavier chuckled. "Took me a good amount of time to grow that beard."

"Not many people have seen you without one," Ursula added.

"That was the idea," Xavier replied.

As they approached the Iron Coast, the road smoothed out.

"That's impressive," Leo said, gazing at the towering three-storey walls and gate.

"Took some skill to make that," Ursula added, her eyes tracing the walls' contours.

The guard waved them through as the giant gates slowly opened, revealing the changes that had taken place over the years. The wagon rumbled down the road towards the docks, the passengers taking in the sight of the various blacksmiths and storage facilities that now occupied what were once houses for the people.

"At least there's a new tavern," Ursula said.

Naval soldiers patrolled past the wagon, casting scrutinising glances at the three occupants.

"Do they know who we are?" Leo asked.

"I'm guessing that's what they're trying to find out," Ursula replied.

"Take no notice of them. Stay focused; we're almost there," Xavier said reassuringly.

"Lord Xavier, welcome," Commander Lynch said as she stood in front of the ship.

"Commander, why are you here?" Xavier asked as he climbed off the wagon.

"The scout who was meant to go with you, he never made it back to Alice Island," she explained. "So I'm your fourth person."

Xavier smiled warmly. "You're most welcome."

Ursula and Leo saluted the commander as they disembarked from the wagon.

"What's the plan now?" Xavier asked as they followed Lynch onto the ship.

"We'll head to Alice Island and board a captured ship, then act as if we're fleeing from the Malsdon navy," she outlined. "However, we're going to crash on the shore. We need to make it look like we took damage, as we wouldn't make it through the docks with just four of us on the ship."

"They expect a ship full of barbarians or dead bodies to turn into Fallen," the ship captain added.

"All right, let's get this over with. On your orders, Captain," Xavier said decisively.

The captain nodded in acknowledgement and began to ready the crew.

*

Late afternoon the crew made it to Alice Island and boarded the ship. They left behind anything that would give them away as knights from Malsdon. Now wearing attire from the dead barbarians, the brave four sailed for the Forgotten Lands. The sea was calm and the day was clear with a light breeze that refreshed them with every hit. The occasional splash of water from a bolt fired from the Malsdon ships following them, reminded them this would be the last friendly act they'd receive for a while.

"Are we ready?" Lynch shouted, pointing at the enemy patrol ships closing in. She scrambled over to a barrel in the corner and lit the fuse.

"You sure that won't kill us?" Leo asked nervously.

"We'll be fine, it'll make it to shore," she reassured him, then signalled the Malsdon ship.

The ship fired one more bolt, timing it perfectly with the explosion of the barrel. The ship rocked violently, knocking them all down. The Malsdon ship turned around, heading back to Alice Island, but the two patrol ships were still closing in.

"What's your plan for them?" Ursula asked.

Lynch looked upon the closing ships then readied two more barrels. "Ursula, I need you to steer the ship to the left and aim for the beach. It'll come into view soon!" she shouted. "Leo and Xavier, I need you to be ready with these barrels in case we get boarded."

The patrol ships came alongside the ship and were almost within boarding range.

"Xavier, we have no choice!" Lynch shouted as she saw the Fallen on both ships.

Xavier looked at the beach then back at her. "Let them board, then we blow the barrels. We can swim the rest of the way."

Lynch looked at Leo and Ursula, who were in agreement. The hooks came looping over and dug deep into the wood, making an uncomfortable scraping sound. The Fallen dragged their ship over, slamming into it as the other ship slowly pulled up on the port side.

"Light it now!" Lynch shouted.

Xavier and Leo lit their barrels as Ursula and Lynch jumped into the sea.

"Stop right there!" the enemy captain shouted as he ordered the Fallen onto the ship.

Xavier and Leo ran towards the back of the ship and jumped off as the Fallen flooded in. The ship exploded violently, causing the four to dive down to avoid the various forms of debris that occupied the sky.

They surfaced to a field of floating wood and body parts; the air was thick with smoke and the smell of burnt flesh making it hard to breathe.

"Let's go, either the smoke will kill us or the other patrol ships will," Xavier said.

"If you find it difficult to swim that length, grab a piece of wood to support you," Lynch said.

They all readied themselves for the tormenting swim ahead.

*

Liliana looked on from horseback as her army gathered at the Iron Coast.

"I'm sorry, my queen, it took longer than usual," River said as she observed the soldiers entering the Iron Coast.

"It's been almost four days; we have to be at sea by tomorrow noon," Liliana replied with a hint of urgency.

"I know. Also, some good news: Jupiter's Moon arrived at Alice Island two days ago, so they should be in the water with the garrison which was stationed there."

Liliana looked down at Shadow, then towards the sky.

"When or if you meet her in combat, don't give any quarter," River advised.

"I know, it's just something Father said to me," Liliana replied, her voice tinged with resolve.

River leant her head encouragingly towards Liliana.

"They see her as a god. Unless we could change that, we'll be fighting the whole island," Liliana said, contemplating their strategy.

"Get some food in you. I haven't seen you eat in a while," River suggested.

"Are you ordering me?" Liliana asked, a hint of defensiveness in her tone.

"No, as a good friend of yours, I'm *advising* you to eat," River clarified, her tone firm.

Liliana snapped at River's reply and the tone of it. "How can I? There's too much going on. What if we're late and I find my father's dead body as we arrive?"

"It's war!" River's voice rose in frustration. "We all lost loved ones. You can't save everyone; just make sure they didn't die for nothing."

A few soldiers looked back as they sharply put their words across.

"I'll see you in the morning," River said as she rode off to calm the situation.

Liliana held her head in her hands. "I have to control myself," she muttered to herself. "This isn't me."

*

The frantic footsteps of men deafened Leo and Ursula as they lay hidden in a mud pile. The closer the men got, the colder they became, their fear escalating as the unfamiliar languages only heightened their anxiety. The sound of steel being driven into wet mud seemed to seal their fate. Unable to see and struggling to breathe, Leo grabbed Ursula's hand tightly, seeking comfort in the face of impending danger.

Suddenly, screams pierced the air, followed by the clashing of steel. The chaos brought a glimmer of hope to Leo and Ursula, even as they remained hidden in the mud pile, their hearts pounding with fear. The sounds continued for a few moments until silence fell like a heavy shroud.

"Ursula, Leo, can you hear me?" Xavier's voice cut through the silence, a beacon of relief in the darkness.

Xavier and Lynch searched every mud pile until they spotted a hand popping out from the top of one.

"Mother's love, they're alive," Lynch said, relief evident in her voice.

They pulled out Leo first, then Ursula, who was worse for wear.

"My lord, Commander, thank you," Leo said gratefully as he knelt down, trying to catch his breath.

Xavier nodded, his eyes scanning the surroundings.

"Leo, I told you before, call me Mona," Lynch reminded him with a smile.

Ursula wiped the mud from her face and patted Leo on the back. "You did well, kid," she said, her tone sincere and meaningful.

"Wipe yourself off and hide the bodies," Xavier said as he threw the swords into the bushes, "We have to get back to the camp."

"You're late!" the guard shouted angrily. "You see the sky? When there's no sun, you come back here!"

The group nodded, pretending not to understand the language.

"There's no point. Stupid barbarians! These workers don't understand anything," the other guard added.

The guard took his wooden club and struck Leo in the face. He laughed cruelly as Leo fell to the ground, clutching his nose. Ursula moved to charge at the guard, but Xavier quickly pulled her back.

"Look here, we've got a live one," the guard jeered. "You better control that wench before we teach her a lesson."

Xavier nodded grimly and hurried Ursula into the encampment, while Mona helped Leo to his feet. Ursula looked back at the guards, who were harassing a group of barbarians who had arrived late.

"Fools! Traitors! They're lucky I haven't killed them yet," she seethed with anger.

Xavier pushed her along until they reached the tent they all shared.

Xavier and Mona sat by the small fire outside their tent, their faces illuminated by its flickering light, while Ursula tended to Leo's injury inside the tent.

"It was too close this time, even the last time. You almost lost your eye," Mona said, her voice filled with concern.

"I know. We're going to need reinforcements," Xavier replied, his tone serious.

Mona took out a map and placed it between them, pointing to a location. "I don't think Artoria is in the makeshift palace."

Xavier nodded. "Everything is too close, and she would have reacted by now." He then pointed to a point on the north side of the map.

"She's living there, inside the fortress?" Mona asked.

"That makes the most sense," Ursula interjected as she emerged from the tent.

Xavier glanced back at the tent.

"He's fine, just resting," Ursula reassured them.

"It'll be almost impossible to get there if the whole Fallen army is on this side of the island," Mona said.

"Don't forget the barbarian warriors," Ursula added grimly.

"We signal the ships, and they'll take three hours to get here. If we're lucky, one hour," Xavier said.

"I'll signal the ships at dawn before the workers get sent out," Mona replied, "While the rest of you blend in. Then meet me on the beach."

They all nodded in agreement, then double-checked their surroundings for any spies. All that lurked were the overworked barbarians droning around the camp.

"Xavier, take this," Mona said, handing over a small pouch.

"Silver powder?"

"Yes. There are small barrels of oil around the camp. If anything happens while I'm gone, it should create a big enough explosion for you all to escape."

They entered the tent after finishing their planning, seeking some much-needed sleep. The tent, like all others in the encampment, was only big enough for two people. However, Mona's and Ursula's lean frames made it easier for them all to squeeze in together.

As they settled down, Xavier sensed an uneasy energy among them. "No one is dying, and we're all making it back. Because I don't want my last night to be squashed up with you three."

There was a moment of silence, then two slaps and a poke followed.

"Any man in Malsdon would die for this situation," Ursula chuckled.

"Right, two of the finest officers in Malsdon," Mona added.

"The smelliest," Leo whispered with a grin.

"With a broken nose, you won't be able to smell us," Ursula teased.

They all laughed softly, the tension momentarily lifted. Xavier smiled contentedly before closing his eyes, feeling a sense of camaraderie and unity among them as they prepared for the challenges ahead.

*

River woke as the sun was rising, the first rays of light filtering through the canvas of her tent. She rose from her makeshift bed and splashed water on her face, the cool liquid awakening her senses. As she dried her face, she noticed a note resting on top of a nearby barrel. She picked it up and quickly scanned the words, her heart sinking as she realised the gravity of the message.

Without hesitation, River dashed out of her tent, her mind racing with urgency. "Soldier, sound the horn!" she commanded, her voice cutting through the early morning air. "And find Commander Aurelia!"

Four short blasts from the horn echoed throughout the encampment, jolting the men from their slumber.

"To the ships, hurry!" River shouted.

A soldier rushed to her side, his eyes wide with alarm. "General, the supplies are still being loaded onto the ships."

"Those ships will have to wait. The first group of ships with soldiers will set sail first," River declared, her voice unwavering despite the chaos unfolding around them. "We're splitting the army."

The soldier looked uncertain. "Splitting the army?"

"We have no choice. Now go!" River ordered, urging him into action.

The men frantically rushed through the gates of the Iron Coast, their movements fuelled by a sense of urgency. Most were still donning their armour as they ran, their faces etched with determination.

"That damn girl," River muttered to herself, frustration evident in her voice, as she watched the chaos unfold before her.

"General!" Aurelia's voice cut through the commotion.

River turned to see Aurelia approaching.

"Get your men on the first ship right now," River ordered without preamble.

"What about the horses?" Aurelia asked, his brow furrowed with concern.

"They'll have to go on the second wave of ships. Now go!" River urged, pushing him along as they hurried to carry out their orders.

CHAPTER FIFTY-FOUR

THE LOST DAUGHTER

"Right, you rats, stand straight!" the guard bellowed, his voice cutting through the air.

The workers slowly lined up alongside the dirt road that ran through the camp, Xavier standing among them in the third row. He watched in silence as the guards ruthlessly beat the workers who failed to stand straight in line.

"Xavier, what's happening?" Ursula whispered, her voice tinged with concern.

Xavier turned his head back towards her, a grim expression on his face. "Took your time," he replied quietly. "And I'm not sure. Maybe they're looking for us."

"Leo is further down the line, and Mona should have signalled the ship by now," Ursula noted, her eyes scanning the scene with unease.

A strange, airy feeling seemed to permeate the camp, and suddenly, a powerful wave of emotions swept over Xavier.

"Xavier, you okay?" Ursula whispered, her voice barely audible over the chaos.

"You worthless things, bow your heads for your queen!" the guard's voice thundered, commanding attention.

Xavier turned his head, his gaze falling upon Artoria, dressed in full white atop a black horse, her presence commanding and formidable. She was followed by her gigas wolf, the creature twice the size of Shadow. Ursula observed in awe as she tiptoed to catch a glimpse.

Artoria halted and beckoned a guard forwards who was pulling a wagon laden with a dead body and various items. With a swift motion, she signalled for the guard to stop, then tipped the wagon over, causing its contents to spill onto the ground. Xavier observed the scattered items, recognising a few they had used for various missions.

"Commander Lynch's missing scout?" Ursula asked, her voice filled with concern.

"Most likely," Xavier replied quietly, his eyes fixed on the scene unfolding before them.

Artoria extended her hand, and with a subtle gesture, she lifted all the items and the body into the air, displaying them for everyone to see. "My people, I'm not very happy with what's been going on," she declared, her gaze sweeping over the crowd.

"She's holding all that in the air without even focusing," Ursula whispered in awe, marvelling at Artoria's abilities.

Artoria singled out pieces of barrel, lifting them higher than the others. "These were used to blow up my forges," she exclaimed angrily, then slammed the barrel remains into the ground.

She then lifted a bunch of swords and axes, her expression darkening. "If I'm not mistaken, these are barbarian weapons, but yet you use them against my guards and your own!"

With a sudden, swift motion, Artoria slammed the swords and axes into part of the crowd, killing a few of the workers. Panic rippled through the crowd as they took a few steps back, their fear palpable in the air.

"Stay where you are!" Artoria's voice boomed, her eyes turning black as her tone became heart-wrenching. "Now, onto the main surprise."

With a swift motion, she lifted the dead body and removed the hood, revealing the person's head.

"This person isn't a barbarian, and he's from Malsdon!" she

exclaimed, her words ringing out with accusation. "He was clever, dyeing his hair black, but his natural silver colour revealed itself to me."

Artoria scanned the crowd intently, searching for any signs of reaction. "This is a message for those scouts still hiding here," she announced with a sinister smile.

With a flick of her wrist, Artoria used her powers to pull the scout's head from his body, then tossed it to Alastor, who eagerly devoured it. She then held the lifeless body aloft for a few moments longer before hurling it at the rows of workers in front of Xavier. As the people fell aside, Xavier was revealed.

Artoria and Xavier locked eyes, the tension between them palpable. Her eyes began to widen in surprise, but suddenly, a guard rushed over and pointed towards the south, breaking her attention away from Xavier. A smile spread across her lips as she ordered the guards who followed her to go with Alastor to investigate.

"Get to work now!" The guard's harsh command rang out, sending a shiver down Xavier's spine.

He watched as the guards began hurriedly ushering the workers out of the camp, their clubs raised menacingly, ready to strike anyone who moved too slowly or dared to meet their gaze.

"Ursula, find Leo and meet up with Mona. I'll be right behind you," Xavier instructed quietly, his voice barely audible over the chaos.

He squeezed her shoulder reassuringly before slipping away into the camp, his movements swift and stealthy.

Ursula nodded and seamlessly blended into the crowd, disappearing from sight.

Meanwhile, Xavier crept around the camp, his senses sharp as he gathered small barrels of oil. A few workers passed him by, their eyes downcast and oblivious to his actions. With careful precision, he collected five barrels, enough for a decent-sized explosion to grab the guards' attention and any other soldiers in the vicinity.

Xavier slowly poured the silver powder on top of one of the

barrels, his hands steady despite the tension in the air. He then carefully led a line away from it, preparing to ignite the makeshift fuse. But before he could even reach for his flint, he was suddenly knocked off his feet by something so silent he couldn't hear or sense it coming.

"I don't think that's a good idea," a voice cautioned, breaking through Xavier's dizziness.

Slowly, he stood up, his vision clearing to reveal the face of someone he both loved and hated. "I knew you saw me," he said, his voice tinged with resignation.

Artoria laughed, her steps bringing her closer to Xavier. "I didn't believe it at first, but I know Liliana hasn't got it inside her to come face me herself. But of course, you'll do anything for your little girl."

"Did you give up Darius to Delilah?" Xavier asked, his gaze unwavering as he met Artoria's eyes.

"What does it matter now? He's dead, and you'll join him soon. You should have stayed on Malsdon," Artoria replied, drawing her sword and circling Xavier, her movements stirring up the dirt around him. "Let's finish this. I promise I won't use my magic on a weak opponent such as yourself."

Xavier stepped back, his hand instinctively grasping an iron rod left behind by one of the workers. "Your swordsmanship was also second best to your sister, so this will be an easy feat," he said, attempting to get under Artoria's skin.

As Xavier readied himself, he noticed Artoria's expression change after his comment. He also observed that she had stopped parallel to the barrels, and the line of silver powder remained untouched before him, undisturbed by Artoria's kicking.

Artoria's smile widened, her eyes glowing black with malevolent energy. With a swift motion, she brought her sword up over her head and swung it down violently, unleashing a rippling shockwave that struck Xavier squarely in the chest. But just as the blow landed, Xavier managed to strike the iron rod against the powder, creating a spark that ignited the silver.

As Xavier was flung backwards by the force of the shockwave, the barrels erupted in a fiery blast, engulfing Artoria within its flames. The additional shockwave from the explosion knocked Xavier unconscious as he crashed to the ground.

*

Ursula and Leo rendezvoused with Mona, who was hiding in a small cave system not far from the beach.

"Her wolf is searching the area along with her traitorous guards," Ursula whispered, her voice barely audible in the darkness as they huddled together.

"We have to hope the wolf doesn't pick up our scent," Mona replied, her tone tense with anticipation. "There are only two ways in: a tiny opening on the beach and the way I brought you two through."

Suddenly, the distant sound of the explosion echoed into the cave, causing Leo to tense up. "Was that an explosion?" he asked, his eyes scanning the darkness.

"That must be Xavier," Ursula said, her voice filled with concern.

Mona rose to her feet, armed only with a bow and a few arrows, then made her way towards the tunnel that would lead her closer to Xavier. "The ships have been signalled. If anything happens, make your way to the beach and pray they're not late."

Leo and Ursula nodded, their resolve firm as they stepped out of the shadows to gather a selection of weapons Mona had gathered, preparing themselves for whatever lay ahead.

*

Xavier stumbled through the dense foliage, his progress slowed by the pain in his leg. The voices grew louder around him, and he urged himself forwards, gritting his teeth against the ache.

"Come on," he muttered under his breath, his hand pressing

against the wound on his leg to stem the bleeding.

As he pushed through the undergrowth, the scent of the sea filled his nostrils, carried by the breeze rustling through the trees. Xavier knew he was nearing the beach, but with it came the realisation that the enemy could be close as well.

A bird's whistle caught his attention, but he paid it little heed, his focus consumed by the urgency of his mission. Suddenly, he felt himself being pulled into a bush, and he tensed until he heard Mona's whispered reassurance.

"Calm, it's me," she whispered, gesturing silently to a passing patrol Xavier had narrowly avoided.

"I owe you one," he muttered gratefully.

Mona examined his wound, her expression grave. "I have no time to dress it," she explained, her hands deftly working to fashion a makeshift bandage from her boot strings and a torn piece of cloth from Xavier's shirt. "This will slow the bleeding, but we'll need to cauterise the wound soon, or you'll lose too much blood."

"Did you hear the explosion?" Xavier asked, his thoughts still consumed by the recent confrontation with Artoria.

"That's how you got the wound?" Mona replied. "You know you have to be careful with that stuff."

"Mona, I had no choice," Xavier said, frustration evident in his voice. "Artoria saw me and confronted me. She's become more powerful. I'm no match for her."

"Any chance the explosion killed her?" Mona asked hopefully.

Xavier shook his head. "She knew what I was doing. She was just taunting me." Xavier rose to his feet, feeling his newly patched leg, his determination renewed. "Let's go."

Mona led the way, their path fraught with danger but their resolve unshaken.

*

"There's too many of them," Leo whispered.

"If we make it to the rocks over there, we'll be able to narrow their numbers," Ursula replied, her eyes fixed on their destination.

They waited anxiously for a gap in the patrol, a brief window of opportunity that would allow them to sprint to safety.

"Run, Leo!" Ursula shouted suddenly, seizing the moment.

With a surge of adrenaline, they burst from their hiding spot and raced across the sand towards the protective cover of the rocks.

Spears and arrows whistled past them, kicking up sand as they narrowly missed their mark. The rocks loomed ahead, their uneven surfaces and slippery terrain posing a new challenge. Climbing them would be treacherous, but it was their only hope of survival.

"We hold them here. Good luck," Ursula said, her usual light-hearted demeanour replaced by a solemn resolve.

"We'll be telling this story in every tavern in Malsdon," Leo replied, his voice determined despite the danger.

As they reached the base of the rocks, they readied themselves for the onslaught. The arrows ceased, replaced by the ominous sound of approaching voices. Suddenly, the piercing howl of a wolf echoed across the beach from the other side, shattering any hope they had of escaping.

"Just hold on as long as we can," Ursula said, her voice tinged with uncertainty as they braced themselves for the inevitable confrontation.

*

"They must be over by those rocks," Mona whispered, her voice barely audible as she pointed towards their hiding spot.

Xavier nodded, his expression calm despite the impending danger. "The wolf and the guards slowly approaching will be a problem. We let them get close to the rocks, then we jump out and attack from behind."

"Lucky the wind is blowing in our favour," Mona said, noting the direction of the breeze. She glanced at Xavier's wound, still oozing blood despite their makeshift bandage.

"I'll be fine," he reassured her.

Mona could see the strain of pain in his eyes. She smiled, though her concern lingered. She knew any vigorous exertion could worsen Xavier's condition.

"Be careful," she urged.

*

"I can see the shore!" a soldier shouted, his voice carrying over the sound of the rushing waves.

"Let the oars down and row!" the captain bellowed, his commands echoing across the deck.

Commander Grey peered through a telescope, his eyes scanning the horizon with urgency. "Faster, men!" he urged, a note of urgency in his voice.

Saya paced the deck frantically, her senses heightened.

"She can sense something," a soldier said, his voice tense with anticipation.

"Yeah, Xavier is in trouble," Grey confirmed, his gaze never leaving the shoreline. "We must increase this pace."

The rhythmic sound of the oars tearing through the still waters filled the air as the ships glided across the surface, their speed increasing with every stroke.

"I can see them!" Grey shouted, his voice rising above the din. He threw down the telescope and picked up his shield, readying himself for battle.

The knights of Jupiter's Moon followed suit, standing behind him with grim determination.

"Secure the beach! Do not give in to fear, show no mercy!" Grey commanded, his tone unwavering as he tightened his grip on his sword.

The knights banged their shields three times in unison, a resounding declaration of their readiness for battle.

Saya stood up, her eyes fixed on the shore as she leant on the side of the boat, waiting for her moment to jump into action. The tension on the deck was palpable as they approached their destination, each member of the crew steeling themselves for the imminent conflict.

*

Xavier, now armed with two swords he had taken from the dead barbarians, continued to carve a path through their ranks, his movements fluid and deadly. Mona, meanwhile, focused her attention on the archers as they emerged from cover, taking them down with precise shots.

"Xavier, more are still coming!" Mona shouted over the din of battle, her voice filled with urgency.

"I'm not worried about them," he replied, his gaze fixed on the wolf who stood menacingly nearby. "Like a true predator, it's waiting for us to falter."

As the barbarians began to rush him in larger numbers, Xavier used the sand to his advantage, kicking it up to blind two of his assailants before dispatching them swiftly. However, dealing with the remaining three proved more challenging, and Xavier felt the strain as he fought on.

Grimacing, he looked down at the fallen foes, a puddle of blood seeping into the sand beneath them.

"Xavier, get up!" Mona's voice cut through the chaos, filled with urgency.

Alastor, the wolf, began to stalk slowly towards them, its predatory instincts keenly honed. At the same time, a dozen more barbarians rushed to reinforce their position.

"Mona, Xavier, the ships are coming!" Ursula's voice rang out as she sprinted towards them, her expression determined.

Mona helped Xavier to his feet, her movements swift and decisive. "We have to get him to the rocks," she said urgently to Ursula, her eyes darting to the approaching threat.

"I can still fight," Xavier said, his grip tightening on his swords as he braced himself for the next onslaught.

The barbarians closed in, their numbers overwhelming as they cut off any chance of escape. At the rocks, Leo found himself surrounded, the situation growing dire with each passing moment. A sense of impending danger hung heavy in the air as Alastor, the massive wolf, approached with lethal intent.

"Steel yourself," Xavier's calm voice cut through the tension, his words a steadying force amidst the chaos. Sensing Ursula's fear, he braced himself for what was to come. "He's after me. Whatever unfolds, run for the rocks. The ships will beach soon."

With resolve in his eyes, Xavier took a defensive stance, prepared to face the oncoming threat. But before the wolf could strike, two darts streaked past Xavier, finding their mark in Alastor's left eye and shoulder. The wolf howled in agony as Ursula seized the opportunity, charging forwards with dual swords. However, her attack was short-lived as Alastor lashed out, sinking his teeth into her arm and hurling her aside with brutal force.

Mona acted swiftly, dragging the injured Ursula away from the fray as Xavier battled against the encroaching barbarians. Despite his valiant efforts, they soon found themselves surrounded once more, facing overwhelming odds.

With Ursula incapacitated and Mona falling to her injuries under the onslaught, Xavier stood protectively over them, his determination unwavering. Meeting the wolf's gaze, he braced himself for the impending assault. But just as Alastor leapt towards him, ready to deliver a fatal blow, the sand exploded into the air, sending both the wolf and the barbarians flying backwards.

Xavier felt his strength waning, his vision growing dim as he knelt beside Mona and Ursula, their safety his only priority. Yet even as darkness threatened to engulf him, he remained steadfast, determined to protect his companions at all costs.

CHAPTER FIFTY-FIVE

POWER OF LOVE

Xavier's eyes fluttered open to the sight of thick fur and four legs looming over him. For a moment, he thought it was Alastor, but as he focused, he realised it was a lioness with brown fur. A deafening roar shattered the air, causing him to wince, but it also drew his attention to Saya and Liliana standing protectively over him.

Liliana drew her twin swords, her movements fluid and graceful as she unleashed a barrage of strikes, aided by her potent magic that pushed the barbarians back several metres. Meanwhile, Saya charged at Alastor, the clash of their titanic forms echoing like thunder. Despite being smaller in size, Saya's ferocity and determination to protect Xavier proved unmatched. With each powerful swipe of her claws, she drew blood from the younger wolf, relentless in her assault.

Alastor, unable to withstand Saya's onslaught, attempted to retreat, but Saya pursued him without mercy. Cornered and with nowhere to run, the wolf grew increasingly desperate as Saya's blows grew more devastating. Finally, with a calculated move, Saya lunged forwards, sinking her jaws into the back of Alastor's neck, aiming for the killing blow.

However, their victory was short-lived as an arrow shot by one of the remaining barbarians found its mark, piercing Saya's side. The lioness' grip loosened as she flinched, and Alastor slipped away, his form limp and lifeless.

As the figure materialised, Alastor sought solace in their presence, rubbing against them in search of comfort. With the remaining barbarians dispatched, Liliana directed her attention towards the figure, her tone firm and commanding.

"Artoria, surrender yourself!" Liliana's voice rang out across the battlefield, her eyes fixed on the enigmatic figure.

Meanwhile, Saya, wounded but steadfast, limped back to Xavier's side, taking her place beside him as a protector and guardian.

"Sister, you are not welcome on my land. Take your people and leave!" Artoria's voice boomed with authority, her stance defiant and unwavering.

A horn sounded as the ship rammed onto the beach, and Commander Grey, along with the knights of Jupiter's Moon, descended onto the sand with purpose.

"Form a defensive formation and find Leo!" Grey's command echoed across the beach, and the knights swiftly arranged themselves into an arrowhead formation with a few spare heading to the rocks.

"For your crimes against Malsdon and the royal family, you will face justice," Liliana declared, her voice resolute as she confronted Artoria.

Artoria, undeterred by the accusations levelled against her, scoffed dismissively. "I will take it that this will only end with one of us meeting our end," she retorted coolly, brushing aside the charges brought against her. "Until we meet again."

With that, Artoria seized Alastor, and in a flash, they vanished from sight, leaving behind a tense silence and the lingering promise of future confrontation.

Liliana and Grey swiftly attended to the wounded, ensuring their safety while securing the beach.

Liliana knelt beside her father, applying her healing powers to mend his injuries. "Father, I'm relieved you all made it."

Ursula, still recovering, directed their attention to the rocks.

"Check on Leo," she urged.

"They're all right, don't worry," Grey reassured her.

"I'm okay, help Mona and Ursula," Xavier interjected, his focus on ensuring the well-being of his comrades.

Without hesitation, Liliana turned her attention to Mona and Ursula, tending to their injuries with skill and care. Xavier, seeking solace, retreated into the water, sitting amidst the gentle waves as he watched more ships approach on the horizon.

"The garrison from Alice Island," Grey informed him, standing nearby as a reassuring presence.

Xavier nodded, his thoughts consumed by the events that had transpired. Saya joined him, her comforting presence a testament to their bond.

"The bond between man and beast," Grey remarked, acknowledging the deep connection between Xavier and his companion.

As Leo approached, supported by the knights, Ursula's energy surged with relief. "You made it!" she exclaimed, her voice filled with joy and gratitude.

Leo acknowledged her with a nod, his gaze meeting Xavier's in silent understanding and solidarity.

The evening cast its serene glow over the beach encampment, with the cold sea breeze weaving through the air. Xavier sat apart from the main body of the camp, accompanied by Saya, who remained steadfast by his side. As footsteps approached, Ursula, Mona, and Leo joined him, settling on the sand to share in the tranquillity of the moment.

"Are you all right, my lord?" Ursula asked, her concern evident in her voice.

"I'm fine," Xavier reassured her, his gaze fixed on the moonlit horizon.

Leo remarked on the weather, acknowledging the brisk wind that swept across the beach. Xavier acknowledged his words with a nod, his hand tracing patterns in the sand.

"I've faced death many times," Xavier began, his voice carrying a weight of solemnity. "But, this time, death almost took me into its cold embrace."

His words hung heavy in the air, prompting a moment of reflection from the others. Mona broke the silence, voicing her thoughts with Xavier's sentiment. Ursula chimed in, acknowledging his role in keeping them alive.

"I'm grateful for all of you," Xavier replied, his gratitude evident in his tone. "And you, Saya."

They remained seated in silence, taking solace in each other's company as they watched the waves dance under the moonlight, the sounds of the bustling camp serving as a distant backdrop to their shared moment of peace.

*

"What are we going to do with these barbarians?" Commander Aurelia asked.

"The scouts have reported that the non-combatants have remained in the camp not far from here," River replied. "The language barrier will be a problem as well."

"I'm sure a few must have learnt our language," Liliana added. "We need to talk with their tribal leaders and make some sort of terms."

"How many roughly are in the camp?" Aurelia asked.

"From the reports and what Mona has told us, roughly eight hundred to a thousand," River replied.

"That could be a great asset or a knife in the back," Liliana said.

"Remember what I said?" Xavier asked.

"Father?" Liliana replied. "We didn't hear you enter."

"The sooner you go, the better," Xavier said.

"How many men do we take?" River asked.

"Take your guard with you, and I'll have my knights nearby," Xavier replied. "You must gain their trust or put them to the sword."

"Father, I can't kill them all."

"My lord, it may be best if you rest a bit longer," Aurelia said.

Xavier stepped up to the commander and looked straight into his eyes. "I've lived among them for days. They've all been lied to by Artoria, promised a better life but ended up as slaves. I saw the longing for death or home in their eyes. Do not forget, boy, I've fought creatures that would make you crumble within yourself. Now muster your guards."

Xavier walked out of the camp with Liliana following close behind.

"Father, stop," she said, grabbing his arm. "You haven't spoken to me, not even a few meaningful words."

"What do you want me to say, Liliana?" he replied sharply.

"To be happy to see me? I don't know what you want from me!"

"I wanted none of this to happen, none of it!" he replied. "So, I'm not the loving father you got to know. You needed the killer, and you got him. I'm here to end this once and for all, even if it requires my death. And then so be it."

Liliana stood there, at a loss for words, knowing that everything he said to her was the truth. But seeing her father as an emotionless warrior was a difficult matter for her.

"Very well, ready your knights. We'll be waiting at the camp exit," Liliana replied sternly, then brushed past Xavier.

"A bit harsh. I know you were in the jaws of death, however," River said as she appeared out of the tent.

"This battle will change my family," Xavier replied, "She needs to do anything she can to make sure it's the outcome everyone needs and not to let her heart get in the way."

"She's not a heartless person, and her father isn't either. That's what drives both of you and why you made her queen: the love for your family and all others," River said. "Now go. I'll see you lot when you return."

CHAPTER FIFTY-SIX

YOU HAVE HER FACE

Angry faces and hissing greeted Liliana as she entered the barbarian camp. Shadow walked tightly beside her, baring his teeth when anyone got too close. The royal guards walked in front with Xavier, Saya, and Commander Grey bringing up the rear. An elderly man stepped out on to the path waving them over to a large tent.

"This must be one of the tribal leaders," Commander Aurelia whispered to Liliana.

Liliana nodded then raised her hand back at the elderly man.

"Greetings, Queen of Malsdon. Please come in," he said.

Liliana followed the old man into the tent, with Xavier and Aurelia following as well.

"Please, sit," the old man said, gesturing to the animal fur on the ground.

"You speak our language well," Liliana said.

"Thank you," the old man smiled. "Artoria taught me at the beginning, then I just picked up the rest listening to conversations between the guards."

"What happened to the other tribal leaders?" Aurelia asked.

"Well, I'm the only one left. The others were mainly leaders of their tribes because of their size and brute strength, so they were taken somewhere, maybe turned into one of those creatures."

"She's making brutes," Xavier said, "I faced one before on Alice Island when I was still a young man."

"I've seen your face before," the old man said.

Aurelia began to ask the old man a question. "Why did Artoria—"

"I lived among you with three others," said Xavier.

The interruption angered Aurelia, but he held his tongue.

The old man laughed. "So, it was you four causing all sorts of chaos. Why are you here?" The tone of the conversation changed dramatically as the old man became serious. "What do you want with us?" he asked, looking straight into Liliana's eyes.

"Your help," she replied.

"Why should we help you? We were lied to before."

"I'm not my sister."

"You have her face, and that's enough for most out there not to trust you."

"What do you want?" Xavier said through gritted teeth.

The old man chuckled. "I want the people of Malsdon to never return once your business is done. I want this island for my people."

"We could make some sort of agreement," Liliana said.

"No, we will make no agreement on his terms," Xavier said.

"How dare you—" Aurelia began.

"Hold your tongue," Xavier said. "Old man, I've listened to your condescending tone, so heed the gravity of mine. Whatever arrangements my daughter makes with you, you will honour them."

The old man nodded as he felt the pressurised energy Xavier exerted. "My queen, what are your terms?" the old man said humbly.

"You will become our vassal. Do you understand the meaning of this?" she asked.

"Yes, I do."

"Good. We'll leave a garrison of soldiers here for your protection and as a reminder."

Xavier handed his dagger to Liliana, who then sliced her

hand, and blood began to flow.

"Honour it in blood," she demanded, handing the dagger to the old man.

He took the dagger but paused for a moment. Xavier looked upon him, not saying a word, as his look was more than enough. The old man cut his hand and then shook Liliana's.

"Even in your laws, this deal is unbreakable," she said. "If you do break it, my father will be back here to cleanse you all from this land. He hates this place, so if he has to come back, no number of gods will save you."

The old man looked into Xavier's cold steel eyes and felt himself grow smaller by the second.

"You haven't told us your name," Xavier said sternly.

"Not on purpose, my friend. You can't say it in your language," the old man replied nervously.

"We'll call you Chief," Liliana said.

He nodded. "Will you stay until I finish telling my people what is happening?"

"Yes, we will," Liliana replied.

The chief stood outside the tent, with Liliana standing next to him. Xavier and Aurelia joined the guards, forming a semicircle in front of them as the barbarians approached. The chief began speaking in their language, explaining what was about to happen. As his words continued to flow, the crowd grew angrier and began making a ruckus.

"If they swarm us, it won't end well," Grey whispered to Xavier. "Shall I signal Annora?"

Xavier looked around at the crowd, many appearing tired and filled with fear. "No, it'll only make things worse."

Grey nodded and scanned for any weapons or projectiles.

The chief held his hand up in the air, showing the blood pact he made with Liliana. Many gasps followed; suddenly, a rock struck the chief in the head, knocking him to the floor. The guards quickly drew their swords and pushed the crowd back.

"Are you okay?" Liliana said as she helped the chief to his feet.

Xavier turned to her and mouthed, "This is the moment."

Her eyes glowed as she held her hand over the wound on his head. As it began to heal, the crowd grew silent, in awe of her healing powers.

"As I said, I'm not my sister," she said as the wound closed.

The chief stood there, surprised and amazed. Most of the barbarians bowed their heads, and the others showed Liliana their wounds, asking for her healing touch.

CHAPTER FIFTY-SEVEN

PARALLEL

"They'll be here soon," Artoria said as she surveyed her Fallen army.

"My queen, you should escape to one of the smaller islands," the guard suggested.

"No, let them come. It ends here."

"We'll have three days, maybe four, my queen."

"Good. When we destroy them, Malsdon will be weak, and we can take it with little resistance," she said confidently. "I can see you have little faith."

"No, my queen, I just worry. If anything happened to you, what would happen—"

"You don't need to worry about that," Artoria said, her eyes glaring at her guard. "You're one of the few who know, and that can easily change."

The guard bowed his head in forgiveness. Artoria looked down on him before returning to her fortress.

*

Ursula looked on as the barbarians helped with the labourers' tasks around the camp. Sipping her tea slowly, she watched their every move with curiosity.

"Captain Annora, you've been summoned," a knight said.

Ursula nodded. "Tell me, do you think this partnership will last?"

"I believe it will," the knight replied.

Ursula took another sip. "Too many things are at play here, and I don't trust them."

"It's possible, Captain. I guess they might be different from the ones that invaded Malsdon," the knight suggested.

Ursula took one last sip, then threw the rest onto the sand. "We'll see."

The knight nodded and waited for Ursula to stand before leading her to the command tent.

"You missed the briefing," Grey scolded as Ursula approached.

"Well, you should have sent for me earlier," she replied sharply.

"You didn't miss much," Xavier added, "But make sure you stay within the camp."

"Yes, my lord," she replied. "What's the plan?"

"Walk with me. Grey, you brief the knights, then meet at my tent," Xavier said.

He led Ursula away towards the edge of the camp. Along the way, they passed a supply cache, and Xavier took a deer's leg, then continued walking.

"Is that Saya's lunch?" Ursula asked.

"Just a little treat. She's had four meals already," he replied.

"Xavier, I don't think the other men will be too happy about that."

"I know I would rather have a well-nourished and powerful lion beside me who could take on twenty men by herself."

Saya came trotting over with her tail raised high in the air.

"For you, my friend," Xavier said, then threw the leg high into the air.

Saya leapt effortlessly, gaining great height to pluck the leg out of the air.

"Wonderful creatures," Ursula said.

Xavier ruffled the fur on Saya's back as she ate. "Yes, they are."

"Sir, I know you didn't bring me here just to feed Saya."

Xavier turned and faced her while resting his hand on Saya's back. "We've been made the vanguard. We break camp tomorrow morning."

Ursula nodded but was still confused by Xavier's actions. "Xavier, is there anything else?"

"You don't have to be in the vanguard with us. I've told Leo that he is staying behind. He has been through enough."

Ursula looked at Xavier, stunned and irritated. "I'm the captain of Jupiter's Moon. I'm not sitting behind as you and my fellow knights are ahead fighting."

"Annora, we've been through a lot in the past few days, more than most could handle or have been through in a lifetime."

"We're not most people. We are knights. I'm with you until the end," she replied sharply.

*

A thick fog appeared with the dawn, and the atmosphere was tense, with only the sound of equipment breaking the silence. Liliana watched as her army got into formation, nodding as Xavier and his knights walked past to lead the army as the vanguard.

"My queen, it's time to get your armour on," Aurelia said.

Liliana acknowledged Aurelia and entered her tent; her armour was placed on a wooden post. One of Liliana's handmaidens began dressing her.

"Do you think I'm a good queen?" she asked.

Aurelia paused, not sure if the question was for him or if she was just talking out loud. Liliana looked at Aurelia, waiting for an answer.

"Oh, my queen. You are the queen we needed," he replied.

Liliana continued to look at him as she lifted her arms slightly so her chest plate could be fitted. "You don't think my mother and father could have done a better job?"

"As your father said, you're the right person to get us through and to the other side." Aurelia picked up Liliana's scabbard and began securing it to her waist. "My queen, we'll follow you to whatever end."

Liliana looked into his eyes as he finished tightening the belt. "It will be a good end," she smiled.

Aurelia bowed, then exited the tent as the sound of horses approached. Liliana handed her crown to her handmaiden before following Aurelia.

The queen's guard got into formation around Liliana and River, then followed the army out of camp.

"The barbarians who are fit to fight were armed and put with the army," River said, "And the rest are helping with the supply train."

"Good work," Liliana said as she offered her hand. "I'm sorry for what happened on Malsdon and leaving without saying anything."

River shook her hand. "You made my life very stressful, but you saved someone we all love."

"I promise I won't do anything like that again."

River smiled and nodded as the horns bellowed a long note when the army hit the path towards Artoria's fortress.

*

Artoria placed the bowl on the table. The guard tried looking to see what was inside but was met with a bone-crushing grip on the shoulder.

"Be careful where you lay your eyes. You may lose them one day," she warned the guard. "You have three days. Take a few barbarians and the Fallen with you to delay their progress, and those left behind can strengthen the defences."

The guard tried looking one more time and was met with a light blast of energy, which sent him through the door.

"You know your orders. Now go!" she shouted.

The guard limped off down the stairs.

Artoria listened to his limping footsteps reach the bottom

before she returned to her bowl.

The bowl was filled with various herbs and other sinister-looking items; she mashed them into a paste, then set it on fire with a click of her fingers. A thick black smoke poured out of the bowl. Artoria's eyes turned black, and she inhaled the black smoke deeply, causing her to shiver. Her voice deepened, and the table shook as she began chanting.

"My faithful followers, it's time to strike. When the protector is away, kill the womb from which I came," she said.

Several voices replied at once to her orders. As the last voice sounded, Artoria crushed the bowl into dust, then gasped for air. She got up and looked through the window with a smile, knowing who was coming to face her and what was about to happen behind their backs.

CHAPTER FIFTY-EIGHT

MOTHER'S LOVE

"Once again, thank you for the wonderful lunch," Layla said.

"I second that," Sabrina added.

Isabella smiled. "Thank you for the company."

Isabella leant against the open carriage window as it sped down the forest paths of the Emerald Meadows.

"Not much to do when the island is at war," Sabrina remarked. "I'm also too old to join in."

Layla chuckled. "We're the old ladies we used to annoy when we were children."

Before Isabella could add a comment, her attention was pulled by one of her bodyguards who was on horseback.

"Are we expecting any army patrols?" he asked.

Isabella poked her head through the open window and saw a dozen riders approaching slowly. "No, they know we patrol within the Meadows, and they patrol the border."

"Maybe they have news on the war?" he suggested.

Isabella froze, thinking the worst. Grave news of her loved ones.

"Intercept them and find out what is going on," Sabrina said, "Take our bodyguards as well."

The six bodyguards approached the patrol, who positioned themselves in the middle of the path. The ladies opened the carriage doors and peeked through, trying to see what was happening.

"They're just talking," Layla said, bending her neck over the door.

"I'm going outside," Isabella said and stepped out slowly.

"Stay in the carriage!" Sabrina shouted.

The bodyguards all turned towards Sabrina's voice, and so did the patrol, then they spotted Isabella stepping out the other door.

Suddenly, blood sprayed into the air.

"Run now!" a bodyguard shouted as the patrol began attacking them.

Arrows flew and crashed violently around them as the ladies ran into the forest. Horses ran wild as their riders were killed.

"Find her and kill her," one of the imposters said.

"They killed three of us," one of them complained.

"It doesn't matter. They died for our queen. Now let's finish it," he replied.

The remaining imposters dismounted and began the foot chase.

The tearing of cloth and the frantic footsteps rang through their ears as the women ran through various bushes and down uneven paths.

"Keep moving!" Isabella shouted.

"Where are we running to?" Layla asked, struggling to catch her breath.

"The border. We're too far from the manor," Isabella replied.

"Isabella, we won't make it!" Sabrina said.

Isabella stopped and checked her surroundings, then pointed to a narrow opening between a few trees. "We'll lure them through there."

"Where does it lead to?" Layla asked nervously.

"The northern border connecting to the Vermillion Sands," Isabella replied.

"The palace border is closer," Layla said.

Sabrina pushed both of them through the narrow trees. "We have no choice. Get any weapons you have out and ready to use,"

Sabrina said as she pulled out a dagger.

Isabella pulled out two short knives and hid behind the tree. Sabrina threw one of her spare daggers to Layla, who hid on the opposite side of Isabella.

"I'm going to lure them through. Make sure you're ready," Sabrina said, then ran off before they could reply.

"Kill her, don't let her escape!" a man shouted.

Arrows whistled and tore through the branches overhead. Sabrina's breathing grew louder as she was followed by multiple footsteps behind her, and she crashed through the narrow opening, falling to the ground.

"I'm all right, don't move," Sabrina whispered as two men slowly entered the narrow opening. She got up quickly, brandishing the blade and luring them deeper into the narrow path.

"Where is she?" he shouted.

"She's long gone," Sabrina replied.

"Liar!" he replied as the two men quickened their pace.

"Now!" Sabrina shouted.

The two women jumped onto the two impostors and stabbed them repeatedly in the back and shoulder. The men struggled, throwing themselves around and into the surrounding trees, but the more they struggled, the more stab wounds they attained until they fell lifeless on the floor. Isabella left her daggers inside the body and grabbed the man's sword, then threw the other to Sabrina.

"Get down!" Layla shouted as she jumped onto Isabella.

A wall of arrows shot down the narrow path, piercing anything in their path.

"On your feet, they're coming through!" Sabrina shouted.

"I can't," a female voice said.

Isabella rolled off Layla's limp body from on top of her. "She's still breathing," Isabella said, her voice shaking as she continued to check her over.

Sabrina looked on in horror at the sight of three arrows stuck in her sister's back.

"Sabrina, you have to cover the path!" Isabella shouted as she pulled the arrows out.

Sabrina slowly moved, still looking at her sister.

"Now, Sabrina!"

Sabrina stood at the path as three more men came through in single file; this gave Isabella time to drag Layla through the path and to the other side.

"No… This can't be happening to us!" Isabella shouted, her breath coming in short gasps. She quickly scanned her surroundings, then gently leant Layla against a fallen tree before checking her breathing once more. "Hang on, Layla."

The clash of steel drew Isabella's attention, and she watched as Sabrina stumbled into view, clutching a wound on her side. Sabrina limped towards Isabella, who met her halfway as the remaining four men emerged from the path.

"Cornered like rats!" one of the men bellowed, laughter accompanying their encirclement of the two women.

"Steel at your front and rocks at your back. You stand no chance," taunted another.

"We can take them. Skill and strategy will prevail in this fight, not brute strength," Isabella insisted, trying to rally Sabrina's spirits.

Sabrina nodded, determination flickering in her eyes. "I may be injured and old, but I'll watch your back as best I can."

"That's more than enough," Isabella replied with a grateful smile. She tightened her grip on her sword, readying herself for the impending confrontation. "Let's do this."

Isabella charged forwards; Sabrina close on her heels. She rammed into the first man, using her shoulder to knock him off balance before engaging the second attacker to her left. Meanwhile, the other two men swarmed around Sabrina.

With each strike Sabrina blocked, another blade found its

mark, drawing blood. Isabella fought fiercely to protect her, but even she couldn't escape unscathed. Their movements were fluid and circular, never exposing their backs to the assailants.

"Isabella, I can't keep this up," Sabrina moaned, blood trickling from her wounds.

Isabella pushed Sabrina back, creating a brief opening, then delivered a swift kick to the closest assailant's groin. In one fluid motion, she severed the leg of another attacker.

"We're not going to die here!" she shouted, rallying her resolve before diving back into the fray.

Blood streamed down Isabella's arm from a wound in her shoulder, her left eye swollen shut, and her legs trembling from exhaustion. Despite her injuries and weariness, she stood defiantly before the two remaining assailants.

The men advanced, their movements laboured. Isabella's gaze flickered to a dagger lying within reach, a desperate opportunity. She dropped to her knees, a tactical move to buy herself some precious time.

"Why are you doing this to us?" Isabella's voice trembled with emotion as she sobbed, her fingers closing around the hilt of the dagger.

"You must die to please our queen," one of the men replied coldly.

"You follow Artoria?" Isabella's question cut through the tension.

"Yes, the true queen, the only queen," he replied without hesitation.

"But you would kill her mother?" Isabella said, her voice thick with anguish.

One of the men recoiled, a moment of doubt flickering across his face. "I'm going to kill her now!" he snarled, lunging towards Isabella with murderous intent.

With a swift and practised motion, Isabella hurled the dagger at her attacker. It found its mark with deadly accuracy, sinking into his neck. A cry of pain tore from her lips as the man collapsed to the ground, clutching at the dagger embedded in his throat, gasping for breath.

Isabella rose to her feet, her gaze fixed on the fading figure of the fallen man, before turning her attention to the last remaining assailant. Wincing with pain, she gripped her sword tightly with both hands.

"Your death will be painful," she declared, her voice steady despite the throbbing ache in her shoulder.

The man's laughter echoed through the clearing as he lunged forwards to meet her challenge. Isabella braced herself, meeting his attacks with skill and determination. Despite her expertise with the sword, she found herself struggling against his strength and ferocity, often forced to one knee under the weight of his blows.

But Isabella was not one to surrender easily. With each strike she blocked, she countered with swift and calculated movements, always keeping the man at bay. She danced around him, using her agility to evade his wild swings and tire him out.

"Stop running and fight me!" he roared in frustration, his swings becoming more erratic as he grew increasingly fatigued.

Isabella continued to move with fluid grace, never staying still for a moment. She kept the man on her right side, a strategic move to maintain the advantage. Despite the pain and exhaustion gnawing at her, she remained focused, determined to emerge victorious from this deadly duel.

The man's wild swings grew slower and more laboured, his body drenched in a mixture of sweat and blood. Isabella, still light on her feet, watched for her opening.

Taking a deep breath as the adrenaline began to ebb, Isabella surged forwards, her determination driving her onwards. The man's swing was slow and wide, a fatal mistake that Isabella exploited. She ducked beneath his blade, maintaining her momentum as she closed the distance between them.

With a swift and decisive motion, Isabella thrust her sword straight through the man's gut. He gasped in shock, his hands instinctively grasping at Isabella, desperation etched on his face. In a desperate attempt to inflict one last injury, he sank his teeth into Isabella's trapezius muscle.

Isabella screamed in agony, her struggles only serving to worsen the pain as the man's bite dug deeper. "Just die!" she screamed, her voice raw with anguish and fury.

Summoning all her strength, Isabella delivered a punishing knee to the man's groin, causing him to gasp and loosen his grip. With a fierce shove, she freed herself, pulling her sword from his gut with a savage yank.

Fuelled by rage and adrenaline, Isabella unleashed a relentless onslaught upon the fallen man. With each strike of her sword, she screamed at the top of her lungs, her blows raining down upon him like a storm. Even as the life drained from his body and he laid motionless to the ground, Isabella continued to hack and slash, her fury unchecked until there was nothing left but silence.

CHAPTER FIFTY-NINE

THE FINAL PATH

"Cover the right flank!" Commander Grey's voice boomed over the chaos of battle.

"Commander, push the line forwards or we'll risk imbalance!" Xavier's urgent shout echoed from the left flank, where the Fallen pressed relentlessly, threatening to breach their defences.

Commander Grey weighed the options for a moment before issuing the command for the first line to advance. However, progress was slow as they found themselves traversing through a treacherous bog, impeding their movement.

Xavier's gaze sharpened, and he gestured emphatically towards the right flank. Without hesitation, Saya burst through the mire, her movements swift and purposeful. With each powerful stride, she sent Fallen adversaries flying into the air, clearing a path for the advancing knights.

"Push them back!" Commander Grey's command thundered, igniting a surge of determination among the knights.

They moved as one, a formidable force, their shields locked together to create an impenetrable wall of steel.

With each synchronised push, the shield wall rose and fell like a mighty wave, driving back the relentless onslaught of the Fallen. The second line of knights, poised and ready, seized the opportunity, striking down their adversaries with precision and ruthless efficiency.

In the midst of the chaos and clamour of battle, the knights remained steadfast, united in their purpose to defend their position and drive back the encroaching darkness.

"All clear?" Commander Grey's voice rang out across the battlefield.

"All clear!" replied Xavier and Captain Annora in unison.

The trio converged in the centre as the main army began its slow advance down the boggy road.

"Good work," Xavier said, offering nods of approval to both of them.

"A few wounded, but thankfully no casualties this time," Annora reported.

"That's fortunate," Xavier said, "The conditions worked in our favour, slowing them down more than us. I have a feeling this bog was deliberately constructed to impede our progress."

Commander Grey nodded in agreement. "Less than a day away?" he asked.

"That's correct," Xavier confirmed, a note of determination in his voice as he surveyed the battlefield, his mind already focused on the challenges that lay ahead.

"This is nasty stuff," River remarked, wrinkling her nose in distaste. "It's going to be a problem for the wagons."

Xavier motioned for his men to continue along the path. "You'll have to use more horses to pull the wagons through," he replied. "Get your boots muddy like the rest of us."

River chuckled. "As general of the army, I'll be making others give up their horses for that task."

"Well, General, I'm going to join my men, and I'll see you soon," Xavier said with a wink before walking off.

"How is he doing?" Liliana asked, appearing beside River.

"My queen, I didn't hear you approach," River replied, a hint of surprise in his voice. "They're doing a great job, and he's focused."

"Always dependable. Make sure the wagons get through in one piece. My guards and I will ride ahead and wait on the other side," Liliana said. "River, be careful. The smell of death and foul intent hangs heavy in the air."

"You as well, my queen. We'll be right behind you," River assured her, offering a respectful nod before turning her attention back to the task at hand.

Minutes stretched into hours as both man and beast struggled through the treacherous bog.

"This is taking longer than expected," Mona remarked to River, her brow furrowed with concern. "Even with the help of the barbarians, most of the army is exhausted."

"Check on the wagons, then we'll move out," River said, "I'll inform the queen."

The knights of Jupiter's Moon, along with their commanders, took advantage of the lull to rest, their weary bodies grateful for the respite. Nearby, the royal guards maintained their vigilant watch, ever alert to any potential threat.

Liliana watched her father as he interacted with each of his knights, a sense of pride swelling within her. "Father, join me for a moment," she called out, gesturing for him to come over.

Xavier nodded and made his way to where Liliana sat, a small distance away from the guards. He settled beside her, his expression calm and composed.

"Are you wounded?" Liliana asked, her concern evident in her voice.

"No, my dear," Xavier replied, offering her a reassuring smile.

"Good. Do you sense what's in the air?" Liliana's tone grew sombre, her gaze searching Xavier's face for any sign of understanding.

"Yes. Your sister's influence is strong in these parts," Xavier replied, his voice tinged with gravity. "Keep an eye on Shadow."

They both turned their attention to Shadow, the wolf companion to Liliana, who paced restlessly, his senses attuned to the unseen dangers lurking in the shadows.

"He was torn away from his brother. In truth, they both should have bonded with one person. So your bond with him will truly be tested," Xavier explained.

Liliana nodded, her eyes never leaving Shadow, a silent vow forming in her heart to protect him at all costs.

Suddenly, a glint of silver caught her attention.

"What is your decision?" River asked Liliana, her tone direct and to the point.

Liliana paused, considering both Xavier's and River's recommendations for their next move. Xavier glanced at his daughter, waiting for her response.

"We march until we reach the fortress," Liliana said, her voice firm and unwavering.

"I'll inform my knights," Xavier said, acknowledging Liliana's decision with a respectful bow before turning to carry out her orders.

River watched Xavier depart before turning her attention back to Liliana. "A siege at night against an enemy that thrives in the cold darkness... Pushing through the bog has exhausted the men... They need rest," River countered, her concern evident in her voice.

"We can't afford to stop now. We're too close, and Artoria's powers have grown. We can't give her any more time to prepare," Liliana insisted, her determination clear.

"I'll relay your orders," River replied, though she still harboured reservations about the plan. With a final nod, she turned to carry out Liliana's command, her mind troubled by the potential risks ahead.

CHAPTER SIXTY

THE DARK OF NIGHT

The night air was chilling, testing the resolve of every individual present, both mentally and physically. Torches flickered, casting feeble light that barely pierced the encompassing darkness. Despite their efforts to ward off the shadows, the unknown still loomed ominously.

As the main army and Xavier's knights merged for the final stretch, Xavier surveyed the surroundings, his gaze lingering on the scattered remnants of their past encounters with the Fallen. "This is where we first encountered them," he remarked, a note of solemnity in his voice.

"As one would say, it's come full circle," Annora mused, her eyes scanning the area with a mixture of determination and apprehension.

"We have your back, my lord," Commander Grey added, his voice resolute as he positioned himself alongside Xavier.

The army pressed forwards, the sound of their footsteps echoing through the night until they reached the opening. The silence was shattered by the thunderous blast of battle horns as they emerged from the path, stepping onto the barren plains beyond.

Before them, the Fallen army, bolstered by Artoria's forces, formed several formidable lines in front of the fortress, awaiting the impending clash.

Liliana, her mind focused and determined, examined the ground as her army passed by, ensuring they fell into formation.

Aurelia approached, concern etched on her features. "Is everything all right?"

"I'm going to test something. Wait here," Liliana replied cryptically, her eyes gleaming with purpose.

Stepping out a few metres in front of her army, Liliana's actions puzzled some of the soldiers, who called out for her to return to safety. Ignoring their protests, she knelt down and placed her hands on the ground, a gesture of defiance and determination.

"Do not submit to her!" a few brave soldiers shouted, their voices echoing across the open plains, a rallying cry for courage and resistance in the face of darkness and tyranny.

Xavier stepped forwards, his torch illuminating the anger etched on his face. "Be quiet, you fools! Why would we come all this way just to submit? If you look beyond your narrow minds, you'll see there's something waiting for us!"

As if in response to his words, the ground beneath them began to tremble, knocking soldiers off balance. Suddenly, holes in the earth erupted, sending wooden spikes hurtling into the air. Dirt and dust filled the air, obscuring their vision, but Liliana, with her mastery of magic, swiftly dispelled the debris with a wave of her hand, revealing the deadly traps hidden beneath the surface.

The soldiers erupted into cheers, their spirits ignited by their queen's defiance and the visible proof of their enemy's desperation. They banged their shields and brandished their weapons, their determination and resolve stronger than ever as they prepared to face the enemy.

"I don't have a fancy speech that will send us into battle without fear," Liliana began, her voice ringing with passion, "But we must take whatever we have and use it. Fear of death, fear of losing a friend, and the fear of knowing that if we fail here, everyone in Malsdon will die or turn into Fallen. My fear will not paralyse me; instead, it will fuel an unbreakable will. No foe can stop or slow us. My will is death and no mercy!"

The men erupted into cheers, their voices joining together in a powerful chorus. Their spirits elevated by Liliana's words, they chanted fervently, their resolve solidifying with each word.

"What say you?" River's voice rang out over the clamour.

"Death and an unbreakable will!" the army thundered in unison, their voices echoing across the plains.

Liliana drew her sword, its blade gleaming in the moonlight, and pointed it towards the night sky. Her eyes blazed with a fierce intensity, reflecting the fire burning within her soul.

"Sound the charge!" River commanded, her voice cutting through the air.

The horns blared, signalling the commencement of the final march. The army surged forwards with renewed vigour, the rhythmic pounding of their footsteps and the thunderous beat of their shields resounding across the barren plain.

"Xavier, your men take the right flank!" River shouted from horseback, her voice carrying over the din of marching. "Aurelia, follow the queen down the centre!"

With their positions assigned, the commanders moved swiftly to carry out their orders, their hearts united in purpose as they prepared to face the enemy and secure victory for Malsdon.

"Archers, now!" River's command rang out.

The archers obeyed, sending a wave of arrows into the Fallen.

"Shields up!" Liliana said, her voice carrying over the din as she hurriedly deflected incoming enemy arrows with her shield.

With a swift motion, she pushed away any arrows that found their mark, determined to protect her comrades from harm. "Double time!"

Despite the relentless barrage of arrows from the ramparts above, they pressed forwards with unwavering resolve.

As they drew nearer, the soldiers tightened their formation, locking shields together to form a protective barrier. With their defences raised, they continued their advance, bracing themselves for the inevitable clash that awaited them at the fortress gates.

The haunting howl of a wolf and the piercing screeches of

Fallen beasts reverberated through the gates of the fortress, signalling their impending release. With a thunderous crash, the beasts surged forwards, crashing into several of the tightly formed formations, shattering their defences and plunging the soldiers into chaos.

Shouts and faint screams filled the air as the soldiers fought desperately to hold their ground against the ferocious onslaught. Amidst the chaos, Saya and Shadow emerged from behind the formation, their movements swift and lethal as they engaged the nearest beasts with unmatched skill and determination.

"Reform the line!" Xavier's voice boomed over the din, cutting through the chaos as he rallied his men to regroup.

Despite the relentless assault of the Fallen beasts and their attempts to dodge the rain of arrows from above, the soldiers slowly began to reform their line, their determination unwavering even in the face of overwhelming odds.

In the centre of the battlefield, Liliana stood resolute, her powers unleashed as she hurled Fallen bodies into the air and unleashed blasts of energy towards the ramparts, aiming to dislodge the enemy archers and disrupt their deadly barrage.

At River's command, the horn sounded, a clarion call that signalled the arrival of Commander Lynch and the scout cavalry. Bursting forth from the path they had taken, they thundered down each flank, their arrival a welcome reinforcement that bolstered the army's spirits.

As the battle raged on, the timely arrival of the cavalry provided much-needed support, gradually pushing back the relentless onslaught of the Fallen.

The knights of Jupiter's Moon shifted their focus to the Fallen beasts, leaving the regular soldiers to contend with the remaining Fallen. Xavier and Annora, their movements fluid and coordinated, dispatched the Fallen beasts with efficiency, utilising the shield and sword technique to great effect.

Yet amidst the chaos, a deep growl echoed through the tumult of battle, catching their attention. Alastor emerged from behind a Fallen beast, his menacing presence striking fear into the hearts of those who faced him. Xavier attempted to acknowledge the approaching wolf, but the relentless onslaught of the Fallen prevented him from doing so, leaving him and Annora vulnerable to the impending threat.

Nerves gripped Annora as she sensed Alastor's proximity, the primal instinct to flee warring with her duty to stand her ground. As she felt the wolf's hot breath upon her, she froze, fear threatening to overwhelm her. But then, in a moment of clarity, she recognised the fur brushing past her face, and with a surge of determination, she regained control of her senses.

As Saya stepped forwards, locking eyes with Alastor, her posture tense and her sharp teeth bared, a palpable tension filled the air. Shadow followed her lead, his confusion mingling with a faint sense of familiarity at the scent of the approaching wolf. They broke away from the main group, maintaining a close distance as they confronted their formidable adversary.

Xavier, torn between keeping an eye on Saya and dealing with the relentless assault of the Fallen, struggled to maintain his focus. The urgency of the situation was underscored by Commander Lynch's desperate plea.

"River, we have to get people inside now! We won't be able to maintain this!" Lynch's voice cut through the chaos, her concern evident.

River quickly assessed the situation, her eyes scanning the battlefield for a solution. "We're not far from the gate!" she replied. "Sound the charge!"

The horns blared rapidly, signalling the soldiers to prepare for a final push towards the fortress gate.

"Shield wall! Push them back. Send them back to whence they came!"

River's command galvanised the men, who locked shields together and began to push back the relentless tide of Fallen once again. However, they remained exposed to the returning volleys of arrows from the ramparts above.

"Liliana, the archers on the ramparts!" River's voice rang out, her sword pointing towards the source of the danger.

Liliana, momentarily distracted, turned towards the ramparts just as an arrow sliced across her cheek, drawing blood. Shock and anger surged through her veins at the close call, fuelling her magic as she summoned a tremendous amount of energy.

With a mighty release, Liliana unleashed her power at the ramparts, the force of the blast causing the ground to shake violently as the walls crumbled before her onslaught. The falling debris crushed any Fallen unfortunate enough to be caught in its path.

"That's our way in!" Liliana's voice echoed across the battlefield, her magic amplifying her words.

With the path cleared, the soldiers rallied around her, their determination renewed as they prepared to breach the fortress and confront their enemy within.

As the line of soldiers pushed towards the opening in the wall, Xavier remained behind, his attention fully captured by the intense standoff between Saya and Alastor.

The lion and the wolf charged at each other with primal fury, their clash reverberating through the air. Saya, fuelled by determination, gained the upper hand, pinning Alastor to the ground and delivering relentless bites to his neck. Alastor cried out in pain, his distress conflicting Shadow, who paced back and forth nearby, his howls echoing with uncertainty.

With a forceful kick, Alastor managed to free himself and attempted to retaliate, but Saya's ferocious onslaught proved too much for him to handle. A vicious swipe from the lion sent the wolf crashing to the ground, his inexperience in battle evident as he struggled to defend himself against the formidable opponent.

Alastor limped away, his breaths laboured as he fought to cling to consciousness. Saya, poised to deliver the final blow, approached with deadly intent, but her path was suddenly blocked by Shadow, his hackles raised and teeth bared in a display of defiance.

Sensing the imminent confrontation, Xavier knew the gravity of the situation. "Saya, kill him, or they'll both kill you!" he shouted.

Saya nodded, understanding the stakes as she prepared to defend herself against Shadow's impending attack. With tense anticipation hanging in the air, the stage was set for a decisive moment that would determine the fate of the last remaining gigas beasts.

As the chaos of battle raged around them, Liliana's attention was drawn to Shadow, whose mind was in great pain. Determined to ease his suffering, she began to move towards him.

"My queen, what's the matter?" Aurelia asked.

"It's Shadow. He's in pain. I must go to him," Liliana replied urgently.

"I'm coming with you," Aurelia insisted.

Through the swirling dust and darkness of the courtyard, Liliana followed her instincts, guided by her deep connection to Shadow. She made her way back, past her soldiers, through the hole she created in the fortress wall, and back onto the barren plains. She stopped short as she spotted her father, Xavier, standing nearby, bloodied and sword in hand, watching the confrontation between the gigas beasts unfold.

"Father, what is happening?" Liliana called out, her voice tinged with concern.

"I warned you of this," Xavier replied without turning to acknowledge his daughter, his gaze fixed on the beasts locked in battle.

"Call that lion off of Shadow now!" Aurelia demanded, his voice stern and commanding.

"No. Liliana, only you can stop this," Xavier said, his tone unwavering.

Stepping closer to the beasts, Liliana held out her hand, a gesture of peace and reconciliation. Shadow, sensing her presence, began to back off, his aggressive stance softening. Saya followed suit, her eyes fixed on Alastor, who lay wounded on the ground.

As Shadow approached Liliana, she placed her hand upon his head, restoring the bond between them. Xavier, meanwhile, confronted Commander Aurelia, asserting his authority with a warning.

The sound of the horn from the fortress pierced the air, signalling their hold.

Liliana turned to Xavier, seeking guidance in the midst of uncertainty. "What do we do with her wolf?" she asked.

Xavier considered for a moment before responding. "We leave him here and kill Artoria. The bond will be broken, and he'll be free."

"I'll come back for him."

"It could work, as the bond with Artoria was forced," Xavier said, "But we'll see."

"General, what is the situation?" Liliana's voice cut through the chaos, her eyes searching for answers amidst the tumult of battle.

"The Fallen have blocked the entrance and most of the courtyard with their bodies," River replied, "And half of them aren't even fighting back."

"She's buying time to escape!" Xavier's voice boomed.

"Escape from where?" River asked, her brow furrowing in confusion.

"There's a path that leads to the cliffs behind the fortress," Xavier explained, his urgency palpable.

"Mona, take your cavalry to the exit," River commanded without hesitation, her gaze flickering to the determined figure of the cavalry leader.

"Commander Grey!" Xavier's call rang out, drawing Grey's attention amidst the throng of soldiers and knights.

"My lord?" Grey replied as he pushed through the ranks to stand before Xavier.

"Show the scout cavalry the exit I showed you on the map," Xavier said, his words laced with urgency.

"I was wondering the same thing. She's stalling for an escape," Grey said, understanding the gravity of the situation.

"Yes, Commander, now make haste," River urged, her eyes meeting Grey's with a sense of urgency.

With a swift nod, Grey leapt onto Mona's horse, guiding the scout cavalry towards the exit.

"Right, we could use an energy wave to unblock this mess," River suggested, turning to Liliana with a look of determination in her eyes.

As Liliana and her guards pushed their way to the frontline, Aurelia offered a reminder, his voice filled with concern. "Remember, just one blast. You have to save your energy."

Liliana's eyes blazed with intensity as she focused her power, channelling it into a single, devastating shockwave. "Stand back!" she warned, her voice echoing across the battlefield.

With a mighty release, she unleashed the bone-crushing force, sending a powerful shockwave rippling through the Fallen ranks, dislodging them from their path and clearing the way for the advancing soldiers.

"Charge!" Aurelia's command rang out, spurring the men into action as they surged forwards.

With swift efficiency, they swarmed the Fallen, preventing them from reforming the block and securing the courtyard.

"Secure the courtyard and the main door!" River's authoritative voice cut through the chaos as she stepped deeper into the heart of the fortress.

"General, some of the Fallen ran back into the fortress," a soldier reported, his voice tinged with urgency.

"River, we'll secure inside the fortress," Xavier said, his resolve unwavering as he prepared to lead the charge.

Annora and the knights of Jupiter's Moon stood behind him, ready to follow his lead.

"I'm coming with you," Liliana insisted.

With a powerful burst of strength, Saya and Shadow shattered the main wooden doors of the fortress. As the doors swung open, a chilling gust of wind rushed out, sending shivers down the spines of those gathered outside.

"Death's kiss," a knight muttered, his voice barely above a whisper, echoing the ominous feeling that permeated the air.

"Let's go," Xavier said, his voice steady despite the palpable tension that filled the darkness beyond the threshold.

With cautious steps, he began to venture into the unknown depths of the fortress.

"Hand me your torch," Annora said, swiftly grabbing a torch from a nearby soldier before following Xavier into the darkness.

As Xavier glanced back to ensure everyone had entered the fortress, he caught sight of Liliana, instructing Shadow to remain outside. A flicker of understanding passed between them, acknowledging the difficult decision that had been made.

"I know it wasn't easy, but it was the right choice," Xavier said to Liliana, his voice filled with a mixture of pride and concern.

Liliana placed her hand gently on her father's shoulder, her eyes reflecting a deep sense of empathy. "No father should have to go through what you're about to do," she said softly, her words carrying a weight of understanding.

"And sisters shouldn't have to kill each other," Xavier replied, his voice heavy with the burden of their shared destiny.

As they prepared to face the challenges that lay ahead, they drew strength from each other, united in their determination to confront the darkness.

CHAPTER SIXTY-ONE

TERRORS IN THE DARK

The group parted into three teams: Liliana and Annora searching the upper levels, the knights of Jupiter's Moon taking the west and east side, Xavier and Saya searching the lower levels.

In the dimly lit room, Annora searched tirelessly, turning over every object in her path without prejudice. "You going to help?" she asked, her frustration evident in her voice.

"You won't find her hiding there," Liliana replied, her gaze fixed on the view outside the window. "She watched everything."

Annora nodded in understanding and continued her thorough inspection of the room. Her attention was drawn to a table with the remnants of a small object sitting upon it. "This smells bad," Annora said, leaning in for a closer examination.

Liliana, sensing danger, reacted swiftly. "Wait, don't touch it!"

With a quick burst of energy, Liliana pushed Annora away from the foul remains, sending her stumbling backwards into the wall with a hollow thud.

"What was that?" Annora exclaimed, startled by the sudden impact.

Liliana approached cautiously, her senses alert as she inspected the mysterious remnants. "Strong dark magic, but I'm not sure what it was used for."

"I guess I must thank you," Annora said sarcastically, rubbing her back where she had collided with the wall.

"There's no need," Liliana replied calmly, her focus shifting to the wall behind Annora. "Let's see where it leads."

*

Xavier relied upon Saya's keen sense of smell to navigate the dark, narrow corridors of the fortress. With each step, the air grew staler, hinting at the depths of the darkness that surrounded them.

Saya paused at the end of the corridor, where they were faced with three closed doors. Instinctively, Saya pointed towards the door on the right, indicating a potential path forwards. However, their attention was soon drawn to the sound of approaching footsteps emanating from the door on the left.

Xavier positioned himself beside the left door, while Saya retreated out of sight, poised to strike at a moment's notice. As the door creaked open, Xavier braced himself, ready to confront whatever emerged from the darkness.

A figure stepped into view, brandishing a sword, but the dim light shielded their features from Xavier's sight. Reacting swiftly, Xavier lunged forwards, seizing the intruder by the throat and pinning them against the wall. However, the figure fought back fiercely, delivering punches and kicks in an attempt to break free.

Just as the struggle intensified, a second figure emerged from the doorway, their eyes glowing in the darkness. Sensing the threat, Saya charged towards them, only to halt abruptly at their feet.

"Stop, Father, it's us," Liliana's voice rang out, her hand soothingly stroking Saya's fur.

Realising his mistake, Xavier released his hold on the intruder, who turned out to be Annora. "You got some good hits in," he said.

"You're lucky; I could barely see a thing," Annora replied, rubbing her sore spots.

"How did you get down here?" Xavier asked.

"There was a hidden door in the room at the top of the fortress," Liliana explained. "I'm guessing Artoria is through this centre door or the one on the right."

"I believe it's the right. Saya targeted that door before you arrived," Xavier told them.

Annora cautiously pushed open the metal door, unlike the others, with Xavier's assistance as she struggled. The smell of death hit them, causing them to stumble back and gag. Saya, ever inquisitive, ventured in first, sniffing around the room. Xavier followed, witnessing the source of their discomfort.

Dozens of lifeless bodies filled the corners, some sprawled across tabletops, while the walls were plastered with blood and other gruesome remnants. Liliana and Annora entered the room, both stunned by the barbaric treatment of the bodies and the state of the room.

"Mother's love," Liliana muttered as she prodded the bodies with her sword.

"They're all males," Xavier said.

"Xavier, what are you thinking?" Annora asked.

Xavier retrieved a lantern from the wall and placed it on a table beside one of the corpses. "All of them are males, muscular and over two metres in height. Yet, we encountered little to no brutes on our way here."

"Father, we found traces of dark magic in another room we searched. Perhaps they're connected—maybe she's trying to create something," Liliana suggested.

"I'm guessing by all these bodies and that evidence, we'll meet that thing soon," Xavier replied grimly.

"Seems there's no secret door in here," Annora said as she finished scouring the room, "I'm guessing all the answers lie beyond that central door,"

Xavier nodded in agreement and gestured for Saya to lead the way out. "We'll find no further answers here."

"Father, considering this place and what these poor souls endured, we have to burn it to the ground, no matter the cost," Liliana said passionately.

"We will, without a doubt."

They passed through the central door, descending another set of stairs.

"Father, was all of this here when you were stuck in this place?" Liliana whispered, attempting to keep her voice low.

"No, my dear, this is all new," Xavier replied quietly.

They proceeded down the stairs until they reached a door, where faint light seeped through the gaps. Saya tensed up, assuming an aggressive posture.

Xavier glanced at Saya, then at the others. "No hesitation, no mercy. It ends here, with us."

Annora and Liliana nodded in agreement, readying themselves as Xavier slowly opened the door. They stepped into a vast open space, pillars scattered throughout, with two rooms at the far end.

"Seems like a training hall," Annora said, surveying the area.

"Yes, it does. But why have it underground?" Liliana asked.

"We'll get our answers," Xavier replied calmly as the doors to the far rooms swung open.

Out stepped Artoria from one room and two brutes from the other. "Sister, Father… oh, how I longed for your company," Artoria said, drawing her sword. "I hope Mother is doing well. She had some unexpected visitors."

Xavier began to storm forwards, but Liliana grabbed his arm, holding him back.

"Father, she's trying to unsettle you," she warned.

Artoria chuckled. "I'm sure she made it out alive. She's a tough one," she taunted, her eyes gleaming with mischief.

Liliana stepped forwards, her eyes glowing vibrantly.

"Now, you don't want to use magic down here," Artoria said, pointing to the ceiling.

"She's right. We'll be crushed," Annora whispered, concern etched on her features.

Liliana smiled and took a few more steps, leaving herself exposed in the open. "That's fine with me. I was always the better one with a sword," she said, provoking her sister.

Artoria's smile faltered briefly before she regained her composure and approached Liliana. With a subtle signal, she directed the two brutes to engage the others.

The brutes lumbered over to Xavier and Annora, wielding claymores with ease.

"You and Saya take the one on the right," Xavier said to Annora, his voice firm but composed. "Stay on the defensive; they tire quickly."

Xavier deflected the brute's heavy strike with his sword.

"I'll try," Annora replied, struggling to maintain her balance after each blow landed.

Despite their efforts, the brutes showed no signs of fatigue, relentlessly raining down heavy blows upon Xavier and Annora.

"Xavier, we have to attack," Annora gasped, her breath coming in short bursts.

"You're right. They're not tiring. Time their swings, and you'll find your opening," Xavier said, his voice steady.

Ducking under a brute's swing, Xavier rolled behind it, keeping a watchful eye on Liliana and Artoria engaged in their own fierce battle.

Suddenly, the brute seized Xavier by the neck, but before it could inflict further harm, Saya leapt onto its back, sinking her teeth deep into its flesh. With a guttural growl, the brute released Xavier, who fell to the ground, coughing.

In a desperate attempt to save Saya, who was now in the brute's grip, Xavier summoned all his strength and swung his sword low, severing the brute's leg. As Saya broke free, Xavier moved swiftly, driving his sword into the brute's face, ending its life.

"Xavier, I need you, please," Annora called out, her voice

tinged with urgency as she found herself backed into a corner.

Rushing to her aid, Xavier stabbed the brute in the back of its legs, causing it to kneel. But as it rose again, Annora stood by his side, ready to face the formidable opponent.

"He's a tough one," Annora said as they adopted a sword and shield stance, launching their attack.

Despite their coordinated efforts, the brute proved stronger and more resilient than its counterpart. Xavier and Annora soon realised their strikes aimed at vital areas had little effect on the brute.

Meanwhile, Liliana grappled to gain the upper hand on Artoria, the two sisters locked in a fierce battle where neither seemed to gain an advantage.

"Killing me won't be so easy, sister," Artoria said, her words laced with defiance as she wiped her bloody mouth.

"You're the reason for all of this, and your death will be your own doing," Liliana replied, her voice tinged with determination.

"But you'll have the death of many on your hands, including Father's."

Liliana, fuelled by her resolve, charged her sword with magic and renewed her attack on Artoria. Sparks flew as their magically charged blades clashed, the air crackling with the intensity of their struggle. Their glowing eyes mirrored the conflict between light and dark, a testament to the internal turmoil raging within each of them.

Artoria began to divert her attention slowly towards Xavier and the others as they gradually overpowered the brute.

"Your fight is here, sister," Liliana said, her voice firm, before unleashing an energy blast that sent Artoria crashing to the ground.

The room trembled for a few moments, but Liliana's actions proved to be the assistance they needed. With Artoria momentarily subdued, the brute fell to its knees. Seizing the opportunity, Annora charged forwards, driving her sword into its chest. However, the brute still possessed considerable strength and retaliated by hurling Annora against the wall.

Xavier, seeing Annora in danger, swiftly moved to intervene. He stabbed the brute from behind, his sword plunging deep into its neck. Despite the grievous wound, the brute continued to resist, as if driven by an unseen force.

Finally, Saya, sensing the urgency of the situation, sprang into action. With a ferocious determination, she seized the brute by its neck and violently dragged it around, wrenching the neck back and forth until it finally separated from the body, bringing an end to the brute's resistance.

Artoria swiftly positioned herself in the middle, adopting a defensive stance between the two rooms.

"We've seen what you've been doing. There's no point hiding what's in the rooms behind you," Xavier said, his voice steady despite the tension in the air.

"Give up, Artoria. You're my sister, and if there's even a small chance where I don't have to kill you, let's take that path," Liliana said, her tone tinged with desperation.

"No prison will hold me, nor will I allow myself to be a prisoner for the rest of my life," Artoria replied defiantly, her resolve unyielding.

Xavier and Annora attempted to manoeuvre around the side to gain access to the rooms, hoping to uncover the truth. However, their efforts were met with Artoria's swift retaliation.

"Fools," she spat, unleashing a violent shockwave that obliterated the pillars on that side of the room.

The resulting collapse sent debris crashing down, filling the space with dust and chaos. Dust filled the air, thick and suffocating, as the fortress began to crumble inwards upon itself.

Liliana struggled to free herself from the rubble, fortunate that she had been shielded from the worst of the shockwave. Crouching low to avoid the cascading debris from above, she retrieved her sword and surveyed the room frantically.

Despite the chaos, Liliana noticed the two rooms remained untouched amidst the destruction. Suddenly, the shifting rubble caught her attention, and she watched as Saya emerged, frantically sniffing for Xavier amidst the chaos. The room trembled once more, the structure growing increasingly unstable.

Amidst the turmoil, the sound of coughing drew Liliana's gaze, and she hurried over to the source.

"Lily, is that you?" Artoria's weak voice called out, her back broken from the collapsing debris.

Liliana swiftly pulled her sister from the rubble and propped her against the wall. "Why would you do that?" Liliana asked, her voice tinged with a mix of anger and concern.

"I can't let you take them," Artoria replied weakly, coughing up blood as she struggled to speak.

"Well, you're in no state to stop us now."

Artoria's eyes glowed with a fierce determination as she raised her hand, attempting to summon her magic. "I'll kill us all," she threatened, her voice strained with effort.

Liliana reacted swiftly, grabbing Artoria's hand to prevent her from unleashing destruction. However, Artoria found a surge of strength within her weakened state, struggling fiercely against Liliana's grip.

"You will not take them from me. We all die!" Artoria shouted.

Saya finished digging up Xavier, but Annora's arm remained trapped beneath a pile of rubble. Despite Xavier's efforts to free her, Annora cried out in agony. Xavier glanced over at Liliana and Artoria, who were still struggling amidst the chaos.

"You're going to have to chop my arm off," Annora said, her voice strained with pain.

"We can get you out without doing that," Xavier replied, his expression determined.

Annora lifted her head to survey the situation. "There's no time, and using magic again will kill us. I can still fight whatever comes out of that door with my good arm."

Xavier hesitated for a moment before lifting his sword and lining it up just beneath Annora's elbow.

"Don't hesitate. Just do it!"

Meanwhile, Liliana brandished her dagger, realising she was too close to use her sword effectively. "Stop now, or I will kill you," she pleaded once more, her voice tinged with desperation.

"You will have to, because I'm going to kill you and Father," Artoria spat, her eyes filled with venomous determination.

Suddenly, a loud scream pierced the air, startling Artoria. In that moment of distraction, Liliana seized the opportunity and plunged the dagger into Artoria's heart. Artoria gasped, her hand instinctively reaching for Liliana's neck, but her grip grew weaker by the second.

"You're my sister. I wanted you dead, but I hoped there was a chance for both of us to live," Liliana said, tears welling in her eyes.

"You caused this, all of this," Artoria whispered, her voice fading as her strength ebbed away.

Liliana stepped back, her heart heavy with sorrow, and turned towards her father, who gave her a nod filled with sorrow and understanding. Then, a voice broke the silence, shattering Liliana's world in an instant.

"Mother?" the voice called out, filled with innocence and confusion.

Liliana's heart froze as she heard the little voice, and she turned to see the shock on her father's face, mirroring her own disbelief.

Liliana turned slowly, her heart racing and her hands trembling uncontrollably.

"Mother, wake up, please," the little girl pleaded, her voice filled with desperation and confusion.

Liliana's gaze fell upon the heartbreaking sight of the child attempting to rouse Artoria, her sister now lifeless on the ground.

Suddenly, a little boy also emerged from the room and rushed to Artoria's side, his cries echoing through the room filling it with sorrow and anguish.

The little girl stood up, her eyes fixed on Liliana with a mixture of fear and accusation. "Mother warned us that a witch who looked just like her would kill her and take us away."

Liliana stood there, stunned into silence by the gravity of the situation. Her mind raced as she grappled with the implications of the children's words, her heart heavy with guilt and regret.

"Answer me now," the little girl said, her tone more insistent this time, demanding clarity in the midst of confusion and grief.

"I'm sorry," Liliana replied softly, her voice filled with remorse and regret.

The little girl's scream pierced the air, her eyes glowing a bright green with a mixture of fear and anger.

"Lily, you have to stop her," Xavier said, his voice filled with urgency.

Liliana held out her hand and closed her eyes, focusing her energy on calming the child. As she concentrated, the little girl began to stumble around, her movements growing unsteady until she collapsed onto the floor, her eyes returning to their normal state.

But before Liliana could fully catch her breath, the little boy turned and lunged at her, his expression twisted with rage. Reacting instinctively, Liliana mirrored his actions, using her powers to incapacitate him before he could reach her.

Xavier and Annora approached Liliana, who stood silently, gazing at the two children before them.

"Mother's love," Annora whispered weakly, her voice tinged with sadness.

"She had children," Xavier said as he examined the boy and girl, his brow furrowed in contemplation.

"The little girl looks exactly like me and Artoria when we were her age, but the boy takes after no one in our family," Liliana added, her voice tinged with uncertainty.

"What about the experiments?" Annora asked, her tone filled with concern.

Suddenly, the room shook violently, the tremors growing more intense with each passing moment.

"We have to go. Liliana, grab the boy," Xavier said urgently as he scooped up the girl.

"Saya found us a way out," Annora announced as the loyal companion dashed towards the room where the children had emerged.

The others followed suit, Liliana pausing for a moment to glance back at her sister one last time before joining them.

They hurried up a narrow stairwell and through a cramped corridor until they reached a locked hatch leading upwards. Annora attempted to break it down with her sword, but it proved futile against the sturdy material.

Suddenly, the door unlocked, and two hands reached out to assist them. The first hand pulled Annora up, but as they emerged, they were met with a voice questioning their identity and the sound of swords clashing.

Saya leapt from the hatch to aid Annora, while Liliana and Xavier rushed out, only to find that Annora had already dispatched one assailant, and the other was held firmly in Saya's grip.

The man gasped as he recognised the children of Artoria. "What have you done to the queen?"

"She's dead," Liliana replied bluntly, her words hanging heavy in the air.

The man cried out in despair. "You're going to kill her children as well?"

"No, they're going to live with us," Liliana said, her tone firm and resolute.

The man's cries grew louder and more desperate, only to be abruptly silenced as Saya swiftly ended his life with a snap of his neck.

"Annora, signal the army," Xavier ordered.

But Annora's response was solemn as she revealed the broken horn.

"We can't be too far," Liliana said.

Xavier nodded, and with a deep bellowing roar, Saya signalled the others, marking their presence known.

CHAPTER SIXTY-TWO

LIVES IN THEIR HANDS

After the collapse of Artoria's fortress and the defeat of her army, the exhausted soldiers of Malsdon began their journey back to the ships. The trek across the Forgotten Lands was arduous, their spirits weighed down by fatigue and the wounds of battle.

In an enclosed wagon, Liliana sat alongside Xavier and Annora, keeping a watchful eye on the boy and girl who slept quietly beside them. River, riding alongside the wagon, broke the silence with a question.

"What are we going to do with them?" she asked.

"I'll take the boy to live in the palace, raising him, and maybe he'll become the king one day. And the girl will stay with Father and Mother," Liliana replied, her voice tinged with determination.

"You'll have to come up with a convincing story to explain their presence to the people," River said.

Liliana nodded, her gaze turning inwards as she considered the implications of her decision. "I'm not worried about the people. It's the children's memories I'm concerned about. I've placed a block on their minds and planted false memories, but only time will tell if it holds as they create new ones."

River nodded in understanding before turning her attention to Annora, who was nursing her wounds. "Annora, when we reach Malsdon, come with me to the Silver Hills. My brother can craft a new forearm and hand for you," River said, her smile warm and genuine.

"You're too kind," Annora replied gratefully, her exhaustion evident in her voice.

"Rest now, all of you. I'll check in again when we reach the barbarian camp," River said, as she rode ahead.

The army finally reached the camp, where the chief greeted them. Liliana stepped out of the wagon, accompanied by River, and approached the chief with a sense of urgency.

"My queen, I hope all is well?" the chief said, his tone respectful but tinged with concern.

"As well as things could be," Liliana replied curtly.

"I take it that the witch queen is dead?" the chief pressed, his curiosity evident.

"Yes," Liliana said sharply, her patience wearing thin.

"And the fortress?"

"Why are you asking all these questions?" River said, stepping forwards with a hint of suspicion in her voice.

The chief stumbled back, caught off guard by River's assertiveness. He struggled to find his words, his discomfort palpable.

"The fortress is destroyed," Liliana said bluntly, her voice laced with a hint of menace.

The chief gasped, his eyes widening in shock as Liliana wasted no time in confronting him.

She grabbed him forcefully, pinning him to the ground and pressing her dagger against his neck. "What are you hiding? What do you know?"

"Nothing, my queen, nothing. I just want to know if the land is safe for us," the chief pleaded, his voice trembling with fear.

"Liliana, let's go," River said, "The ships are waiting."

Reluctantly, Liliana released her grip on the chief, casting a final glance of warning at him before walking away. "The garrison will be here in three weeks," she said before departing, her queen's guard following closely behind.

As the convoy moved on, the chief watched with a mixture of disdain and intrigue. Once they were out of earshot, he gathered himself and quietly issued a command to his followers. "When they're gone, search the ruins and battlefield for any signs," he whispered, his eyes fixed on the direction of the enclosed wagon where Saya and Shadow were following closely.

*

The captain of Liliana's ship greeted her, and Xavier watched on as they spoke. Liliana turned around and signalled to Xavier to bring the children aboard. Everyone around them was moving with purpose as they all longed for the comforts of home. Xavier and Commander Grey boarded the ship with a child over their shoulders.

"Place them down below in my quarters," Liliana said as Grey and Xaiver hurried past.

Liliana gazed solemnly as the last soldier of her army boarded their respective ships, their departure marking the end of a gruelling chapter in their journey. Her eyes drifted further inland, where she noticed the chief observing their every move with a watchful eye.

"He's going to be a problem," River said, joining Liliana's side and echoing her concerns.

The ship jerked as it was pushed off the beach and into the shallows, the gentle rocking serving as a reminder of the tumultuous events that had transpired.

"The garrison will keep him honest," Liliana replied, her voice steady despite the underlying tension.

"And if that isn't enough?"

"We'll cross that path if we have to."

*

Xavier and Liliana stood vigil over the sleeping children, their faces etched with concern and uncertainty.

"What are we going to call them?" Xavier said, breaking the heavy silence that enveloped the room.

"We don't even know if they were created through dark magic or born like regular children," River said from the doorway, her expression troubled.

"Are you afraid of them?" Grey asked, his voice laced with curiosity.

"They won't awaken unless I choose to awaken them. Please, come and join us," Liliana said, gesturing towards the seats.

"How about Cassandra?" Xavier suggested, his voice carrying a note of strength and resilience.

"A powerful name," Grey said, his approval mirrored by the others in the room.

"Now, for the boy," Liliana added, her gaze thoughtful as she considered the sleeping child.

"Prince Hector," River proposed, her eyes lingering on the boy with a mixture of admiration and apprehension.

Liliana rose from her seat, her demeanour solemn as she addressed the group. "If they regain memories of their past lives, we may have no choice but to eliminate them without hesitation."

"We'll need someone to accompany them," Xavier said, "A personal bodyguard who understands the situation."

Commander Grey stood up, his resolve evident in his expression. "I'll watch over the girl. It makes the most sense, considering I'm already here and we'll be in the Meadows."

"Are you certain, Edward? It may complicate your duties as commander of the knights," Xavier said.

"It's a sacrifice I'm willing to make for the greater good. Personal ambitions must take a back seat," Grey replied, shaking Xavier's hand before retaking his seat. "And what about the boy?"

"Commander Aurelia will be his guardian," Liliana said, her voice unwavering as she assigned the task to the trusted warrior.

"Yes, he's already your protector, so safeguarding the prince will come naturally," River added.

"And I'll be nearby as well," Liliana added softly, her commitment to the children unwavering.

As they sat in silence, the rhythmic sound of the waves crashing against the ship provided a backdrop to their contemplations. Xavier's gaze lingered on Hector and Cassandra, wondering what destiny had in store for them in the uncertain future that lay ahead.

*

The horns resounded as they neared the dock, stirring Xavier from his slumber. Startled, he found Cassandra lying on him, her presence unexpected but not unwelcome.

"I woke them up. It's better if they walk out with us," Liliana said gently, her fingers running through Hector's hair as she spoke.

"What's wrong, Father?" Cassandra asked.

Xavier's eyes met Cassandra's bright green gaze, and a tear escaped his eye. "I'm okay," he said, his voice tinged with emotion.

"Cherish her childhood. In essence, she's your granddaughter. Treat her as you would have treated me and Artoria," Liliana said, her words carrying the weight of unspoken truths. "No one will question her identity. Cassandra, the daughter you kept hidden."

"Cassandra, we'll be home soon," Xavier said, his gaze tender as he met her joyful smile.

"We'll hang back for a while, to attract less attention, before we make our way to the wagons," Liliana said, her tone authoritative yet filled with care.

As they prepared to disembark, Xavier held Cassandra close, feeling a sense of responsibility and love swell within him for the child who was his granddaughter, and for the chance to raise a daughter, the chance that was stolen many years ago.

CHAPTER SIXTY-THREE

HOME

The Iron Coast was quiet as the ships docked; only officials and army personnel were allowed into the naval base. Isabella stood near the docks along with Sabrina, both still nursing injuries from the assassination attempt.

As tired soldiers disembarked and trudged past them, beginning their long journey home, Isabella couldn't help but reflect on the toll of endless warfare. "Years of ceaseless fighting… These men and women have nothing else on their minds but the warm embrace of their loved ones," she said sombrely, her gaze following the weary procession.

More soldiers and knights streamed out of the docks, paying little heed to Isabella and Sabrina, perceiving them simply as two women standing nearby. However, their attention was quickly drawn when Annora approached them.

"Lady Isabella, Lady Sabrina, what happened to you?" Annora asked, her concern evident as she halted beside them.

Isabella's expression softened with concern as she noticed Annora's injured arm. "What happened to your arm?"

"The price of war… For some, it's cheap, but for others, it's costly," Annora replied, "I'm afraid I ended up on the more expensive end of the spectrum. Now, what happened to you two? And where is Lady Layla?"

"Isabella and I were attacked by followers of the witch queen," Sabrina replied, her voice tinged with bitterness and resolve.

"And Xavier and Liliana?" Isabella pressed, her concern for her family evident in her voice.

"They're still on the ship," River interjected, offering a brief explanation. "I'm sorry for what you've endured."

"We're just grateful to be alive," Sabrina replied, her voice carrying a hint of relief amidst the turmoil of their experiences.

Two wagons barrelled down the road, their speed causing some soldiers to leap out of the way, casting angry glares at the driver.

"Slow down, you fool!" River shouted, "Are you trying to kill someone?"

"Sorry, General," the driver replied sheepishly, clearly rattled by River's reprimand.

Isabella couldn't shake the feeling of unease. "River, why do my husband and daughter need to travel in enclosed wagons?"

"My lady, all will be revealed in due time," River replied cryptically, her expression giving nothing away as she turned to walk back towards the docks.

Isabella watched her go, frustration mounting within her. She knew River was keeping secrets, and she couldn't shake the feeling of dread that lingered in the air. As the wagons sped on, she couldn't help but wonder what awaited them at their destination.

Isabella's frustration dissipated as her eyes caught sight of Xavier and Saya approaching from the docks. A spark of hope ignited within her, but it quickly turned to dread as she noticed the solemn expressions on their faces. Their eyes met, and Xavier hurried towards her, his concern evident in his every movement.

He scooped her up into his arms, but Isabella winced in pain. "Careful, dear," she cautioned, her discomfort palpable.

Xavier gently set her down and began to check her over, his attention shifting to Sabrina. "What happened?"

"We were ambushed by imposters posing as army patrols," Sabrina explained, her voice trembling with emotion.

Xavier's gaze moved between Sabrina and Isabella, a sinking

feeling settling in the pit of his stomach. "Where's my mother?"

Neither Isabella nor Sabrina could bring themselves to answer immediately, the weight of the news too heavy to bear.

"Izzy, please tell me," Xavier pleaded, his eyes searching hers for the truth.

Isabella took his hands in hers, her tear-filled eyes conveying the devastating news before she spoke a word. "She protected me… By the time our patrol found us, she had succumbed to her wounds."

Xavier fell to his knees in stunned silence, his world crumbling around him. Sabrina and Isabella knelt beside him, offering what little comfort they could as they held him close in their shared grief. In that moment, the weight of their loss hung heavy in the air, a painful reminder of the sacrifices made.

River guided the hooded figure of Cassandra towards the waiting wagon. Saya stationed herself by the door, her gaze fixed intently on the young girl as she boarded.

"She's okay now," River assured Saya, but the lion remained vigilant, ignoring River's words and maintaining her watchful stance beside the wagon.

Commander Grey approached, followed closely by Liliana and her guards, who formed a protective circle around her and Hector as they made their way towards the wagon.

"Xavier, it's time!" River's voice carried across the bustling scene, prompting Xavier to rise from his kneeling position, breaking free from the embrace of Isabella and Sabrina.

Xavier's eyes swept over the gathered group, his gaze lingering on Annora, who stood in the background with tears glistening in her eyes, clearly affected by the news of Layla's demise. "All of you, let's go."

With resolve in their hearts and determination in their steps, the group moved towards the waiting wagons

"Aurelia, go gather the horses with the guards," Liliana said, "I must speak with my family." With swift movements, she guided

Hector onto the first wagon before approaching her parents.

Meanwhile, Grey and Annora leapt onto the second wagon, taking their places next to the driver, ready to depart. As the Leo family gathered together, a sense of sombreness hung in the air, each member grappling with their own emotions in the wake of recent events.

"Mother, what happened to you?" Liliana asked, enveloping her mother in a tight embrace.

"We're okay, but your grandmother didn't make it," Isabella replied, her voice heavy with sorrow.

Liliana's confusion was evident as she looked between her parents, seeking answers in their expressions.

"Artoria sent men to try to kill them," Xavier explained, his words punctuating the air with a weight of their own.

Tears welled up in Liliana's eyes, and Isabella moved to comfort her daughter, offering what solace she could in the face of such tragedy. As they stood together, united in grief, the bonds of family served as a beacon of strength amidst the darkness that surrounded them.

"Father, when are we leaving?" Cassandra's voice broke through the sombre atmosphere as she opened the wagon door.

Isabella and Sabrina were taken aback by her sudden appearance, their eyes widening in surprise.

"She looks just like you and Artoria did at that age," Isabella said. "Why did she call Xavier 'Father'?"

"It's not what you think, Mother," Liliana replied quickly, attempting to quell any potential misunderstandings before they could escalate.

"Get back inside, dear. We're coming," Xavier said to Cassandra gently, a hint of sadness flickering in his eyes as he spoke.

Cassandra offered a small smile before obediently retreating back into the wagon.

"Cassandra and Hector were Artoria's children," Liliana said, "I wiped their memories and replaced them, so now Hector believes I'm his mother and Cassandra believes Xavier is her father."

A moment of stunned silence enveloped them as Isabella and Sabrina processed the shocking revelation.

"Lily, you said 'were'," Isabella said softly, her voice tinged with sorrow.

Liliana bowed her head, the weight of her decisions heavy upon her shoulders. "Mother, I tried to offer her another path, but she gave us no choice."

Isabella reached out, gently grasping her daughter's shoulders in a comforting gesture. "I know you would have done everything you could to save her, and I'm sorry you had to make such a difficult decision."

Emotions ran high as the gravity of their situation sank in, the clash of war and family colliding in a tumultuous whirlwind of conflicting feelings.

"Right, everyone into the wagons," River said, taking charge of the situation and guiding them forwards with a sense of purpose.

The two wagons sped out of the Iron Coast and into the forests of Malsdon, enveloped by the serene silence of the woodland. Inside the wagon, the only sound was the rhythmic creaking of the wheels against the rugged terrain. Saya positioned herself in the middle of the wagon, her watchful gaze fixed upon Cassandra.

Xavier gently poked the lion in the stomach with his foot, prompting her to turn and face him. With a reproachful glance from Xavier, Saya obediently lowered her head, settling down at everyone's feet.

"Cassandra," Xavier began, addressing the young girl.

"Yes, Father?" she replied cheerfully, her eyes bright with curiosity.

"This lady sitting on the right of us is Lady Sabrina Panthera, and she is my aunt. That makes her your great aunt."

Cassandra nodded in understanding and offered Sabrina a warm smile. "You're pretty," she said sweetly, earning a delighted chuckle from Sabrina.

"Thank you, little one," Sabrina replied, returning Cassandra's smile with equal warmth.

Turning her attention to Isabella, Cassandra's inquisitive gaze fell upon her. "You're pretty as well. Who are you?"

Isabella's heart swelled with affection as she looked at her husband and then back at Cassandra.

"She's my wife and dearest friend. That means she's your mother," Xavier said gently, a softness in his voice.

Cassandra's smile widened, and with a burst of excitement, she jumped onto Isabella's lap, causing her to startle slightly.

"I believe you're going to grow up into a beautiful woman," Isabella said tenderly, wrapping her arms around Cassandra as the young girl nestled in her embrace.

CHAPTER SIXTY-FOUR

FOR EVERLASTING PEACE

"You've been through a lot, my friend," Belthazor said.

"Where am I?" Xavier asked.

"You're right where you fell asleep."

"Why are we in the Meadows Forest?" Xavier asked.

"It's your dream," Belthazor chuckled, "Walk with me for a moment."

Belthazor and Xavier walked through the forest; the sun glowed through the leaves as the wind whistled a sweet tune.

"How's the girl?" he asked.

"It's only been a month, and she's growing so fast, and so is her power," Xavier replied.

"Yes, and so is her brother's power. However, I sense no more dark magic within them, but I still can't sense how they came to be."

"I'll keep an eye on her and keep her safe."

"I know you will. They're important, all three of them."

"What do you mean? What's going to happen next?" Xavier asked.

"Evil never sleeps, my boy; it always finds a new master," Belthazor said, then faded away.

"Belthazor, come back…"

"Father, wake up!" Liliana shouted.

Xavier jumped out of his sleep to find Liliana standing in front of him, wearing a white leather outfit with gold trim, blocking the sun.

"Sorry, dear, for not greeting you. I must have dozed off after visiting Mother and Father," he replied.

"At least they'll forever be in each other's company," Liliana said, trying to be positive.

"They died protecting their children, like any parent would." Xavier stood up, letting out a big yawn followed by a stretch.

"You know, Father, you're becoming more like a lion. Falling asleep in the fields and yawning like one," Liliana said jokingly.

Xavier smiled and looked around the field. "When I was younger, I would just lie here with Saya and Jupiter, taking in all that the Meadows offered us. Right, I'm hungry, let's head to the manor; it's almost lunchtime."

Xavier began walking down the hill, and Liliana followed. She smiled as she saw the joyfulness return to him.

"Where's Shadow and Hector?" he asked.

"Back at the palace, training with River," Liliana replied.

Xavier nodded and continued walking; Liliana looked at him, wondering why the mood had shifted slightly.

"Did he speak to you?" Liliana asked.

"Yes, I'm taking it that he spoke to you as well."

Liliana nodded. "I just want this to be over. I want peace. I want to spend afternoons with you and Mother," she said, letting her frustrations out.

"My dear, I've seen for myself now that evil will always find its way to desperate souls to corrupt. Peace will always be a temporary thing."

Liliana felt disheartened, and her head dropped.

Xavier placed his hands on her shoulders. "As a father, I will always protect you, my daughter. As a knight of Malsdon, I will always protect my queen. For as long as I live, my dear."

Liliana raised her head. "I love you, Father."

Isabella and Cassandra stepped outside the manor's doors and waved them in.

"We have an afternoon right now together as a family. The rest will come, I promise, so let's enjoy the one we have now," Xavier said as he saw Isabella and Cassandra.

Liliana looked at the joy on their faces before they stepped back in. "This is what we've been fighting for."

"What everyone will be fighting for up until the end of time, my dear."

ACKNOWLEDGEMENTS

With the purest of hearts, I would like to thank the following people:

Gloria, my mother, for her never-ending support and belief in me. Shawn, my little brother, for his love and support. To my Rebecca, for her patience and belief in my story. Alex Louca, little does he know, his many English lessons helped me—even if the kids weren't paying attention, I certainly was. To my family and friends who sent their positive vibes and encouragement. To Kristina and the Publishing Push team for helping me along the final steps to become a published author.

Most importantly, my father, Michael, and my Grandma Blair, for without their unwavering belief in me and my story, what started as a dream and ended as my first book wouldn't have been possible.

And to you, the reader, thank you for picking up this book and immersing yourself in my world. Welcome.

N.K. NASH

Printed in Dunstable, United Kingdom

70365297R00255